1st SIGNED 20^a

1st book

The
Mango
Opera

TOM CORCORAN

The Mango Opera

ST. MARTIN'S PRESS

NEW YORK

A THOMAS DUNNE BOOK.
An imprint of St. Martin's Press.

THE MANGO OPERA. Copyright © 1998 by Tom Corcoran. All rights
reserved. Printed in the United States of America. No part of this book
may be used or reproduced in any manner whatsoever without written
permission except in the case of brief quotations embodied in critical
articles or reviews. For information, address St. Martin's Press, 175 Fifth
Avenue, New York, N.Y. 10010.

Design by Ellen R. Sasahara

Library of Congress Cataloging-in-Publication Data

Corcoran, Tom.
    The mango opera / by Tom Corcoran. — 1st ed.
        p.   cm.
    ISBN 0-312-18628-2
    I. Title.
    PS3553.06444M3   1998
    813'.54—dc21   98-4808
                                                       CIP

First Edition: June 1998

10 9 8 7 6 5 4 3 2 1

Acknowledgments

Special thanks to Norman and Shirley Wood for sparking my fascination with Key West lore, and to David Wolkowsky. Also thanks to Carolyn and Jim Inglis, Diane and Rich Roca, Carol and Harold York, Nathan Eden, Benjamin "Dink" Bruce, Kim Works, Cherie Binger, Richard Badolato, Mary Jo Melone, Rick Hayward, Sterling Watson, John Boisonault, John Leslie, P. J. O'Rourke, Marty Corcoran, Sebastian Corcoran, and especially to Dinah George.

There is a trigger that makes the day begin and all life end and it breaks like a glass rod. It lies at the middle of everything that breathes or dreams. It will bend and break, and when it breaks it is night.

—Thomas McGuane
Panama

1

"Rutledge, I have to move back in."

I was barely awake.

Annie Minnette stood at the screen door in shorts and a blouse that looked slept in. She blew upward to dislodge a damp strand of hair that hung across her forehead like a scratch in a picture, but the hair didn't move. She held two crumpled paper sacks full of clothing, and her left hand clutched the neck of our antique balalaika. Her dark brown leather tote, stuffed with cooking equipment, hung from her right elbow.

I was lost for words. Birds chirped and spring morning light played through the porch screens. Annie's car idled loudly in the lane. Her pale green eyes held all the sorrow in the world.

"I don't have time to explain," she said. "Ellen is dead. A man from the county who smells like cigars is waiting back there to talk to me."

"Ellen?"

"My roommate." She clenched her teeth. "She's dead now. Take this stuff. I've got more in the car."

Annie jammed the bags toward my hands. She hurried to her VW Beetle convertible, pried a suitcase out of the rear seat, and jumped backward as it fell over the side. It gouged a dent in the rear fender and landed hard in the gravel.

"Shit." She stared down at the suitcase and shook her head

as if the fallen bag symbolized her life to this moment. "Alex, would you get this?"

She didn't look up or wait for an answer. She flung two pillows onto the suitcase, got in, popped the brake lever, cut a U-turn, and sped away with her head mashed against the seat back, the wind tossing her long brown hair. Someone had painted an underwater scene all over the car. Coral, sea fans, blue water above grassy sand. I fetched her suitcase and wondered if I should deliver it directly to the bedroom that we had shared for almost three years.

Annie had been out of the house for twenty days. So far she had explained nothing, though I hadn't begged for an explanation. The day after she left I decided to ride out the storm in silence. My nights had been liquid, with an adamant departure from light beer and a renewed allegiance to Mount Gay rum and soda. It's not like me to slog in the muck of self-pity. Dirtying the plight rarely draws sympathy from the person responsible for the gloom. I held no affection for the cynics and rummies of the bar scene, but I couldn't concentrate on work and couldn't stand being alone in my own house.

The thermometer, the only dependable gauge of life in Key West, headed back up the scale. The sun glared through the pine trees across the lane. Its rich yellow light angled into the porch and spread a glow over the philodendron, the asparagus fern, the aloe and bougainvillea, her pet dracaena. Annie had given her plants names and had thought of them as first-string companions. I believe she'd engaged them in discussion groups on leaf fullness and the combat of root rot. The plants were the only part of her that had not vanished that Thursday afternoon. Each night since then, on returning from the downtown saloons, I had expected to find the plants gone, too. Now she wanted to return, under emergency conditions. The cynic in me warned that her return could simply be a temporary comfort stop. There also was the chance that she'd come back to the plants rather than to me. I dropped her bags on the living room floor. She had packed them. The next step was hers. The balalaika went back to its hooks above the kitchen door.

I needed to force daylight into the tunnel. Eight o'clock was too early to focus without three minutes in the outdoor shower and my morning slug of Cuban coffee. One thing for sure, I felt short on information. "She's dead now," hadn't revealed much. Had Ellen suffered a heart attack, a drug overdose, or an accident? The presence of the police indicated something sudden. Drive-by shootings had never caught on in Key West. Traditional crimes of passion and revenge were seldom fatal, due to assailant drunkenness and inexpertise.

My bet went to suicide. If a crime had taken place in a shared apartment, the police would not have allowed Annie to depart with four bags of personal belongings. With suicide there would be formalities, but not urgent ones.

As if anything might be urgent in Key West.

As if anything might be formal.

I had constructed a four-by-four-foot rain forest outside my back door. Here the plants were mine. Like the exposed plumbing, they were not exotic. I let my brain ramble as I soaped, and mulled the dead woman's name. Years ago at a party I had met an attractive, dark-haired woman named Ellen Albury who had managed the Public Defender's office. Her name had appeared several times since then in newspaper articles. A recent piece in the *Citizen* had lauded Ms. Albury as a champion of the wrongly accused. Something about street people being picked up for crimes that plainly required boats and trucks. Logic held that Annie, who was on track to a law partnership at Pinder, Curry, and Sawyer, had met Ellen Albury through that maze of legal maneuvering and hourly rates that fed on the island's insanity.

I pulled on a clean shirt and shorts, checked the phone book, and found an address for E. Albury in the 800 block of

Olivia. Twice in the past week, short-cutting from downtown to the Overseas Market, I had seen Annie's VW parked in that stretch west of Frances and adjacent to the cemetery. Now I knew where Annie had been living. I hated the thought that Ellen Albury had died.

I wear several hats to earn a living taking pictures. The only photographer worth a damn in the Lower Keys is an underwater ace, so I refer open ocean work to him while I go for anything above mean high tide that promises a profit. Anything except babies and weddings. Too many mothers of babies and brides are photography experts. My best jobs, while sporadic, are for magazines and ad agencies. Lower in my preferences is police evidence work. To ensure that the mortgage is paid, I back up the full-time photographers for the Monroe County Sheriff's Department and the City of Key West Police Department. Hour by hour, there isn't much difference between taking pictures of restaurant place settings and documenting crime scenes. Each is an "f-8 and be there." Show up and press the button. There's no glamour, but I don't have to coax anyone to pose or smile. Some gigs get weird, but that's part of living in crazy-ass South Florida. I've always suspected that my photos have leveraged insurance claims more often than they've solved crimes or helped to win convictions.

I know all the detectives in both departments. The county sheriff employs a diverse crowd. From week to week I deal with Peter Falk imitators, cowboys in black T-shirts and Tony Lama boots, intense military personalities, and a few slow-motion lifers. The city tends to hire less qualified but more motivated cops. Avery Hatch, a senior investigator with the Sheriff's Department, always smells of cigars. He carries large Palmas in his shirt pockets, expensive Dominican Republic numbers as big around as a baby's arm. I'd heard that it had taken an official reprimand to stop his lighting up on the job.

The idea of Annie's grieving alone did not sit well. Nor did the image of her fielding Avery Hatch's usual barrage of intimidating crap. If Ellen Albury was the deceased and Annie was dealing with Hatch, it made sense to check it out. It had nothing to do with instinct. It definitely didn't promise a paycheck, and I have no stomach for the faces and ceremonies of death. Chalk it up to chauvinism and nosiness. I hate bullies, I wanted to be there, and it beat sitting around the house wondering what the hell had happened.

My old Mustang fastback comes out of its garage only for trips off the Keys. That left a choice between the lightweight bike and the 500cc motorcycle. Factoring in the law-enforcement mind-set, my choice went to the authority of a motor. If the Albury woman had taken herself out, the Olivia Street house would be swarming with relatives. I would pass quickly and keep on going. If the place was a crime scene, my duffel full of camera gear would get me inside the door. At that point, I would have to script my moves on the fly.

Around back, I pulled the blue tarp off the motorcycle and shook the yard bugs out of my helmet. The neighbor's brown-and-white spaniel poked her nose and sad eyes through the fence and whimpered for attention. As I scratched her forehead her eyes became more alert and twitchy. After a half minute of revival she got antsy and raced off to chase lizards.

2

To avoid traffic on Eaton I cut over to Southard and joined ten or twelve bicyclists headed downtown to begin the workday. Through my helmet I heard birds high in the trees, pet macaws and Quaker parakeets that had escaped or been abandoned. The sun's angle, the dust-free air, the vibrant foliage begged a photographer to remain outdoors. Cumulus clouds were spaced apart in a rich blue sky. Even the island grass was more lush, the streets washed cleaner by recent rains. A morning far too pleasant for death, I thought, then wondered what sense that made. Death comes every day and gives no one a choice. Unless, of course, someone exits by her own hand. A low palm frond whacked my shoulder as I dodged broken pavement closer to the cemetery.

I coasted to the stop just past Poorhouse Lane. Indeed, someone wanted to talk to Annie. Six official-looking sedans sat along the curb two hundred yards up Olivia in the stretch of old cigar rollers' homes called Roberts Row. Annie's VW was among them. I eased up the narrow one-way street. Years ago when the city had widened this section of Olivia, they chopped back the sidewalk on the south side and left the utility poles in the roadway, two feet from the curb. Three cars could fit between each pair of poles. There wasn't a space for the motorcycle. I parked on the sidewalk a couple of houses down and approached on foot.

The gods of red tape must have been smiling. The first face I spotted was Monty Aghajanian's. A few other men and women, most of them city officers, stood alongside a white picket fence. One comes to recognize the routine, the long faces and occasional smirks, the wait for the coroner's team.

Aghajanian had been a neighbor on Dredgers Lane before he became a cop, back when he was selling used cars. We'd shared a lawn-mower shed, a set of jumper cables, a dented Weber grill, and volumes of self-glorifying "This-One's-True" adventure yarns. His promotions through the Key West Police Department ranks came in the late 1980s. Five years ago he'd made detective. A year ago he was accepted by the FBI. But suddenly the state of Florida yanked his badge, and to Monty's utter disappointment the FBI backed off. The deal had reeked of fix and politics. The chief of police, to challenge the state-level power brokers, had rehired Monty to be the department's public-relations liaison. More than disliking his new posting at the city, Monty missed the street action. But a wife and new baby and large mortgage had him wedged in. In civilian clothes he looked neat and athletic. At five-ten he was a powerful piece of work, as squared away as the uniformed officers, and more fit.

"Morning, Monty," I said quietly.

He nodded. "I am grateful, bubba, that you did not put 'good' in front of the word 'morning.' Two reasons."

"Two dead people?"

"No, one. Ellen Albury. The pretty one from Milt Russell's office."

"I haven't seen her in a long time."

"Someone used the Cablevision wire to tie her wrists to a boat anchor in the front room. They handcuffed her ankles together. Covered her mouth and nose with duct tape. It took her a while to suffocate."

"Ugh."

"Yeah. Your ex-girlfriend found her like that."

Now I understood Annie's abruptness this morning. "She tell you it's 'ex'?"

"She found the body when she came in a few minutes after seven." Monty's expression went neutral, to the stoic pose that law officers assume when they deliver bad news. "Said she was living here, but she'd spent the evening elsewhere. A name was mentioned. You might say her alibi is tight."

"Seven this morning?"

Monty realized that he had touched a nerve. "Sorry, Alex. You look like I kicked you in the nuts."

"Where is she now?"

"The backyard with the sheriff's deputies. Hatch and Fernandez."

Inside the city's jurisdiction? "This isn't the county, Monty."

Aghajanian's eyes grew vacant. "Hatch and Fernandez represent the multi-agency Monroe County Violent Crimes Task Force. They're trying to link it to that ugly one on Stock Island a few days ago. They're fishing, trying to connect this Albury woman with the other victim."

I pulled two 35-millimeter cameras out of my bag and looped their narrow cloth straps over my neck. "This Stock Island murder is news to me. Forsythe must have handled it."

Monty scanned Olivia Street, the die-hard habit of a watchful cop. "How's work?"

"One article assignment. Zip shit for advertising. I'm drifting in the creative doldrums. My cameras are going dry."

"Like my brain. This desk job is not my idea of adrenaline rush."

"How goes the appeal?"

"I've about given up. The FBI has age limits. Another six months, I'll be thirty-eight. Sometimes you get the wienie."

Sometimes the wrong people get the wienie.

"What's the other reason it's not a good morning?"

"I had Sam Wheeler booked for a half day out by Woman Key." Monty checked his watch. "By now, that first hook and release was history. The first Coors was upside down in about fifteen minutes. I ask you, bubba, how often I get a day to fish, to go screw off on the shallow salt water? One good thing, Sam won't peg me for the deposit."

"City need photos?"

"Ask Chicken Neck. He's hiding in that Taurus with the A/C blowing down his custom-made royal-blue polyester shirt. Waiting his turn."

"Must tighten his jaw, having to wait for Hatch."

"I think Neck is over that wife thing. He knows the hell Avery Hatch is going through with that woman, paying for his long-dickin' the hard way. Anyway, Neck's got him a new deal with a fat Cuban lady. Between you and me, Chicken Neck is laughing at Mr. Hatch. Like he did him a favor by snarfing his old lady. 'Course, the two of them aren't going out of their way to be friends."

"I'm going to go see how Annie's holding up."

"Come visit at the city someday soon. We'll get a ropa vieja down at Lechonera." Monty's face went grim again. "One other thing, bubba."

"What's that, partner?"

"Don't get weirded out when you go in the front room. That dead woman and your girlfriend? Could have been twins."

Hearing it was weird enough.

I didn't want to get involved talking with Chicken Neck Liska, the ranking detective with the Key West Police Department and America's last remaining throwback to the days of disco shirts and gold chains. I approached the idling squad car, pointed at my cameras, then pointed to the house. My luck dropped ten points. He motioned me over and cracked his window.

"Yah, go by the back door and act busy and hurry them

county dipshits. Tell 'em they can bullshit later. We got real work to do. Don't touch the front door or any windows or light switches." Liska ripped a single rectangle from a paper-towel roll and wiped sweat from his jowls and neck. "Don't touch a fuckin' thing. Tell the sweaty one with the Honduran horsecock in his fat mouth to air out the joint, too."

The shotgun house at 812 Olivia represented a hundred years of Key West. Built to rent to immigrant cigar makers a century ago, it had been restored to lease for top dollar today. Many homes in Old Town had been refurbished, some elegantly, some not. They were set close together, close to the sidewalk. The unrestored ones were easy to spot with their rusted, unpainted tin roofs.

I loaded color in one camera, black-and-white in the other, shot a few frames of gingerbread trim and window shutters to establish location on the film, then headed around back. Alongside the board-and-batten building, spiderwebs from croton bushes snagged my camera bag. Sparse grass struggled in the packed, sandy soil. Someone had dumped two boat batteries back in there, a touch of poor housekeeping that did not meld with what appeared to be a recent renovation. I rounded the corner.

Avery Hatch had heard me coming. He glared over his shoulder. "Those city wussies sent your ass to give us county men a hint." Spittle and flecks of cigar-wrapper tobacco rode his lower lip. "We're stinking up their show and they're late for coffee break." He turned back around and used the palms of both hands to smooth the hair above his ears. A quick application of brow-sweat hair gel. A webbed plastic chair suffered under his weight.

Billy Fernandez, an equally unsociable Sheriff's Department detective, slouched, bored, in a similar chair next to Annie Minnette. Billy was in his early thirties. I'd watched his hairline work its way backward an eighth inch every twelve months since I started part-time work with the county ten years ago. Billy's thick mustache made him look as if a black caterpillar had crawled onto his upper lip and died there. I hadn't seen him change his expression in years.

Annie gave me a narrow-eyed "What are you doing here?" stare. I looked away. A rusted washing machine occupied a concrete slab next to the back door. A mildewed Pawley's Island rope hammock hung between two sapodilla trees.

"So?" said Fernandez.

"Thought I'd get a few before Riley's people arrive." I pulled a small flash unit from my bag.

Hatch turned again. "Look here, Rutledge. Cootie Ortega left ten minutes ago. He was trying to beat the black-bag squad, too. And you know what? He even had on a shirt, official as hell. It said 'Crime Scene Unit' on the back. Blue shirt, white lettering. You're not wearing an official shirt. Did the city call you, or is it you need snapshots for your personal collection?"

Avery had always thought of me as a post-hippie beach bum who couldn't possibly deserve a job with the county. The idea that his income and mine came from the same till didn't fit his self-image. He waited for my response. It was a good question. Neither Monty or Liska had mentioned Ortega.

I locked him eye-to-eye. "Most of us understand that Cootie's the mayor's wife's cousin," I said. "Nobody at the city has the balls to fire him. Every time he works, the evidence gets trashed in court. Like Forsythe working out of your Marathon Substation. Marathon's a big town now. You ought to be able to find somebody with a brain. But the county calls me only when Lester's busy. The city calls me when they don't want their case flushed down to Castro with Cootie Ortega's evidence and the rest of the city's shit."

"Gentlemen." Annie stood. "It is time for our talk to end."

The pain and finality in her voice settled it. Fernandez dragged himself out of his chair, and Hatch flipped through a small steno pad to amend his notes. Annie walked toward the rear of the yard.

I let myself in the jalousied back door, wondering whether Annie Minnette was grieving for her lost roommate or reminiscing about the night she'd spent with her tight alibi. I could learn his identity without much trouble. I wasn't sure I wanted to know. I sure as hell would rather hear it from her.

The kitchen smelled of paella. Odors and steam from five generations of Cuban meals had impregnated the walls. A Fantasy Fest poster from 1985 hung between varnished pine cupboards. My boat shoes squeaked on the hardwood floor in the narrow hallway. A pair of black-and-neon-yellow Rollerblades lay against a discount-store stereo. Pictures of strangers sat on glass-topped wicker tables. A peace lily in a red clay pot needed watering. Someone had stepped on a video cassette of *Angel Heart*.

I had made it inside. I had bullshitted my way into documenting a murder scene for no good reason. I had no real desire to view the deceased, no need to build a corpse portfolio. So much for curiosity. This job made those sensitive portraits of rock stars and authors a piece of cake.

Ellen Albury's body lay between two chairs in the living room. Someone had found the charity to cover her face with a section of cloth. I had to lift it to take the photographs. Aghajanian had warned me. I am sure that he had meant facial similarities, though death had distorted her features, but there were others. Either Ellen owned an identical Mickey Mouse T-shirt or she had borrowed the one that Annie treasured. She had Annie's high cheekbones and shoulder-length brown hair. Even the hipbones were the same, the high-rise underpants, the shape of her thighs, the pubic outline.

"Hey, Rutledge!" Billy Fernandez ambled down the hallway twirling his keys on one finger. "Different anchors have different names, right?"

"Yeah." I gathered my composure.

"Whad'ya call that one, bubba?"

I looked over to check. "A fifty-pound Danforth."

"Ah, yeah. How you spell that?"

It occurred to me to spell f-i-f-t-y. Someday I would print bumper stickers to distribute in Florida that said, IF YOU CAN READ THIS, YOU'RE WAY AHEAD OF ME! I spelled "Danforth."

Billy wrote it down. He left without a thank-you.

Once I started photographing, I viewed objects in the room, including the late Ellen Albury, as items in the viewfinder. I've learned to use my camera as insulation. Documentation requires objectivity: you remain detached, an arm's length from the situation. I worked with both cameras and framed out a series of overlapping shots with each one. I took note of furniture that appeared out of place or too perfectly placed. I shot details of cigarette stubs and debris like the chewed toothpicks and disassembled Bic lighter on an end table.

I finished the color film first and dropped the OM-2 into my bag. I exited the back door, found no one in the backyard, took a shot of the hammock in black-and-white, and walked around to the front. Larry Riley, Monroe County's ponytailed medical examiner, leaned against the picket fence and sipped from a ceramic mug. No sign of Annie's Volkswagen. An ambulance had claimed its parking spot.

Chicken Neck Liska emerged from his climate-controlled Taurus and began to escort two younger investigators into the house. He held out his palm. "Give me the film. I'll have Ortega develop it for us. Quicker that way."

The last person I wanted touching my work was Cootie Ortega, the cousin of the wife of the mayor. He was an odds-on bet to overdevelop, expose, or scratch my negatives. But Liska had me in a bind, and the film was my ticket out. If he wanted it, I had to give it to him. Or explain in detail what I was doing there in the first place.

"I shot a roll of black-and-white." I turned my back to the sun, rewound the film, and popped open the OM-4. "Favor. Don't hold it in the direct sunlight."

"Invoice me. The usual."

I recalled Liska's inaccurate but constant reminders that I made more in an hour than he did in a day.

"It's only nine o'clock, Rutledge. Have a nice day at the beach."

I packed my photo gear as I walked back to the motorcycle. I couldn't help thinking: What if Annie had been home? What if she'd walked in as the murder was happening? She may have treated me like crap, but she didn't deserve harm. A bigger question also loomed. If the two women were so similar, could Annie have been the target instead of Ellen Albury?

Annie's wake-up knock on the door had been a surprise. The next ninety minutes had shot my day to hell. The beach did not sound appealing.

Nothing sounded appealing. I headed back to the house.

3

For the past four or five years, Sam Wheeler and I have met for lunch on the Wednesdays he hasn't had a charter. He tended to be fully booked; our routine tended toward the Wednesdays with the nastiest weather. For a while we'd skipped around, field-testing new restaurants as they appeared on the island. But the skimpy gut luggage posing as cuisine, promoted as healthy, had driven us back to our old standby, the Half Shell Raw Bar at the old shrimp docks.

Back when Bob Hall shucked thirty dozen a day and Cowboy Ron sang country classics, locals had kept the place alive. Even after the Half Shell had become a popular tourist spot it never lost its dependable menu. The place was decorated with road signs and hundreds of old vanity license tags lined up to read as statements. Eight on a wall near the entrance stated: OOH YEP KILROY GONE HOP ON ISLANDS DAILY. Two plates above the restroom door proclaimed TINKLE CRISIS.

In recent years the Half Shell had become center stage for a mischievous day-shift bartender. A survivor of the Fort Lauderdale party-bar circuit and the mother of two grade-schoolers, Peggy Sue Peligrosa dispensed seafood, street directions, drinks, slander, and off-the-wall gossip. Anyone not an island resident was a Griswold—after the family in *National Lampoon's Vacation*. A tourist with a sense of humor and a respect for the tip jar could gain acceptance. Locals got the worst of Peggy Sue's jokes, honesty sessions, and hangover harassment. Her voice was loud but not grating, and Sam and I came for the entertainment as well as the food.

I met Sam at noon. He climbed out of his '69 Ford Bronco as I coasted my bicycle onto the tarmac at the foot of Margaret. Sam's rust-perforated truck had evolved into rolling poetry: a starboard list, aluminum cans a foot deep in the pickup bed, a coat-hanger antenna, and its interior awash in business cards, unopened credit-card offers, and sun-roasted coffee cups. Wheeler earned top dollar as a light-tackle guide. He lived in a modest house and collected military retirement pay. He could afford ten Grand Cherokees, but he took pride in sticking with the old seacoast refugee. He'd hired a local artist to paint "Eddie Haskel Edition" under each windowsill.

The Bronco's hinges were shot. Sam lifted the driver's-side door to hook the latch. "I spilled steaming café con leche in my lap," he said. "I braked to miss some dimwit from Broward, and I can't sue for groin damage. Pepe's doesn't have a million dollars."

I wedged the bike into a rack near the wharf's edge and chained the frame to a crossbar. Sharp odors from the basin— rotted fish and decay—wafted on the fluky breeze. "I got up early and I saw a dead person."

"You got involved in that, too?" Sam tugged on his long-billed ball cap. "I lost a charter with Monty Aghajanian. He wants to make it up next Tuesday. I think I got a conflict."

"He told me that he'd missed the trip. Genuinely pissed."

We worked our way past a clutch of elderly tourists crowded in the Half Shell's doorway. A Little Feat song played loudly as a hostess with a crew cut pointed us toward two stools at the far side of the bar. Peggy Sue sounded an ahh-ooga horn and reached into the beer cooler.

As we reached the empty stools, Sam twisted his face into a

scowl. "How come this place always smells like last night's beer?"

"I don't know, Sammy." Peggy Sue turned to someone behind the oyster bins. "Hey, Backassward, was it slow last night?"

"Yep, slow," someone mumbled.

"There you go, Sam. You called it. We're still serving last night's beer. I always said you had a good nose."

Sam's grin became an uncharacteristic leer. "That's not what you raved about a couple years ago."

Peggy Sue planted a hand on her side-slung hip. "You remember that far back, big boy? You got me when I was a baby. I didn't know any damn better. Why is a new husband like linoleum?"

Sam shook his head. "I've heard it. But first I lived it."

Peggy Sue grinned and snapped open our beers. She dropped them on coasters in front of us and turned to another customer. "Corn and slaw with that flounder, ma'am? Put hair on your chest. Make you horny and dance in church."

Wheeler had ten or eleven years on me, but his physique—that of a lacrosse or rugby player—went beyond the picture of health in the Keys. He was thick through the neck and shoulders, with huge forearms and beefy hands. You could not accuse Sam of being unkempt, but his sandy hair never looked as if a brush had come near it. His rugged face stayed tanned except for the reverse raccoon areas around his eyes where sunglasses shielded the skin. He went tropical formal: always a threadbare but clean denim work shirt, long khaki trousers, Topsiders without socks, and a pair of high-dollar polarizing specs, either on his face or suspended on a nylon lanyard.

Sam had been to Vietnam and preferred not to discuss it. After years of friendship, I knew only that he had received the Silver Star for bravery. He'd never offered details. Other vets had told me that a Bronze Star was special, but a Silver Star, if you lived to pin it on, indicated a whole other level of action.

"The dead girl was Annie's new roommate."

Sam perched his cap on the counter. "How did they do her?"

I told him about the duct tape, anchor, cable cord, and handcuffs.

"Came equipped for the job, eh?"

"And I just realized that something bugged me about that anchor. It was identical to the one on *Barracuda,* the boat I rode to Mariel." The Mariel Boatlift, the odd influx of Cuban refugees in 1980, had almost cost me my life. It had filled the media with emotional hoopla and flooded South Florida with immigrants. I was paid two thousand dollars for taking pictures, but I'd spent ten days in a Cuban harbor trapped on a boat with four other people and barely survived a vicious storm during an overnight trip home with another twelve refugees aboard. It had cured me of war-zone journalism.

"Mariel." Sam turned to face the waterfront. His eyes squinted and he looked to be conjuring up volumes of ancient details. "Long time ago."

"Stamped indelibly in the gray matter."

"Where was Annie when the roomie got it?" said Sam.

"Spent the night elsewhere, according to Aghajanian."

"Meaning not your place, either."

"Correct. And now she wants to move back in."

"And that's okay with you?"

Good question. "Call me ambivalent. All this caught me by surprise. You catch me thinking about forgiveness, remind me to be pissed."

Peggy Sue approached with an order pad. "You talking about that murder on Olivia? I heard it on the radio. Kinky girl that worked for the lawyers?"

Sam quit staring at the docks. "Kinky?"

"Not being kinky myself, I don't know firsthand. You spank me if I'm lying. But you know, you hear stories. By Cayo Hueso standards she was normal as apple turnover. She came in every so often, sometimes for lunch with people in office-worker clothes. Sometimes at night with different guys. She was fun to have around."

Sam and I ordered grouper sandwiches, and Peggy Sue drifted down the bar to chat up two ponytailed carpenters from the wood shop on Caroline. Sawdust was sprinkled in one guy's beard. The man with the blue bandana around his head was missing the tips of both index fingers.

Sam turned again toward the docks. "What kind of inquiry was going down on Olivia Street?"

"You ever see those photographs of five or six toothless hillbillies in hitch-up overalls and crooked ball caps, leaning on shovels and grinning like idiots? The caption goes, 'Our Helpful and Courteous Staff Is Always Ready to Assist You.'"

"I'm way ahead of you," he said. "In the Army the MPs were the ones too dumb to scrub latrines."

"Sam, this is an island. Connected by road to that thumb of a crowded mainland, but a real island surrounded by salt water. With cruise ships, speedboats, shrimp boats, Navy ships, and regular old motorboats."

Sam waved his arm toward the waterfront. "Lobster boats, sailboats, and big white yachts."

"And houseboats and dinghies. Billy Fernandez grew up here, and the dummy doesn't know a Danforth from a trailer hitch."

"Much tradition has washed out to sea. The brains of the forefathers are out there energizing the phosphorescent plankton. These days they know more about frozen pizza and remote controls, and less about navigation and tidal action. Sad, sad."

Two more beers appeared in front of us. Sam's broad, sunburned hand pushed his empty to the far edge of the bar, then grabbed the fresh bottle like a lifeline. "I gotta quit this three-beers-at-lunch bullshit. This is a day's quota."

"You make it sound like doctor's orders."

Sam toned down his voice. "Last time I saw him, he asked

about my habits. What've I got to hide? I told him four or five beers a day, which I've been proud of since I quit the hard stuff. 'What about weekends?' he says. I tell him, 'Pretty much the same.' So he says, 'About a case and a half a week, then?' and I agreed with him. So he taps on his calculator for a minute and says, 'That's seventy-eight cases a year. A hundred and seventy gallons.' That's what got me."

I tried to imagine the weight of a hundred gallons of beer.

Sam waved his bottle at me. "What percentage of my last fifteen years has been spent taking a leak? How many hundreds of hours with my pecker in my hand, waiting for my used beer to rejoin the ecosystem? Hell, I've even carried beers into the john so I could keep drinking while I peed out the last one. Go into Fausto's and check out gallon milk jugs. Whatever they got, imagine a hundred and seventy of them and think of your kidneys." Sam hoisted his Amstel, took a long sip, and said: "Monty Aghajanian told you about Annie's alibi?"

I looked over and nodded.

"Aghajanian's pretty straight, isn't he?"

"I'd trust him down to the wire," I said.

"Tell me the deal on the city getting sued by that car thief."

"The city's insurance paid the twenty-five grand, except the guy isn't spending his money the way he wanted. He's supposedly up in Raiford for an armed robbery on Big Pine."

"I can't remember why it all went down."

I had to think for a minute. "It was right after Monty joined the force, nine or ten years ago. Out near Searstown he blue-lighted a Firebird with no headlights. The joker bolted over Cow Key Channel, past Boca Chica, all the way up to Summerland. Some deputies stopped traffic on Big Pine and two FHP troopers wedged their Mustangs onto a bridge to form a blockade. The Firebird stopped, but the jerkoffs in the car wouldn't get out."

Sam laughed. "They took themselves hostage?"

"Monty parked so they couldn't retreat, and he's in a big adrenaline huff. He tapped his flashlight on a side window to get their attention. The window shattered. It wasn't intentional, but Monty reached in and unlocked the door and pulled one guy out of the front seat. A minute later three guys are facedown and cuffed on the pavement."

"With you so far."

Our fish sandwiches arrived as "Brown Sugar" faded into "Kodachrome" by Paul Simon—a favorite of mine for all of its lyrics, not just the photo reference. We decorated our fish with the rabbit food, plugged some Pickapeppa Sauce and ketchup to the side of the fries, and dug in.

I took my time with the first bite, then continued. "The scumboys bonded out like it never happened. The next morning Nicky Bryan, ace attorney, boogaloos into the chief's office. Affidavits from three douchebags, glossy pictures of the busted window, and a hospital report. One guy had to have a glass particle removed from his eye. No permanent damage, but he wasn't the driver, so he wasn't charged with anything. He's filing police brutality charges against Aghajanian. A manufactured case, pure and simple. The city settled. The punk waltzed with twenty-five thousand and the Key West Police Department gave Monty a month's unpaid vacation." I took a second bite of the fish.

"Jesus."

"It gets worse. An assistant federal prosecutor up in Miami gets in the act. Name of Michael Anselmo."

Sam sneered. "Now working out of Key West."

"No!"

"Yes. He fishes Captain Turk on the *Flats Broke,* that Maverick in the slip next to mine. I figure this guy's been an asshole since he learned to tie his shoes. Turk's almost throttled him once or twice."

"Well, he's a born crusader. Gonna defend our Constitutional rights until his butt bleeds red, white, and blue. He couldn't tolerate a rogue cop whuppin' on a citizen. Son of a bitch got a grand jury to indict Officer Aghajanian on a civil-rights beef."

The noise in the bar jumped a couple of levels. The passing Conch Tour Train blew its whistle, and Peggy Sue answered with her ahh-ooga horn.

Sam wiped his hands on a paper towel and pushed his plate to the far edge of the bar. "I knew he was an asshole, but not a dangerous gaping one."

"Monty had to hire Jimmy Pinder, but Pinder took it on for free because he already had a hard-on for the prosecutor." I looked down. I still had half my sandwich to go. "Anyway, Anselmo put the pressure on Pinder. Said he was going to see Monty's ass in jail if he didn't cop to a misdemeanor in return for dropping the felony."

"Nothing subtle about the boy." Sam pointed to my food but motioned for me to keep talking.

"So much for Pinder's hard-on. Monty pled the misdemeanor. But the judge asked for a conference. Turns out the judge didn't see much merit in the case. When he found out that Anselmo had laid on heavy pressure, he went ballistic. Back in the courtroom he ripped Anselmo to shreds, in front of the jury and all of the people waiting for other cases to be heard. Anselmo got a professional slap in the face, in public."

"So the misdemeanor plea cost Monty his badge?"

I shook my head. "Monty'd already done his suspension. The plea had no effect on his job. Shit, he got promoted to undercover narc not long after that."

"Yeah. I've seen him unshaved, dirty clothes, looking like a zonk."

"But jump ahead two years. All along, Monty's applying to the FBI. He gets rejected twice. He starts to think it's because he's a white male instead of an Asian-Hispanic hermaphrodite or something. He didn't hide the misdemeanor, so I guess the

Feebs figured the past is past. Finally they called him back for a physical and a sit-down test like graduate-school SATs. They said it was a go, and gave him a date to report to Quantico for basic training. Monty and his wife put their house on the market, he gave notice at the city. They started to celebrate. He even bought a new car."

Peggy offered us two more beers, and Sam shook his head. He held on to his empty, just to have something in his hands. "We still haven't gotten to the badge deal?"

"Right. So Milt Russell, Ellen Albury's boss in the Public Defender's Office, is up at the Federal Building in Miami. He runs into the butthead. Anselmo says, 'How's my friend Aghajanian?' Milt told him about the FBI and, to quote Milt, Anselmo 'reacted unprofessionally.' Which means he threw his briefcase down a hallway and sucker-punched a tapestry that fell off the wall into a potted plant. He ranted and raved and drew a crowd, then bellowed, "We'll see about this FBI bullshit," and disappeared into his office. Next thing Monty knows, some state police standards commission reopens the old civil-rights complaint. He has to appear in front of an FDLE review board in a hotel dining room somewhere up near Jacksonville. On the spot, the FDLE yanked his badge."

"At which point the FBI pulls the plug . . ."

"Yeah. They tell him no way. So it's a double slam, just because of a chance conversation in Miami. Monty's out of the FBI and he's off the police force."

"And he can't prove shit that Anselmo dropped the dime."

"What's to prove, Sam? The review board did the dirty work."

"Anselmo gets revenge for being cussed out by the judge. Off-the-wall revenge, but revenge."

"Sometimes the wrong team wins."

Sam tugged his hat onto his head. "Monty pissed in a large way?"

"Monty's dreamed about the FBI since he was twelve. He made the grade and, poof, it went away. It proves you can try to be normal, and still get sucked into the craziness. Sex and politics, religion and cash. Mix any two and watch 'em crash."

"You just make that up?" he said.

"I think I did. I also finished my lunch. Why is Anselmo in Key West now?"

"The way Captain Turk tells it, the man's not happy."

"Maybe he got caught dishing his shit in Miami and they put him out to pasture," I said. "Even though shitheads usually win in that town."

Peggy Sue slid my empty plate to one side and caught me eye-to-eye. "I can tell this murder's got you going."

"How so?"

"You're out of uniform. You're always in shorts, T-shirt, sneaks, ball cap, and camera. The last ten years Alex Rutledge has looked like the universal goddamn tourist. The ultimate tacky camouflage. Today, no camera."

"I used it too much this morning."

She realized that she'd touched a nerve. "Sorry."

"Not your problem." I smiled. "But I wish I had a picture now. You're the brightest star of the day."

"Ooh," she said. "One more remark like that and I'll brighten your nighttime, too." She pointed toward the screened window that faced the parking lot. "Too bad you two didn't make bigger pigs of yourselves. Somebody slipped in and paid your tab."

Thirty yards away Annie sat in the VW, her head tilted back against the headrest, her sunglasses reflecting the midday sun.

"I'm out of here, anyway," said Sam. "I've got to hose out fish boxes."

I slid off the barstool. "Me, I wish I could stay."

4

"They asked all the wrong questions." Annie's right hand rested lightly in the crook of my left elbow. Her fingers pulsed with tension. I felt her shoulder push me along toward the water.

We'd left her Volkswagen in the parking lot and braved the shrill blare of country music from the Wildlife Bar & Grill to walk the litter-filled wharf toward Land's End Marina. "They poured out this cobwebbed Joe Friday routine," she said. "And whenever they popped a question that might get them somewhere, they settled for a lame answer. I mean all of them. First those two dorks from the county . . ."

"The cigar and the mustache."

". . . then the city detectives, Liska and a guy I've seen around but I didn't get his name. Except they were nicer about it, because they knew me. But all any of them wanted were lame answers. They already knew what they wanted to hear." She pulled a strand of hair from her eyelash. "I tried to fill in their favorite blanks. I wasn't trying to be evasive, but it kind of worked that way. And that goddamned Avery Hatch called me Ellen two times. The first time he did it I corrected him. He said, 'Oh yeah, Ellen's the dead one.' The second time he said, 'My mistake.' As if it could have been someone else's. Like he'd raised his hand to acknowledge a basketball foul. How do those lazy shits justify their salaries?"

"They're not paid to be protocol experts."

"Put me up against them in a criminal defense. I'd chew their strategies into pieces and spit them back into their brief-cases. They'd be dead meat."

"You talk like you've got an idea who did it."

"I don't have the smallest clue. Alex, I never realized so many people lived aboard these boats."

The live-aboards had chained bicycles and mopeds to the post-and-hawser safety rail at the head of the pier. The dozen or so Conch cruisers were flame-painted, polka-dotted, and sculpted with fish ornaments. One sun-bleached blue bike had a sticker on a wooden box behind its seat: "Don't Re-Elect Anyone."

Without the breeze that had swept the morning sky, the midday air felt thick and warm and damp. We stepped around obstacles on the dock: orange shore power lines, propane tanks, dinghies flopped turtle, pitch-stained hoses, yellow extension cords. Paraphernalia for the escape from civilization. The vagabond lifestyle suddenly appealed to me, though I knew all about the high turnover rate among dreamy-eyed mariners.

A gull flock lifted off the swaybacked tin roof of the Turtle Kraals work shed and swooped the waterfront toward Schooner's Wharf. Annie's eyes followed the birds. "On one hand," she said, "I can't imagine anyone wanting to hurt her. On the other, I have to say that it doesn't surprise me."

I questioned her remark.

"She'd played around when she was younger. Dated weird men over the years, to hear her stories. Heavy characters—the coke-spoon crowd, a few redneck losers. But nothing was stolen. And I don't think a thief would get so evil about how he did it."

"So, you think revenge or jealousy?"

"Well, it's for certain that somebody was pissed at her. And it's going to get confusing. The forensic examiners will come to the conclusion that she was probably raped. But I happen to know that she spent the early-evening hours screwing her tush off with someone she knew."

"There's a boyfriend?"

"Last count, four or five. Each could have a motive, but the man she was with last night has a witness to his departure and his whereabouts the rest of the night. They didn't ask me about that."

"And he was with you the rest of the night," I said.

"Not exactly. Not what you mean."

She had a habit of double-jumping my thought patterns. "I'm glad you know what I mean, Annie," I said. "My brain's been on hold for almost three weeks, so I haven't had a clue what's on my mind."

I earned a scowl and large portion of silence for that remark.

Smells of diesel fuel, paint, and exposed barnacles wafted over the pier. The metallic slap of shrouds against aluminum masts intruded on the peace. Over the years the weather had worked on the dock. Much of the two-by-six planking had warped and splintered. But all of the slips were claimed. Boats with names like *Psychic Ward*, *Orion's Melt*, and *Adios M.F.*

Safe-harbor suburbia.

At pier's end we sat on someone's fiberglass locker. Rubber boat fenders squeaked against the dock pilings. An antique biplane buzzed low over the Navy Pier. A man in a frayed Panama hat putted past in an inflatable Zodiac powered by a four-horse Yamaha.

"Let me ask this," I said. "You arrived at my house with luggage. Who let you leave the site of a murder investigation with all your personal belongings?"

"Good. That's the kind of question I wanted out of Billy and Avery."

I waited for her answer.

She shrugged and looked downward. "I stashed it all in my car before I called 911. I figured they'd gift-wrap the house with yellow 'Police Line' tape and not let me take the clothes I wear to work. My practical side scares me sometimes. It's always so cold-blooded. I didn't scream when I found her. I made sure no one else was in the house, I threw up, and I knew for absolute certain that I couldn't stop her from being dead. So I packed my stuff in the car and threw up again and called the police." Annie turned back toward me. "Oh, shit. Some of my clothes are still in the trunk. They're all going to smell like gasoline."

We stood awhile, soaking up the midday warmth. Everything in my line of sight had been built since my arrival on the island, most of it in the past ten years. The Waterfront Market, the Hyatt, the Galleon resort, the new marina behind the breakwater. The superstructure of a cruise liner rose above the former Thompson-O'Neill shrimp processing plant—now a complex of sailmakers' lofts. I had become resigned to the inevitability of change in Key West. I had ranted about it, though the Waterfront Market had proved to be a blessing. I hadn't wanted my relationship with Annie to change, either, but I saw no way to retrieve it. I stood a foot away from her but felt as if she were gone. Like a dead person.

I'd felt lucky to have found her. She and Becky Till, central Florida natives and senior-year roommates in Tallahassee, arrived in Key West seven years ago, thirty hours after their senior-year final exams. They had rolled down the Seven Mile Bridge on the second wave of AIDS warnings, hitting town intent on turning eight years of higher education into two waitress jobs and as much safe sex as they could handle. Along with their bicycles and enough money to fund first and last months' rent plus a damage deposit, they had brought six Hefty bags full of clothing that would mildew before Christmas.

"I remember telling Becky to kill me if she ever saw me riding one of those smelly mopeds," Annie had once told me. "And Becky ordered me to cut off her face if I caught her in one of those booths selling time-share condos. She said she'd rather clean motel rooms. Better to spend all summer picking pubes out of drains. I remember asking her why we didn't think about being motel maids before we spent our parents' money on tuition."

Their first night in town a drunk in the Full Moon Saloon informed them that he had been evicted from a cottage on Grinnell for nonpayment of rent. If the young women showed the landlord actual cash money in the morning, they could claim an A-plus house. It had a front porch, three ceiling fans, and a tub with legs shaped like claws grabbing baseballs. Plus a marijuana bush out back among the crotons and new jacarandas. He planned to sleep in his car until his ex-wife arrived a week later with enough dough for a suite in the Casa Marina. The young women got the place.

Becky lucked into a job at a croissant shop her first day on the hunt. It took Annie a week to land an evening shift in a Duval Street store full of Guatemalan blouses. Over the next few months they kept company with a long parade of male friends. They learned to ride sailboards, cook exotic shrimp-and-rice recipes, and navigate the Old Town back streets on their bikes. They picnicked and sunbathed nude at Woman Key. They learned island history. They danced until four in the morning in the gay discos. They also grew weary of the carnival, the lack of direction. Within eight months, Becky had met and become engaged to a computer programmer from Denver. She'd gone to live in Colorado. And Annie was back in Tallahassee working toward a law degree.

After passing the bar exam, Annie accepted a position near her parents' home, with a company specializing in marine law. After six months in West Palm Beach and a brief, tumultuous affair with the firm's youngest partner, she found herself needing more slack and less traffic.

29

When she left Key West to attend graduate school, Annie had given no thought to returning, short-term or long-term. After a few months working in West Palm she realized that the Island City offered what she needed: in her words, "a laid-back atmosphere and an honest chance to get ahead." She quit her job and drove south. I met her at the deli counter of Juan Mayg's the day after she hit town for her second go-round. The next day we ran into each other ordering sandwiches at La Bodega. She said, "Two restaurants in a row without '-ery' at the end of their names." I respect a sense of humor. I was in love before she finished the sentence.

"I need to get in touch with Mr. and Mrs. Embry." Her expression held no emotion. Her frazzled hair and puffy face— normally signs of a long workday—told me that the events of the morning had caught up with her.

The names didn't click with me.

"Ellen's mother and stepfather. They live out on Staples. I guess the police broke the news to them. I haven't talked to them yet."

"Who was your alibi?"

"You're bringing up our agreement to be honest."

"Agreements are agreements." I began to walk toward the parking lot. A crewman on a custom-hull thirty-six-foot charter boat snagged mooring lines off pilings as the boat backed to the dock. Someone tried to hand us brochures that touted a catamaran sunset cruise.

Annie walked close to me but stared straight ahead. "I suppose you've told me about every lover in your past. I mean, hell. You're tall and handsome. You're built to survive volleyball, deep-sea diving, a night of dancing. Around here, after ten P.M., their skirts reach for the sky and their heels grow hinges and their knees go east and west. I can understand women being attracted to you, especially in this town. You've been open, in general, but I'll bet there are women I don't know about."

She was right. There had been several who had grabbed my heart and held on like they'd meant it. "You've even met two or three," I said. "Seen pictures of most of them."

"But there've been omissions, correct?"

"Goddamn, you sound like a lawyer. You and your words. Look, I've been single all my life. If we figured one lover a year since I started making love with women, which is not necessarily true, you couldn't count all of them on all your fingers and toes. What was I supposed to do? Submit a roster?"

"Let me keep last night to myself awhile, okay? That's all I'm asking. I'm not real proud of myself right now."

I couldn't argue with a line like that.

"Did a lot of folks know you were sharing a place with Ellen?"

"It's not like I went around announcing it. A few people asked why they'd seen my convertible parked on Olivia. That's part of living in a small town. Can we be roommates again?"

"Until you can find another apartment?"

She rolled her eyes upward. "Uh-oh, he's mad at me."

"You don't think there's something that needs explaining?"

"It was something I had to do. I wanted space."

"Did you find it?"

"Not yet. Not all I need, at least. I sit on the beach at lunchtime and that helps. I wouldn't call it meditating. That sounds a little too alfalfa sprouts. I think it has something to do with restlessness and worrying about the future. And fighting the fact that I love you."

Attempted sucker punch. I refused to respond.

We went back to the house so she could unload the rest of her clothing, and so I could retrieve my messages. Chicken Neck Liska wanted me to stop by his office at the police station before the end of the day. A man with a polished voice of

31

concern had called from Annie's office. A magazine in New York needed me to overnight the slides I had promised three days ago.

Annie washed her face, changed her blouse, and briefly inspected her plants. Then she drove away.

I unlocked my bicycle and ventured back out into Paradise.

5

Duffy Lee Hall, an old Full Moon Saloon drinking companion who processed film at a drugstore on Simonton, promised secrecy and hurry-up with the color roll that I'd held back from the police on Olivia Street. For the hundredth time we exchanged opinions on Cootie Ortega's professional abilities, then Duffy Lee shooed me out of his darkroom.

With a certain amount of dread I headed for Liska's office at City Hall.

I chained my bike to a handrail at the Key West Police Department's Angela Street entrance as Larry Riley, Monroe County's medical examiner, parked his olive-drab fifties-vintage Jeep in the red zone next to the curb. A breeze tossed the shrubs that had hung in since the city's last budget-conscious landscaping effort. Cloud shadows raced down Simonton. Birds screeched and sang in the old Peggy Mills Garden across the street.

Riley grabbed several manila file jackets full of legal pages and computer printouts, climbed out, hitched his jeans, and joined me on the sidewalk. "Got a sec?" He turned his ball cap so the brim faced forward.

"All day. Liska asked me to drop by. I don't see this meeting as a brick in the foundation of my career."

"Someone said you knew the deceased woman."

"Not really. We'd met a while back. She'd been my girl-friend's roommate for the past several weeks. Sort of a domestic upheaval at my house."

"Sorry to hear it. I'd like to chat with your girlfriend. I knew Ellen in high school, but I need some recent background before I complete my report."

"Her name's Ann Minnette. She found the body."

"Oh. I know Annie." A puzzled expression flashed across his face, then vanished. "I never connected the two of you. I also need detail prints from your scene photos. Did you get close-ups of the wire knots around the wrists, the handcuffs on the ankles?"

"Got it all."

"Good. This one's a doozy. I guess Ellen was into some weird shit, at one time or other."

"That showed in an autopsy pre-lim?"

"Old rope burn marks on her wrists and ankles. A few other things. But nothing too recent. It's probably old news in this town. Or boring news, I mean. People still talk about that article in *The Citizen* when the police had to pull apart those two lesbians fighting on St. Paul's steps over a rainbow-colored nine-inch dildo."

"Key Weird earned its name the hard way."

"Play on words," said Larry. "You never know when this kind of stuff might be connected to a murder. In this case there are other considerations."

"Evidence of recent sexual activity? That kind of thing?"

He wheezed a half-laugh. "You reading my mind or my mail?"

"Annie told me an hour ago that Ellen had entertained someone during the evening hours, and that he could be ruled out as a suspect. She knew that Ellen was fine when he left, and that the man hadn't returned during the rest of the night."

Larry thought about that for a moment. "She say much else?"

"About what?"

"I thought I'd found bruising in the pubic region. On closer inspection, it was a two-word tattoo under her muff: 'Daddy's Girl.' Who knows what that means. It's not a fresh tattoo. It could be ten years old. Her mother married Forrest Embry twelve years ago, and she said that Ellen's father's been in and out of town since the seventies. Let's hope that 'Daddy' is an old boyfriend. Plus, I found two other tattoos and some scars from old punctures. Nipple rings, one labial ring, some body piercing here and there. All of it looks to be a few years old. Maybe a previous lifestyle."

I wondered for a moment why the medical examiner would give this type of information to a civilian. "Annie didn't mention that kind of stuff."

"You think I'd be off base to suggest a forced sex act?"

"I wouldn't tell you to destroy evidence. Who knows what happened after the boyfriend took off? But something was going on beforehand."

"Someday, some way," he said, "I'm going to find a way to make this job more fun."

Inside the glass doors I waved to Marge Sayre, the youthful fortyish receptionist behind the protected enclosure. On normal days Marge radiated cheer. Today she looked harried. She stood and waved a handful of message slips. "Both of you boys need to return calls to the county. Something ugly near Bahia Honda. I think they need you up there."

Riley and I sorted through identical rose-colored slips, "Please Call Back" notes from Sheriff Tommy Tucker at his office and Detective Billy Fernandez on a mobile prefix. There was one pay phone on the wall.

"Help yourself, Doc."

Riley's forehead furrowed. He punched in a number. "Gonna be a long day," he said to the wall.

Marge Sayre sat down and returned to some kind of macrame project. "Shame about Ginny Embry's daughter."

I nodded. I was trying to eavesdrop on Riley, for a preview of the dilemma thirty-five miles up the road.

"She'd been doing so well the past few years." Marge adjusted her wire-rimmed bifocals. "We would see her all the time, in and out, always busy, always happy. I don't know what Milt Russell's going to do without her."

Riley turned around, his expression pure disgust. "You want to ride up there with me? Bunch of volunteers working Coastal Cleanup found a fresh one near the south end of the old bridge. Another young woman, killed elsewhere and dropped during the night. They want you to document."

"I'll need to stop at the house and get my satchelful of gear."

"Where do you live?"

"Off Fleming, up near White."

"No way I can put off a couple things here." He waved his bundle of files. "Ride your bike home and I'll pick you up in ten minutes. Unless you'd rather not get beat to all get-out in that Jeep."

"I don't mind open air." Sometimes business required the qualified lie. I loved open air, but I hated Jeeps. They made me feel vulnerable, as if I were sitting on a barstool traveling at highway velocity. But I wanted a chance to pick Riley's brain regarding the murder. I also saw the ride as an excuse to postpone my meeting with Chicken Neck Liska. "I'm at 422 Dredgers Lane."

"Next door to Carmen Sosa?"

"Two houses down, same side. My favorite neighbor."

"Carmen Ayusa, my high-school girlfriend. Married Johnny Sosa during my freshman year at USF and that was that."

Carmen had never mentioned Larry Riley. Over the years

she and I had developed a wonderful friendship. We'd tried once to be lovers, not long after her second divorce, but we couldn't get it to feel right. It might have been my reluctance to become an instant daddy. Maria Rolley, Carmen's young daughter from that second marriage, was the darling of the block. With Carmen's work hours, the child divided her time between her own home and that of Carmen's parents across the lane at 413. Even in the years since Annie's arrival, Carmen and I had continued to be each other's confidant and morale booster.

Twice he'd mentioned the high school. I'd never realized that Riley was a Conch. Not many had lost their Conch accents. Fewer still had become doctors.

As usual, the ride up through Cudjoe and Summerland and Big Pine Keys provided culture shock. Living in Key West you become lulled into the idea that you are removed from the real world, in both a philosophical and geographical sense. You live in the Gulf of Mexico and are part of the nation only in that your money is decorated with Presidents' faces and you dial long distance direct. But once you get about ten miles up U.S. 1, where the wildlife and vegetation are doing their damnedest to survive the whirlpool of civilization, you realize again that true isolation means no other humans. You wonder how the pioneers survived the Everglades and the Keys, how anyone managed to live here in 1850 or build that railroad almost a century ago. Beyond problems of food and water and shelter, those people sure as hell couldn't drop into a 7-Eleven to buy bug repellent, or gather supper when the ocean was snarling with a tropical wave. Or make a quick appointment with the dentist.

There was little traffic on the highway. I balanced my satchel on top of my feet so the Jeep's vibrating floor pan would not rattle my equipment into a scrap heap of minuscule camera parts. With his long-brimmed ball cap facing backward, Riley drove under the limit and said little. A moderate head wind buffeted the open car, so a conversation would have been difficult. On

Big Coppitt a sedan with a yellow county license tag passed us, honked, then raced on ahead. Riley yelled something about his assistants becoming the next two victims of the Overseas Highway. "They can't do diddly till I get there, anyway."

Mangroves baked in the heat and gulls coasted above tiny peninsulas. Sunlight reflected vibrant lime and pale purples off bottom sand in shallow basins on either side of the road. In the back country the wind had churned the water to a milky pea-green. We would get an occasional rank whiff of beached seaweed—then a draft of cooler air on a maverick breeze. For a while I kept my eyes upward, hoping to spot an osprey or spoonbill. Offshore in Hawk Channel, two commercialmen dieseled toward Key West. Beyond the reef, east of the Western Sambos, the superstructure of a northbound freighter poked above the horizon. Crossing a bridge in the Saddlebunch Keys, I spotted the orange-and-blue sail of a Windsurfer hammering across wave tops a mile to the southeast.

A small pull-off area remained on the Atlantic side of the highway where the road used to angle down to the old trestle-style Bahia Honda Bridge. It was hard to spot. The occasional sharp-eyed tourist would park and amble down the rocky slope to photograph the twin palms near the tide line, or wonder about the stubbed end of the bridge that went fifty feet and stopped midair. We arrived to a snarl of vehicles, marked and unmarked, parked haphazardly in the upper lot. The small slab of broken pavement at the lower level was blocked by a half dozen more cars and a Ford ambulance. The tops of nearby palms clattered in the breeze that had shifted slightly to the southeast.

Riley angled into a narrow slot between two highway patrol Crown Vics, shut off the Jeep, and turned his ball cap frontward. "When I was a kid there was a tollbooth on Big Pine," he said, as if the remark fit a conversation he'd been having in his head. "You had a special taxpayer decal on your windshield, you didn't pay a buck. Goddamned skeeters ate up toll collectors, but those guys knew everyone from Marathon to Mile Zero."

I trailed Riley down the gravel path toward the waterline. Detective Avery Hatch, accompanied by an occluding gust of cigar smoke, fought his way up the rocky trail. "Stogie fix, boys," he barked. "You're in charge till I get back. We got a dead Hispanic this time, kind of a *Twin Peaks* job. Remember that goofy-ass TV show? This darling puts a new meaning to 'all tied up.'"

Riley winced. "How long's she been in the water, Avery?"

"She was never in the water. She's high and dry. Somebody dropped her off and she never caught the bus."

I stopped Hatch. "Why am I here?"

Larry Riley looked at each of us, then continued walking downhill.

Hatch pushed his cigar off to leeward. "What you said about Monroe County being cheap, about Forsythe not being very professional? The detectives are aware of his shortcomings. But his scrawny salary makes room in the budget for Kevlar vests. Meanwhile, we got two dead females in one day. If the two are connected and we got a nut killing women in the Keys, it'll make national news sure as shit. I don't want to look like a butthole by blowing the case. I consider you high-priced insurance."

I'd been called worse. I continued down to level ground, through sparse grass to a thin strip of dirty sand, then crossed a high-tide weed patch littered with weather-beaten four-by-fours and white plastic bleach bottles. I found it easier going on the wide rocky ledge.

Thirty yards to the southwest and fifty feet from the waterline, Larry Riley peered into a huddle of reporters and EMS people and deputies in a hammock of mangroves and spindly pine saplings. As I approached, Larry walked toward me and set his briefcase on a boulder of brain coral. "Damned if it doesn't look like that TV show. Plastic wrap, blue face, and everything. All we need is fluttery music and a station break."

I dropped my camera bag next to Riley's clipboard. I was in no rush to join the viewing. I grabbed two cameras, a battery pack, and a flash unit, then set the exposure and f-stop dials on my equipment and checked my film settings. After taking a moment or two to scan the horizon beyond the reef, I approached the group surrounding the corpse, slipped between two glum deputies, and glanced down.

Oh, damn, Julia. Don't do this to me, goddammit.

There are times when you want everything to go blank. But your mind shoots off in its own directions, making the moment and the whole world more intense. She had been so full of sense and spirit, so fluid, graceful, so hard to please. She could be erotic one minute and cinnamon-sweet the next. Then she would go tomboyish and pretend not to understand her own allure, not to believe in her own beauty or wit. She did it all as if flipping a switch, as if she did not care.

On the second day I knew her, in 1977, she had cooked paella to help celebrate the purchase of my new home on Dredgers Lane. She had told me, "I'll sleep in your bed tonight if you promise three things: Never tell me you love me, never ask me to live here, and never ask me to marry you." In spite of the strong cooking vapors, she'd smelled of a delicate rose perfume. Her green-gray eyes had watered from singed spices. I told her I would promise her anything. "Then," she replied, "you must promise not to forget this conversation in the morning."

Spoken as they were, I should have recognized the standard rules for a union of convenience.

Detective Billy Fernandez nudged me. "You gonna get these snapshots, bubba, you gonna stare at the net buoys all afternoon?"

40

"Is that Forsythe over there?" I asked.

Fernandez scratched at his dead-caterpillar mustache. "That's our boy," he said. "Wearing his street shoes in a puddle of water. He's a dumb fuck. Those shoes are forty-nine bucks at Upton's."

"I'm going to need a minute or two. Let's let Forsythe finish his work."

I looped my camera-bag strap over my head and walked up the beach.

6

So I'd flaked on the photo job. I knew I couldn't press the button, sure as hell couldn't focus. I'd deferred to Forsythe and his budget lenses and waterlogged wing tips. Larry Riley showed concern as well as curiosity. He found me on the concrete seawall beneath the blunt stub of the old Bahia Honda trestle bridge. I was dangling my legs, watching the choppy turquoise sea scramble itself into a blur. My thoughts had bounced back to Annie at the property-line hedge in Ellen Albury's yard, her eyes pissed and confused. I wasn't ready to envision Julia's face or wonder how she had died, or whom she had last seen with her sweet green-gray eyes.

"You had a thing with this woman?" Riley sat next to me, facing away from the water. He did a good job of holding a neutral tone of voice.

"Ancient history," I said. "I once rode in a Porsche that went a hundred and forty-five miles an hour. Being with Julia was like three times the speed limit. It didn't last long."

"Cuban girl?"

"Born down there, a couple years before Castro made his move."

She had told me the background. Her mother's family had been in wholesaling and her father had become an anti-Batista go-between, moving aircraft repair parts from the CIA to the rebels. When the Castro revolution succeeded, the mother's clan, along with Julia and her sister, fled to Miami, while the father kept his two sons in Cuba. Later the father crossed up his Communist comrades and was thrown into prison. The sons escaped to Miami in the seventies. The old man was released a few years later. I'd forgotten the details, but somehow he'd made it to Florida by the early eighties.

"Her father's first name Raoul?" Riley's feet shuffled in the sand and dirt.

"Raoul Balbuena, right. Some kind of civic or political honcho in Miami."

Riley grunted. "In the *Herald,* just last week, there was an article. Raoul's been a hero in Miami for years, being an ex–political prisoner. But he's speaking out against the trade embargo, so the diehards are calling him a traitor to the cause. Demonstrating whenever he appears in public." Riley paused and blew out a puff of air. "Now his daughter turns up dead on the beach."

It didn't add up that someone would kill Julia to make a political statement. "Got to be a flawed connection."

"It's an ugly way to make a point," he said. "You can bet the sheriff's going to get hammered by the media."

"Even the anti-Castro nuts, the militants, they wouldn't bump off a man's daughter for revenge. I mean, doesn't Castro's sister live in Miami?"

"How'd you hook up with her?" Riley was fishing for conversation, trying to coax me back to his Jeep so he could start home.

"In '77 and '78 I bartended at Lou's on Duval. One afternoon she strutted in and ordered a 'fucking quadruple margarita, straight up, and hold the goddamn salt,' unquote. I mean strutted, like she'd had lessons from the hot-pants chiquitas on Collins Avenue. Instead of the margarita, I made her a Cuervo Gold with soda and a chunk of key lime. She liked it."

"I could use one right now."

"It was slow in the bar. I refilled her drink four or five times. We poured out our life stories until I got off at sundown. She walked home with me." I still remembered the heavy smell of night-blooming jasmine on Caroline Street that evening. "She slept on the couch the first night. We spent the next day on my boat and after supper that night we went gangbusters. It lasted eight days."

The breeze faltered for a moment and I felt an untempered blast of the afternoon heat. The buzzing traffic on the highway reminded me that the rest of the world was rolling along, oblivious to Julia's death, oblivious to my loss. I saw no point in occupying the crumbling seawall for the rest of the day. I stood and followed Riley uphill toward U.S. 1. His Jeep was the only vehicle in the upper lot where the tangle of cars had been parked. Two cars and an EMS ambulance remained in the lower area. "She go running back to Lauderdale?" he said.

"She hooked up with Ray Kemp, one of the other bartenders. He wound up owning a charter boat—*Barracuda*—out at the Bight. Left town years ago."

"I remember the boat. I don't recall Ray Kemp."

"They started yakking one day while he and I were working the bar. They fell in love on the spot, like a soap opera. She didn't even wave good-bye. He quit his job a day later. I didn't see them for a couple of years."

Riley gave me an odd look, then pulled onto the road behind a southbound Yugo towing a homemade trailer. We drove into the late-afternoon sun. The breeze had picked up—a tailwind, so our conversation did not have to fight the buffeting. "Doesn't sound like you were impressed, the way they handled it," he said. "You still upset?"

I wasn't sure why Riley wanted to keep this going. But I hadn't thought about it in years, and I felt more like talking than clamming up and stewing. "At first, poof, she was gone," I said. "No explanation. I would've kept on with the relationship. But she'd made it clear from the start that sex was all she wanted. Plus, you know, the age difference mattered more back then. How could I get angry? She wanted real romance."

Traffic had snugged bumper-to-bumper in the double-yellow sections. We finally hit an open straightaway, and Riley pulled to the right so a stake truck full of crab traps could go around. "So they stayed to themselves?" he said.

"Maybe she was ashamed of herself. I kept expecting to look up one day and see them pushing a baby stroller down Duval Street. He went to work on *Barracuda,* then quit and earned some quick money offshore. He came back to Garrison Bight with a bagful of dollars and bought the boat and made himself captain. I hooked up with him during the Mariel Boatlift."

"Nineteen-eighty. I was in med school, in Gainesville."

"I was in the thick of it, trying to be the ultimate photo-journalist. When the rush to Cuba began, Julia talked Ray into using *Barracuda* to go after her father. I went to take pictures for *Newsweek.* I made an enemy of Kemp, and I almost bought the farm."

Riley was surprised. "She went to Mariel, too?"

I nodded.

"How come suddenly you were back in touch?"

"A *Newsweek* editor showed up on the dock and hired Sam Wheeler's *Fancy Fool*—that old Bertram Sam used to charter. *Barracuda* was out of the water getting prepped at Steadman's for Ray and Julia's trip. But the editor met Ray on the dock just before *Fancy Fool* left. The guy wrote Ray a check for five grand and told him to hire a professional photographer and bring him to Mariel. Ray was going anyway, so the money was a sweet little bonus. They asked me to come, to be *Newsweek*'s man with the camera. I don't know why. Maybe to heal the old wound, a peace offering. I don't know. We wound up getting stuck down there ten days, anchored in Mariel Harbor. Ray and Julia had a falling-out during the trip, but I made two grand."

The highway widened to four lanes in the section that fronts Boca Chica Naval Air Station. A half mile later the carful of ME staffers passed us, then the Ford ambulance in a quiet, unlit transit mode. I forced myself not to dwell on what the ambulance carried. Neither of us spoke until it was out of sight.

"Her father come back on *Barracuda*?"

"No. We brought in twelve refugees, but not him."

Riley tilted his head toward me. "You have anything to do with their falling-out? Or am I being too nosy?"

"From what I saw, the split was inevitable. Ray's bullshit on the trip pushed it over the edge. I didn't get in the middle."

Riley crossed the bridge above the charter-boat docks, zipped a yellow light at Eaton, made a couple of lefts, and stopped on Fleming at the top of Dredgers Lane. Sam Wheeler's truck and Annie's convertible were up the lane in front of my house.

Riley pointed at the Jeep's door, to help me find the handle. "When was the last time you saw her?"

I thought back. "Late '85. She came down with a boy she'd been living with in Boca Raton. College-jock type, at least six-six. Hell, she was five-two. Jesus, Larry. I've talked myself hoarse."

"No problem. Stories like yours help to humanize my job. I get to be a hard case, fighting depression, looking for the bright side of life. It gets ridiculous. I almost named my sailboat *Aw Topsy Tipsy*. Say hello to Carmen for me."

The Jeep's transmission whined through the gears as Riley drove up to White Street. I stood on Fleming, jiggling my camera bag, watching a drunken bicyclist fight to keep his balance as a raucous motorcycle sped past. Something nagged at me, and after a moment's thought I decided that it had been Riley's tone of voice when he asked me when I'd last seen Julia.

The yellow lights in the windows of my house were beacons

of comfort. I wanted to crawl into my cave and stop all the craziness.

Sam, Annie, and Carmen sat in the glow of the oil lamp on the screened porch, the porch no wider than the deck of a small boat. The first thing I noticed was the liter bottle, my stash of Calvados, on the porcelain tabletop. Annie, in her office clothes minus shoes, her pale green eyes red and puffed, cradled a snifter in one hand. Sam sipped from a can of beer. Carmen sat in the old redwood chaise, her legs crossed at the ankles, her eyes focused straight ahead. She, too, had been crying.

Sam handed me an open beer. He must have taken it from the fridge when he heard the Jeep pull up. "Monty called," he said softly. "Said you'd identified the body."

"A nasty day. Is this what I missed by being too young for Vietnam?"

"Carmen went to high school with Ellen." Annie's voice sounded thin. "They knew each other in twelfth grade."

"I just rode down the Keys with Larry Riley."

Carmen also held a snifter. She looked up and I caught her eye. "You never told me about him," I said.

"Ah, Larry. The first of many missed opportunities in this life. Painful, we were so innocent. Sweet Jesus, we were innocent."

"He sent his regards."

Carmen swirled the brandy with her forefinger, raised the glass in salute to the memory, and tilted back for a big gulp.

"I'm sorry about your friend Julia." Fatigue and defeat weakened Annie's voice. "I'm sorry about our friend Ellen. And I'm sorry but I have to go lie down. Thank you for taking care of my plants." She lifted her hand so I could help her from her chair.

"My mama watched the news on the cable." When sober, Carmen did a better job of masking her nasal Conch accent.

"They sayin' Julia's murder could start a civil war in South Florida. Her daddy vowed to avenge her death."

Sam's eyes followed a lizard up the screen. I sat, exhausted, on the cushion still warm from Annie.

"I was born in Key West," Carmen continued. "I speak English and Spanish every day, even at work in the post office. Three of my grandparents were born in Tampa, and some of my great-grandparents were born in Key West or Tampa. I've always been a Cuban, other Cubans treat me like one of them. Still, I don't know what's going on in Miami."

My two cents: "The Hong Kong of the hemisphere."

She agreed. "Those people wave a flag, it belongs to another country. They made their big money in Florida while they argued over that property Fidel took thirty-five years ago. He didn't make that land into some private estate. What are the rich people in Miami going to do, fly down there on jets and take it back from the farmers and their children? Anyway, I have to get up at four-thirty so I can stuff mail in the boxes at six-fifteen. But I'm going to buy a dog, even if it barks all night and wakes up my neighbors and its shit smells up the lane. And I'm buying a gun."

Carmen stood and carefully placed her snifter on the table. "Now I can be like every Cuban housewife in Key West. I will carry a little pistol in my purse on the pretext that it will protect me from hippies stealing my jewelry. Of course, you boys know, the real reason the housewives keep their weapons is so they can threaten to shoot their cheating husbands where it hurts the most." She wobbled when she started for the porch door.

I reached to steady her. "Let me walk you home, sweet woman. We can't be too careful."

I was back in a minute and a half. Sam hadn't moved a hair. "Two damn murders in one day, and no suspects in sight," he said.

"Two murders close to home, as they say."

"Right in your lap. You got a certain look in your eye."

"I'd like to have a few words with the fucker who did Julia."

Sam held his arms as if holding a machine gun, making his empty beer can the pistol grip. "Crazies with the fervor of patriots. Nasty people with automatic weapons. Times in Miami have changed, amigo. We Anglos wouldn't stand a chance. How about the Albury murder? You want to get snoopy, you could make more headway with that one. Even though you didn't know her."

"My schedule is not bursting with alternatives."

"Think with care, friend."

"Don't I always?"

Sam hesitated. "I'm too busy fishing to keep score."

We sat for a minute and Sam cleared his throat. "Another subject. You will be proud of me. Hearing your story at lunch got me riled, as did the two extra beers I drank with a foul conscience. So I hustled my butt down to the *Citizen* and found a lady who listened to a few choice questions. Like where does someone who doesn't work for the state of Florida, an assistant federal prosecutor, get the traction to convene a special session of the Florida Board of Training and Professional Standards? And where does that board get the balls to decertify an officer who's risked his life undercover for three years? Those questions, in a more diplomatic format, are going to show up in print. I also went to the *Herald*'s news office and did the same dance."

"You can't be sure what's going to show up in print," I said. "They make promises they don't keep."

Sam shifted his eyes to the ceiling. "I got a dinner date tomorrow night."

Wheeler and his women. He won their hearts, and they came back to him again and again, but not one had inspired his settling down.

"You sleazeball. I'm going to offer you another beer and I'm going to have one myself."

"I'll pass." His broad shoulders slumped slightly as he pulled the empty out of its foam insulator. "I need to drive up to Sugarloaf to see an old client who's in town, but not fishing this time. He's dying of some disease. Cancer, I suppose, but he won't talk about it. He started fishing with me in the early eighties, and it took him only two years to stop being a patronizing prick. Ever since then we've had great times, three trips a year. He turned into a kickass light-tackle angler."

"Well, I'm going to have at least one more."

Sam stopped outside the screen door. "Whatever it takes, bubba. I am sorry about Julia."

I leaned against a doorjamb on the porch, sipped a beer that I didn't need, and studied the living room. Lots of memories. It had been my hideout, my office, my reading room, and party central. Before Annie had come along I'd slept more often on the sagging couch than in the bedroom.

Annie's sleepy voice came from the dark. "Rutledge, who are you talking to?" She walked out of the bedroom in a short T-shirt and panties.

"I guess to myself."

"It's nice to hear you talk." She picked dead leaves from a philodendron and delivered them to the kitchen trash. Then she sat in the bamboo rocker and gathered her legs up to her chest. Her disheveled hair gave her beauty a spontaneity, a firmness. We looked at each other and listened to sounds in the neighborhood, air conditioners and rattling palm trees. In the dim light her eyes didn't say much. After a minute she stood, adjusted the underwear elastic under her bottom, and walked past me to the porch.

A few moments later she leaned against me and rested her hand in the crook of my elbow. "This may not be fair," she said, "because I wouldn't answer a question of yours this afternoon. I've never heard you mention Julia. Carmen said that she'd meant a lot to you."

"She spent seven days in this house, the first month I lived here. Then she went to live with someone else. I've never analyzed, deep down, how I felt about her, except I liked having her around at the time. And I missed her. She was on the boat I rode to Mariel. I saw her again ten or twelve years ago. I guess I had her filed under 'unfinished business.'"

"Did you ever wish you could finish the business?"

"Before I met you."

"Never since?"

"Today. When I realized it was impossible."

Annie moved closer and rested her forehead against my chest. "Can I ask a favor? A big one?"

"I know what it is. I was going to ask the same thing."

She took my hand in the softness of hers and led me into the bedroom. A moment later, pulling off her T-shirt, she stopped with her hands still in the armholes and hung the garment across the top of her head. "Don't you wish that making love could bring back the dead?"

Talk like that had drawn me to Annie from the beginning.

I moved closer and reached behind her to push down her underpants. She stopped me. She wanted to remove my clothing first. She fumbled a moment with the buttons, then opened my shirt and pressed her breasts against my bare chest. Her kiss slowed us and, second by second, her mouth erased three weeks of anger. I wanted simply to hold her, to pull her closer, to lock her to me until I could forget her absence, her fading, her silence.

We held each other, hardly breathing. Her lips formed words against my shoulder. I wanted the panties off. They reminded me of Ellen Albury's dead body. Annie pushed my hand inside the front elastic, then turned my wrist to aim my fingers into the folds. The dampness, her openness, begged a shift from distrust to the faith of love. Her warmth melted the boundary between wariness and submission. She tugged me to the bed. The underpants slipped to her ankles as she let herself fall backward.

I gazed at the soft skin of her belly and thighs and wondered for a moment if this was a fresh start or some crazy finale. I bent to kiss and nudge with my tongue the skin of one breast, from the bump of a rib upward to the nipple. A minute later, as my mouth moved down that sweet line from her neck to her navel and farther, I caught myself recalling Julia's smooth olive skin.

Annie must have sensed my wandering. She shifted and pushed my head downward, then cried as if in pain and pulled me back toward her face. Her eyes took me away from Julia and demanded my presence. Her surrender and compliance erased everything else from my mind.

7

This piece of theater had played on my brain for twenty days.

Annie had invented a morning game. She had worked on timing, perfected her routine. She would get up first, and after her shower I would watch her dress for work. That was it. There would be no talking or eye contact, and my pillow-height point of view was wondrously exaggerated by her five-nine height. She would begin by untangling the underwear, then perform exquisite hop-steps as she looped her slingshot panties over one foot and the other. Some mornings I would get a rear view of this stage; other mornings she would face me but still no eye contact. After she had adjusted the panties for comfort, smoothing them over her upper thighs, she would choose a bra. She took her time with its positioning and snugging, taking each breast in a full handhold to ensure its exact place in the cloth cup. Then came the blouse selection, the shoes and bracelets, the flow of the sun-streaked brown hair that would go anywhere she wanted it to go. After Annie had buttoned her skirt—always the last step—and had left for work, I'd head to the kitchen for my Cuban coffee.

I wanted this morning to be one of those. Along with the slow-motion lovemaking that had closed out the night, the voyeuristic ritual would affirm that our romance still had a chance. If I still wanted to take that chance. I felt Annie get out of bed. Smells of mangoes and figs drifted in the morning air. The traffic on Fleming sounded urgent but far away. I can't recall how long she'd been out of the room.

Then she was back in the room, nudging my foot with her knee.

"You come out here and deal with him." Her voice was a forced whisper. "I walk around bare-assed for five minutes before I realize he's out there. It's that goddamned detective with the smelly cigars."

"Is he smoking one now?"

"No, but he looks like he wants to."

Resplendent in a sky-blue guayabera shirt, navy-blue trousers, and white dress shoes, Avery Hatch had made himself at home on my porch. The Keys section of the *Miami Herald* covered the table—he'd moved the nearly empty Calvados bottle to a plant shelf—and he sipped coffee from a McDonald's cup. Torn sugar packets and empty nondairy creamer thimbles littered the lounge-chair cushion. Light filtered through the hanging plants and reflected off a faint sheen of mousse in his mod pompadour. His right breast pocket held four large dark-colored cigars.

I stood in the doorway in my jockey shorts, scratching my stomach.

Hatch threw out the first ball. "I find out after all the rigmarole at the Olivia scene that you and the Minnette lady are friends." He twisted his head to peer into the house, then turned to face me again. "My compliments. Then I dwell on the fact that I don't know shit about this Albury case, which, as the pivot man for Monroe County's Violent Crimes Task Force, I need to know."

I refused to respond.

Avery hunched forward for a sip of coffee, taking care not to drip on his shirt. "You identify the corpse in the sand. It's okay you didn't take pictures. I understand you're under a strain, the shock and all. But Forsythe, in his words, either overexposed the film or underdeveloped the film or vice versa. I know when he uses technical words it's an excuse for a fuckup. So in his pictures the deceased looks like a Norwegian blonde instead of a Latina brunette. Like I said, it's okay you didn't take pictures. But I wonder could I learn more about this magnificent world by sitting here and drinking my third cup of burned coffee and listening to you talk about said deceased. You follow me?"

A verbal response would give him permission—after the fact—for helping himself to my porch.

Hatch figured out that I had no reason to speak. "Since we got the unique circumstance of you and Miss Minnette in the same house, I want to listen to both of you talk. You sure sleep late."

Now he was going to sit there and critique my schedule. "You got big feet," I mumbled. "I had a long day yesterday."

He twisted his neck to look around his thigh. "Size-ten foot, size-eleven shoe. Sale at Burdines. They were out of tens. We married guys don't have the incentive to stay in the sack much past the rooster hour. Do me a favor."

More strategic silence.

"I killed the open speaker in the car so the two-way radio wouldn't rile the neighborhood. I pride myself in community service, being sensitive to the populace. You mind flipping your scanner to the county freak?"

"I don't own a scanner."

He shot me an expression. Phony surprise. "And you work for us?"

"I try not to be on constant alert. I'm a photographer, not a groupie."

"We can provide a beeper. We got beepers out the ying-yang."

I stared at him with the dumbest expression I could muster.

"Go fix your coffee," said Hatch. "I can wait. This is kinda nice out here. I had a cubbyhole like this, I'd go terminal lazyass myself. All you need is elevator music. Light jazz. A little bare-boobed Tahitian girl with a paper fan."

He looked too comfortable. And smug, on the Monroe County time clock. In that regard, I couldn't forget that the man authorized paychecks, though I planned to reconsider my commitment to crime photography. In this case I had no legal problems, but I wanted some information myself. I told myself to hold my tongue and keep an open mind.

Wrapped in a robe, Annie tiptoed into the kitchen as I measured out Cuban coffee. "What does he want?"

"Why are you sneaking around? He knows you're here. Now he knows you've got a birthmark on your inner thigh."

"I just want to know what he's after."

"He wants to hear us talk. So far he's been sociable."

"I think we can count on this not being a social call."

"You afraid of something?"

She thought a second. "Him in general. Wasting my time."

"We'll get it done quickly." I called out to Hatch: "You want cup number four? It's high-test. Like they used to make at El Cacique."

"I'd spend the rest of the morning in the john."

"Lovely man," said Annie. She spun and headed back to the bedroom.

"Mind if I use your phone? I gotta call in." I heard Hatch shuffle on the porch, then step onto the hardwood living room floor.

"It's on a long cord," I said. "Could be anywhere."

"Sounds like the people who work for me."

Audible punctuation from Annie: the bedroom door slammed shut.

I carried my Bustelo out to the morning breeze while Hatch made his call. The close-up of Julia in the *Herald* looked recent. She looked like an executive being promoted, a real estate broker joining the Million Dollar Club. The headline went for the sensational, calling the murder TWIN PEAKS–STYLED. No photo accompanied the two-column LOCAL LEGAL WORKER FOUND SLAIN article about Ellen Albury.

Hatch returned to the porch, fumbling with his pocketful of cigars. Annie walked out behind him, dressed for the office. She'd pulled back her hair with an antique silver barrette. She looked great.

"This going to take long, Detective?" Her words had that courtroom ring, the resonance that made her sound like a different Annie.

"A minute or two. You and I kept missing each other yesterday."

"I hadn't realized that. I recall a Q and A session in the backyard on Olivia."

He pushed the newspaper aside and pulled a three-by-five card out of his shirt pocket. "You'd been gone less than two minutes when I stopped at the Embry house. And your car was leaving the Federal Building when I arrived to speak with the assistant federal prosecutor. I grabbed your parking space, and I thank you for that. You'd been to his office, too."

Hatch's attitude and words were crowding the edge of accusatory. Worse, he had referred to Michael Anselmo, Monty Aghajanian's nemesis. It shouldn't have surprised me that Annie might know Anselmo, but I didn't like where this was going.

"I had a number of appointments yesterday," said Annie. "As you know, I got a late start."

"Yes, ma'am. We all got a rough start yesterday. My timetable was screwed from the time I got up."

"So what do you mean, missing each other?" she said.

Hatch glanced at me, then looked off through the screening. "I had a few more questions for you, that's all."

I didn't want to butt in, but I didn't like his tone. "What are we trying to nail down here?" I said. "You're talking about a murder inside the city limits, you're talking about Bahia Honda, which is in Monroe County, and you're talking about a federal prosecutor. That's three separate jurisdictions."

Hatch checked the bottom of his Styrofoam cup, grimaced, and decided against a last sip. He fumbled again with his cigars, then turned to Annie. "I need to double-check the timetable, for one thing. We know you discovered the body at 7:08—according to your statement—but the 911 call didn't come through till 7:25. Also, according to our tracing system, the call didn't originate at the Olivia Street house. You called from the home phone of Michael Anselmo."

Annie nodded in agreement.

I felt tall walls crumbling around me. I knew what she had been afraid of.

"So, what the hell?" Hatch's eyes locked on her.

"That's your question?" snapped Annie. "'What the hell?'"

"We're not stupid people, Miss Minnette."

I had to agree.

Annie turned red but maintained a poker face.

Hatch splayed out his hands as if to calm things. "Let me make myself clear. You are not a suspect, Miss Minnette. You've got an alibi. I'm sorry if I offended either of you. I'm just digging for information. Here's another question, Miss Minnette. Did you know that Miss Albury's biological father, Pepper Neice of Riviera Beach, was convicted of the sexual abuse of young girls?"

"Oh, Jesus." She exhaled, disgusted.

Hatch checked another three-by-five card. "According to the court's records, neither conviction involved his daughter. Some people in City Hall recall that he skated in that regard at least twice. Once when she was in grade school, and again later. He was a gentleman of the shrimping trade. A deckhand and a real late-sixties dock bum. Mrs. Embry—the former Mrs. Neice—met him in Captain Tony's Saloon. She married him a week later and divorced him a year after that. Out came Ellen. Daddy was in and out of town until he got busted with a naked nine-year-old playmate of Ellen's in '75. He did a scoot in Raiford, then moved to Shallotte, North Carolina, to resume his career in the shrimp business. Seven years later he was back.

"When Ellen was about fifteen, she moved out of her mother's home and into his. At that time there were two domestic dispute calls over a period of weeks with no complaints filed. Then she moved back into her mother's house. A short while later he got nailed again with a minor. This time the judge plain fixed him. He didn't get out of prison until three weeks ago."

Annie's eyes had dampened. She took a seat at the end of the chaise, put her elbows on her knees, and rested her forehead on her hands. It took her a moment to speak again. She sat up straight. "I have a huge caseload. I missed an entire day's work yesterday, and you allow that I am not a suspect. Can we meet later in the day, in my office, to discuss all this?"

"That'd be fine," said Hatch, "but one more thing. I got a call from Mrs. Embry last night. She and her husband had gone to the Olivia Street house to pack up her daughter's belongings. She said that she found a few things that belonged to you—surprisingly few things for someone who had lived there. And she said that an expensive bicycle is missing. It had been a gift from them to Annie . . . Ellen, sorry. They suggested if we could find the bike, it might help us find the murderer."

Annie showed me a frozen expression of disgust, then spoke to Hatch with forced civility. "I borrowed the bike. It's safe, and I'll make sure that it's returned to the Embrys. How about one-thirty this afternoon?"

"Okay."

She ducked into the house and reemerged with freshened lipstick and her briefcase in hand. She leaned to kiss my cheek, caught my eye for an instant, but looked downward. "Hang in with me, Alex," she whispered. "This is a tough one. I'm glad to be back."

She went out the porch door. Hatch and I sat listening to the VW speed through the stop sign and accelerate up Fleming.

"I take it you've got a problem with Michael Anselmo," said Hatch.

"I knew I had a problem. I didn't know it was another lawyer."

"Sometimes I think the women on this island are affected by sea air," he said. "Been a mystery since my first piece, they all want to sneak around, give it away to geeks. Pisses me off bad. Only way to get even, lemme tell you, you knock down strange and bang it regular. Only goddamn thing that works."

I wanted another cup of Bustelo. I went into the kitchen and came out with a bottle of beer. Twelve ounces of self-indulgence to fend off stupidity.

Hatch sneaked a glance at his watch. "Starting early?"

"Not my usual routine."

"You don't have a scanner."

"Never will."

"Nobody down at the city contacted you yesterday. I know because I just called and asked. With no scanner, how is it you happened to show up at Olivia Street, camera in hand, ready for work? How'd you know?"

"She told me."

"She called you from Anselmo's?"

"She showed up right here on the doorstep with her suitcases. She was afraid you'd quarantine the Olivia Street house and keep her clothes. She put her stuff in her car before she made the first emergency call. I guess she decided to leave it all here instead of Anselmo's. She said you were waiting for her back on Olivia. Why is this a surprise to you?"

Hatch smiled and shook his head. "Loaded her car. That explains the delayed call to 911. Before I could start taking her statement, she had to go to the bathroom. I told her she couldn't use the one in her house, so she said she'd be right back."

"She came here. But she didn't use the bathroom."

"If I ever need a lawyer, I want her number."

Five sips into my beer, I caught myself wishing for elevator music, too.

"Speakin' of the bathroom, mind if I drain the dragon?"

"All yours."

While I waited for Hatch, I looked again at the photograph of Julia. It could have taken me into an all-day daydream, except that a headline on the same page caught my eye: COP RISKS LIFE FOR YEARS, STATE SAYS NO THANKS. The opening lines described the revocation of Monty Aghajanian's badge and his original problem with the car thieves. Perhaps this would shake some action out of Tallahassee. Three cheers for Sam Wheeler.

Hatch eased himself back into the chair. He pretended to clear his throat and attempted a sympathetic approach. "Tell me about Julia." He tapped the paper next to her picture. "I want to get a feel for the woman, to understand her personality, her views . . . enough to consider theories and reject impossibles."

"You want the two-hour version?"

"Five minutes or less."

I summoned the daydream. "Where to start? A moral version of the whore with a heart of gold. I mean, she played it tough, streetwise, but she was normal under the facade. Better educated than most of the women who show up in this town. I was around her for a week in '77 and eleven days' worth of Mariel Boatlift bullshit in May of 1980. We fell in lust, she went for another guy named Ray Kemp, she lived with him until Mariel, and she went back to Miami. In the mid-eighties she came here with a boyfriend and looked me up. We had rum drinks down at Louie's on the Afterdeck, said good-bye, and I never heard from her again."

"She ever talk about her father's politics?"

"Just that he'd been one of Fidel's boys until the Commies decided that he wasn't so faithful and put him in the clink. I don't think we talked about him the last time she was here."

Hatch stared off in thought for about fifteen seconds, then heaved himself to his feet, smoothed the wrinkles in his trousers, and readied the cigar he would light the instant he left the porch.

"Bad things happen in threes," I said. "You waiting for the third shoe to drop?"

"You count the dead girl on Stock Island five days ago, you got your three. Or you could count three in one day with that attempted car-jacking yesterday afternoon. You hear about that?"

I shook my head.

"Story's been told fifty times down to the city, and all the deputies got it memorized. Lady at Key Plaza walks out of the pet store. A guy grabs her, he's waving a big fillet knife, wants her keys and wants her in the car. Cool lady ignores the knife. She unbuttons her blouse to show him her titties. The idiot's drooling through his fake beard, she nails him with a tear-gas zapper on her key ring."

"Catch the guy?"

"He ran off. Nobody around to chase or identify him except the lady. But like I said, he's wearing the false beard. She buttons up, walks back in the pet store, and asks them to call the police. Like there was nothin' to it at all. She's been in town for years. You know Shelly Standish?"

I knew Shelly Standish. But I didn't say so.

Hatch handed me the cellophane cigar wrapper. "So I won't litter your yard." He stepped outside and let the porch door slam.

He'd walked about fifteen feet when I said, "You recall the victim's name on Stock Island?"

Hatch stopped but he was facing downwind, so he didn't

turn. "Sally Ann Guthery. Another one in her late thirties." He finally fired up his cigar.

I knew how old she was. Exactly how old she was. A small coincidence we'd discovered. She and I had shared the same birthday. Same date, same year.

The tall walls that had been crumbling began to fall down on me.

8

Sam Wheeler swore he would never allow a cellular phone near his skiff unless a client had health problems. "Contrary to bad lyrics and old movie scripts," he'd said, "you can run *and* you can hide. Imagine some natty angler on the flats, whispering to his colleagues about rate of return while fifteen permit tail by . . ."

To stay in touch with customers and his darling companions—Sam's term—he kept an old rotary style on the dock, plugged into a jack he'd installed next to his shore power box. When he was on the water he'd stash the phone in a dock locker, and an answering machine did the dirty work.

I got the machine: "Gone fishing. I'll be back when I return."

"Rutledge. Call me."

I called Monty Aghajanian. He was in.

"Saw your name in the paper," I said.

He breathed out a false chuckle. "Once in a while my problem comes up. It's because I've gotten to know the media people."

"Anything helps." I decided not to mention Wheeler's mission with the newspaper reporters.

"Nothing ever comes of it. Bernier—my buddy in the FBI—saw the article. He called to say that the door was still open if I get recertified for my badge. It gets to be a vicious circle. I've been around four times already, like penalty laps in gym class. I've learned not to get my hopes up."

"Gotta keep plugging."

"Always. Chicken Neck asked me did I see you."

"I had to run to Bahia Honda for that one, so I missed him."

"Man, I was sorry to hear. I saw her name, I knew you'd hit it head-on."

"Thanks. I floated some anguish over that woman."

"Goddamn shame. They're saying Cubans."

"Oh, I hope not. I mean, I don't much care who did it beyond I want him caught. But such a waste. What do you know about this Shelly Standish thing? I heard a story from Hatch, first thing this morning . . ."

"The insensitive rumor here at the city is that she's going to be the new spokesperson for Hooters."

A knock at my screen door. Carmen Sosa, in her post-office uniform. I motioned her in. "Has this fake beard struck before?" I said to Monty.

"No, but he must be an Einstein. An '81 Buick on its last legs, held together by primer paint and duct tape. Carjacking doesn't make sense when there's only one road off the island."

"That murder on Stock Island the other day, I missed it in the news. Any suspects, witnesses?"

Carmen went straight for the coffee. I covered the microphone end of the phone. "I'm out of cream. Why aren't you at work?"

"Split day," she said.

"You sound like you got the Hatch disease," said Monty.

I uncovered the phone. "I hope not. What do you mean?"

"It's either a conspiracy or a serial killer. Down here at the city we're not buying the theory."

"Well, shit. It's strange enough when Annie's roommate and my ex-lover are killed on the same day. But I know Shelly and

I knew Sally Ann. I mean, I dated both of them way back when. I slept in both of their beds. I didn't offer those facts to Hatch, but this is getting too close to home."

Carmen rolled her eyes at my admission, as if I were tallying my macho conquests. She carried her espresso to the bamboo rocker and settled in.

"You live in a small town, Rutledge," said Monty. "You could drive yourself crazy thinking like that."

"How can I ignore it? Three direct hits and a near miss."

"Logic tells us you're the prime suspect."

"Let's rule me out for the moment and discuss the real possibilities."

"Okay, how many people would connect you with Julia? That was how many years ago, fifteen, twenty? Before you answer, figure how many people know about you and Shelly or you and Sally Ann. Bear in mind, this is Key West. Everybody's too screwed up to remember that far back. Including, I hate to tell you, Shelly and Sally Ann. Second, there's so much wild thing going on, who keeps track? Third, why would anyone pay that much attention to your love life? I mean, who cares?"

Monty had a point. Take everyone who ever knew all three women and find who in that group might connect them to me. It came down to me. And maybe Annie, though I could not recall what I had told her during our truth sessions.

"Monty, it's not going to stop bothering me. Let's say there's a connection, direct or remote. What comes next?"

"Where does Ellen Albury fit in? You barely knew her."

"Mistaken identity. You said it yourself. They could have been sisters. If the wrong person got killed, Annie's in trouble right now."

"Remember Merle Williams, the chief when I was first hired?"

"Yeah. How could I forget?"

"His favorite saying was, 'Stack up the ifs.' *If* there's a conspiracy or any connection. *If* there's a serial killer lurking out there. *If* anyone knows about the connection to you. *If* Ellen was the wrong person. *If* he's still in town and he's going to strike again. Then, yes, you're right, Annie's in danger. In my judgment, to put it bluntly, five ifs don't mean squat."

"That's what I needed to hear." I said it like I meant it, but I didn't feel any easier. Just the "in-town" *if* was enough to worry about. "Thanks for putting up with my paranoia," I said.

"No problem, bubba."

"One more thing, Monty. Any idea what Chicken Neck wants?"

"No. He's got Milt Russell in his office right now. I heard them saying how the Public Defender's office gets threats all the time. People they represented, cases they lost. The old routine, 'When I get out of prison, I'll get you for this . . .' or 'I know where you live . . .' Could be they want to dig out all those files, check out those old threats one by one."

"Tell Chicken Neck I'll come by after lunch."

"You get paranoid for any new reasons, bubba, you call me."

I hung up and sat on the sofa, opposite Carmen. She looked as content as a human could be, stroked out, shoes off, her Latin loveliness compressed into her five-four height. Though she would not escape the spread of middle age, she would always carry an erotic grace and an intelligent, playful spirit. She wanted more out of life, every day, than most of the women who had grown up in Key West. She knew that there was a larger world beyond Stock Island, outside the island social scene.

"Aghajanian misses his job," I said.

"The guy who got screwed out of his badge?"

I nodded. "And the guy behind the shafting is the one who's been slipping Annie his hard bargain."

Carmen's jaw dropped. Her eyes slitted in a grimace of disbelief. "She knows he's the guy?"

I shrugged and nodded again. "What's a split day?"

"Five of us share shifts with Richie Mooney. He's in a wheel-chair and he can't get the county van until seven-thirty. So he can't load PO boxes in the mornings. I do it once a week. It gives me almost a whole day off, and I make up my lost hours on Sat-urday. Richie gets enough hours to be considered full time, for the benefits and all."

"Uncle Sam didn't make that one up."

"He doesn't know it's going on. Kind of a palace revolution. You through with the phone?"

"You need it, go ahead."

"You going to warn Annie that she might be in danger?"

"I guess I should do that first."

"What about me? You and I were lovers."

"You feel left out?"

"I want to know should I buy that pistol before noon."

"We did it once. I never told a soul. You already said you were too wasted to remember what went on. A true compli-ment, I might add."

"I remember you got the rubber twisted and you had to open a new one. Your flag slid down the mast, but we fixed that. Anyway, we did it twice."

"That hand job in the hot tub? You wouldn't even take off the top of your bathing suit."

"My mother could have walked into that yard at any mo-ment."

"Your Catholic guilt just eats you up. At two A.M. your mother's going to come around your house on skinny-dip pa-trol?"

"I still rate a warning about this serial killer who's attacking your old girlfriends."

"Ellen Albury received threats from convicts who felt that their prison time was the result of poor representation. We talked last night about how Julia Balbuena's family is involved in a Cuban turf war. The guy who tried to abduct Shelly Standish sounds too loose to pull off the murders. I don't know anything at all about Sally Ann getting killed."

"You're repeating what Aghajanian just told you. Warn me. Please."

"Don't run into any walls while you're looking over your shoulder."

"Sometimes I hate you."

"I love you always. Please be careful. Just in case."

"Thank you."

I knew Carmen's habit of squinting and squaring her face. If her eyes are cold as steel, it's time to clear out. A sparkle means mischief.

"We need a contingency plan, Alex. We need a list of every girl you've slept with, so we can do a mass mailing. Call it a blanket warning. If you can't afford the postage, I can float you a loan."

I spotted the sparkle. "You're a laugh a minute."

"Can I ask something personal, seriously? Why so many girlfriends?"

I had to think about that for a moment. "It took a long time to find Annie. Sometimes they bugged out on me. Different reasons. Two or three times it clicked, but then it would shut off a few months or a year later. It wasn't like the same problem over and over again. Either I wasn't their dream date or they weren't mine."

Carmen tasted her coffee and scowled. "Annie's your dream date?"

"Was. Closest thing since before I went in the Navy. Now probably not."

"Let me suggest that you warn her in person. Sort of a woman's move, not so much that you want her back, but you might have to drum up a list."

"Monty told me not to dwell on it."

"And you told him that it wasn't going to stop bothering

69

you. You want me to help you solve the murders, so you can stop sweating?"

"The police are out there working on it. You're not dependable, anyway. You've turned into a raving gun fanatic."

"I know you too well. If you see any connection, you have two choices. Give the police your list of possible victims, or chase down the murderer yourself. You'll pick choice B."

"Let's cross that bridge when we get to it."

"Somebody crossed it already. Twice yesterday."

The row of restored buildings in the 500 block of Whitehead offers a fancy address to two title insurance companies, two law offices, a real estate broker, a licensed private investigator, and a quickie marriage chapel. The wood shutters and railings are bright, the signboards subdued. The gingerbread is close to authentic. The sidewalks are in better repair than in other sections of the downtown historical area. Pinder, Curry & Sawyer sits mid-block, fifty yards from the main portico of the hundred-year-old red brick Monroe County Courthouse. I lucked into a metered space for the Kawasaki my second time around the block.

Lucette, the young Pinder, Curry receptionist, wore a yellow Walkman headset and a thousand bucks' worth of gold jewelry. As I entered she regarded me as if she might follow a dust mote.

"Here to see Ann Minnette." I hung my helmet on the gaudy umbrella stand in the corner behind the door.

"What? Like I think you're here to see Benjamin Pinder? Every time you come in the door you're not here to see Annie? You hear that her roommate's like dead? And Annie's tied up right now."

Alarms went off in my brain. "Who's she with?" I started for Annie's office door.

Lucette reached up. "Wait, dude. She's with Mr. Pinder."

I had already flung open the door. It banged against a

springy-sounding doorstop. Pinder and Annie were huddled over her broad desk, surveying a computer printout. Both jumped.

"I hate to bother you, but when did you borrow Ellen Albury's bicycle?"

"Pardon me?" Annie's bewildered expression bordered on fear.

Benjamin Pinder also was shaken by my entrance. His pinched face spread to horror and his arms began to rise in self-protection. "I've got a call to make before ten." He was out the door before he said the word "before."

Annie struck an all-biz pose. "Let's not get into this right now, Alex. I owe you an explanation. I wouldn't blame you if you threw me out of your house. But I can't deal with this now."

"I don't want to get into anything except one question. All I need is a one-sentence answer. When did you borrow Ellen Albury's bicycle?"

"About nine o'clock the night she was killed."

"Where was your car?"

"This is question number two." That attorney tone of voice.

"Where was your car?"

"In front of the house on Olivia."

"All night long?"

She nodded.

"Okay, look. I don't want to argue, and I'm not here to evict you. It's your house as long as you need to be there. But something is going on. You might be in danger."

"Please, Alex."

"You ever hear me mention Sally Ann Guthery?"

"Yes. And I know. She was killed in that trailer court last weekend. The detectives asked me if I knew her. I didn't know her from Madonna. The fact that you dated her years ago means nothing."

"How about Shelly Standish? She was attacked yesterday."

"You've talked about her, too. I can see where this is leading. Was she hurt?"

"She outsmarted a thug. Is my imagination trampling my common sense?"

"Alex, I don't want to live in fear. I don't worry that a germ has my name on it. I keep a positive attitude. I eat bacon. I sometimes swallow tap water when I rinse after brushing. You're making too much of this."

I wasn't convinced.

"We're in shock from yesterday," she said. "My mind has been off in every direction. Maybe your imagination could send mine a postcard when it takes a minute to cool off." She began to straighten her papers. "I've got the funeral tomorrow, and then I can start putting this behind me, a little at a time. Can we go to dinner tonight and put our minds somewhere else?"

I nodded yes. "Please tell Benjy Pinder I'm sorry for my rudeness."

"Benjy forgives you. Trust me on that."

I'd thought I might grab a take-out sandwich at the Pier House Market and go home for a couple hours' work. Instead, I headed the motorcycle down Whitehead. Joe Cocker wailed from the jukebox at the Green Parrot. Two old black men on bikes rode slowly through Bahama Village. A tourist family posed next to the historically null cupola that had marked the Southernmost Point for twenty years. I turned east along the Atlantic side, then around to Louie's Back Yard, where I parked it. I've often turned to boat rides to work out mental knots. My own personal flavor of hydrotherapy. When a boat is not available, a walk works wonders.

The bowlful of bad news and crazy coincidence in my head did not mesh with Annie's on-again, off-again flakiness. She'd said that she'd fought the idea that she loved me. Fought like a maniac, I supposed, frolicking with Michael Anselmo. The fact that I'd spent twenty nights in smoky saloons before last night's reunion added to the confusion. Now she refused to acknowledge even the remote chance of danger.

Perhaps she was right: I had overreacted. Not necessarily foolishly, but too protectively. Hell, I was not her father. Maybe I needed to back off.

I cut through the boat rental area at the Casa Marina, drank a quick rum and OJ at the cabana bar, and kept walking. The positive ratio of bicycles to rental cars at Higgs Beach announced the fade of the winter tourist season. As did the percentage of topless women among the hip-to-hip sunbathers.

By the time I had reached White Street Pier, I had chilled out and begun to juggle my priorities. I had filled the mental blackboard with imperatives. I hadn't intended to become a sleuth, and I probably would stink at it. But I saw no other choice.

I spit in the ocean for luck and headed back.

9

Chicken Neck Liska sat behind his desk in a high-backed swivel-and-tilt chair, staring out at the city parking garage and breathing through his nose. We'd said our hellos. From the questionable comfort of a government-gray steel-and-vinyl chair, I observed his contemplation. I sensed that the wait was part of his message. He wanted me to know that he was perfecting his phrasing. Out on Simonton a car with a loud bass amplifier passed slowly. Metallic threads in Liska's vintage Nik-Nik shirt caught yellow-green flashes from the fluorescent lights. His face had been shaved imperfectly and his eyes drooped like a turtle's. I wondered if his occupation had aged him beyond his time.

"We got four ex-boyfriends: two with domestic violence records and the other two not exactly first-class citizens." Liska now focused on his mildewed mini-blinds. "Those are the ones in town or alive. We got the kiddie-diddling father, one Pepper Neice, fresh out of prison, released ten days ago, negative contact with his parole officer. Bastard's vanished, but he could've dropped back in town." Liska reached across the desk. Without looking, he slapped a stack of manila file pockets. "We got twenty-odd violence-prone indigent losers who claim their convictions were conspiracies between the Public Defender and the police department. We got a B and E punk who likes to hit the homes of single women after they've gone out for the evening.

There's a chance he's the dirtbag who wound a Cablevision cord around a blue-haired lady's neck to force a rape. We're fucking lucky he didn't kill that one. I'll have the Olivia Street fingerprints cross-referenced by the NCIC database at four o'clock and a first draft of Riley's ME report by five o'clock." He turned to face me. "You can tell the public we are solving the hell out of this crime."

"I don't work for a newspaper."

"I wonder who you work for."

I just looked at him.

"To summarize, everyone on the island who is mobile, and not in jail or visually impaired, is a suspect, although there is trace evidence of heterosexual activity, which in this town narrows the field considerably. All we have to do is cull the innocent. The troops are praying for someone to step forward and confess. It ain't likely."

Liska clicked his head one notch sideways to check for my reaction. I didn't move.

"You're supposed to be on our side, Rutledge." He hefted a glass jar full of dollar-sized Peppermint Patties and offered me one. I picked two. The obvious answer was that both the law-enforcement career and his recent divorce had taken their toll on his health.

"And you're holding back evidence."

I still had nothing to say. But my solid ground had begun to quiver.

He went back to gazing out the window. "I'm a fabulous detective. I didn't get into an office on the north side of the building with my own phone and a door that shuts and a salary that lets me drive a Lexus by being dumb. I didn't get here the old-fashioned way, by being related to somebody in power. I did it a new way. I walked the beat. I wore a dark wool uniform in the heat of the day right square in the tropics. I drove dumpy squad cars that smelled like mildew and axle grease and cat piss—

sometimes ten, twelve hours a day—before the city's budget allowed air-conditioning. I kissed more Cuban tushy than you ever saw. I pulled some shit, and I played the game. I took chances, I evened scores, I gave people a break now and then. I gave a lot of people breaks. Now I got this office, it means something. After all that practice, I notice things, I follow up."

Chicken Neck's phone rang. He ignored it for a moment. "We've worked together too long to bullshit each other. I don't need to know today why you kept them. But why don't you plan an explanation real soon. Bring me the color five-by-sevens." He popped the receiver to his ear.

I stood to exit the office. Liska raised one arm to get my attention, then held his palm over the mouthpiece. "They pulled a match on the prints from Olivia, the front door and an ashtray. Pepper Neice. The missing father."

"Jesus, her father?"

"What is it, 'Friends and Family'? You never know, bubba. Hate, revenge, love, jealousy, and the weather. You tell me. I just type reports." He waved me out and returned to his conversation.

I passed through a labyrinth of four or five open cubicles where detectives faced dim computer monitors or stared at their desk calendars. The whole place smelled like a locker room. Not your standard television sleuths. I took the concrete stairway and waved to Marge Sayre on my way out.

At the pharmacy Duffy Lee apologized for spilling the beans. "I owe Neck a lifetime of favors. He asked me, I had to tell him. I printed you an extra set of four-by-sixes. They're in the bag with your negatives."

I bummed a manila envelope, sealed Liska's prints inside, then dropped them off with Marge Sayre. I took a roundabout route home and passed the house on Olivia that Annie had shared with Ellen Albury. Someone already had posted a FOR

RENT sign on the porch. The traffic up Truman went slow-motion, single-file. Yesterday's tourists, fleeing the carnival. When I reached the four-lane stretch where it became North Roosevelt, I twisted the throttle and shot toward the next intersection. Frustration.

Immaturity. And no left turn at First Street. I cut into the gas station on the right, hooked left into the rolling traffic on First Street to catch the green across Roosevelt, and sped over the Garrison Bight Bridge. Sam's *Fancy Fool* bobbed in its slip, covered by a tarp. No sign of Sam or the Bronco.

I found two messages at the house. Sam's voice, weary: "Back to Sugarloaf to visit Doyle. The idiot wants to skydive before he dies. He's hired a Cessna out by the Bat Tower. Got a cash client in the morning. Talk to you."

Annie said: "On second thought, I don't feel like eating in public. Deal: You buy and I'll fry. Anything in the white-wine category. Love you."

Love you? Her portion of the next mortgage payment?

I chided myself for my cynicism and pledged to chill out. I had nothing to lose by wagering the benefit of the doubt. I biked to Fausto's for a dose of island culture and a buggy full of groceries.

By the time Annie had parked out front I'd uncorked a Chardonnay, set out a plate of golden lumpfish roe, and brought the coals in the grill to a neon red. The Flying Burrito Brothers, Dr. John, Van Morrison, John Hiatt, and Michael Hedges rotated on the CD player. Supper would be grilled tuna steaks, green beans, and a chowder of shucked clams and corn kernels.

I was invited to sit on a stool and watch.

Annie spooned six or seven herbs into a coffee mug, then mixed in olive oil. "I guess I'm guilty of failure to communicate."

"Well . . ." I hesitated. I didn't want to slam her admission by agreeing too wholeheartedly. "Not so much in frequency as substance."

"Which means . . . ?"

"While you were gone I missed seeing the message light every time I walked into the house."

"I get it. If your phone didn't ring, it was me."

"You used to call me a lot. While you were gone, nobody did."

She stuck the olive-oil paste to the tunas and parked them in the fridge while she mixed the chowder. This involved serious prep work: a flail of onion and green pepper, celery, butter, cream, a vicious-looking jalapeño, flour, bacon, leeks, red and yellow peppers, bay leaves, tiny spuds, basil, sea salt, corn, and clams. Finally she took a breather. "You said you wanted to get to know me better."

"Yes. I want to pose tough questions and demand straight answers."

"Go ahead."

"I want to know dirty tidbits about your sex life as an adolescent. I also want to know the beliefs and rules by which you face this gross, mundane world. I want to accumulate and stockpile facts, the better to manipulate you into never leaving me again."

"Fair enough." She put some of the ingredients in a pan and stirred the rest into a tall pot. "I think that the Ten Commandments are the foundation of democracy. I believe democracy is the only efficient arena for capitalism. I believe that capitalism allows me to enjoy Quaker Oat Squares and Tropicana juice for breakfast. I knew how to masturbate on a bicycle seat when I was in grade school. I wore padded bras until I was fifteen years old. Aside from that, I can't stand tailgaters in traffic, I hate the smell of Pine Sol, and I don't like to fuck on a full stomach."

"Some of those I already knew. Everything but the bicycle seat and the Commandments."

We finished the first bottle of wine before the tuna steaks hit the grill. She was stone sober. I was having fun balancing on the stool. But I shaped up to face the food. It is the rare meal that provides a window to profound elegance. When all five senses dance, when fifteen flavors form a truce and six or seven scents dominate, you have symmetry. I wanted to race back through time and thank that tuna face to face. I promised I would wash the dishes and drive the VW to the Dairy Queen. She informed me that I could wait until morning to drive anything.

After we stacked the dishes, she became morose.

"Down in the face," I said. "Thinking about tomorrow?"

"The cemetery is where I like to walk. I was just thinking, I've never been sad in the cemetery."

"There's a chance it was her father."

"They found out he'd been around?"

Had I left the theater for two minutes and missed a shift in the plot? "You knew about him?"

"I knew he'd been in jail. I didn't know why. That's why Hatch's story shook me so bad. It explained a lot of her problems. That's what I thought about all day, why I didn't want to go out tonight. He came around a week ago. She told him he could have five minutes to speak his peace and then he had to leave. He was with some other guy who was driving a new pickup truck. The other guy waited outside. Her father wanted to say he was sorry in person. She accepted it and he went away, no problem. Ellen never mentioned him again."

"Why didn't you tell this to Avery Hatch?"

"I just wanted to get away from him. He gave me the creeps."

"I'm going to Coral Gables tomorrow for Julia's funeral."

"I wondered if you might. I'm going to be busy with

the Embrys and the people from work. And you didn't know Ellen."

"How do you know that?"

"We talked about you. She remembered meeting you a couple of times. Once during a yard party at the Woods' house and once in a restaurant. She thought you were a great guy but too tame for her."

"How am I supposed to take that?"

"As right on the money."

10

Annie awakened on Friday in a nasty-ass mood. She complained about sand on the hardwood floor, the shower temperature, the coffee temperature, a lost earring, dust bunnies under the bureau, and the neighbor's spaniel that always barked at garbagemen. There had been no repeat of Wednesday night's lovemaking, no morning-after tenderness. I had read that women do not want solutions to problems as much as compassion, so I locked my face into sympathy and kept my trap shut. After several more tirades, Annie announced that she wanted to work at the office before the one o'clock graveside service for Ellen Albury. The VW convertible pulled away. I began my day all over again.

Julia Balbuena's obituary had appeared in Thursday's *Herald*. It had taken three tries to connect with an English-speaking employee at the Diaz-Suarez Funeral Home in Coral Gables. Four o'clock service, today, at St. Joseph's Catholic Church. Palmetto Expressway to Bird Road, east to Red Road. There would be no cemetery service. They'd cremated the remains. I faced a five-hour drive, including time I needed for two errands en route. Then a four-hour return in Friday night's southbound rush of weekenders.

Transportation in Key West runs to the personal statement. Offbeat cars, wild paint schemes in paisleys, Day-Glo Mondrians, seascapes, and cartoon faces. Twelve years ago I paid a bargain price for a '66 Mustang with a Shelby competition suspension, disc brakes, and a 306-horsepower motor. When new it had been a high-dollar, Candyapple Red, "special customer" Hertz rental unit at the Jacksonville airport. During the seventies its second owner had campaigned it in some kind of fender-bending sports-car circuit. Hence the bargain price.

The curse: about ten years ago Shelby Mustangs shot up in value. First they became hot collector's items. Second, they became ripe targets for theft. So I paid for a blah-brown paint job, stacked the flashy aluminum wheels in a closet, and installed primer-painted junkyard replacements. With its emblems removed the car looks like any other beat-up Mustang on its last legs. I can drive it up to America, park anywhere, and hold a speck of confidence that it will be waiting for me when I'm ready to drive home. Still, I pay five hundred a year for special insurance and I have to hide it in a run-down garage behind Carmen's house. It costs about a hundred a year for speeding tickets in the Upper Keys. Factoring in the fun makes those tickets a bargain.

I trust that the car's appearance is not a reflection of my personality.

Out of consideration for the neighbors I waited until after nine to back the Shelby out of Carmen's yard. It took me an hour in front of the house to change the oil and check its other vital fluids. By the time I had showered and dressed, it was time to join the northward flight of feather-footed snow-birds on U.S. 1.

The phone rang as I went out the door. I had the urge to let it go. I waffled.

"Hey, sailor."

"I thought you had a charter."

"We started in the Marquesas," said Sam, "but some funky weather came out of the north and churned the water. I got worried about a choppy ride home. My client was turning green, anyway. What's up?"

"I'm about to attack the long and ugly road. Thought I'd go to Calle Ocho and pay my respects. But there's a bunch of stuff going on."

"I've got news, too."

"You go first."

"The lady at the *Citizen*? Marnie Dunwoody. She checked out Anselmo, made some calls, knocked on a few doors. Nothing hit until this out-of-the-blue call from a state representative, some mid-Florida progressive redneck. He talks up Anselmo. Asks if she doesn't have better things to do than bother a man who's dedicated his whole life to helping the little guy. Tells her he knows that she's been shopping Orlando and St. Pete for a better job. Lets her know he's always ready to help a hard-working journalist."

"The best freedom of the press that money can buy."

"Well, that sucker lit a fire that he's going to regret. She's on the damned warpath, and she figures that there's something the public—that would be the 'little guy'—needs to know about Michael Anselmo."

"Hot damn, Sammy."

"Match that, action man."

"I don't know about matching. But Ellen Albury's pervert father just got out of the Big House, and they found his fingerprints at Olivia, inside and out. That hurts my theory that some lunatic was snuffing my ex-girlfriends, even though Annie doesn't believe he's the one. Second, Mr. Anselmo has been the cocksman in the woodpile."

"Go back ten steps on the girlfriends."

"I found out yesterday, Sally Ann Guthery was the woman killed in the mobile home out by Oceanside last week. I go back so far with her, I remember the Bee Gees on her record player. Shelly Standish was attacked at Key Plaza on Wednesday afternoon. Attempted kidnapping, or carjacking at the least. I took her to the New Orleans Jazz Festival in 1979. So with Julia, and then the odd chance that the murderer mistook Ellen for Annie, I generated this half-assed idea . . . You get the picture."

"You're reaching, but I'll hold judgment. What about Anselmo?"

"That's where Annie was spending her time."

"You mean . . . oh, hell. She needs to be disciplined like a child. Shave her head and cut off her allowance."

"I've got two hundred and eighty miles to think about it."

"I'll talk to you in the morning if this weather keeps going downhill."

I remembered to call Chicken Neck with version two on Pepper Neice.

The drive up the Lower Keys was a mixture of moderate traffic and great scenery. I got stuck on Big Coppitt behind a slow LeBaron convertible, a remnant of the Avis fleet that had swamped South Florida in the early nineties. I finally found a straight two-lane clear of traffic. The Shelby took to the quicker pace like a strong horse, wanting air as it crested smaller bridges. It squatted in sweeping curves and overtook in one jump a convoy of three minivans from Maine. The oil pressure and engine heat gauges remained in their comfort zones. The car did not break a sweat.

I passed the old tollbooth location that Larry Riley had pointed out. It occurred to me that the highway patrol had created a new collection spot. On holiday weekends, at the south end of the new Bahia Honda Bridge, a dozen black-and-mustard cruisers took orders from an airplane at two thousand feet, the speed trap a bona-fide tribute to tax-supported enterprise. Where had the troopers been when someone was depositing Julia's body on the beach, fifty yards from their cash-register operation?

I pulled into the upper parking lot at Bahia Honda. I wanted photographs from different angles, from the highway and the bridge. It took twenty minutes to reenact for myself how someone might dump a corpse without being seen from the road. I stepped off the route a vehicle would take downhill from the turnoff. Thin grass grew through the pavement. Yellow and purple wildflowers decorated the slopes and Styrofoam and broken glass littered the ground, along with several Pampers, balled-up and ripe. The lumpy narrow surface made a sharp right and led to a graffiti-emblazoned concrete barrier. The aerosol scrawls informed me that an urban posse had visited. That made about as much sense as Ping-Pong in the space shuttle. To the right of the barricade a two-track path rose to a clump of tall bushes. The beaten saw grass led to a gravel section thirty feet beyond the barricade.

I looked upward to the road. Passing drivers had a direct view in daylight. After dark it would depend on headlights and the moon. Tuesday's rains had stopped late. The skies in the Keys had cleared. The moon was waning, so the visibility factor was a toss-up, but the silhouette of a person carrying a body would be certain to draw attention and passersby could easily have seen a car or truck down where I stood. I backtracked to the clump of high brush and fixed that spot as where the killer had concealed a vehicle.

Anyone carrying a body toward the west, into the flat open area, would hit a dead end of dense berry brambles. The slippery rocks between the brush and the grassy spot where the Coastal Cleanup volunteers had found Julia would present even more problems. The only other choice was to backtrack fifty yards to the twin palms, then walk the open path that Larry Riley and I had followed two days earlier. Someone had taken a huge chance of being seen, or else had brought Julia's body to the beach during the rainstorm. I wished that I had some photos to show whether her hair and clothing were rain-soaked.

I walked around volleyball-sized lumps of algae-flecked brain coral, over sandy, torn sea grass, then westward on the ocean-scrubbed rock surface and turned the corner onto higher ground. Beer bottles and milk jugs littered the small mangrove and scrub-pine hammock. Off in the weeds lay a busted Igloo cooler, a child's flip-flop, and a crusty old hibachi grill. A plastic grating from a window-mounted air-conditioning unit lay among some funnel-shaped sponges. Bumblebees worked the purple flowers in patches of shade.

I walked to the waterline and stared off beyond Sombrero Reef Light in the direction of Mariel, Cuba. A dozen net markers floated within two hundred yards of the rocky beach. I ached with the thought of what had happened to her.

Here's to you, sweet Julia Balbuena. You deserved better than this.

I tallied the pieces of the puzzle. The careful truss-and-wrap job made it obvious that the murder did not occur on the beach at night. The killer had not left Julia's body in a Dumpster or in the trunk of a stolen car, or weighted it and dropped it into the sea from a bridge. It had been deposited out of sight, but not so far that no one would find it. The killer had wanted her body to be found. I would bet that whoever negotiated the hammock in darkness was familiar with the area.

After-the-fact photos wouldn't help at all. I headed back to my car.

Billy Fernandez was sitting on the Mustang's rear bumper. I recognized his angle of slouch. He wore new-looking jeans, a white T-shirt, and black plain-toed uniform shoes. A ball cap with a sheriff's star was pushed back so its visor pointed upward. Billy played a ragged toothpick back and forth, from one side of his mouth to the other, as if tickling the feet of his dead caterpillar. He'd parked his copper Oldsmobile close to the road.

"Looking for anything special, Rutledge?"

"That's right. Anything special." I pointed to the bumper. "You mind?"

Fernandez stood and brushed the seat of his Levi's. "For someone so shook and tuned out the other day, you're all of a sudden hot for details."

"I knew the woman, Detective. I have questions that need answers. I'm not trying to crowd your gig, if that worries you."

"You know this place? You and your girlfriend come up here for picnics and all? Explore the hidden trails? Quiet splash in the surf, moonlight walks with the sand fleas?"

His angle had gone too far south. I didn't respond.

He shook his head and laughed to himself. "I try to be too much like the movies. That was a bullshit thing to say." He paused for a second or two. "But you might want to practice answering that kind of question, you find yourself close to another one of these."

"Every minute you people at the county pay attention to me, you're getting farther away from someone who kills people."

He spit out the toothpick and rubbed his mustache with his index finger. "You gonna make the funeral on time? Never seen you in long pants, bubba."

I took his remark as a good guess. I didn't ask what he was doing there.

Fifteen miles later I stopped at the Monroe County Sheriff's Substation in Marathon, a single-story adobe-tinted building with a red-tiled roof and token palm-tree landscaping. I wanted to check out something in Lester Forsythe's photographs of Julia Balbuena's body. I slid the Mustang into the last parking slot out front. Inside the glass doors, an officious clerk with a severe crew cut informed me that Lester was at lunch and expected to return in ten minutes. After I'd waited fifteen in the welcome air-conditioning, the clerk offered the fact that Lester always ate lunch across the road at Dinah's Kitchenette.

I found Lester alone in a booth reading a swimsuit magazine and holding his BLT together with all ten fingers and thumbs. The upscale tourist might not appreciate the place. Six patrons sat in the booths, four sat at tables, and two held down the truncated counter. Four greenish fluorescent overhead units cast a moldlike pallor on the food. The exhaust fan on the far wall had not done much of a job in recent years. The odor and sheen of burned cooking oil had long ago fused into the restaurant's fixtures.

Forsythe was in his mid-thirties. He had the face of a sixteen-year-old, a hairstyle straight from the bell-bottom era, with long sideburns. His eyes were too close together, his bulky shoulders more flab than muscle. He recognized me and inclined his forehead toward the opposite seat, inviting me to join him. A speed-of-light waitress in cut-off jeans and a black tank top had a paper place mat in front of me before my bottom hit the seat. I nodded "yes" before she asked if I wanted coffee.

"How's it going up at this end, Lester?"

No way he could stop chewing to answer. The place mat showed an artist's interpretation of a sportsman's life. A hook and line extended from the gaping jaw of a huge freshwater bass. The line looped to the bowed pole of an angler in a canoe. A slogan at the bottom: "Try Our Bait Shack and Sushi Bar Out Back."

Lester cleared his mouth and washed back the chewed food with iced tea. "Same old shit, Rutledge." Even his voice sounded like a teenager's.

"Sorry I bagged out on the action the other afternoon."

"No sweat, Rutledge. Larry told me that you knew the girl. I can dig that you couldn't deal with it. I can dig that. I don't know who screwed up and called you anyway. Obviously, I had it handled."

"You bet, Lester. But I'm curious about some things. I'd like to look at your proof sheets. Whenever you finish up here."

"The two sets are already checked out. Hatch and the, um, neighbors . . ."

"I wondered if the FBI would get involved."

". . . but I just printed a full set of prints. Five-by-sevens. They ought to be dry by the time I finish my Jell-O. Man, all these murder cases . . ."

Lester worked up a sweat just crossing the five lanes of U.S. 1 in the midday heat. To kill his thirst he purchased a one-dollar Coke from a machine at the substation entrance. Inside, in a small darkroom at the end of a well-lighted linoleum-floored corridor, he pulled the prints from bulldog clips strung on a taut wire above the sink. The contrast and detail stank. He'd had to correct for his bad negatives. Like a rank rookie, he'd failed to back himself up with fill flash. He also had managed to include his own shadow in several of the shots.

"Great stuff, Lester."

He almost blushed. "I always say, ace output is job security."

"You are so right on."

But I found something. Four photographs taken after the examiners had unwrapped the plastic. A thief had not killed Julia. I recognized the small ruby ring that had belonged to her grandmother. During a magnificent twenty-four-hour period of our week together in 1977, the ring was all she had worn. She'd flashed it while joking about the sexiness of partial nudity. This time around, the ring looked cold against her colorless skin. There was one other thing. The knots in the yellow polystyrene rope were perfect bowlines and double half hitches. Not many murderers cared about nautical correctness. This killer knew the knots most useful at sea.

I ran the gauntlet of Marathon's fast-food strip and continued northward under a mixed sky. Ominous black and violet clouds hung low and pushed to the southeast. Scattered white clouds coasted higher, blowing almost directly west, and pale blue patches offered rare sunshine. A small single-engine taildragger wobbled toward a crosswind landing at the municipal airstrip. Colorful snapping pennants flew from trailers that housed instant real estate offices. Above Duck Key, near Mile Marker 75, eight wading fishermen cast into waves on the Atlantic side. The road narrowed to two lanes and I felt fortunate to be heading up the Keys. On Friday afternoon half of South Florida comes the other direction, southward to weekend homes or three-day parties on Duval Street. I knew, of course, that I'd face a long return trip to Key West.

Forsythe's photos were still on my mind. I probably wasn't paying proper attention. I sensed something, though, then saw a U-Haul truck, sixty or seventy yards ahead, pull onto the highway to block my northbound progress. The truck lumbered northward, barely increasing speed, hardly moving at all. Even the Shelby's brakes would not stop me in time. But I saw an escape route: an opening in the oncoming lane. I slowed and pulled left, crossing the double-yellow to clear the U-Haul.

Then, just as suddenly, a quarter mile away, a massive dump truck pulled into the southbound lane and headed right for me. I was hung out on the wrong side of the road, blocked by the U-Haul, looking face-to-face at a head-on. Wasn't time supposed to slow in moments like this? Why hadn't I seen this coming?

I've always preferred to solve traffic problems with my gas pedal instead of the brakes. I knew my Shelby's capabilities. But this time I needed more road than the trucks were giving, more acceleration than fourth gear would deliver. I dumped the shifter into second. Too radical. The tach banged to the red line, and the rear tires chirped as the gearing braked the car. I quickly jammed the lever up to third and felt the engine's torque kick as I came alongside the U-Haul. Its driver, by slowing, would give me room to jump safely back into the northbound lane. But the orange-and-white truck accelerated as if trying to pace me. Why wouldn't the asshole slow down? Three hundred yards ahead, the dump truck, dark and huge, also increased speed. Didn't these sons of bitches see me?

Two choices. Somehow clear the U-Haul, yank it to the right and regain the northbound lane. Or aim left for the shoulder and hope to keep control in chuckhole dirt and broken pavement. The Shelby shuddered as its engine strained in third gear. I was doing sixty-five, a nose ahead of the truck, but barely making ground. The whole mess was turning into a squish job. My only option was the shoulder. I warned myself not to brake with my left wheels on dirt and my right wheels on pavement. The mismatched traction could spin the car into the mangroves or else broadside into the dump truck. The thought came to me that I would miss Julia's funeral if I was dead.

I lifted the accelerator. My left front wheel hit dirt and gravel. But the dump truck jerked right, toward the same piece of turf. If the dump-truck driver went for the shoulder, neither of us could avoid a collision. Surely he could see the danger, too. But the truck slipped into the gravel, blocking both the on-coming lane and my road-shoulder escape route. I was back to my original dilemma. Using the brakes would kill me.

I regained the pavement, pressed the gas, and wondered if my foot might push through the floor of the thirty-year-old car. Still in third, to my relief, I began to gain ground. The U-Haul must have peaked its built-in governor. My rent-a-racer stank of heated grease and boiling antifreeze. The car vibrated with strain. Twenty more seconds at these rpms, and my engine would turn into a grenade. I aimed for the sliver of daylight ahead to my right. The road's center line passed under my car. I felt my right rear fender scrape along the corner of the U-Haul's front bumper. With a crunch that sounded like a shattering taillight lens, I cleared the U-Haul and looked upward. The dump truck had swerved back to its left, almost as if its driver wanted to hit me. I needed another two feet. I was running out of pavement. Then, quick as a crash and inches away, the dump truck passed. I was still on the road, accelerating.

I looked down. Eighty-five miles per hour. I lifted, dumped the clutch, and prayed that my engine would not melt down. I tried to exhale but there was nothing there. I tried to inhale and could not remember how. My fingers felt locked to the steering wheel, frozen in place.

Nothing made sense in the rearview mirror. One truck was skidding in dirt, but I was not going to hang around to make a scene about my near demise. Where were the cops when you needed them? I pulled the lever into fourth gear, settled down to sixty, and hoped that the sweat would dry before I entered St. Joseph's Church.

Finally, I took a deep breath.

I hadn't been in Coral Gables for years. The city had not changed, except for narrower tree lawns on the widened main roads and even more construction. The wonderful palms and oaks and Spanish moss still thrived. Executives with perfect hair and skinny telephones welded to their ears drove Japanese luxury sedans. Latino wives and girlfriends piloted German cars, full tilt each direction on every street. There was no way to see ahead in traffic with every car's rear window tinted black. And woe was unto those who dawdled in Dade County's sphere of anarchy, who hesitated to read a street sign, or who changed lanes at less than full throttle.

Fortunately, the directions I'd received were right on the money. I found the church in a neighborhood of large two-story Spanish-style houses, each with thick burglar bars caging its ground-floor windows, each with a sign in the yard touting the security company that backed the homeowner's right to privacy. Six neckless two-hundred-pounders in bulging suits patrolled the church parking lot. In Dade County, security exists for show as well as protection. My car was directed to the end of a row of somber older-looking sedans. Sent to the back of the bus. Not allowed to park near the Infinitis and Town Cars. In Miami, even in paying respects to the dead, there is a pecking order.

No big deal. I had arrived alive. I angled the rearview mirror so I could see to run a brush through my hair and knot my necktie. I began a new attack of the sweats, probably brought on by my proximity to a place of worship. I grabbed my suit coat, patted the Shelby on its roof, and walked to the funeral.

11

My background is plain vanilla and white bread. I grew up the second of three boys in a Midwest Protestant family. Cleats, snot rags, dirty laundry, bad sneakers, and illicit fireworks filled the house. We were force-fed primary virtues: honesty, grades, quiet, and frugality. Spiritual matters came under the heading of convenience. Except for Palm Sunday, Easter and Christmas, church attendance hinged on good weather and a parent not too hung over to drive. It's no wonder that the architecture and drawn-out ceremonies of the Catholic Church have always intimidated me. I associate a higher power with higher ceilings. Authority and mahogany hand in hand.

Then there's the rump factor. The few Catholic funerals I'd attended had lasted longer than my deceased acquaintances would have tolerated had they not been the subject of the Mass. To me, a lot of up-and-down. Opinion: The reading-and-response never caught the real spirit of good-bye. This service promised to be different. The massive St. Joseph's chapel, the mystery and ritual and Spanish ceremony would fit my feelings for Julia Balbuena. I was glad that I had come. I'd made it with fifteen minutes to spare.

As those who've not been in touch with the deceased will do, I signed the small leather-bound register and found a seat toward the rear. The oak pews were three-quarters filled. Solemn

Latin men wearing the tobacco-tint eyeglasses popular in Central America shook hands. Women in black lace mantillas nodded forlorn hellos. The older children looked to be caring for the elderly or tending to young siblings. I sensed no surreptitious business being transacted, and just a trace of political seating and deferral. Few tears were evident. A sense of wariness pervaded.

To the side and two rows back sat a group of professional-looking people, including several black women and two older men, no doubt the group from the office, Julia's co-workers. Behind them sat a group of blacks. The men looked thin, like so many Haitians, and wore loud ties. Perhaps Balbuena family employees. There were not many single men seated alone. Until a bearded man in an ill-fitting sport coat entered, I might have laid sole claim to the ex-lovers' category.

I recognized him through the beard. I had once seen almost two weeks' growth; Ray Kemp hadn't shaved during the Mariel ordeal. But he'd gone gray in the years since. I had never seen him without a suntan. He hadn't missed many meals, either. The sport coat was either the veteran of a previous decade or a number from a secondhand store and contributed to his looking several notches down the far side of seedy. Kemp hung toward the rear of the church, sat apart, and did not appear to notice me. I had just decided to move nearer to him when the organ music began. I remained in my seat. Until someone rose to speak in English of Julia, I spent the time studying stained-glass-window images. Several related to how I had felt in the past forty-eight hours.

Thirty minutes into the service, I looked around. Kemp had slid out the far end of his row and was headed for a side exit. We had not been in touch for years. I wanted to say hello. I also wanted his views on Julia's murder.

I almost didn't catch him. I found him in a sedan about seventy-five feet from the church doors. The security goons must have found his new Pontiac acceptable. Maroon with red upholstery, the color of so many rental cars, and clean. He'd left the driver's door open to cool the interior as he fumbled to insert the ignition key.

"Ray." I started to perspire immediately in the afternoon heat.

Kemp looked up, looked baffled, then showed genuine surprise. "Not in a million years . . ." he said. He climbed out, pocketed the keys and extended his hand. The years had scrawled webs of age lines around his eyes. Along with graying, his hair had thinned and headed aft. His shoulders were rounded, his posture poor.

"Been a while, Captain Kemp. They talk about you in Cayo Hueso, you know. People wonder what happened to you. Not just the bill collectors . . ."

"Yeah, I don't know." A smirk appeared and vanished in an instant. "I've promised myself a Key West vacation for years. I wondered who was still left down there. Every time a new Buffett album comes out, I get homesick."

"Every time one does, ten thousand more tourists hit Duval Street. You wouldn't recognize it. You know Phil Clark died, don't you?"

"Well, I thought so. I caught something in Jimmy's lyrics a while back." He scratched at his beard and shook his head. "What got him?"

"Drowned in San Francisco Bay. Overextended the party."

"How'd he get that far from the Keys? Of course, I say that. I'm near Seattle, still trying to live a storybook life. Kind of like Phil always did."

"He was hiding from bondsmen and lawmen and ex-wives. Fake name and all, bartending in Marin County."

"I tried bartending after I left Key West. No way, José. I built a spec house in the Carolinas and, dumbass me, I followed a young bimbo out to Bremerton, Washington. I lost track of

96

her, thank God for that, but I've been fishing out of Port Angeles for . . . I don't know . . . eight years. Off-season, I'm into vehicle recovery. Motor homes, big vans, delivery truck repos. I even got domestic and bought a house. You still taking pictures?"

"I'm still at it." Unless there's a dead body on the beach.

"I figured you'd be famous by now. Articles about you in *Time* or *GQ.*"

I shook my head. "Fame sucks. How'd you hear about Julia?"

"Local papers up there. Something hits the press wires as a 'Twin Peaks Copycat Slaying,' it gets picked up in Washington State. That's where they filmed most of those segments. Man, it broke my heart. I can't begin to tell you how often I've thought of that woman. They were all supposed to drift away and not be memories. If I had to think of all of 'em, my brain'd weigh fifty pounds. She never did go away. Not for me."

"Well, I always felt something, too. Enough that I drove all this way to remember that I'm not much for religious rituals. I've always wondered when they'd phase in the collection plate at weddings and funerals."

"They figure who might have done it?"

I told him about the father and the Cuban-American intramural spat. "I guess there's been other violence, but nothing like this."

"You couldn't get me to live in Miami. Hell, Rutledge, you couldn't pay me to leave where I'm at. You want to know a secret? It doesn't rain all the time in Seattle. They keep the myth going so the place doesn't get crowded out by tourists and big money."

"I remember in the Keys, back about '75, they would have piggybacked tourists down the highway just to sell postcards. We should have had our own rain rumor. A permanent hurricane warning."

"Yeah, maybe that would've helped."

The conversation stalled. The reunion had sputtered out.

I waved my arm in a direction away from the church. "You want to go grab a beer?"

He checked his watch. "Like to, but I can't."

"Ah, the mating call of the Monroe County woman."

"I'm out of here in an hour and forty minutes. The only flight I could get, unless I wanted to stick around until Tuesday. This time of year, the job calls. I've got to turn in this car to East Coast and—"

"No sweat, Ray. Good to see you. Hurry your ass back down this way. Man, you wouldn't believe some of the old crew. Sid's running Sloppy's, and a bunch of people are on the wagon. Norman's still got the *Petticoat III*. Even Trucker's got a nine-to-five."

"That I do not believe. I'll bet Tripper's still peddling bad acid down on Telegraph Lane."

"See, your memory hasn't drained out completely." I reached to shake Ray's hand and we paused to look each other in the eye. Many years had gone down the pike. There had been moments, after Ray and Julia had found each other, and during the Mariel trip, when I'd hoped never to see the man again. Time has a way of healing even the most painful wounds. Somehow we all become comrades in survival.

As our hands came apart I felt no calluses. I glanced down, then back at Ray's eyes. In a brief moment I saw another look. The look of a man with too many secrets and too many failures. We promised to stay in touch, to look each other up, somewhere down the line. I did not mention Sam Wheeler, nor did I offer an invitation to bunk at my house should he visit the Keys.

I passed a hefty security gentleman as I returned to my car. His leather pouch was the perfect size for a weapon. Probably a cellular phone. He would conceal his weapon under the expensive suit coat. People began to walk out of the church. I had missed the grand finale. Julia would understand. She might even appreciate this five-minute reunion of two ex-suitors.

On the drive up to Miami I had promised myself a culinary treat. I found a shopping area, parked in front of a combo Laundromat and Cuban deli, and ordered two espressos to go. The first to burn my tongue and bring beads of sweat to my forehead. The second to taste like heaven and keep me awake until I'd returned to Dredgers Lane. The middle-aged woman behind the counter wore gold necklaces and bracelets and rings and had the flashing Cuban eyes one reads about in old books, hears sung about in ballads. She bounced back and forth between mile-a-minute Spanish with another lady and taking my order in perfect, unaccented English.

As she worked the espresso machine, I thought back to my chance meeting with Ray Kemp. Our reunion at the church had started to bug me. Considering the animosities in our past, I couldn't help feeling that the meeting had been too easygoing. Something had not been genuine. Ray had looked like a doughboy, with the pasty skin of a long-term couch potato. He claimed to have lived a life of manual labor, but his shoulders had grown close together, as if his upper body had atrophied. His hands had not been those of a seagoing man, though I knew Ray was familiar with knots and lines and hawsers. After all these years, he had reappeared. At Julia's funeral.

Outside the deli I put one of my coffees on the Mustang's transmission hump and carried the other to a phone booth near the sidewalk. I swatted gnats and dialed a local number.

"Thank you for calling East Coast. How may we help?" A pleasant singsong voice. A surprise in Miami.

"Manny Cline, detective division, Miami-Dade." I tried to sound as bored and snide as possible. "We got a possible hit-

and-run on a tag that DMV-Tallahassee says is one of yours. Let's see, HV2-74G. Maroon sedan. Can we check that, and get us some rental-record particulars and a vehicle status report?"

"Hold, please." I waited about thirty seconds. "Sir, that car's already been turned in. There's no damage on this report."

"Well, you better look again. What's the operator's number?"

"Um, MI072551-04569."

"Jesus, what state is that?"

"Michigan."

This was too easy. "Oh, shit." A profane word for the cause of authenticity. "What city in Michigan?"

"Saginaw."

"Saginaw, Michigan." I used my Columbo exasperation. "Okay, what's the street address?"

"4901 Stockton Street."

"Operator name?"

"Frank R. Johnson."

"What'd he do, Visa, what?"

"Lemme see . . . MasterCard. By the way, Detective. Our garageman just inspected the car again. He says there's no damage anywhere."

"You're lucky. You got less paperwork than me. Thanks for your time."

I called Monty, got no answer, and left a voice-mail message asking him to start scouting the names Ray Kemp and Frank R. Johnson. See what the NCIC data bank might tell us about Ray's past. About that time of day Sam was almost always on the dock. I tried him. Again, no answer. I said, "I found a rat, but it may not be the right woodpile. Home by ten. Call if you're still awake."

It took far too long to leave Miami. Friday rush hour went in every direction. The old shortcut into Florida City, along the western edge of the metro area, had become a horticultural mega-mall. I cursed the Magic City and let my sour mood fester until I hooked up with six or eight Florida weekenders just below Card Sound Road. They towed flat-bottomed speedboats behind new pickups, and ran between seventy and eighty to the top of the Keys. I reached Mile Marker 106 in time for a fifty-dollar sunset.

Crazed traffic or not, it felt good to be on the road home. The blat of the Mustang's tailpipes echoed off bridge railings. The sea air fresh from the late-afternoon rain carried pungent barnacles and beached seaweed. I saw running lights on several small fishing boats changing positions on the bay side.

Even in traffic, the ride down the Overseas Highway, after dark, drags on. You wouldn't think paradise could lull you to inattention. I didn't want to drift off as I had earlier that afternoon, when I'd almost daydreamed myself into a bloody wedge between those trucks, so I tuned in an AM station from Cuba for some meringue music and regretted my limited Spanish.

My mind kept juggling the facts. The knots and their possible link in the murders of Ellen and Julia clamored to offer a giant clue. I also played back in my mind my conversation with Kemp, trying to recall what we had said, every word he'd used to respond to my chatter. It was time to process another thought—one I had kept submerged until after the funeral: Annie Minnette was the common denominator. She had heard me speak of Sally Ann and Shelly. Though she claimed never to have heard of Julia, I recalled having included Julia in several retellings of the Mariel ordeal. The closer I got to Key West, the more I found to consider, the less sure I felt about what I knew.

A stained towel hung over Barracuda's *cabin window to block reflections off the greasy waters of Mariel Bay. Facedown, my nose pressed into a musty life jacket, I recalled smells of boyhood— military-surplus duffel bags, soggy pillows in tents, hand-me-down slickers. Sweat puddled under my stomach and soaked into my* three-day-old shorts. A rhumba tune floated across the water. People on a nearby boat discussed Jimmy Carter and the fifty hostages being held in Iran. A wind shift brought the relief of a cooling zephyr, an invitation to drift into a nap where five minutes delivers three hours' rest.

But Barracuda began to shudder with the wind. I pushed aside the towel. Upwind, beyond the shallow hills to the northwest, the sky had darkened. Other boats began to swing with the stirring air. After nine days as captives of Third World paper pushers, we'd looked for ways to kill the boredom. This would do it.

I hurried aft. Julia Balbuena snatched clothing from makeshift hooks. The temperature dropped. In nests of boats clumped at center harbor, men hung over railings and fought tangled anchor lines. On the elevation that faced the Gulf of Mexico, patches of casuarina whipped and Australian pines thrashed in the wind. Nearer, I heard ominous whistling in the shore trees, flapping canvas on sailing vessels, the throaty sputtering of diesel engines.

In the forward compartment, suspended in sleep, the captain embraced a stuffed laundry bag. I did not wish to know its contents.

"Crank the motor, Captain," I said. "Time for drastic measures."

Ray Kemp's voice growled from deep slumber: "Look who's giving orders. You forget I own the boat. You're just the hired help."

"It's bad weather. We need to move. Get up and drive now, or your boat'll be trash in ten minutes."

He rolled over, listened to the havoc a moment, and grabbed for his keys.

On the foredeck I laced my Topsiders as gusts kicked paper high in the air and tore shirts and towels from other boats' clotheslines. The boat hung on sixty feet of anchor line. Trying to haul it in, I strained against what felt like thirty knots. I needed help from our one good engine. Cold pellets of rain stung my arms. The wind pitch dropped. Cuban soldiers, our guards on the hillside a quarter mile north, scattered to escape a menacing wall of water.

On the flying bridge, Kemp cranked the ignition. The Chevy V-8 coughed, then smoothed out. Ray slipped Barracuda into gear and eased ahead. When the anchor line was straight up and down, I yanked us free and hauled the anchor on deck. With a crescendo of swirling rainwater, all hell broke loose.

"Full throttle into the wind, Ray! Go toward that shoreline! Jesus Christ! Get us behind those trees!"

Kemp still looked half-asleep and dazed.

Visibility dropped. Horizontal rain slammed. A large lobster boat loomed out of the downpour, dragging anchor, bearing down on Barracuda. A collision would throw me into the water, could sink both boats. A gust spun the lobsterman. Our luck: her anchor line parted. A moment later she slipped within a two feet of our starboard rail, then cleared astern and disappeared into the gray.

Ray straight-armed the maelstrom to shield his eyes. The boat pounded into the shallow, wind-driven surf. "I can't see a damn thing! Tell me if we're getting close!"

I grabbed an inch-wide gutter above the canted windshield and hunkered down. Julia reached through the opening and pushed a nylon windbreaker into my hand. I fought gusts to jam my arms into the flapping jacket. More than providing warmth, it blocked the stinging rain.

Off to port a group of water-filled outboards maypoled around knotted anchor lines. Beyond them a shrimper had crashed another nest of small boats. Men in the water fought to stay afloat as volumes of water tumbled through the fierce wind. To either side I heard strained motors and faint yelling, boat bells and foghorns. Within my short visibility, scummy whitecaps pitched boat cushions, Styrofoam coolers, plastic chairs, fishing floats, and milk jugs. As we closed on the shoreline, the lee under the treetops began to favor Barracuda. The howling wind dropped its intensity. Even with the continuing heavy downpour it became easier to move around, to hear.

"Get near the beach," I yelled. "I'll throw the anchor."

Hunched behind the narrow windscreen, Kemp waved to ac-knowledge me. Then he stood to call out, "I'll put her aground. Tie us to a tree."

A moment later Barracuda's *bow sliced between two gnarled clumps of mangrove root. Her keel crunched woefully, and I flashed for an instant on the hull's failing during the trip homeward. Back to real time: I passed the anchor chain under the bowrail, jumped into the shallows, and sank to my knees in black muck. I feared that I would continue downward, slurping into dark, chemical decay until I too dissolved. One sneaker pulled off in the silty goo as I freed my legs and worked to gain a foothold. One rank shoe, I thought, will now sink to China. Someone there will use it. I scrambled five yards, swung the Danforth around the joined trunks of two pines, and looped it around the trailing chain links. For the first time in nine days I knelt on solid ground. In my underpants, one sneaker, and a thin jacket.*

A clicking noise behind me. The other American captains had followed our example. Anchor chains will fly. I needed to separate the chain from the rope so I could secure the bow line to larger trees.

I also needed to catch my breath.

Close by, another crisp metallic snap. An AK-47 automatic rifle barrel lay six inches from my forehead. Its black, webbed shoulder strap flipped about in the gusty wind. The young Cuban soldier's blue-cold hand shivered at the foregrip.

Flashing red and blue lights filled the rear view. No siren. I hadn't noticed headlights, if he'd used them. An ambush. A goddamned sneak attack. I looked down at the Shelby's dim speedometer. Seventy-five. Ah, well. Pay the piper.

As I pulled to the shoulder, the deputy blasted me with a spotlight bright as the sun. He took his time getting out. Calling in location, running the tag against the hot roster. We were somewhere near Grassy Key. My engine made ticking sounds as it cooled. A light sea breeze drifted out of the west. The air had chilled behind the afternoon's front.

His flashlight played the backseat and passenger area. I kept my hands on top of the steering wheel. "Moving right along, sir. Twenty over the limit gets costly." I was relieved to see that he was a sheriff's deputy, not the FHP.

"With my mind a million miles away." A hundred and thirty miles away, and a hundred years ago. "I guess I wasn't paying attention. Not much traffic tonight," I added, to help my case and offer a local's point of view. The deputy was huge, black as the rural Florida night, military-perfect. I'd seen him before, in a courtroom where we both had testified for the prosecution. Another downside to the evidence gig. Having to show up in court and swear to the jury that my pictures were my pictures.

"Please hand me your driver's license and registration, and step out of the car."

Oh, shit. The whole drill. We walked around to the side of the road, to be clear of traffic. He held the light so he could read the license. The officer's name tag said SAUNDERS.

"Six-two, one eighty-five?"

"Three years ago." It was time to heed Sam's beer sermon.

"Look, Mr. Rutledge, I don't care for excessive speed on a public roadway, especially in an older vehicle. You've got new tires, but you got that equipment factor working against you. Right off, you got a tail lamp lens about to fall out. But that's not why we're here."

Seventy-five is not why we're here? "Great. Why are we here?"

"Before I say anything else, I'll tell you your friend is okay."

"My friend is okay?"

"Ann Minnette."

"You pulled me over to tell me that she's okay? What's not okay?"

"You'll have to get details from our detectives, Mr. Rutledge. I understand you know several of them. As I have it, her car was stolen this afternoon. The thief went a short distance and a bomb exploded. The kid lost part of his leg. The city police think it was intended to kill Miss Minnette."

I was lost for a response. A media murder, then a car bomb. Murders and bombs were out of my league. Like it or not, my league was expanding.

"She's with two friends, waiting for you at the Marathon Substation. Can I count on you to obey the speed laws?"

Fat chance. "Can I get an escort?"

Saunders got a look in his eye. He knew he was asking for trouble.

"Thank you," I said. "And one other favor. Could you call ahead and ask Lester Forsythe to meet me there?"

"The geeky snapshot man?"

"That's the one. It's kind of important."

12

Saunders led with flashing lights but no siren. The official beige license tag on his black Mustang GT read SEIZED. Following a sheriff's vehicle down the Middle Keys at eighty should have been a hoot. I just wanted to go faster. My mind worked to fit this new complication into the puzzle. My categories had been ex-girlfriends, knots, and Ray Kemp. Add a new one: explosion.

At speed, we took twenty-five minutes to reach the Marathon Substation. Saunders whipped a U-turn and headed north. I went left and stopped between two green-and-whites to the left of the building. I glimpsed Sam Wheeler's Bronco behind a van around back, out of sight from the highway. Hurrying inside, I almost flattened the crew-cut desk clerk departing in civvies, smelling like a magazine cologne insert. He pegged me with a hostile glare and kept going. All trimmed out for Friday night in Marathon.

Sam stood to one side of the foyer sipping a Coke. "You made good time."

"What the hell happened? Why are you here?"

"She parked her car at your house and walked to the funeral. Everyone in the cemetery heard it blow. One of your neighbors was in the Sunbeam Grocery when it went off, right at the corner of White. Annie didn't even know her car was missing until the neighbor ran down Fleming and told her. My first impulse was to get her the hell out of town. We got this far. Carmen suggested we flag you down, so you'd know, so you wouldn't get home to an empty house."

"The car thief took the blast?"

"Some kid, a Filipino, or Hawaiian. Been in town a week. They say he was fortunate. It was a dud pipe bomb, or an amateur job. The doctors are trying to sew his ankle back together."

"The bomb was meant for Annie?"

Sam shrugged. "That's the cautious way to look at it. Unless you want to figure the kid brought the bomb with him. He told the cops it wasn't his. He'd never stolen a car before. Monty's checking the computer. Annie's in that office over there, talking to her parents long distance. Carmen's in there, too."

"Where do we go from here?"

"For now, Annie's taking your crackpot theory to heart. She volunteered to go out of town for a few days. They gave her a leave of absence from work. I told her she could stay at my cabin up in Alabama. A couple weeks in Butler Point is good for the soul."

"She'd fall in love with Baldwin County and never come back."

Sam looked away. "You complaining?"

A door opened in the hallway. Carmen peered out, mimed an expression of relief, stepped outside and closed the door. "Someone in there to see you." Then she whispered, "Be calm. Just be calm."

"Rutledge?" A voice behind me. Lester Forsythe in a lime-green tank top and a pair of plaid Bermudas that I wouldn't wear to scrub a Dumpster.

"Lester. Thanks, partner. I hate to ask this of you, but I need to look at your photos of the Guthery scene. The one on Stock Island."

"You got me down here at this hour for that? Kind of un-cool."

"It's real important, Lester. Or I wouldn't have dragged you away from the barbecue. Your pictures could solve the case."

"How'd you know where I was at?"

"Friday night, Lester. I figured it out." I turned to Carmen and Sam and pointed at the door where Annie waited. "She still on the phone?"

Carmen nodded yes.

"One minute, I'll be back."

Tonight the hallway reeked of fast-food grease and dark-room soup. "How did this one die, Lester?"

Lester shook his head. "Dr. Riley's still working on the lab re-sults, or else he's keeping it to himself. I heard two rumors. One was lethal injection. The other was a pinched artery in the neck."

Forsythe had done a better job with his automatic flash unit in Sally Ann Guthery's mobile home. He did not have full-sized prints. But the thumbnail-sized images on the proofs were clear enough to view through a magnifying loupe. The killer had tied Sally Ann to a vinyl recliner, bound her ankles to the chair legs, and stuffed a wad of patterned material into her mouth. She wore what appeared to be a housecoat or a robe. Maybe a flan-nel nightie, spread open to show black bikini-style panties.

My most vivid memory of Sally Ann came from a Hal-loween party. She had dressed as a conehead Brownie Scout. Late in the night, in full costume, she had danced a credible hula on a local dentist's kitchen counter. She'd always been fun. I had lost track of her, and I wondered how she had wound up in a dumpy trailer on Stock Island.

At the bottom of the proof sheet, almost as an afterthought, Forsythe had included four more photographs. The rope and knots that held Sally Ann. Double half hitches at each chair leg. Perfect, identical, double half hitches.

"Appreciate your time, Lester."

"Mind if I ask what you're looking for? If it's the rope, I already checked and it's different from that girl on Bahia Honda."

"That's what I was looking for, all right. Should've asked you first."

"This girl, she looked kind of slutty, if you know what I mean."

"Right off, I don't know what you mean."

"The black underwear. It's a sure sign."

"You're quite the detective, Lester."

Forsythe looked pleased with himself. At this point, blowing him out of his job would be my prime incentive to continue working with the detectives.

"One last thing," I said. "Has there been official determination of rape in any of these recent murders?"

"I have no idea," said Lester.

I could tell that Lester had a perfect idea, but wasn't about to let on. And I had to wonder: If the Sheriff's Department or Medical Examiner's Office knew of a rape threat in the Keys, in addition to a possible serial killer, why hadn't they told the newspapers?

Annie looked a wreck. Her eyes were discolored and puffed, her hair flipped askew as if she had been combing it with her fingers. Her expression looked too exhausted for fear, but lost and dazed.

"My poor convertible. The poor bug. Like a cigar that blew up and tore itself halfway back to the end by the lips. The emergency-brake handle went through a window at Island House."

She stood and I held her in my arms. "At least you weren't in it."

"I feel like I was. I feel like a peeled grapefruit."

We held each other for a minute. On Carmen's advice to be calm, I held back fifty questions I wanted to ask. For almost a minute.

"How long were you away from the car?" I said. "Can you figure it out?"

"I was almost late for the funeral. I was at the Embrys' house, and I made the mistake of stopping one more time at the office. Then I made the mistake of taking one call from a client."

"At the office, where did you park?"

"Around the corner on Fleming, in front of the real estate place. When I got to the house, I had to use the bathroom. I changed my shoes and walked to the cemetery, the Frances Street entrance. The service lasted, what, twenty-five or thirty minutes?" She looked over my shoulder at Carmen. "All told, I was away from it forty-five minutes, a little more."

I couldn't imagine someone having the brass balls to plant a bomb in a car in broad daylight on Dredgers Lane.

I asked what was next on the calendar.

Carmen spoke up. "Sam offered us accommodations on Mobile Bay. But we had another idea. Less of a drive."

Carmen and Annie exchanged conspiratory glances. I could tell that they had formulated an invincible plan. I saw the glitter in Carmen's eye. The ladies had planned a road trip. This would be their move. Their ideas would prevail.

Annie pitched the basics. "Carmen has a cousin, a gay guy. He lives in a quiet area in North Miami. Like a compound of elegant houses."

"It's called the Enchanted Forest." Carmen offered a smirk of irony.

"It's not as far to drive. We can sit around the pool. No one will bother us, and no one will find us there."

Sam couldn't resist. "Aren't you afraid little fairies might spring out of the glens and hollows and steal your suntan oil?"

"Cute, Sam," said Carmen. "We don't tell fag jokes anymore."

"I know. I live in Key West. But you name a subdivision the

Enchanted Forest, you're asking for it. I don't care how enlightened we are."

"Well, that's where we're going." Annie tried to give me a pleading look. It came off as desperation. "Can I borrow your car?"

Carmen wrote down the address and phone number in North Miami. We arranged to pass messages through Carmen's mother, Cecilia Ayusa, and, as backup, through Sam's dockside answering machine. Carmen asked us to help the police find the murderer. If she missed work beyond Wednesday—she pronounced it Wen-ez-day, like a true Conch—she would be docked sick time. She preferred to use her sick time shopping the malls in South Miami in September.

Annie and I spent another couple of minutes in the substation parking lot before we went our separate ways. The north wind rattled the grove of palms in front of the library next door.

"I was going to cook pasta and clam sauce tonight," she said. "I never got to the store. I wanted to sleep next to you. I wanted to explain more about the last two weeks."

"Three weeks."

"Okay." Her hand slid down my back. Her thumb hooked into my belt.

I said, "I wanted to sleep next to you and not ask questions."

"I love you, you know."

Another sucker punch. This one connected. Then I remembered something. "Call me when you get to Miami, okay?"

She said okay.

"Ellen Albury's current boyfriends? I assume Liska got their names from you. Tell me over the phone. I want to write them down."

As we kissed good-bye a tree bat flew past our heads.

13

Sam drove the Bronco slowly out of Marathon. After a BMW passed us in the double-yellow stretch over Knight's Key, he stuck the speedo needle on fifty and steered to counter cross-winds over the Seven Mile Bridge. I couldn't think of anything to talk about. I wasn't so much taken by the nighttime ocean view as run dumb by a long day. At the south end of Bahia Honda, Sam flipped his signal, waited for a northbound van to clear, and turned into the parking area where that morning I had run into Detective Billy Fernandez.

"This it?"

"Yes," I said, and wondered again why Fernandez had re-turned to Bahia Honda. Certainly the deputies had cleared the scene of all possible evidence. Billy hadn't been surprised to see me walk uphill from the tide line. Obviously he'd run my license tag through the Sheriff's Department computer.

Sam yanked the emergency brake, took the keys, and walked the incline toward the stubby end of the old bridge. Instead of following, I retraced my path from that morning. In less than a minute I'd figured out what I should have guessed earlier. The headlights of cars approaching from either direction could be seen from just above the clump of vegetation where the mur-derer's vehicle must have been stashed. With patience, anyone could have carried Julia's body undetected to the beach.

I got my suit coat from the Bronco and caught up with Sam on the seawall between the bridges. In the lee of the abutments, the water's surface looked as if someone had scraped it level with a spatula. We were far enough from the newer bridge so that little road noise marred the peace. The stars were clear in the dark sky and Orion's Belt hung over the reef. The Pleiades, the pint-sized daughters of Atlas, danced above us.

Sam began with the questions. "What was that hurry-up meeting with Lester Forsythe?"

I told Sam about the knots in each set of photos. He asked a few details and agreed there could be a link, a psycho with nautical knowledge and a strange category of victims.

"It still could be a fluke," he said. "Coincidence."

I waited. In spite of the Pepper Neice connection, I was back to my original theory. Assuming I could count on Carmen, there was a chance that I might recruit my second ally.

Sam watched the lights of a motor cruiser in Hawk Channel. "I learned years ago not to trust coincidence," he said. "What do we do on boats? Go with worst-case scenario. We pay too much for equipment. Over-prepare for safety. We buy extra food and fuel in case we're out longer than we expect. So let's call the psycho concept our worst case and roll with it. Where does it go?"

"That's the bitch. What makes anybody want to kill my old girlfriends? 'Course, with a psycho, it's a bad start to look for a logical motive."

"You think of anyone's got it in for you?" he said. "Somebody out for a shot of revenge? You ever screw somebody out of fifty bucks? Eighty-six a drunk when you worked on Duval? Cut somebody off in traffic? Fuck a married lady?"

"For living where I do, the way I do, I don't get into much shit. You know I don't play games, Sam. I mean . . . I said to Annie yesterday, the day before, I hate to deal with fuzzy information. I want positive and negative. I want black and white.

Up and down. Yes, no, hot, cold. Sweet or nasty. I'm a fool for definitions. Oh, goddamn . . . did you warn Shelly Standish?"

He waved a hand to calm me down. "I talked to her. You got calls to make besides that one."

I'd already thought of that. The prospect hadn't sat well. "Shit, I never kept a little black book. There can't be many of my old flings around, anyway."

"Just call and tell 'em straight: 'Your life may be in danger.'"

"What did Shelly say?"

"She said she could handle herself. Look, if your theory holds water, the threat is survivable. These ladies can go away until something's solved. They can arm themselves. Take precautions."

"Well, there's no dodging it. But here's the real pisser. If I'm right about this, they'll regret ever knowing me. If I'm wrong, they'll all figure I'm two degrees shy of a right turn. There'll be talk. I'll never get laid again."

Sam chuckled. "On the subject of fucking," he said, "what happened between Annie and Anselmo? She confess to something?"

"Not until she was forced to." I wished Sam had not brought it up. Once again I found myself dealing with the mental picture of Annie bouncing under the faceless attorney. "It came out during a face-to-face with Avery Hatch, yesterday morning on my porch. He was prowling around town the other morning after Ellen died and kept running into Annie. One place was Anselmo's office. He'd also established that she'd called 911 from Anselmo's home number. The other pisser is, I can't decide how to react. I want to forget it's happened. But it has. And I can't."

"The ability to forgive has its limits. Go back five spaces. Why was Hatch at your house?"

"He had some background questions on Julia Balbuena.

Said he wanted to form a picture of her in his mind. He thought it would give him a better feel for the case."

Sam shook his head and kicked a chunk of seawall into the shallows. "He's full of shit. How long have you known Hatch?"

"A few years—five, maybe seven years."

"If anything, he knew Julia better than you did."

I couldn't imagine two worlds more different. "You've gone a step too far for my brain."

"Follow this," said Sam. "Before he was a deputy, in the mid-seventies, Hatch was a charter captain out of Garrison Bight. We all knew him. He owned a boat called *Bamboozle*, which he renamed *Barracuda*. He went broke gambling on college football, the second-worst-kept secret on the docks. He sold the boat to Ray Kemp to pay his debts."

"The worst-kept secret on the docks?"

"Kemp's source of purchase money."

"You mean what I think?"

"He ran a goddamn flotilla for two years," said Sam. "I knew about one shrimp boat for sure. There was talk he'd bought two of them at a bankruptcy auction up in Tampa. He was supposed to've had three crews in thirty-five-foot sailboats running to the Guajira, hauling bales of pot back up to Key Largo and Hilton Head and the Chesapeake Bay."

"How could I not have known that? I made a point of not paying attention to him, I suppose because of Julia. But Jesus, Sam. Boatloads?"

Sam puffed his cheeks and exhaled. "Ray made a bunch of money before it got to be cocaine and guns and body bags. Then he dropped out. He was one of the few who never got caught. Far as I know, he skated like a hockey star."

"I saw him today."

Sam glanced in momentary disbelief, then turned back to the water.

"Looking his age," I said. "Paunchy, gray, receding hairline.

Said he's been out in the Northwest, fishing workboats. Here's the weird part. He didn't look like a seafarer. I made a call before I left Miami. He'd rented his car under a false name. Frank R. Johnson of Saginaw, Michigan."

Sam laughed. "Probably easier to come up with a new identity than to launder Samsonites full of cash. He's living on a yacht somewhere, what'll you bet, having his meals catered, manicures, eating grapes one at a time."

"What the hell, Sam. I was around. I knew what was going on back then, who was involved. Kemp went big-time and I had no idea?"

"Craniums have only so much room for storage. They get full, they either reject the incoming or unload old stuff. People get amazed I don't know one TV star from another. Hell, I memorize the top ten tunes, I might forget to brush my teeth, wipe my ass."

"You think Kemp's still hot? I don't know how the statute of limitation works."

Sam shrugged. "My understanding, crimes go away except for murder and tax fraud. You should stick to armed robbery and declare your income."

"Did Ray ever sell *Barracuda*?"

"Matter of fact, to a maniac I knew from the war. I introduced the two of them. Ray practically gave the boat away. My buddy was going to run it out of Ocean Reef. Come to think of it, I never heard from that guy again."

The mention of Ocean Reef reminded me of something else. "I almost got killed this afternoon, up around Mile Marker 80."

"Don't tell me. A drunk pulled out of a restaurant parking lot."

"Close. A truck pulled out northbound. I jumped the center line. Another one pulled out southbound. Almost as if it had been timed that way."

"Now they're after you instead of the women."

I ran that idea through the risk tables. Long odds, but I'd promised myself to unstack the "ifs." "You think Hatch pretended not to know Julia in order to gather evidence?"

"Or to gather evidence that he wants to hide. Or wants to orchestrate so he looks like the ultimate sleuth. Wasn't he up here, too, when she was still on the beach?"

"He was here when Riley and I drove up. We arrived, he was just ducking away for a smoke break."

"I thought you made the official identification of the body."

Even down low, out of the wind, I felt a chill. "Politics. I don't know."

"Avery would know his knots," said Sam. "All the time he spent on the water. He'd know his knots."

"And he may have had a hang-up with Julia, back somewhere in the past. But that doesn't give him a motive to mess with Annie or the others."

Sam looked off toward the southern horizon. "I remember in the Bull and Whistle, when it first opened in the early seventies, a folk singer would play a tune called 'The Devil's Took Miami, and He's Movin' Up the Coast.' That title always stuck in my head. I figured he had the right idea, but he fucked up his geography. Key West is where the devil did his apprenticeship."

"The bartenders are shrinks, the shrinks are all hopheads, the hopheads are vegetarians."

"Right you are. The machine works between the left wall and the right wall. No such thing as right or wrong, or yes or no. Makes me think of the half hour before sunup, the false dawn. It isn't light, it isn't dark. It's ten thousand shades of gray."

"Nice speech," I said. "A good book title, *Ten Thousand Shades*. Where does it leave us?"

"You've made a connection between three murders that the police may not have made. We suspect that Hatch can't be trusted, for whatever reason—good guy, bad guy, conniver."

"Conniver for certain, whatever the rest of it."

"It's a strong shot that there's someone killing women who are connected to your past and your present, but the police may not want to buy it. We know something's fishy with Ray when he rents a car under an assumed name. And we can tie Hatch and Kemp together in the past, with the boat sale."

"Back to, where does that leave us?"

Sam started up the slope to his Bronco. "It's time to circle the wagons and shoot back. You've sworn a hundred times you'd never do police work. But like it or not, you're involved. So . . . I'll help."

We drove across Cudjoe Key, then past the Sugar Loaf Lodge. I asked about the friend, the old fishing buddy Sam had visited.

"Doyle's gone back to Bloomfield Hills to kick the bucket. A good man, I swear. Truly a good man."

In spite of the higher speed limits, the last twenty miles into Key West are the longest.

14

My T-shirt was drenched in sweat when the alarm jolted me awake at six-thirty. A neighborhood rooster urged the sun to toast away the gauze, then a siren wailed down Eaton, paramedics en route to another pre-dawn heart attack in one of the hotels. After kicking and tossing all night I had slept maybe three hours. My dreams had swirled with boat hulls pounding into arching waves, explosions, laugh tracks, and Annie riding an old-fashioned bicycle along paths in the cemetery, through pastoral, sunny sections and gusty downpours. I had wanted to open my eyes and find her next to me, or performing her reverse strip tease in front of the mirror. No dice. My eyes were still fatigued from my round-trip to Miami. A chalk taste filled my mouth.

I called Monty Aghajanian to arrange a seven-thirty meeting and breakfast. He was barely awake: "For this on a Saturday morning," he said, "I will fish two days with Sam."

The backyard reeked of cat spray. Showering under the unmoving trees, I stared at the mildew on the back of the house. I could not muster much in the way of analytic thought. A commercial jet pierced the island sunrise on final approach. You would have to be a determined vacationer to leave Miami at five forty-five.

Fifteen minutes later I carried my coffee out to Sam Wheeler's Bronco. He handed me the Florida Keys section of the *Herald*.

CAR BOMB: BLAST RIPS BUG. The scene photo gave no real detail. The short article filled ten inches in two columns. A sidebar below the middle fold: ISLAND CITY OR INNER CITY?

"It gives some background on Annie," said Sam, "but it doesn't mention her connection to Ellen Albury. Someone didn't do their homework. Sure as shit, they'll have it by tomorrow."

"Did they speculate on the bomb?"

"The detectives suggested that the thief may have, quote, stolen the car to deliver the bomb to another target."

I could have said horseshit, but we both knew it already. I wheezed out a long draft of air and tried not to dump my coffee as Sam bounced down White Street. We stopped at the police department's Impound Compound on Flagler. A tall chain-link fence surrounded a field behind a paint- and body shop near the high school. I did not doubt that the city of Key West leased the lot from someone's partner's cousin. Squinting into the glare of morning sun, I made out the canted silhouette of the VW. The morning's first wind gust kicked up dirt devils. The humid air became warmer by the minute. My coffee was only half gone and completely cold.

Monty arrived two minutes later with the key to the padlock. All-business and nervous about going in. "Let's make it quick. I'm not positive about your access here."

The driver's-side front fender of Annie's Volkswagen bulged outward, the metal shredded as if a cherry bomb had blown inside a tin can. The front tire had melted, and the fire had charred and peeled the car's paint—except for the rear fender that Annie had dented when she'd dropped her suitcase on Wednesday morning. The radio hung by two wires from the dashboard. The plastic steering wheel resembled a flowing sculpture, turned upward like the brim of a cowboy hat. Damp ashes and clumps of ripped insulation coated the seats. Brown stains had matted in the carpet under the pedals.

Sam found the remains of the apparatus that had attached the bomb to the left-front wheel well. A stainless cable sling, two turnbuckles, and two U-bolts were fixed to a steel plate the size of my hand. The duct tape used to hold wiring in place had shredded and melted. A prime example of an oceangoing jury-rig. No car thief had built it.

I asked Monty and Sam to cast their shadows on the wheel well so the direct sun wouldn't throw off my fill flash exposures. I should have waited to shower. Sweat poured out of me as I ran through a roll of color and a roll of black-and-white. Monty looked relieved to relock the gate. I asked if he'd had any progress on recertification since the newspaper piece. Sam high-signed me not to let on that he'd stirred the pot.

"No word," said Monty. "It's getting near crunch time with the FBI."

I walked two hundred yards to the Mañana Deli on Bertha Street while Sam and Monty reparked their vehicles next to the restaurant. Jorge, the owner, wore running shorts under his apron and black high-top sneakers. He handed out laminated breakfast menus. "Not one of 'em shows this morning," he said. "I bring these girls in Saturdays, college girls from Virginia and New Jersey, give my Cuban ladies a day with their kids. These girls can't add or subtract, they cost me my ass, they shortchange the friggin' State Attorney. It's embarrassing. I cook, I bus dishes, I wait tables, I give correct change. Don't let the door hit you in the boongie on the way out."

We made it easy for him with identical orders. Spanish omelets, chorizos, grits, Cuban bread, cafés con leche. A Cuban conga song on the kitchen radio faded to "Hey Baby," by Bruce Chanel.

Sales-pitch time. Sam sat back and I did the talking, concentrating on knots and rope because they were hard evidence. Monty snapped his face into a shrewd expression, as if sooner or later I would trap myself in some lame theory or flaky cop logic. He'd already blown off my girlfriend concept, so I had to circle back to that. Our cafés con leche arrived. I closed out by describing what he'd seen for himself. I explained the nautical nature of the sling under the VW, how it was typical of spare-parts-and-duct-tape repairs made offshore. Risking redundancy, I noted that jury-rigs and knot knowledge go hand in hand.

As he stirred his coffee Monty let the haughty expression slide. Either he agreed something was fishy or he was being po-lite. He rubbed his jaw and shook his head, manufactured lit-tle gestures to delay his response. He scratched at the vinyl tablecloth and fiddled with Sweet'n Low baggies, shook the Tabasco and twirled a plastic ketchup dispenser. Finally the food came to the table.

We'd managed to sell Monty so far. The three of us dug into the food, and Monty said nothing until he had taken his last bite.

"I told you to stack the 'ifs,'" Monty said with a mouthful of grits. "Now you've gone sideways on me. I think you're out of the 'ifs' territory with the knots. The rental car, there's no way to know if someone named Frank Johnson—a friend of Kemp's—leased it on his own credit card, then let Kemp use the car. By the way, neither name showed up in the computer. But I'm worried that the ME's lab people haven't found some other connection—the cause of death, the stomach contents, finger-prints, whatever. At least they haven't told us about any con-nection. We don't even know if she was raped or not. Come to think of it, they haven't told the city shit. Not that that's un-usual."

"Okay, Monty," I said. "Put that on hold. And forget that when you told me to stack the 'ifs,' you also said that Annie wasn't in danger . . ."

"Hey . . ."

"Hey, at the time I agreed with you. No problem."

"You mention it, how can I forget it, bubba?"

I waved it off. "How well do you know Avery Hatch? What do you think of his professional abilities?"

Monty leveled his eyes. "I don't know where this is leading. It's dangerous to start thinking you can do a cop's job better than a cop."

Jorge brought another round of coffee and took our empty plates.

Monty continued. "Not a soul this side of Tavernier will argue that Avery's not a premium butthole. But he's tallied heavy cases over the years. I heard he got pushed to prove himself when he first got on. Matter of fact, the worst one on his case was Billy Fernandez. Now he's his damned partner. Hatch busted that dork in Marathon that was raping grandmothers. That case got into surveillance and late-night legwork, DNA, and a complicated setup. He also sniffed out that houseful of Peruvian hitmen on Sugarloaf Key, with enough armament and explosives to overthrow Hialeah. They had to evacuate the neighborhood, but they took that fort without a shot. Those weren't gimmes, either one. Those busts took talent and smarts and guts. A sixth sense, a cop's sense. So, overall, he's a pro—one of the best in Monroe County. And honest, as far as I know. That what you wanted to hear?"

"Okay."

"You asked what I thought. Plus, I'll grant you, he's a butt-hole." Monty thought a moment. "Am I supposed to ask, 'Why do you ask?'"

"I told you he came by my house Thursday morning."

"When you found out about the old girlfriends."

"The reason he came by, he wanted to get a feel for Julia Balbuena. He wanted to understand her personality—enough to help solve the murder."

"With you so far."

"Does that make sense, from a law-enforcement point of view?"

Monty nodded. "It's one approach."

"Sam told me last night that Hatch used to own *Barracuda*. Avery sold the boat to Ray Kemp when Ray and Julia were living together. That makes it, he's known Julia since '79, maybe earlier."

"No guarantee that he knew her." Monty shrugged. "He did business with Kemp. That doesn't guarantee anything."

Sam said, "She'd be on the docks once or twice a week. They spent plenty of days together, fishing and cruising. Hatch knew her, believe me. He drooled over her."

Monty exhaled, then gritted his teeth. "So, he was yanking your chain. He heard that you reacted funny to seeing her on the beach. He thinks you're a potential suspect."

"He was there when Riley and I got there, and he didn't know for sure that I'd even show on the beach. Riley could've shown up without me. Why didn't he identify her the minute he arrived on the scene? Would hiding her identity help him solve it? Was he going to let her be a Jane Doe?"

Monty looked at Sam, then back at me. We had him. "You have just made my day more complicated. I'm not even a law officer anymore." Monty reached for the check but Sam nailed it first. I dropped a five for the tip. Jorge could buy a fresh apron.

Monty said he'd get back to us.

Sam pulled into Dredgers Lane and stopped in front of my house. He reached down, pulled a small metal cash box out from under his seat, unlocked it and lifted out a .380 Walther PPK. "I've got another one of these at the house. Why don't you borrow this one for a week or two. Contingency, whatever."

"Whatever," I said, though the idea of needing it depressed me. What had become of my peaceful tropical outpost? I wrapped it in the classified section of the *Herald* and took it inside. The only hiding place that came to mind was a bookcase. I slid it behind a row of novels organized alphabetically by author. Gardner, Gerber, Gifford, Grafton, gun. Then I crossed the lane to the Ayusa home to see if anyone had heard news from the Enchanted Forest.

"Piggyback!" Maria Rolley ambushed me from a porch hammock. Eight years old and big enough to cause horseplay injuries. "Carry me in, Alex. You can see my new books."

"Your nana take you to the store?"

"Of course not. I got them from Ranger Rick."

Cecilia Ayusa reported that Carmen and Annie had called a few minutes after eight. Everything was fine, and Carmen had interesting news. They would call back around three o'clock, but I should not worry if I was busy elsewhere. Cecilia handed me a slip of paper with five names: Ellen Albury's boyfriends.

I extracted myself from Maria's world of excitement.

I sat at the porch table to make my own list. Someone could accuse me of promiscuity. I crossed off the one-night stands, where no one could have known. I eliminated one who'd died when a drunk in Sarasota blindsided her car. Three of them had left years ago and had made no contact since. It came down to five names. It was rude to call early on a weekend morning, but it improved my chances to catch them at home.

I began by practicing a set speech. Sorry to bother you. I'm not calling you for a date. No, I don't have AIDS. I edited the story, and reminded myself to use key words like "coincidence" and "careful."

I got on the phone.

Andrea Woodhouse, angelic face, thin legs, and two-thirds wacko. Her response: "Ah, shit, I don't need this kinda crap. Here, tell my husband." I fumbled that one, but the guy took it straight, calmly, and said thank you.

Laura Tate, wispy blonde, tough-talking, invented the word *erotic.* She left me to go back to her old boyfriend, though that one didn't last either. She was not at home. I couldn't invent a plausible message. I left my number and asked her to call me back as soon as she got in.

Jody MacLean, World's Tallest Woman, elegant, sailboard expert, crazy as a loon. She was appreciative of the call, very concerned, at present involved with a guy who owned a new restaurant on the old Navy property. I told her about Annie. She suggested we have lunch when this blew over. Pals forever.

B. J. Stein, surgical nurse at Florida Keys Memorial, used to smoke at least five doobies a day. Once when out of work, broke and lonesome, she had cured the blues by charging a three-hundred-dollar dog to her over-limit MasterCard. She'd loved James Taylor music in the bedroom. She sounded pissed, and said she couldn't afford to miss work because of a stupid death threat.

Polly Banks, grew up near Intercourse, Pennsylvania, and loved to tell about her hometown's proximity to a town once called Blue Ball. A dedicated bimbo, an aerobics instructor with a yardful of tropical plants. "Would I be safer if I came over and stayed with you?"

Two heartbeats after hanging up the final call, the phone rang. "Mr. Rootleg?" A moderate Spanish accent. No, we do not want chinch-bug spray, aluminum siding, flood insurance, a stock portfolio review, an interior paint program, a discount restaurant coupon book. I hung up without speaking. They call them courtesy calls but they want your money.

I had made five calls. Four out of five had connected. The warning was out. Painless, so far.

Another ring. "Mr. Rootleg" again.

Benefit of the doubt. "Okay, this is Rutledge. What are we selling?"

"Please hold for Mr. Balbuena."

I'd been rude again. Why the father?

"Mr. Rutledge?" He got it right.

"This is Alex Rutledge."

"My name is Raoul Balbuena." He had less of an accent. Almost no accent. "I am the father of Julia Balbuena."

"Yes, sir. I recognize your name. My sympathies."

"Thank you. My son and I are visiting Key West. We would like to talk with you, if you have the time."

The leather guest book at the church. Julia may have mentioned me to her family. Did they know about the other women?

"Of course I have time."

"Will you join us for late breakfast at the Hyatt Hotel?"

The hotel property filled the water's edge where Simonton Street used to dead-end at the Marine Railway Shipyard. Years ago, ocean vessels in need of repair were piggybacked onto a railroad carriage chassis and winched out of the water on tracks. I had explored down there when I first arrived on the island, and had kept the discarded sign I'd found: DO NOT ANCHOR BETWEEN TRACKS. These days Simonton runs straight to a boat ramp. The Hyatt is surrounded by manicured tiled driveways. The location boasts four stories of pastel paint, gingerbread, and potted plants. I had never mastered the hotel's maze of exterior pathways, but they all wound up near the water. I followed one past the check-in desk and around a group of room-service carts. Detective Billy Fernandez hurried past me on his way out. He gave me a cold-eyed nod, said nothing, and tilted his head toward the dining area as if to say: You're next.

15

Black crows on a veranda jammed with seagulls: the three men stood as I neared their table on the crowded open porch bordering the Hyatt dining room. Each wore a business suit with a dark tie and hard shoes. Men dressed that way in Key West tended to be bank examiners, attorneys scheduled for court, con artists, or out-of-town FBI agents. Raoul Balbuena introduced himself, then his burly son Carlos and Emilio Palguta, a gnarled character I guessed to be in his mid-fifties. Palguta shook my hand as if unaccustomed to the gesture. At five-ten and two-thirty or so, he had a neck too large for his collar and the build and movements of an ex-fighter or weight lifter. I guessed that Carlos had been one of the muscle boys in the Coral Gables church parking lot. His handshake was rough, his swagger controlled in deference to his father.

A bulky man himself, Raoul looked near seventy, with a full head of salt-and-pepper hair. He possessed a sternness born either of his years in Cuban jails or repeated studies of Brando's Don Corleone. Judging from the kowtow of the son and the mouth-breathing associate, Raoul Balbuena came off more as thug than civic leader. I don't know what I expected Julia's father to look like, but this wasn't it. In his attempt to dress like an executive, he'd wound up looking like a mob boss.

He motioned for me to sit in the rattan chair with the most

expansive view. I'd removed my sunglasses for the introductions, but replaced them to counter the glare off the Gulf of Mexico. A waiter cleared away a used cup. Several sugar bags had been torn to shreds. Billy Fernandez, minutes earlier, in this position. Another waiter appeared above me with a tray. Coffee, pastries, and orange juice. I asked for an Amstel beer.

"You are welcome to anything on the menu, Mr. Rutledge." Raoul made it sound like an order rather than an invitation.

I declined. The men had finished their meal. But they were in no hurry to discuss matters at hand. One never knows if slow motion is a facet of Old World custom or a test of nervousness for the odd man out. I rolled with it. Living in the Keys had taught me patience. This was suddenly looking like a tough-guy showdown, and I felt the need for some kind of weapon. Patience would do. I settled into my seat and took a reading. Palguta had the mottled taupe skin of a recent prisoner. His fifty-dollar haircut did not fit his rheumy, wary eyes and angular face. He stared at me with an expression of disinterest that I took to be a sample of how he viewed life, or death.

I began with an honest expression of sympathy. "Your daughter and I knew each other a short time. I have never forgotten her."

Raoul looked me straight in the eye. "Thank you. Were you in love with my daughter?"

"She found her way into my heart. A part of me died yesterday."

Raoul nodded. "She told me about your coming to Mariel, the bad weather and the evil people. She said she could never know for certain, but she thought you had saved her life. She mentioned your name in recent years."

"But she never came to visit."

"That's true. She never did. Are you comfortable in that chair?"

I nodded, knowing that they'd arranged for the glare in my

face. The waiter arrived with my Amstel and more coffee for the others. No one spoke until he had left. I let the beer sit untouched.

"She was independent, as was her mother," continued Raoul. "In the years since I arrived in Florida, she has been a great friend to me, much more than her mother, as well as a respectful daughter." He gestured to his son. "Carlos?"

The brother extracted a folded manila envelope from his inside pocket. He removed several photographs and slid them across the table toward me. The picture on top was a rear view of my Mustang parked in the church lot, its license plate clearly legible.

The no-necked goon with the leather pouch under his arm. It hadn't been a gun or a cellular phone. He'd had a camera.

The next photograph was a long-lens shot of Ray Kemp talking to me in the church parking lot, Ray facing and my back to the camera. A different angle. There'd been more than one photographer.

Raoul continued. "You were kind enough to sign the small book inside the church. And your name was on the police report because you identified Julia. But this man did not sign the book. Do you know his name?"

"Ray Kemp. He and Julia—"

"Yes," he interrupted. "Another name from Julia's past that we recognize. The captain of the boat you took to Mariel. But we never have met this man." He took the photo from me, and stared at it. "We want to talk to him. Did you know that Ray Kemp was in trouble with the police?"

"I know that he was involved in smuggling marijuana. My impression has been that he was never caught."

Raoul's expression turned grim. He motioned for Carlos to continue.

The next photograph showed a rear view of the maroon rental car as Ray drove away from the church. The next was the

Pontiac's license tag, enlarged from the same negative as the previous shot. Good darkroom work. The print was as clear as a close-up: HV2-74G.

"It's a renter, from East Coast," mumbled Carlos. His first words, with more of an accent than his father. It had been Carlos who'd called me "Rootleg."

I was still amazed that Ray had used a fake identity to come to Julia's funeral.

"You know where to find Mr. Kemp?" said Raoul.

"Kemp rented the car using a false identity."

"Yes. Johnson, of Saginaw, Michigan."

"I called directory information last night. No such name in Saginaw."

Raoul nodded. "No Stockton Street either."

They had been as successful as I with East Coast. "Ray told me he's been living in Port Angeles, Washington, for years."

Carlos began to write in a small notebook.

I continued. "He didn't say much else except that he's been a commercial fisherman and a repo man specializing in motor homes. This was the first time I've seen him since . . . I don't know . . . '81, '82."

Raoul shifted his chair and leaned closer to me. "I want to find the man or the people who killed my daughter. The police believe that it was one of my political enemies. We have been talking to a detective with the Sheriff's Department, and I will quote what he said: 'Murders are murders. They happen all the time.' In my life, Mr. Rutledge, I have learned not to trust the police to do a good job. In Cuba they did not work for the people, the citizens. They worked for the people in power. In the United States the police are overworked. They are not paid enough money. No one can do a good job with those conditions."

I agreed.

"I am involved in political talks which anger many of my

shortsighted former countrymen. I am aware of threats made against me. But that is not what happened to my daughter. No one wanting to hurt me would dress up the dead body of my daughter like a television murder victim and deposit her remains a hundred miles away from Miami. My political enemies are too powerful to bother with theatrics. They would begin by ruining me at the bank. They would have me arrested for any one of a dozen false reasons. They are too busy to drive down the Keys. Even the most evil of them would only have beaten her and left her in a Calle Ocho sandwich shop, propped at a table, playing dominoes with the broken, drooling, stubborn old men who despise the past and cannot understand the future."

Carlos shook his head. "They would not have killed her. We are Cubans. Not Colombians, not Peruvian animals."

Raoul aimed a glare at his son, then relented and nodded.

There was one more photograph. Ray stood at the Pontiac's open trunk. He held his undersized sport coat over an open piece of luggage, what we used to call an AWOL bag. The trunk appeared full of large duffels and boxes.

I studied the print. "A lot of luggage for a quick trip to Florida."

Emilio reached into the pocket of his suit jacket and another envelope appeared on the table.

"We want to find the person who killed my daughter."

I ignored the envelope. "As do I."

"We want to locate Ray Kemp, to clear his name in this regard."

Punch his ticket, too, I thought.

"We would like your help, here in Key West."

"I'm not on a jam-packed schedule."

"We would not ask for your time without compensation."

"Forget it."

Raoul took the notepad from Carlos and flipped a page.

133

"Please excuse our snooping. You have a six-hundred-and-fifty-dollar mortgage payment due the sixth of every month. You have been late in mailing three payments in the past twelve months. Your telephone bill averages over seventy-five dollars per month. Your utility bills exceed two hundred dollars per month. You have been overdue twice since January on payment to the city of Key West."

"Bad planning," I said. "I'm okay with money. Sometimes I forget to mail checks. Look, I'll help you find Ray Kemp. I'll do anything to help find Julia's murderer."

Raoul took a new tack. "We will offer a five-thousand-dollar reward for the person who finds the brutal monster responsible for this death."

Why fight? "We'll talk about it later."

"Is there anything you know right now that might help us?"

"Nothing," I said. "But let me ask two things. You said you saw the police report on Julia's death. Which police officer signed the report?"

Raoul cleared his throat to stall, then said, "Detective Billy Fernandez was the officer of record."

"Did you show these photographs to Fernandez?"

"No." He pushed himself out of his chair and extended his hand. "We will give you three telephone numbers to call and a credit-card number to use."

I stood and shook his hand. "Fine."

"We'll keep you informed of our progress as well."

It did not look all that fine to Emilio Palguta. I reached down for the bottle of beer and took my first sip. "Sounds great. Why does this man look like he wants to shoot me?"

Raoul glanced at Palguta. "I don't pay this man for charm. He sees the reflection from one tooth, he bites the neck below it."

"I promise not to smile at him."

I took the Amstel with me.

16

Eleven A.M. by the clock atop old City Hall. I had been awake four hours and it felt like twelve and I wished I'd taken the Balbuenas' offer of food from the menu. The beer helped fill the void where my stomach used to be.

I needed to reach Laura Tate, wispy blonde, ex-lover. No privacy at the Hyatt breezeway phone, but I used it to call home to my message machine:

"This is Marnie Dunwoody at the *Key West Citizen*. It's nine-forty on Saturday. I would like to talk to Ann Minnette about the death of her former roommate and the theft of her car. Please call me at 291-1241."

As Sam had predicted, someone had done her homework. A pleasant voice. The same woman who was checking out Monty Aghajanian's certification flap with the state of Florida.

"Robert Osborn, Sunstate Insurance. I need to meet with Miss Minnette regarding the accident involving her 1975 Volkswagen. My number in Marathon is 744-7400. The best time to call back is Monday morning before ten. Thanks."

"Ann, Marnie Dunwoody again, calling from the *Key West Citizen*. If it's possible, I'd like to talk to you this afternoon, before four o'clock. Please call me at 291-1241. Thanks again."

Can't happen. Should I call?

"If you would like to place a call, please hang up and dial again."

Phantom messages. All the time.

"Alex, this is Bob Bernier, a friend of Monty Aghajanian. If you could give me a call sometime this weekend, I'd appreciate it. 291-5501. Thanks." Monty's buddy in the FBI.

I chugged the Amstel, tossed the bottle in a trash can, unlocked my bicycle from the Hyatt employees' rack. Over at the Pier House the phone booth in the hall, just inside the south parking lot entrance, would give me privacy. On Front Street clouds of dust tumbled behind turtle-paced minivans and convertible rentals. The midday heat put a clammy sheen on my skin, trapping airborne dirt in a thin paste that only five showers would remove. Or an hour's swim in the salt waters of the back country.

No such privacy. I'd never noticed that the booth had been removed from the Pier House hallway. Another chunk of history gone. From that small cubicle people had cut deals, lied to bosses and mates, confirmed assignations. I walked past it one night in the eighties and found a middle-aged couple, nude below the waist, making love in the booth. The man was talking into the phone, the woman sobbing as she bobbed up and down . . .

Outside the Chart Room I found a new pay phone where the garbage cans used to be kept. No eavesdroppers around. What the hell.

"Laura, Alex Rutledge."

"Oh, God, Alex, it's been . . . God, it's been years. Wait a minute. Is this the call every woman in Key West dreads?"

"What is it?" I said. "Old boyfriends are the gong show of life? I'm not calling about a disease, I'm calling about a threat. Can we continue?"

"Have you gotten weird on us, Alex?"

I realized this would be easier face-to-face. "No, but the world around us is getting weirder by the minute."

"I know. I gave some Lithuanian tourist a sympathy fuck until five-thirty this morning. I'm tired and sore. I smell like Third World BO. Where are you?"

"Down by the Chart Room."

"I need a Bloody Mary. Would you bring me one? What's it like at the Pier House?"

"The place is full of tourists, lathered up and broiling. The place smells like a big vat of piña colada and baby oil."

"Let's do something we haven't done in years."

"I thought you were sore."

"You haven't changed. Let's meet for a Bloody Mary at Sloppy Joe's."

"Any day but today. Look, I have to explain something to you."

"Will it wait until you bring me the drink? Stoli with extra Tabasco, two limes, no celery. I still live on Amelia."

"You really need it?"

"It's the only thing that will put me to sleep. I have to get up at sundown to go to work. I'm back to hostessing."

"One of the new restaurants?"

"The Packet Inn. It's an all-you-can-eat. I've got an application at Kyushu."

The Chart Room Bar had become a local hangout in the seventies, when David Wolkowsky, the original Pier House owner, converted a motel room into a miniature saloon. Six barstools, three tables, a first-class view of the Gulf of Mexico. The tiny lounge had provided a safe haven for a crazed assortment of yachtsmen, drug dealers, treasure divers, and politicians. There had been nights when an unknown songwriter had strummed his guitar and sung for drinks. After finding success he had included the bar's name in a well-known lyric. But things change. A certain soul, a camaraderie, had evaporated over the years.

I drank another beer while I waited for Laura's Bloody Mary, and chided myself for moping about the "old days" of only twenty years ago. Fifty years ago what was now the Pier House waterfront had seen huge ships come and go. The SS *Cuba* and SS *Florida* had provisioned and taken on passengers bound for Havana's exotic adventures. Seventy-five years ago, Aeromarine Airways had occupied the property. The company had flown passengers and mail to Cuba in leftover World War I seaplanes. Fifty years before that, the United States government had run a ship coaling station. Key West had been a marketplace, a hub of commerce for a century and a half. I suddenly felt small, devoid of perspective, bemoaning the shifting moods of a fifteen-by-twenty-five-foot gin mill.

I had just left a murdered woman's father—a man with a tough history of changing politics, a treacherous looking henchman, a punk for a son, and an envelope full of money. The father wanted to buy a solution to a crime. I knew South Florida. He stood a good chance to succeed. Money had bought change in Key West. It also bought all kinds of justice.

Dangling Laura's drink in a paper bag, working the bicycle's gear lever with my thumb, I pedaled across the island. A bike ride on Simonton is the real-life equivalent of a fast-moving video game: you dodge ruts, bricks, Rollerbladers, broken pavement, stray coconuts, mopeds, and fallen fronds. At the Eaton Street light I squeezed between parked cars and traffic to pass the Conch Train, an Isuzu pickup towing a boat trailer, and two convertibles. A Mercedes-Benz 400SEL sedan at the head of the line waited to turn left and head out of town. The old man was in the backseat, Palguta driving. Carlos Balbuena sat low in front, punching numbers into a cellular phone.

Laura Tate had lived in the same place for years. Amelia

above Simonton, near William, is lightly traveled, even by Key West residents. Her cottage sits behind another home, protected from island noise by a small rain forest, a snarl of vegetation she used to call Lizardland. One evening, years ago, we spent hours sitting in beach chairs under the canopy of trees drinking sangria that she had chilled in a thermos bottle, and listening to homemade cassette compilation tapes borrowed from a disc jockey friend. When the wine was gone we'd tried to make love down in the dirt and back to nature, until a frog jumped onto her forehead and scared the wits out of her. We managed to shower off the filth and finish the sex without falling in the bathroom, and we fell asleep on the living room floor. After sunrise a flash downpour had struck. I still can picture her racing out the door, running naked in the yard, laughing and scrambling to save the tapes and the ghetto blaster from the rain.

She answered the door wearing a flimsy tank top, men's boxer shorts, and a backward ball cap. Cute as ever. Pink skin, a weariness in her eyes. She held a large black penis-shaped dildo in her hand.

"Do you know how to fix these?"

I eyeballed the upright phallus and offered the response of a concerned physician. "Hmm. What seems to be malfunctioning, young lady?"

"It's supposed to be a three-speed model. All I get is full tilt, like a damn Joy Buzzer. Doesn't do a thing for me, high speed."

"Have you tried using older, worn-out batteries?" I handed her the bag with the Bloody Mary.

"I think old batteries were the problem in the first place. I didn't use this thing for a long time while I was dating Tripper Wilbanks, 'cause I didn't need to. Then the dummy got caught with a briefcase full of blow, and he had to go to camp. Meanwhile the batteries leaked, you know, that orange goo stuff, so I put in new alkalines. Six bucks at the pharmacy, you believe that? Six bucks. Ever since, full speed. Kind of reminds me of that Lithuanian boy last night. Open throttle, all the way."

Laura fetched me a nail file so I could clean the internal switch and battery contacts. I settled onto a sofa and dismantled the plastic dick while I explained about the murders, the attempted abduction, and the shredded VW. I blabbed on with all the details while I scratched away corrosion. Laura was flopped back into an old beanbag chair, sipping from the Bloody Mary and poking around in her mouth with the straw. Her threadbare tank top permitted the occasional review of near handful-sized breasts. Her nipples pointed outward like push-pins and the boxer shorts were askew just enough to flash wispy hints of pale pubic hair. I must have needed someone's ear. Or else I did not want to abandon the view. I even threw in the parts about Raoul at the Hyatt and Ray Kemp at the funeral in Coral Gables. I mentioned that rape may have been a partial motive. Finally I stopped talking because there was nothing left to tell.

The coal-colored dork was operational. I needed to get out of the cottage before I succumbed to the scenery. Laura looked at me, stone-faced, making sure I had finished. She began to giggle and apologize at the same time. Something in my story, something in the tale of murder, had struck her as amusing.

"Let me in on it real fast," I said.

"I'm trying to say I'm sorry. Oh, Jesus . . ."

She leaped from the chair, dropped her cup on the table, pushed down her boxers and went running for the open door of the bathroom. An exquisite moon, those perfect buns that I had loved to palm as I fell asleep the nights I had spent in the next room. I heard her hit the toilet seat, and listened to the splash as she urinated. Out of breath and wheezing, she patted her bare feet on the tile floor.

She walked back into the living room. "Nothing you haven't seen before . . . But don't look, okay?"

I looked. The flat tummy, the little blond welcome mat. She turned her back, stepped back into the shorts, and bent to pull them up.

This time I should have looked away. Things began to get crowded in my shorts.

She composed herself and sat back down. "This town. This crazy town."

"No argument there."

"I get on laughing jags, I wet my pants. Ever since high school."

"It never happened when I was around before."

"It comes and goes. Like an allergy. Some years I'm allergic to cats, some years I'm allergic to pollen. Some years I pee."

"What was so funny?"

"I didn't know about you and Julia. Up until the day Ray met her, he was sleeping in my bed. Back when I lived on Seidenberg, in that second-floor apartment I rented from Maggie What's-her-name. The Maggie that moved to New Orleans."

"I never saw that apartment."

"So she dumped you and Ray dumped me the same day. We didn't know each other until five years later. Almost like we got our revenge, but it was too late by then . . . And now you think Ray's killing your ex-girlfriends?"

"I know, it doesn't make any sense at all."

"Would he kill me, too? I mean, he doesn't know about us. And I'm his ex-girlfriend. Would he kill me, too?"

"I don't know. I don't know for certain that it's Ray doing it. I've got a good idea, but he was in Miami when Annie's car blew up, so he couldn't have done that. All I wanted to tell you was, please be careful. Something's going on. I can't tell you to leave town, to lock yourself in the house, or anything else. All I can do is what I just did. Warn you."

"He never acted like the killing type."

I thought back to Mariel. "No. Just foolish in the face of disaster."

"Will you lie down next to me until I fall asleep?" Her eyes drooped.

I remembered her remark about still smelling like Eastern European body odor. "Why don't I take a rain check, tuck you in, and lock the door behind me?"

"You promise? The rain check?"

Before I left Laura's house I borrowed her phone. Bob Bernier thanked me for returning his call. "How's your afternoon look?" he said. "Can you spare me a few minutes?"

"Anytime after three-thirty."

"You up for a beer at Louie's?"

"Sounds fine," I said.

"Four?"

"I'll be wearing a Bimini T-shirt."

I looked in on Laura. Sound asleep on top of her bedspread. I had a feeling that the rain check might save my sanity sometime soon.

Back on the bike, I rode that section of Virginia Street east of Windsor Lane that remains so Cuban and original. I did not want to race traffic on Truman, so I turned at the stone fire station at Grinnell, zipped the stop sign next to ChiChi's Bar, and cut around the cemetery. I put some effort into it, getting up speed, blowing through pools of vermilion petals under the poinciana trees on Frances. I quickly built a sweat and felt a few kinks and knots work themselves out of my back muscles. All this intrigue, plus Laura's sexual radiance, had boosted the pressure inside of me. I wanted to uncork the ache without making any dumb mistakes, unwind without diluting what had turned into a sense of purpose. I would shed the superfluous details and focus on stopping the threat. I wanted to make sure that someone paid for all this damage and death.

142

I felt as if I had accomplished five percent of those things by the time I turned onto Dredgers Lane and coasted into the yard. I could blame some of the ache on exercise. I had burned off the morning beers.

Cigar odors wafted from the porch.

Avery Hatch in a tank top and a pair of shorts. A warm-weather ensemble similar to Laura Tate's. Not the same effect.

17

Sheriff's Detective Hatch delivered a massive belch. "Too much goddamn lunch," he said. I refused to respond. His intrusion had tossed my mood. I rolled the bicycle around back, locked it to the tree, threw the tarp over it. A million things on my mind, Avery Hatch not on the list. The neighbor's spaniel whined at the fence. I ruffled the hair on its head. It licked perspiration from my fingers. Unquestioning trust in the dog's eyes.

A Slurpee cup teetered on the edge of the porch table, cigar ashes stuck around its rim. "You came here to talk about your gluttony, Avery, and you walked," I said. "Your car's not in the lane. You wanted to ambush me?"

He shook his head. "Kiwanis pancake brunch at the AARP. Five goddamn dollars, I wanted my money's worth. I felt like walking off the maple syrup. My car's around to that lot by White Street, by Southard."

"Ah, but you're sitting down. Why here?"

Hatch sat up straighter in the chair. The wicker creaked in complaint. "Ask questions, like before," he said. "Why else? What do I do every fucking day of my life? I ever got time for social calls? I come here to pay my respects?"

"You want to know what the Cubans said, go ask your partner. Billy'd be happy to share his perspective." I entered the porch but remained standing. He didn't take the hint.

"What Cubans we talking about?"

"I hope the rest of your questions have more substance."

Avery shot back: "Rutledge, y'ever know Sally Ann Guthery?"

Here we go, I thought. "A few years ago. Took her out a few times."

"You didn't mention that Thursday morning when I told you she was the victim on Stock Island. I think you already knew she was the victim." Hatch looked impassive, as if he were reading a menu. I foresaw a one-man tough-guy, good-guy routine.

"I didn't know until you told me," I said.

"Where were you the night she was killed?"

"How the hell do I know? I don't know what night it happened. Even if I knew, I don't think I could come up with an answer."

"You don't know where you were?"

"The last couple of weeks I haven't paid much attention to myself. I've been through a period of personal distress. I sure as hell haven't kept a diary."

"So I take it you don't want to even attempt an alibi. I suppose you know Shelly Standish, too." He'd begun to spit his words.

"Now you're guessing, Avery." I walked inside and continued talking as I went to the refrigerator. "You heard from Lester Forsythe that I asked about the Balbuena and Guthery evidence photos. Shelly Standish, you're just guessing. Maybe that's what you do every day of your life. You guess."

"What'd you learn from the photographs?"

I returned to the porch and chugged from the OJ carton. "Somebody knows how to bend correct knots. Knots that don't slip, and similar knots in each case. You noticed them yourself, didn't you? You know enough about knots."

Avery's pause was long enough to convince me that he hadn't noticed the knots in the photos. But he decided to fake it. "Gimme some goddamned news," he said. "Did you forget that we live on a fucking island? Thirty-five thousand year-round residents right here at sea level. Elevation zero. Adventures in Paradise. Nautical Wheelers. Everybody and his brother knows knots. You think that's a clue, you got a long way to go. Where were you last Tuesday night when Julia Balbuena was dropped at Bahia Honda and Ellen Albury was offed in her living room?"

"See, everything's been sort of hyper since Wednesday, so that one I know for sure. But let's play with this fact, Hatch. I dated Shelly Standish, too, a few years ago. One way or another, I'm linked to every one of these crimes."

"So why shouldn't I arrest your ass? I think you've been screwing with the evidence."

"Look at yourself, Avery. In my goddamn chair, suffocating the plants with your two-and-a-half-buck hand-rolled cigar, insinuating that I might be a suspect in three murders. Where's your common sense? I'm a photographer. I got no chips on my shoulder except you're getting close to being one. I get drunk, I don't hurt people, I fall asleep. Do they pay you for this crap?"

He waved his hand to interrupt. I wouldn't let him.

"You've cranked your intuition around to the idea that I might murder a few friends and leave a broad trail to my own doorstep. It'll read good in the newspaper, won't it? 'Crime Wave Suspect in Custody.' So I freeze in fear. I scamper out and hire a three-piece lawyer. But Avery, it's a waste of pissant paperwork. You know I'm not your bad boy. If all you want to do is a shit job, take a hike. I've got important things to do around here. I've got to clean the crumbs out of my toaster. Three days of dishes in the sink. Pour pennies out of the Drambuie bottle and stuff them into rolls of fifty each. Scribble my account number on each roll."

"No need to be a wiseass, Rutledge."

"I've got to run a load of throw rugs through the washer and dryer. I need to refold my underwear and dust the windowsills. Use the carpenter's level to make sure all my framed artwork is hanging straight. Come to think of it, I've got to check the air pressure in my bike tires." I took another slug from the OJ carton. I didn't offer to share.

Hatch kept quiet.

"Okay, Avery, now that I've got your attention, I'll turn this sideways and ask my own question. I'll tell you in advance that I asked this of several people in the last day or so. Why did you pretend not to know Julia Balbuena?"

He went for the calming effect of breathing through his nostrils. "What do you mean, pretend?"

"Why didn't you identify the body? Tell me that."

Hatch's hand went for a cigar in the pocket, except there was no pocket. His eyes roved around at the three-foot level. They fixed on a small monstera plant in a weather-beaten Star Wars wastebasket.

"I'm a good detective. I told you that once, Rutledge. I'm good."

"I've heard other people say that, too. I'm glad you agree."

"I knew from 1980 that you had the hots for Kemp's girlfriend. Ray told me about it. She wanted to be friendly after the three of you got back from Mariel. She kept wanting to invite you for dinner or meet you for drinks. He had to convince her that you were a pest, and you wouldn't settle for friendship. You'd get possessive and grabby like you'd been when she dumped you for him.

"Ray Kemp asked you to go to Mariel because he figured you were over it, but afterward he had you pegged. He knew you were going for the goods. He told me about it, and I never forgot. Why the fuck do you think I had you come all the way from Key West when Lester was on the scene at Bahia Honda? You think I bought that bullhockey about you being expensive but good?"

"So the detective recognizes a body on the beach," I said. "He doesn't tell anyone who she is. But he remembers that Rutledge knew her half a lifetime ago. The detective thinks: That irrational freak. He's always in trouble. Always five or ten miles over the limit. Who cares if he's worked for the Department and the City for years? Who cares if he's never had so much as a jaywalking citation? Wouldn't it be great to set him up? Test the bugger to see if he perpetrated a few snuffs out and about the Lower Keys?"

He shrugged and gave a faint nod.

"Too far-fetched, Hatch. Julia Balbuena knew a thousand people in her lifetime. Maybe two thousand."

Now his head nodded nonstop. "That's how I do a good job. I fetch far. This time I fetched back six hours to where your girlfriend's roomie is toast. And you're rumbling around the murder venue like somebody official."

"Which I am, from time to time."

Hatch heaved himself out of the chair and shuffled toward the screen door. "Self-appointed, it appears. You a cop groupie, Rutledge?"

"I would be, but I can't afford a scanner."

"You think we don't know about your odd jobs? You stole a sailboat three years ago."

"Funny, Avery, the loss wasn't reported. Maybe the captain in possession wasn't the rightful owner. That was a favor for a friend. And I recall a Sarasota insurance investigator saying—in confidence, of course—that several deputies, your colleagues, were partners in a boat brokerage in Port Charlotte. They sold out after I recovered that yacht."

Hatch started to say something, but changed his mind.

"Avery, you believe what you want, but Julia and Ray split up not long after the Boatlift. You didn't see me beelining for Miami back then. Why would I want to kill her fifteen years later?"

He let the door slam on his way out. I stared up the lane as he waddled off toward Fleming.

A Cuban cadet in a blue uniform held the dripping AK-47. His poncho flapped against a pine sapling. His hands shook and one of his mismatched boots kept slipping in the mud. Only the weight of the weapon ensured his balance.

Mother of God, I thought. I am here for a quick down-and-back. Now I am eye-to-eye with where the bullets come out. I will sign the confession. I don't want to die in my skivvies in the rain.

I went back to the anchor chain and the Danforth, concentrating on the chore at hand. I wanted the trainee not to feel threatened. I wanted the emergency of the moment, the mariner's priority, to be more urgent than a sentry's duty. Even to look again at the boy would challenge him. I did not wish to put my life under the trigger finger of this teenager. He acts brave as he confronts the Yankee invaders, I thought, but he's shivering and he's new at this. My legacy is seven thousand slides with no copyright stamps. I will make him wait to shoot me until I have finished tying these knots.

One more problem. If the wind shifted, as it should after an abrupt front, it would push Barracuda *farther onto the beach and trap her in bottom ooze. We would need to free the boat. Untying knots wouldn't do the job fast enough.*

I worked to separate the Danforth from the heavy rope. Two soldiers holding AK-47s joined the young one. To maintain a shield of confusion, I made my task more complicated. I freed the anchor chain, tethered the rope to a broader tree, then turned bowlines around an adjacent trunk. Without facing the soldiers, I hefted the anchor and chain and retreated to the boat.

Through the slit of a cabin window I spotted Ray holding my camera to his eye. Christ, I thought. Taking snapshots of me, of my impending death in my Jockey shorts and this soggy windbreaker, on my film. With kiddie-cadets in the background. Let's all get shot now. Get it developed and charge my account.

"Give me a knife," I shouted toward the rear of the boat. "In case I have to cut this line in a hurry."

Ray lowered the camera and pushed open a top-hinged window. "If you say so, commando. It's your beachhead."

That's it, I thought. It's my boat now. Until I get off—if I make it back on—I will make the decisions that count. This captain is shit for brains and a child to boot. I moved back through the muck, charading for the soldiers, using hand signals to indicate caution. The rain let up. Ray came to the bow holding the blade end of a carving knife.

"Toss it near the bushes, over there." Somehow I mustered a calm tone. "Don't hit the Cub Scouts."

The knife landed flat. Without looking at the cadets, I walked four steps and jabbed the blade deep into the dirt next to the tree trunk. I turned to the soldiers, made a cutting motion over the rope, pointed to the knife, and made a pushing motion toward Barracuda. *Even Castro's conscripted grunts could understand that I had taken action for safety rather than aggression.*

I waded out toward the stern and hauled myself back aboard. I found Julia hunkered down on the afterdeck, her face a flood of tears. Ray Kemp sat in the cabin, proud of himself, patting my camera like a puppy.

I had packed the photos in an Army surplus ammo box, watertight and bug-proof. Two hundred slides from Mariel Bay. None had been published because another photographer, another survivor, got back to Florida first. He made the magazine's deadline and I ate six rolls of Kodachrome. A welcome-home meal.

A week later the Mariel Boatlift was old news. I'd never sorted or filed them.

I checked them one by one with a magnifying loupe. Some weren't too bad. I'd been trying to show differences and disparities. Filthy old shrimpers and workboats had nested in groups of eight or ten around two or three main anchors. Alongside them were luxury yachts and beamy sailboats designed to beat SORC racing class rules. Hundreds of filthy, battered fiberglass outboards had gathered in clusters as well. Sprinkled about the bay, underway, were Donzis and Cigarettes and Scarabs. Rich and poor waited in the same line, like the urinal lines in the Orange Bowl. We waited for the corroded bureaucracy to act. A rare victory for Castro's flawed system of all for all.

In one series of shots Ray mugged for the camera and displayed a finger count of our days in port. Long ago I had put this group in order, to show a mutual friend Ray's state of mind during the ordeal. On a sunny morning with two fingers in the air he looked fresh in a clean T-shirt. By four fingers he appeared frazzled, brushing his teeth as he grinned for the photo. Eight fingers flashed on a gray morning as he embraced and pretended to smooch an upright mop.

On the ninth morning, well after sunup, his hair matted and nasty, Kemp clutched a liter bottle of Havana Club Rum. He'd begun the bender the previous evening at sunset. It had included a midnight swim in the bay full of turds, oil scum, and garbage. Ray came away lucky from that one. The Cuban marines patrolling all night in motorboats had promised to shoot anyone in the water. On the tenth day he'd reached around Julia's waist and jammed his arms down into her shorts. Ten fingers extended outward from the bottom hem. She bore an expression of disgust. Even then I could see the beginning of the end of their relationship.

I finally found the sequence I wanted. The half-dozen Ray

had shot while I crawled through silt and mangrove roots trying to secure *Barracuda* to the shore trees. In the lee of the trees, the storm was a mere downpour. The Cuban soldiers who surrounded me looked malnourished. They appeared fearful, but willing to defend the homeland. There I was, carrying the anchor and chain back to the boat after I had removed them from the bowline. The Danforth anchor, with its dull, scratched aluminized finish. The big gash in its fluke where it had grabbed another anchor or a chunk of a wreck.

The duplicate Albury murder-scene prints from Duffy Lee were in a desk drawer. I didn't have to check them, but I did to be certain. The surface texture was the same. The gouge across the fluke slashed at an identical angle. The Danforth was the same size. It was the same anchor.

That son of a bitch.

How had Ray learned about my friendships with these women? Why the women? Why not just me? Why now, after all these years?

At five minutes to three I walked across the lane and knocked on Cecilia Ayusa's door. The puffy breeze fanned her wind chimes. The garlicky smell of boiled yuca drifted through the screens. Rhumba music, the kind that Carmen loved to play mornings after romantic encounters, played in a back room.

Cecilia came to the door wiping her hands on her apron. She pushed a few stray hairs off her forehead. Also one of Carmen's habits. The women were like sisters, with Cecilia twenty pounds heavier and twenty years older. Always ready with a laugh, a bawdy remark, a brilliant smile, a sympathetic shoulder. I often accused her of spending her entire life in the kitchen. I had learned a few years ago that Cecilia was an expert diver. She'd grown up with three older brothers who were lobster-hunting legends. Two had moved to Tarpon Springs to become sponge divers. They had quit while still in their thirties, and retired back to Key West after the Boatlift dust had settled.

"You look like a dead person," said Cecilia. "You need to eat and sleep and make love and get a sunburn even if you catch a cancer."

"You have a way with words."

Bilingual like her daughter, Cecilia could reconstruct English on the fly. Like many native Key Westers, she could mold it around Cuban idiom, Caribbean Spanish, traces of Bahamian phrasing, even urban slang. The crazy hybrid mix communicated exactly what the speaker wanted to say, made room for frank statements and hard truth. Many mistook it for a Bronx accent.

"They call yet?"

She pointed at the receiver. "That phone gonna ring in ten seconds."

And it did. Cecilia grabbed it first and let fly with a barrage of questions. Then it was her turn to answer a few. Yes, Maria was fine. She had spent the day on a boat in the Snipe Keys with her uncle and cousins. Finally Cecilia put me on.

"Annie?"

"She went outside to turn off a sprinkler. We've got our little assignments around here."

"How's it going? You had something to tell me."

"Better me than her. You told me that the guy who gave Monty Aghajanian the shaft was the guy she was seeing?"

"I recall that."

"We've been talking about things. When she told me the man's name I started to think, I know that name from somewhere. I figured it out."

"He gets his name in the paper."

"No, not that. You know, when you're alone in the post office at six-thirty in the morning, with only one or two other people, putting up the mail and sticking it in the boxes? You don't have a whole lot to think about. After a while, you get to know people by their mail. You follow me?"

"So far."

"You see things, you remember them, you see them again a week later, a month later. I can tell you the name of everyone in Key West who gets *New Yorker* magazine. I know who doesn't pay their bills and who gets letters from collection agencies in Marathon and Miami. I know when women get their child-support checks. I know who's got money in a half dozen mutual funds and who's getting mail from people in prison. I can tell you if someone's got a gold credit card or American Express. Who's got relatives in Cuba or Germany. It's not like I've got a photographic memory, but after a while you know everything that's going on with those boxholders."

"Which brings us back around to Michael Anselmo."

"Right. He's been Box 6705 for about three months. He gets personal and business mail at that address. The strange thing, and why I noticed his name when Annie told me about him, he's been getting weird postcards for the past couple of weeks. They're old picture postcards from before postcards were glossy. They used to call them linen cards. Anyway, they're always addressed in pencil. But they're not from a prison, which is the usual tip-off with pencil addresses."

"Okay."

"They've been postmarked all over the place, from New York to Missouri to South Carolina, and all over. And this is what me and my co-workers have been noticing. They all sound threatening, like 'Your day is gonna come,' and 'Everybody got to go sometime,' and 'Bend over and kiss your ass good-bye.'"

"I agree, that's weird."

"We even spied on this guy. He reads the cards and looks worried as hell, and he stuffs them inside his sport coat or suit jacket and goes away. One said, 'You never hear the bullet that gets you.' We expected him to bring that one to the Postmaster's attention. Anyway, I thought this was a strange coincidence, you might be interested. Annie just walked in the door."

I could hear the receiver being handed over.

"Hi."

"How goes your vacation in Miami, Florida?"

"It's paradise and it sucks. Carmen and I had a wonderful day, and I have sunburned boobs and a sore throat from talking so much. But I want this death-threat crap to stop."

"I think Ray Kemp may be the bad man. The captain of the boat I rode to Mariel. He was at the funeral yesterday."

"At Ellen's funeral or Julia's funeral?"

"In Miami."

"So how could he have put a bomb in my car?"

"I thought about that. He got to the funeral just as it began. You walked to the cemetery just before one o'clock. He was in Coral Gables at four. That's three hours to plant the device and drive up the Keys. He'd have to hurry, but it's possible."

"Where is he now?"

"Last I saw him, he claimed he had to hop a flight to Seattle."

"But he could be in Miami right now."

"He also could be in Key West. By the way, a reporter from the paper has been calling and leaving you messages."

"Like I've got something Earth-shattering to reveal to her readers . . . Look, can you come up here tonight? I still haven't had a chance to explain things face-to-face. If you still want to listen to me."

I had started the day at six-thirty, dealt with Monty, the Balbuenas, Laura Tate, and Avery Hatch, and I still had another sit-down ahead of me. I waited too long to answer her.

"Is this like 'No'?" Her voice thin.

Our romance was turning into a Bosnian cease-fire. Assuming she was sincere, it couldn't hurt to hear her side of things. "Can I bring wine?"

"Not if it slows you down."

18

Bob Bernier, Monty's friend in the FBI, had claimed a table under a sea-grape tree at Louie's Back Yard. Fifteen or twenty other people sat closer to the water on the restaurant's Afterdeck and stared at the ocean as if any minute it might perform a back flip. Alert to my entrance, Bernier recognized my shirt, pushed his chair back and stood to identify himself. He was my height, just shy of six-two, though more slender. The way he moved made me think of a football halfback. I pictured him as sturdy but quick.

We shook hands like opposing captains on the fifty-yard line. Bernier's thick forearms looked as if he had grown up pitching hay bales. He wore horn-rimmed eyeglasses, a blue button-down short-sleeved shirt, and dark cotton slacks. His ash-colored hair showed advanced effects of male-pattern baldness as well as a home-grown trim, the unnatural curve made by electric clippers above the collar. I've always wondered about the fifty-thou-a-year guys who go to the missus for cash-saving touch-ups. Bob Bernier's aura of straightness was not so much the stereotyped bureaucrat as one of those cloned fellows who bike around town in a white shirt and tie handing out religious tracts. Still, he was observant and not immune to life's pleasures. The regulars at Louie's knew that the table he'd picked offered the best view of sunbathing women at Vernon Street beach.

The waitress headed our way.

"Name your poison."

I ordered a Mount Gay rum and soda in a tall glass, and we sat down.

"Monty couldn't make it," said Bernier. "Some kind of family deal."

"You've known him a long time?" I said.

"Not all that long. We linked up on a couple joint ops maybe thirty months ago. Back when he was single. It's not often that the bureau works well with local law enforcement."

It's not often, I thought, that a Fed will admit to the tradition of friction.

Bernier continued. "For some reason Monty and I hit it off. We were good at sharing info. He was a first-rate police officer." Bernier slid his chair closer. "Let me get right to it, Alex. First off, I'm on the fence. So far the Bureau has no jurisdiction in this case. ATF is here because of the bomb, and FDLE because of the link between the bomb and the Albury murder. By the way, you should warn Annie Minnette that the ATF investigation may delay her insurance claim. They haven't let the adjuster near the car. For the record, you didn't see it up close or take pictures this morning."

I tried not to show surprise.

"Don't worry. Monty's not in any kind of jam. That was city business. It changed to federal business before noon."

"Okay."

"Meanwhile I'm here for . . . let's call it 'guidance.' We're keeping a watch on all this political drumbeating in Dade County. Monty tells me that you've turned up a few interesting details regarding the Balbuena murder."

"It's been a busy day, Bob. Avery Hatch from the Sheriff's

Department just dropped by the house to accuse me of being a serial murderer."

"I hope you denied it."

The waitress arrived with my drink. She refilled Bernier's iced tea. I'd have felt more trusting of the meeting's unofficial nature if Bob had been drinking something alcoholic. But he was the lawman most removed from local politics, most capable of an overview, the person with the power to pursue every angle. Except for Monty, I couldn't think of another badge to trust.

I spun the web for him, including the knots, my call to the car-rental agency, my warning calls to the five women, and the arrival of the Balbuenas with their photos. I mentioned seeing Billy Fernandez at the Hyatt. I told him how Sam Wheeler had blown Hatch's ruse regarding his not having known Julia. I let Bob compare the slide from Mariel and the print of the anchor in Ellen Albury's front room. I offered the possibility that Ray had triggered the car bomb, then driven straight to Miami for Julia's funeral.

We watched a young woman race shoreward on a sailboard. To reverse tack she steered into the wind and pirouetted forward of the mast to gain the starboard rail. She wore a neon-red thong bikini and mooned the Afterdeck as she sped away on an offshore gust. Returning to check on our drink levels, the waitress affected an expression of admonishment for our being interested in the windsurfer's bum, then walked away with a twist of her hips, confident that our attention had shifted.

Bernier got back to business. "Ray Kemp acted like your long-lost friend in Coral Gables. But Avery Hatch told you that the guy disliked you in the old days. Distrusted you with his woman. Now he's your pal again?"

"I treated yesterday like a reunion, too. On the trip home from Mariel, it wouldn't have bothered me to see his sorry ass washed over the side. He was dangerous on his own boat. I guess time smoothes out the rough spots."

"You don't think Kemp ever went down?"

"At one point in '78, early '79, I could have named you three dozen of the boys involved. Back then I didn't know Kemp was one of them. I found out yesterday he was a major player. If I'd known, I never would have gone to Mariel on his boat. If he's been to prison, I never heard about it."

Bernier looked back toward the water. "Did you get involved?"

Dodge this bullet: "There wasn't a man on the island who didn't think about it. I was lucky. I started to make money with my photography. I turned down a couple of rides."

Now he turned back toward me. I sensed the care he was taking not to lose the conversational tone. "You make it sound so casual. The 'boys' and their 'rides.' They weren't afraid of being turned in?"

"It was a convoy mentality, like truck drivers speeding in packs. The scammers thought they were immune. They were all coming home with suntans and grocery sacks full of cash. I guess they figured no cop could stop them all."

"Wide open."

"You bet. Guys who'd been waiters at Tony's Fish Market showed up in new BMWs. Spreading around the wealth got them laid like rock stars. Their girlfriends all sported Rolexes."

"And they never thought the IRS would get on their backs?"

"I don't think they were thinking. In their eyes, they'd beaten Mother Ocean all the way from Florida to South America and back again in small sailboats. They'd had to dodge Colombian pirates and bad weather and the Coast Guard . . . like living their own adventure movies. But there'd never be a Jimmy Buffett lyric about them. So they told the tales themselves."

Bernier nodded. "Internal Revenue was a million miles away."

"Plus," I said, "around here a lot of law-enforcement people were directly involved. Nobody held back. Eventually, all of the boys got popped, including the cops, usually by the snitch system. I never heard Ray's name. Not once."

"So if we took him down, it was somewhere far away. Or else he played the system into Witness Protection. And he bought the boat with drug money?"

"I assume so. Easy enough to cover. He had a job. Not many scammers had real jobs, and I can't remember any other charter captains getting involved. They all found floaters . . . small potatoes."

Bernier screwed up his face.

"A boatload of smugglers would see the Coast Guard on the horizon, they'd push the pot bales over the side. It was cheaper to lose the load than pay lawyers or do prison time. The evidence drifted away with the currents. A lot of people found them. The charter captains would haul aboard a soggy bale, their customers got a free day of fishing, and there was a number the captains could call. A van would come by the Bight docks after dark. The captain would collect two or three thousand cash. Tropical enterprise. Nobody looked down their nose at it. They called the bales 'square groupers.' Somebody even printed 'Save the Bales' T-shirts. Picture of a guy with a harpoon on the foredeck of a Hewes flats skiff."

"Christ, Rutledge." Bernier tilted back his iced tea. "You've got your details down pat on these operations."

This diehard bastard could not believe that I wasn't a bad guy. I wondered if I'd made a mistake spilling out my evidence gems. "Believe me, Bob," I said, "there was no social stigma, and there were no secrets."

That stopped him. He became silent. I did not interrupt.

"So when did Ray leave Key West?"

"I don't know. One day I realized he hadn't been around for a while."

"You know if he sold the boat?"

"To a military guy. Friend of a friend of a friend. I'm not sure when."

Bernier took out a notepad and a gold pen. "Any idea of his full name?"

"Raymond, and there's a middle name. He had his passport in Cuba. The middle name was Irish, an O'-something, because I called him by that name and he got pissed. Not O'Rourke or O'Hara. Something out of the ordinary, like O'Johnson, or O'Clinton."

Bernier wrote and I looked around. The bartender was leaning over the bar to eat a salad. The waitress put out red and green candle jars in preparation for the evening cocktail hour. Two barflies I knew as Stacy and C.J. stood among the stools near the waitress station. A slow day. Post-season.

"What do we do about Avery Hatch?" I said.

Bernier thought about that one for a moment. "That visit an hour ago was less than official. In Case One, he either knows something, or he wants to steer the suspicions toward you."

"And Case Two?"

"Maybe it's what he said before. Maybe he's a good detective. Maybe he's on the level."

"Even when you consider his past connection to Kemp?"

Bernier looked up at the sea-grape tree, then made another note. "Yes, that's strong." He looked back up toward the tree. "On that train of thought, Alex, it's not unusual for police officers, no matter their background, to harbor deep, unexplained rage." Bernier turned to face me. "You know the man. Do you think Monty Aghajanian is capable of committing a violent crime?"

I wanted to make sure Bernier believed my response. It was my turn to look up into the sea-grape tree. It wasn't to ponder the possibility of Monty's being a murderer. I was counting to twenty.

"No, I don't think so," I said in a firm, quiet tone.

"Did he date many women?"

I thought a moment. "I remember two before he met his wife."

Bernier looked again through the photographs. "Balbuena's picture, that shot of Ray putting his coat in the packed trunk of the rental car. Where would Kemp have kept all those boxes of boat equipment? Someone's home? He sure as hell didn't fly into Miami with a fifty-pound anchor."

"The gear on that boat was ratty. He'd have no reason to keep it."

"We're assuming he hasn't lived around here all along."

"Here's the zinger. How did he get the names of my ex-girlfriends?"

"Let's work on that. Who would know their names? Did you ever tell any of these women about the other ones?"

"Sometimes I've introduced them to each other."

"Your current girlfriend. Does she know . . . ?"

I didn't want to start a wild-goose chase by suggesting Annie as the source of the names. "We've been open about telling each other things. We understand that everyone has a past."

"No jealousies?"

Good question. "It's the growing process. You learn to be a good partner. Some things you learn from some people, some from others. It all adds up to make today's relationship all that much better."

Bernier looked at me with a cocked eye. I had to admit to myself that it sounded pretty corny.

"Now that I think about it," he said, "she couldn't be the source anyway. If someone wanted to kill girlfriends or if he wanted to kill his source, either way he wouldn't have done the wrong person. Ellen Albury wouldn't have been hit. I say all this assuming the killer is not female. Can you think of any drinking pals you might have confided in, talking about the ladies?"

"Plenty of people have seen me with one woman or another. Sam Wheeler's met most of these women, at least in the past six or eight years. Or he's heard me speak of them from time to time."

"Okay, but you've described him as a close friend. Is there anyone else you can think of?"

"Who knows who talks about what? I'm out in a bar or a restaurant with one woman or another over the years, the bartenders may remember one or two. But who would keep track, make a list?"

We ran out of ideas. I considered telling him about Michael Anselmo's odd postcards, but that was another topic for another day. I didn't want him to lose his focus on the immediate danger. We sat back to finish our drinks.

Bernier told me that he'd put in nine years with the Bureau, the first six in the upper Midwest, and was shooting for twenty-two. He'd retire at fifty-one, in Costa Rica if the country hadn't been discovered and spoiled by then.

"Alex, you're a civilian. But you're under a probable threat to your safety, so you'll be kept informed, warned if we see anything coming your way. To a certain extent, we'll compare notes with the city and county. If Monty wants to share anything, that's up to him. Can I keep your photographs a few days?"

I couldn't think of a reason not to let him have them.

"Let me ask you one more thing, Alex." He stared at a bare-breasted young woman who'd sat up on the beach in order to refasten her bikini top. "Where are you from, where'd you grow up?"

"Cleveland Heights, Ohio."

"The Midwest. And you've been here how long?"

163

"Oh, twenty-plus years."

"Okay, tell me. What's all this 'bubba' stuff? Everybody calls everybody else 'bubba.' It's about to drive me bananas. Is this a figment of the Waylon and Willie legacy, or does it come from the Nashville Network?"

"Near as I can tell, it was here before Patsy Cline."

"So it's a local thing."

"I agree, it doesn't make much sense. The roots of this town go back to the Bahamas and to Cuba, not to Hattiesburg, Mississippi."

"I hear it in federal court. Defense attorneys talking to prosecutors and vice versa. They butter each other up by calling each other 'bubba.' It's almost a prerequisite to getting down to business. It drives me bats."

"When they start using it on you, you'll know you've been accepted."

"They didn't tell me this in graduate school."

A base-level fatigue began to creep into my muscles and my mood. It would have been easy to blame the rum, but common sense told me I had not been good to myself for almost a month. Stress, travel, and lack of sleep never used to bother me much. I'd always banked on a personal theory of relativity: the quicker your speed, the slower time passes. In other words, the faster you live, the longer you live. It was proving to be a bogus notion.

Exercise is supposed to help. But I'd labeled the bike ride to the Hyatt and to Laura's as my workout for the day. If I hadn't ridden the Kawasaki to Louie's, I might have blown off my next whistle-stop. One more ride past the Bight to try to catch Sam at the dock. My traffic-avoidance program took me out Washington to 1st Street, and left to Charterboat Row. I found the deadpan captain hosing down his skiff next to the houseboat restaurant in the corner near Roosevelt Boulevard.

"Get a chance to relax?" Sam looked at me more closely and knew the answer.

"Things are flying by a mile a minute," I said. "You're going to just love a couple of these tasty details. Before I tell you about Julia's father offering a fat reward for Ray Kemp on a platter, I will give you the juice on Michael Anselmo receiving threatening postcards in the mail."

"After the doofus I had in the boat this afternoon, I need some fun."

For the second time in ninety minutes I explained what I knew. Then I tagged Carmen's post-office recollection with the fact that Marnie Dunwoody had called about the dead roommate and the car bomb.

"Isn't it wonderful to find someone in this town doing her job?" Sam coiled the water hose and stowed it in his dock locker. We caught a whiff of bilge soap from down the dock. Sam pointed out a hefty woman with her hand in the back pocket of her thin cotton pants, scratching her ass like crazy. "You ready for a cold one?"

"I'm ready for twelve hours with my head under the pillow."

"Go do it."

"Wish I could. My penis brain won't let me. Miami calls."

"What happened to our pledge to solve the mystery?"

"I'm thinking about it every waking minute. And I'll be back on the clock Monday morning."

"People get murdered on Sunday, too."

"We can't be psychics. He wants to hit, we can't stop that. I think the kind of work we need to do requires places of business and civic offices that aren't open until Monday."

"Did Annie ever explain anything?"

"I'm not sure I caught the gist of it. Something about being pissed off that she loved me."

"That makes you the one at fault. You asked me to warn you if you flew too close to forgiveness."

"I got snared in the web the other night."

Sam got pensive, and looked back again at the woman in the white pants. "Maybe I need a night or two in some kind of web. It's been a few weeks."

19

I rolled into Dredgers Lane in second gear. The copper Cutlass
Ciera was angle-parked up near the house, its nose tucked into
an overgrown croton bush. I let the Kawasaki coast to a stop.
Through the screening I could see Detective Billy Fernandez
staring at me from the lounge chair on my porch.

"How do I put a stop to all these surprise visits?" I said.
"Cut the fucking porch off the house and tow it out the Northwest Channel?"

Billy clutched a *Sports Illustrated* swimsuit issue. Dandruff
flecks covered the shoulders of his black muscle T-shirt. He
didn't answer and his arrogant, mustached TV-cop expression
didn't change. By a count of empties, he was four beers into a
six-pack of Heineken. That late in the day I was sure there'd
been a previous six-pack, maybe two. A mix of fashion cologne
and rank perspiration escaped the porch and tainted the yard air.

I kicked down into first, eased the cycle around back, and
peeled off my helmet. The spaniel's glum eyes peered through
the fencing. I wondered if I wasn't looking into a mirror. Afternoon shadows and fingers of orange sunlight shimmered in the
crabgrass. An electric guitar somewhere in the neighborhood delivered respectable Stevie Ray Vaughan riffs.

The walk to my door was getting longer by the day.

Fernandez tilted back for another swig of beer. I figured the

ICE logo on his ball cap for a rap group until I recalled that Island City Electric sponsored a baseball team in the youth leagues.

"We need to compare notes, bubba." He slurred his words. "You don't know what kind of slicks and badasses you're dealing with."

Why this? "I'm getting to know you too well, Billy."

"Coño, I'm not who I mean." Billy squinted and tapped the neck of his beer bottle against the table edge. "This ain't no goddamn Mickey Mouse scenario, bubba. You follow?"

I stared back.

He shifted his sitting position and brought up a modest burp. "I tell you 'bout chitchats they start in Spanish, they stay in Spanish," he said. "That's a Miami code they use to make it Latin against Anglo. They get Hispanic Metro cops to go bad that way like, you know, bending the law falls under a category of political action, you follow me? The caca ever hits the fan, they hang the kids out to dry. I got this acquaintance on the Metro-Dade force, ex-vice, ex-homicide, he's done two years Internal Affairs. Knows the fuckin' scene inside out. Even talks Yiddish, a few words. I call him last night and out of his head he pulls nicknames. You wanna know this?"

Did I have a choice? I took a beer and Fernandez offered the opener on his key ring. "You got me rolling," I said. "Let's see where it goes."

Billy perked up and tried to focus. "Carlos Balbuena, the kid?"

"Right."

"Right. Also known as, get this, Charlie Balls, the man to see in the Grove and the Gables and South Beach for quantity crystal meth. He's sewage. Almost for sure the man behind three homicides. And he's a puncher. Big into personally stomping street addicts who don't pay his runners. Hangs with a bunch of rich Cuban boys, drive top-of-the-line Japanese cars with gold-plated trim. Their girlfriends all look like WASP girls from the university or the country club. Except for their women, these boys hate anyone not Cuban. They hate Colombian, they hate Puerto Rican. And they pay to train this bunch of jerks who want to abduct Castro, teach 'em how to crawl in mud and throw grenades in the Everglades. So these para-militaries are the rich boys' muscle, and they don't give a rat's ass who they mess up. Now you want to find out about Emilio Palguta."

"Okay."

"Like I say, no Mickey Mouse, right? 'Ogunito,' the name from santería. You know, Cuban voodoo. The god of the forge and warfare."

I tried to imagine a Cuban swordfighter. "Blades," I said.

"Fuckin' A, bubba. Ogunito likes the sharp edge. He likes to spring bad for the simple fun of it. He's in Broward now because Dade kicked him out. Back then he did little shit. Melted stolen coin collections, made gold and silver coke spoons to sell to the head shops. He put vans in vacant lots near the canals to offload Cigarette boats after mother-ship trips. Did time upstate. Last ten years he lives the good life, a made guy in Dania. He and the old man Raoul, they go back to the jungle, blood-brother rebels in Camagüey, eating leeches, wiping their ass with ferns, fighting for Fidel's little dream."

"They're looking for someone who killed the man's daughter. She was a friend of mine. We're working the same side."

Without a breeze the porch had become stifling. Sweat streamed from Billy's forehead. He pointed the bottom of the beer bottle in my direction. "How much they offer you, bubba?"

"How much they offer you, Billy?" I said. "Are we working against each other? Is that why you're here?"

Fernandez pondered his answer. He scratched his stupid mustache, and I wondered which way the dead caterpillar faced, if Billy was picking its nose or its ass. "Three bills to leak a few things. Five to drop a dime when we make an arrest. Ten grand to let him escape." He paused again. "They pumped me a grand for scene details on the Guthery and Albury cases. Little pocket change."

It wasn't the beer talking. He was bragging, thrilled to have learned his dollar value in the bribery market. The potential income was clouding his vision. He'd been a cop too long to ignore the obvious. He was setting himself up for a lifetime of blackmail.

"You got family, Billy? Wife, kids?"

"Ex-wife, two boys. Over on George Street." His voice dropped as his brain shifted into a different gear. He lifted his ball cap, then showed me the ICE logo. One of the boys played in the youth league.

"You're looking for a way to collect their cash, Billy."

He shut up for a moment. Mopeds and motorcycles made a racket over on Fleming. "You should remember one thing, bubba, this one thing. You can't get me in trouble, but I can get you out of it."

Somehow I knew he'd used that line a hundred times before. "You saying that I'm headed there, or I'm already there?" I said. "Or do you think I'd turn you in for helping the Balbuenas?"

"Like you say, bubba. The same team."

"They offered me five to snoop around Key West."

Billy snapped out of his stupor. He grabbed the cardboard container for another beer. "A bird-dog fee? Five hundred or thousand?"

"What's the difference? I turned it down."

"You notice, these girls, nobody's saying official cause of death."

"Now that you mention it."

Now he looked smug. He popped the bottle cap with his opener. He almost whispered, "You know Avery wants to come down on you?"

"Avery's been diddling around, not making a whole lot of sense."

"He makes more sense than you think, bubba. Sometimes you know he scares me, he makes so much sense, you follow?" Fernandez began to jingle his key ring. "So he talked about picking you up for questioning. My partner can be a fuckhead sometimes. You could hear the knock on the door. This is not a good time to be holding concealed."

"I look like the type to carry a gun?"

"Maybe you should." After a long swig his glassy eyes met mine. "Just don't get caught."

"How long have you known Hatch?"

"I jumped city to county in '80. He came to the county in '81."

There was no way to be sure if Fernandez had known Ray or Julia. I didn't want to ask. The time frame suggested he might have. "Find anything at Bahia Honda?" I said.

"Only you." He pushed himself out of the lounge chair and leaned against the doorframe. "You should back off. Back away, bubba. Don't forget these talks we have."

The talk had consisted of slurred advice from a man who complained about tactics used to turn good cops to crime, then, like reading a menu, explained his options for making illegal pocket change. Fernandez lumbered out the door with his half-finished beer looking no different than a thousand drunks he'd arrested for staggering out of the Boca Chica Bar. He left his empties and his magazine behind.

The last thing I said was not to spin his tires in the yard. In Key West real grass is harder to grow than the Jamaican variety.

Raoul Balbuena had dictated a message to my machine. He'd spoken with his ex-wife about Ray Kemp, and she had told a strange story she'd heard long ago from Julia. Raoul thought I might find it interesting. Before Julia left Key West, Ray had become angry at a neighbor's dog. The dog's owner worked a night shift, and the dog barked all night every night and kept Ray awake. One midnight Ray had gone next door and duct-taped the dog's mouth shut. The dog had died.

Raoul had drawn a parallel, but did not explain his knowledge of Albury crime-scene details.

I packed a waterproof duffel and listened to the phone ring as I headed for the door. Again, against good judgment, I answered.

"You sound out of breath," said Bob Bernier.

"I'm blowing town for the sake of my optimism."

"Far?"

"Near. Going to Miami for a couple days. See what I can make of this half-assed romance of mine."

"I need to ask one more question. Was Kemp ever in the service?"

"I told you all I know."

"You said he sold his charter boat to an old friend from the military . . ."

". . . an old friend of Wheeler's," I said. "But now that you mention it, Ray and another captain in Mariel got into war stories, recognition games about places in 'Nam. You couldn't tell by the way he acted on that trip, but I got the impression he might have been in the Marines."

"Well, he doesn't fit our type profile for serial crime. That gives him some distance. But not much."

"So where'd the bomb come from?"

"The big leagues. It was a mix of commercial mining explosives. Tovex and Drivex. They look like greasy white sausages, crimped at both ends with metal staples, nasty to handle. They're hard to get, except in West Virginia, in any hardware store. At least that was the case a couple years ago. The law may have changed by now."

"How was it set to blow?"

"Two different ways. An electric blasting cap and an M-100 firecracker, both wired to filaments in bulbs like they use in taillights. The bulbs were wired to the brake-light circuit. Broken glass, intact filament. Once the driver hits the brakes and holds his or her foot down, the bulb would last about forty seconds in the open air. It'd glow white-hot and light the M-100 fuse. Plus, when the bulb burned out, it'd trigger the electric cap. Crude, rude, and fail-safe. Either way the explosive gets a boost."

"Why wasn't the thief blown to hamburger?"

"German engineering, the way the factory pieces together sections of VW convertibles. That and luck."

"Why West Virginia?"

"Who knows? It's solid rock, and people need holes for their outhouses and graves and coal mines."

"I've got to go, Bob."

"Can I ask a favor?"

I told him he could ask.

"You're a focal point. I'd like to put a man in your house until you get back. We'll bring in groceries and bed linen."

And search my house for evidence of my involvement in pot smuggling, you chickenshit bureaucrat. On the other hand, I felt reassured having someone looking out for the homestead. Plus, I had nothing to hide.

"I'll leave a key under the Christmas cactus," I said. "Be prepared. The neighbors are going to ask who you are. Tell my houseguests there's no cream for coffee. It's been a few days since I've been to the grocery."

I did not have the energy to push it. I found a speed just above the limit and put my brain on cruise control. In the Key deer slowdown zone on Big Pine, I zeroed in on one question. If the ex-girlfriend link was real, what had I done to provoke all this ugliness and violence? Nothing came to mind. And knowing nothing about the killer or his motives, there was nothing I could do to change it. All I could do was try to stop it. I quit thinking again.

Except for the beam of the cycle's headlight, my ride through the desolate areas of the Keys and across the longer bridges was like being aboard a sailboat at night, up close to the flavor and moods of the sea. Ships' lights glowed in the distance and gave the only clues to the horizon. At the south end of Marathon a wobbly pickup truck pulled in front of me as it departed a bar. A double downshift and a swerve cleared me from danger. Two close calls in two days, though this had been the lesser of the two. It would have done no good to confront the loadie in the GMC. Sooner or later a semi would T-bone his pickup, shatter his legs, bounce his skull against the roof, and the *Herald* would have another five inches to fill.

An hour later, behind a line of traffic north of Jewfish Creek, I laughed at the brake lights, the slowing, the movement to the right in the four-lane passing zone. The tourists' radar detectors had picked up Southern Bell's microwave tower on Card Sound Road. For once, the locals could speed up and go to the head of the line. I hit the Turnpike in Florida City, turned east on 836 behind the airport, and connected with with I-95 near the center of Miami. A friend once told me that cycle riders in Miami are classified as targets of opportunity. Traffic was light and my last few miles were easy. I found the Enchanted Forest address about twenty after eleven.

Carmen's cousin lived in an elaborately lighted home in an area bordered by canals. The motorcycle engine had buzzed me into one large nerve ending. I felt shaky on solid ground, like a sailor who steps onto the dock after a long voyage and becomes seasick from lack of rolling motion. A jovial man answered the door. My height, probably in his mid-thirties, he wore silk pajamas and a short inch-thick terry-cloth robe. He looked like a blond stand-in for the Marlboro Man. If this guy is gay, I thought, I'm Nancy Reagan.

He introduced himself as Thadd, "with two *d*'s."

Well, maybe so.

"Give me your things and let me make you a drink. You've been through so much turmoil, and I like the name Alex. I like any name with an *x*. Max, Rex, Tex, all of them. Of course those have only three letters and you have four. You must be a wreck." He put my helmet and duffel bag on a chrome-and-leather love seat in the foyer and led the way into the kitchen. "The girls and David have gone to bed. Not together, of course."

"I could use a plain beer and first a bathroom."

Thadd pointed. "Mi casa, su casa. We leave before eight for Key Largo, so sleep as late as you like and ignore the telephone. Our machine will pick up."

I turned a rheostat to light the bathroom. Seashells in a glass jar, pastel wallpaper, metallic accents, shell-shaped soaps, a philodendron wandering up one wall, spray bottles of cologne on the counter. Like a hundred thousand others in Florida. I looked into the mirror. Haggard. Four days in a whirlwind. Little sleep and a predawn alarm seventeen hours ago. My eyes, mouth, and facial skin drooped. Ah, yes. The springer spaniel.

Annie stared as I entered the kitchen. Her mouth smiled but her sleepy, sad-sympathetic eyes sent a cross-message. Thadd had vanished and Annie held the beer I'd requested. She took a sip before she handed it to me. I kissed her forehead.

"I want to hug you," she said softly, "but I'm too sunburned. I'm sorry."

I chuckled. "You're not accustomed to being a tourist."

"You're right, and it's not the life for me. I'm going stir-crazy. Thadd said good night and to put your big motorbike in the garage. I think he likes your big motorbike."

"Can I see your sunburn?"

"Yes, but you'll just want to do something. Let's do it in the morning, after we talk."

"I still want to see."

She opened her robe and showed me. She wasn't completely right about wanting to do something. She was a beautiful sight, and I could have spent hours just staring at her, but I wanted to hear what she had to say. I kissed her again on the forehead and went to move the Kawasaki.

20

The bedroom's second-story screened veranda overlooked a large free-form pool. Glossy patterned tiles surrounded the pool and reflected the yard's accent lighting. In underpants and T-shirts, Annie and I lay in side-by-side cushioned lounges under a slowly turning fan. The fan rustled the potted plants that lined the floor along the porch screens. A massive thunderstorm painted the sky to the north, and through a break in the trees we watched the light show roll down the East Coast. Lightning streaks jumped between tall thunderheads and split and stabbed downward. Ahead of the weather the streetlights of Hallandale painted a weird neon glow on the cloud bottoms.

We sat there and didn't talk. It was time for the Big Discussion, but I was too fatigued to begin and she was too full of nerves. We listened to frogs and the distant buzzing of traffic.

Annie and I had mastered abstract communication. We almost always got along well, but we had tended to stockpile stubborn pride. Her mother once said that our romance reminded her of her own in-laws. They were such bad drivers that the only reason they'd lived beyond sixty was they'd never met each other coming the other way.

She broke the ice. "Did you dream about me while I was living on Olivia?"

I wondered whether this might be a great time to lie my ass

off. "Well, no," I said. "My sleep wasn't deep enough to register a dream. I can tell you that I missed the balalaika."

"It's not like either of us can play it."

We had bought the three-stringed instrument in the gift shop of a Florida museum that had exhibited the treasures of the Russian czars. It had been one of those afternoons when everything felt right. We'd spent hours wandering, holding hands, speculating about wealth, ogling other people's money. "It's important to have cultural decorations," I said. "My life feels larger when the balalaika is on display."

She rested her hand on my forearm. "Am I a decoration?"

"A loaded question requires return fire. I learned that from an attorney."

"Fire away."

"My life felt larger when you were around."

She squeezed my hand. "Okay, past tense. What's the next thing on your mind?"

"For two years you've said that you love me. On Wednesday you said that you'd been fighting the fact that you love me. Are you fighting the fact or the process?"

"Oh, Alex, I don't know how to answer your questions. You analyze things so much."

She had a point. I wasn't sure where I'd drummed up that one.

She moved her hand back up my arm. "You've always been much better with words. I mean, I say what I feel but I don't expect it to stand up in a court of law."

"As I hinted a moment ago, you've been trained in techniques for that line of work. You're supposed to be able to weave words into bullwhips, aren't you? Turn a caress into a sucker punch? Let's try this. What do you like least about me?"

"Loading up, are we? Okay, sometimes you breathe through your nose when you sleep. It's like a jet stream across the pillow. It wakes me up. What do you like least about me?"

178

"Falsehood by omission."

She flinched. "I don't even know what that means."

"Of course you do."

"If not saying things is the same as telling lies, who can ever be innocent?"

"Very good. Now we're into situational ethics."

"I know where you're going with this."

"Then you can drive," I said. It was time for my safety net. I wanted to believe, if only until morning, that she felt remorse.

The thunderstorm reached North Miami and the light show intensified. Jagged zaps leaped between the low and high clouds. Thunder shook the house and smells of electricity filled the air. Taller pine limbs began to bend and whip and whistle.

Annie shifted to a matter-of-fact tone. "I was infatuated with Michael. I knew that you disliked him. For obvious . . . well, for selfish reasons, I couldn't bring up his name. I guess at first I was trying to cover my ass. I was hedging my bet. If he turned out to be a bad bet I didn't want to lose you. I moved out because I didn't want to get involved with him while I shared your house. Am I making sense so far?"

"Okay." So much for legal preliminaries. The groundwork of the argument.

"Since then I've tried to blame it on tropical ennui. Or some other wispy notion that doesn't explain anything. I admit it, I was taking too many things for granted. I assumed that I could move back into your house without a problem. I figured you'd forgive me. Now it looks like you might not."

The price one pays for not being combative. "The toughest thing to forgive is your silence," I said. "You didn't tell me a blessed thing. You didn't say squat. There've been times in my life when I've felt lost. This variety of lost was a new one."

She hesitated. "After I realized how badly I'd acted, I was afraid you'd tell me to stay the hell out of your life. I was thinking that at Ellen's funeral."

Lightning flashed and the afterimage left me seeing Annie in the amber and green tones of a color negative. I smelled approaching rain, the breeze ahead of the storm less humid than the still air of five minutes earlier.

"You didn't help things, by the way," she said. "Why didn't you turn into a pestering jerk? I wanted you to grovel and act like a whiny asshole, or get jealous. You didn't come around looking for me, causing scenes, throwing bricks through my windows, chasing me through restaurants."

"You've been watching daytime TV." The rain began with a bright flash and a crack of thunder. The yard lights flickered and went out.

She remained quiet a minute or two, then said, "Getting involved wasn't what I expected it to be. It went downhill after the first couple of days."

"Please. No box score."

"I don't mean to sound like that. I'm just trying to say that after weeks of pondering, it dawned on me that most of the time I was away I was thinking about you."

"Now you're coming out of the woods. I like the sound of that." Fatigue was setting in. My responses felt as if they were floating to the surface rather than snapping to mind. The whole house had lost power. Without the ceiling fan, the porch became close and smelled of mildew.

"Can I explain one more thing?" said Annie. "About that last night I stayed with him? Before I found Ellen?"

"Okay." This might throw her back into the forest. Another bolt of lightning struck nearby. For an instant the pool glowed quartz-blue. The thunder rattled the house. I wondered if the ceiling fan might fall in my lap, but the concussion diminished.

The waves of raindrops on the shingled roof forced Annie to raise her voice. "I got spring fever on Tuesday. I came home from work early so I could drive out to County Beach and soak in the sun and play tourist. I walked in the back door and they were doing it in the kitchen. Michael and Ellen. My boyfriend and my roommate. Right on the floor. It's sort of weird to watch a man's butt bounce up and down on your kitchen floor. I didn't recognize him at first. But he stopped and looked over his shoulder at me. All he could say was, 'Oops,' and all I could do was run away. But I had nowhere to go."

"What time was that?"

"Four-fifteen, four-thirty."

"So where *did* you go?"

"I drove up the Keys. I got to the other side of Marathon and asked myself where the hell I was going. I stopped for a margarita at that Holiday Inn where the road turns off to Key Colony Beach, where my parents' friends, the Gordons, live. Then I drove back into Key West and watched the sun set into the Gulf."

"How did you wind up on Ellen Albury's bicycle?"

"I was tired of driving and it was dark and I wanted to go home. But I didn't want to talk to Ellen. I didn't want to be pissed anymore, and I would've gotten that way if we'd had to face each other. The house was lit up. I could see her walking in the living room and down the hall. It looked like she was alone. So I left my car in the street and took her bike. We both had keys to it. I thought about riding over to your house, but I didn't have the guts for that either. Anyway, I went down William Street. Right away I met Michael coming the other way on his bicycle. He claimed he was coming back to Olivia to find me and apologize. He asked me to come to his house to talk it out, so I did. The truth is, I only wanted a place to sleep, and I didn't think he'd be in any kind of shape to want sex. His house was the safest bet. For a coward like me."

"So you cavorted in his Jacuzzi, slept in his bed, and you became each other's alibi."

"Why would he need an alibi?"

"I don't know why either of you would need one."

"We talked all night long. We talked until the sun came up. Both of our stomachs were growling, so we ate some cereal and he drove me home and dropped me off. That's when I found Ellen."

Another crack of thunder was followed by a drawn-out rumble. The storm had passed to the south, and the air quickly took on a deeper chill. A thick mist filled the night.

Just before we fell asleep, Annie whispered, "Please forgive me."

I nodded my head against her shoulder. I wanted to tell her I would try, but I fell asleep before I came up with the exact wording of my response.

21

In spite of our stockpiled fatigue we both woke early, actually refreshed. Marked horribly on my face by the perforations and patterns of pillowcase ruffles, I suffered Annie's ridicule and review. To bury my shame I proposed that we make love while attempting not to aggravate her sunburn. Within minutes we had confirmed that the skin least accustomed to direct sunlight was most strategic in our endeavors. We also determined that she needed to face away, on top, so that I would not be tempted to touch where the sunburn hurt most and she would not be tempted to laugh at my engraved skin. The view convinced me that forgiveness has its blessings. When we came up for air I was informed that the doilylike imprints on my face had vanished.

After hearing Thadd and David's car back out of the garage we pulled on shirts and shorts and descended to the kitchen. Carmen was wrestling with a steaming skillet on the stove. She pointed at the counter. "The guys left us a pot of Cuban."

The *Miami Herald* was on the counter. The yard looked inviting, a clear sky after the rain. "Anyone mind if I take my coffee on the deck?" I said. "I long to repose on a tropical daybreak next to a trickling fountain and abundant pool, wallowing in the many pages of the mullet wrapper. I will start with the first section, which is mostly Burdines ads. News, bras, news, bras, news, bras."

"I never knew this side of you," said Carmen. "You're full of shit in the morning. Outside, now."

The phone rang. We stood there, looking back and forth at each other.

Annie waved it off. "Thadd said the machine would get it."

"What if it's my mother?" said Carmen.

I shrugged. "Go for it."

She handed me the spatula and hot pad and grabbed the receiver. "Thadd and David's." A heartbeat later: "Hi, Mom." She stretched the phone cord back to the stove and shooed us out.

Annie and I went to poolside. The bright tiles and yard colors glowed, reds and greens, even blues in the shadows. Oleander and jacaranda shimmered in the light breeze. Annie positioned a chaise under an arbor of bougainvillea and covered her legs with a towel. We divided the paper. She selected the Business pages with their cover story about career moves.

I pointed at the headline. "How's yours going?"

"Building. But it's on 'pause' right now."

"Would you like to be here in Dade County, kicking ass with the big boys?"

"I'm not so sure."

"You don't hunger for bigger territory, a little fame and glory?"

"Somewhere down the road. Professional pride, and all that. First I need to figure out which road leads to progress."

That hit home. "I know what you mean. Sitting here on my butt, I'm not getting any closer to finding a murderer."

"That's not your job, is it, Alex?"

"I haven't gotten the feeling anybody else is doing it."

I was either a jump ahead of things, or a stride behind.

Carmen leaned outside. "Another call came through, Alex. This guy keeps asking for either you or Sam Wheeler."

I hurried into the kitchen. "Sam?"

"Captain Turk of the *Flats Broke* here. Sam Wheeler give me this number."

"What can I do for you, Captain?" Gulls in the background. He was at the Garrison Bight pay booth.

"Do it for your buddy. They come and hooked his butt fifteen minutes ago. Bunch of deputies and plainclothes, got they guns out, even the girl deputy. Run off half the customers on the dock. Sam told me this number. Said to tell you."

"They say why he was arrested, Captain?"

"They didn't say, but I hear tell there's another lady murdered downtown last night. You don't think ol' Sam's caught up in that?"

"No. Did Sam give you any message?"

"Nope. Just the number. And that he's off to the hoosegow."

"Thanks for calling, Captain."

Captain Turk clicked off. Carmen and Annie stood inside the sliding glass door, staring at me, afraid to ask.

"Another dead woman, and the county has taken Sam into custody. I can't imagine the two facts are related."

Annie's reflexes took over. "I'll call Benjy Pinder."

I shook my head. "First thing, I'm going to finish my coffee. In the half minute it takes to do that, I'm going to decide the order of about five phone calls I need to make in the next five minutes. Are there two phone lines into the house?"

Carmen looked around. "I think three. David's an interior designer. There's a business line in his office and a fax line that has a regular phone hooked to it."

"Okay." I eased past the women, walked outside, and looked upward. It's amazing how valuable a simple blue sky can feel when you consider how little of it is seen by people in jail. The coffee had become cold. I carried it inside to the microwave and pressed the buttons. Annie sat on a stool next to the counter, doodling nervously on a scratch pad. Carmen began to wash the pan and her dishes.

"Here's the plan of attack," I said. "Monty's home number is on a small list in my wallet. Annie, if you could try to get him on one line, I'm going to call Sheriff Tucker on this one. Carmen, let's see what your mother can find out about this new murder. And Carmen, after you talk to your mother, please try to book me a noontime flight to Key West."

The microwave beeped and startled me.

"You can't drive back?" said Annie.

"Flying is sure as hell faster than dealing with U.S. 1."

My first call was to Sheriff Tommy Tucker. He'd campaigned on the promise that he would always be available to the electorate. It took five or six minutes to weave through the county switchboard to the top man. They finally rang through to his home.

"Tucker here."

"Alex Rutledge, Sheriff, in Miami. But I just got word that a friend has been detained by your deputies."

"You must run with an ugly crowd, Mr. Rutledge. Remind me to review our business relationship."

"Sheriff, I've been working with Avery Hatch and Billy Fernandez on these recent—"

"I know. And I don't have time to talk to you right now, Mr. Rutledge." The line went dead.

So much for accountability.

"Alex?" Annie called from another room.

I found her seated in a large, airy study cluttered with wallpaper samples and carpet swatch books. As I entered she finished her conversation and hung up the phone.

"Monty's wife says he left an hour and a half ago. But he said if you called, to get in touch with Bob Bernier. Something about . . . about Michael Anselmo." She inhaled and shivered, then rested her forehead in the palm of her hand. "Something that happened a long time ago."

Carmen joined us. "My mother'll call us back in ten minutes. My daughter is behaving like a maniac. Annie, are you going to hate me? American had two standbys, but they're almost a sure bet on Sunday, so I booked one for myself."

Annie shook her head.

"I wouldn't go except for Maria . . ."

"That's okay." Annie looked up. "It's normal. She misses you. You're not in any danger down there. You did me a favor by bringing me here. I was thinking, maybe I'll drive up to West Palm and visit my parents."

I called Bob Bernier and got his machine. I called my own number, got my machine, and asked anyone to pick up if they were still staking out the place. Bernier answered and had a bitch of a time shutting down the "record" mode. "Okay, okay, I got it now. I wondered if you'd call, or if you'd heard."

"Tell me."

"Three things. Big ones," he said. "First, Wheeler's at the county."

"I know that."

"I figured you did. I'm to blame, but not on purpose, I promise you. I was invited to observe an all-agency sit-down last night. I mentioned to Hatch about Sam's being privy to the identities of your lady friends. I also mentioned that Sam helped set up Kemp's sale of his charter boat. Avery raised the possibility that, as middleman, Wheeler took possession of the *Barracuda* equipment, like the anchor they found in the Albury scene. Then he linked the special knots to Sam's oceangoing knowledge. He figured he had enough to move on. Monty says the city's keeping mum, but Liska and the other city detectives think it's a lame call. Unless the sheriff's people come up with something else, something real to support it, I'm not going to pursue it. By the way, we picked up Ellen Albury's father, Pepper Neice. It looks like he'll alibi out. Anyway, one way or another, Sam should be sleeping in his own bed tonight."

"Okay. That's one thing."

"Item number two. You know about the murder on Eliza-beth Street?"

"I know there's a dead woman."

"Okay. I'm going to say a name, Alex. We both know there's a chance . . ."

"Just say the name, Bob."

"Mary Alice Noe?"

"Aw, shit, shit, shit."

"Another ex-girlfriend, or just someone you knew?"

I thought back. "Neither." I looked around. Annie and Car-men were outside in the hall. "When was that earthquake dur-ing the World Series game in San Francisco?" I said. "October, '89? That was the night she dragged me out of the Chart Room and took me home. She was engaged to some guy who was out of town, and she wanted one last fling. God, she was good-looking. Long blond hair, wonderful shape. I remember her talking to the bartender, looking over at me. Then she came over, blatant as hell, and said, 'Jerry gave you the stamp of ap-proval. You want to go somewhere and get high and get naked?' I couldn't believe my luck. That was it."

"One night?"

"Yeah. She loved the guy and didn't want to screw up the re-lationship. I don't remember his first name. Something Noe. She married him, but I heard later they got divorced. I've seen her around town, in Camille's and at the movie theater. I think both times I was with Annie. We just smiled and said hello to each other. It was the original painless one-night stand."

"Who could have known?"

"I'll think on it, but I can pretty well promise I never told a soul."

"Not Sam?"

"Not Sam. Not Annie. Not a soul." I waited a moment; Bernier didn't say anything. And I wondered how Annie could be so certain that Carmen was in no danger in Key West. "I'm ready for the next bummer, Bob."

"We did some work on Kemp's background. He was busted up in Dade in '82, in a sting called Operation Snapper. They had videotape, informants, an alleged murder. It was a conspiracy to distribute four tons of hashish. Kemp's arrest got turned into an information deal. Witness Protection, fake name, a new residence, the whole kit. It'll be a few days of paperwork and arm-twisting to dig deeper."

"Monty's wife said you'd learned something about Anselmo."

"Anselmo was the prosecutor. He was in on the sting from the word "go." We aren't sure, but it's odds-on he okayed the Witness Program for Kemp. Looking back, it's possible Kemp got a free ride. They didn't need any more informants. They had enough evidence to pack 'em away for years. But Kemp got immunity anyway. There was also a problem later with one of the detectives on the case. He got sent away for confiscating cash and never turning it in."

"Smells like low tide in the canal. What does Anselmo say?"

"We're sitting on it until tomorrow. Are you coming back?"

"On American. I get in at twelve-forty."

Bernier paused. "I'd like to keep your house another day or two."

What did he know that he wasn't telling? "I'll camp out on Sam's couch."

"I'll contact you there tomorrow, midday."

We had fifty minutes to catch the plane.

Carmen knew a quick way from the Enchanted Forest to the airport. I drove the Mustang down Dixie Highway and over to I-95. Traffic was light on the toll expressway to LeJeune Road. Minutes later Annie kissed me good-bye at the curbside check-in and drove away. With my duffel and her paper sack full of

clothes and toilet articles, Carmen and I looked like street people. A young black baggage handler made a crack about her
"Haitian Haliburton." The woman at the ticket counter didn't
bat an eye. Processing passengers to Key West, she must have
seen all kinds. We got adjoining seats.

I didn't relax until we were airborne, over the water. As the
plane banked to the southwest, I looked down on Cape Florida
at the southern tip of Key Biscayne, at the parallel patterns cut
by the east wind across the wavetops. For years, an offshore
community of stilt houses, spare platform camps, had dotted
the tidal flats. They'd offered a touch of the old Florida that on
the mainland was now paved and developed. But Hurricane
Andrew had erased Stiltsville.

About the time we leveled out, Carmen nudged my thigh.
"Look, friend. It's time for a heart-to-heart, okay?"

This sounded like personal business, and I wasn't in the
mood.

She continued, "Anybody ever tell you that your woman's a
flake?"

"No. But you're about to explain it, aren't you." This had
nothing to do with springing Sam.

"Let me tell you, and this figure of speech does not come
from the women's movement. She tends to skirt the truth with
a full skirt."

"Is that like embellishing reality?"

"It's like talking crap. Her mind rolls in and out like the
tide. She talks about her great dilemma. She loves you but she's
mysteriously, physically attracted to Mr. Anselmo. And that's
what I call bullshit."

"Is it sexist to suggest that a man might accept that concept?"

"She was head over heels for this guy—enough to move out
on you—and then she caught him fucking Ellen Albury the
night Ellen died."

"So I've been told."

"She tell you the details? About how his butt was doing the up-and-down dance and Ellen had her thumb in his behind?"

"She told me parts of that . . . and he looked up and said, 'Oops.'"

"Did she tell you that the bastard finished his downstroke? Right in front of her face. At least he could've pulled out. Pardon my explicit frankness."

I caught myself, for some reason, trying to calculate Annie's point of view. Had it been a side view like an R-rated movie, or straight up the middle, toes to crotch, like a porn shot? Just as quickly I decided I couldn't care less.

Carmen went on. "Later that night he fell all over himself to apologize. He blamed it on Ellen. He said she'd seduced him. He tried every scam in the book to get back into Annie's good graces. They stayed up all night long, drinking wine and talking about their relationship, how she still had feelings for you and that he would make allowances for that. He wanted her full-time and he would never be unfaithful again."

"Where does the bullshit come in?"

"She loves you. She caught this guy fucking her roommate. And she's still in a dilemma?"

"That's what it sounds like."

"Hello? From a man's point of view, it's a dilemma. From a woman's point of view, take my word, it's pure bullshit. You're either in love or not."

"It's possible to love more than one person."

"See? That's a man's point of view. Your woman needs a set of values."

"I think she may have had some before she went to law school."

"Are you still in love?"

"I don't know anymore. Maybe I'm just in need."

"Maybe that's the whole problem, a man your age." Then

Carmen tacked on another question. "You said you had a lot of girlfriends because it took so long to find Annie. Was she the only one that ever clicked? Has there ever been another woman that made you feel something?"

"Yes. But all she gave me was one lay and a hand job in a hot tub."

That put a squint in Carmen's eyes that I'd never seen before. I'm not sure where in my brain it came from, but I realized as I spoke that I'd told the truth.

"You said Annie was the closest to the real thing since you were in the Navy."

"Yes, and you were giving me a bunch of shit when I said that. I left you out as a matter of spite. Anyway, this is a rank time for me to be out hunting a new girlfriend."

Carmen stared straight ahead, at nothing. I glanced at her expressionless face and caught myself flashing ahead to the rest of my life, imagining what it might be like to spend it with her. The overall picture was not unpleasant. Then I wondered if Annie might get in touch with Anselmo, might let it be known that Bernier had information about events from "a long time ago."

Someone had left the Keys section of the *Herald* in the seat-back pouch. I pulled it out and spread it open. Citizens versus the EPA. The EPA versus the citizens. The county versus the state. In the lower left-hand corner, a short two-column piece:

BROTHERS COLLIDE
—UPI, Key Largo
Brothers Luis and Umberto Ruenes, each heading a different direction on U.S. 1, collided one mile south of Layton on Friday afternoon. Umberto Ruenes, 33, of North Key Largo, told the Highway Patrol that a gust of wind pushed his four-ton dump truck into the path of the eighteen-foot U-Haul truck driven by his older brother near Long Key.

Luis Ruenes, 35, of Tavernier, suffered a broken collarbone and fractured arm when his leased U-Haul left the road at approximately 50 mph, collided with two concrete utility poles and destroyed a roadside seashell market. Umberto Ruenes regained control of his dump truck and suffered no injuries. There were no injuries reported at the unattended shell stand. The Florida Highway Patrol estimated damage to the U-Haul in excess of $16,000. An investigation is continuing.

A gust of wind?

Who knew that I was traveling U.S. 1?

Annie . . . Carmen . . . Sam . . . Bob Bernier . . . and Billy Fernandez.

Detective Billy Fernandez.

22

Above the Key West baggage ramps: BIENVENIDOS A CAYO HUESO." A literal translation: "Welcome to the Island of Bones." Indeed.

Our plane taxied past bright rows of private aircraft tethered to recessed eyebolts. Everything moved in slow motion, shimmered in the intense heat of high noon. The ground crew waited in the shade of an overhang until the last minute to approach. As the plane halted, Carmen leaned her shoulder against mine, tilted her head my way. Solidarity and support. "Can you drop me at home before you check on Sam?"

"You feel like calling your friend Larry Riley?"

"And?"

"Exact causes of death for each of the four women. And anything he's held back from the media or the police. I can't lose the feeling there's a puzzle piece waiting to come out of the closet, for want of a better expression. No one official has mentioned rape, for instance."

"It's not like he and I are *intimate* friends, you understand."

"The way things work in this town, that's a plus."

She looked puzzled. "You mean disease?"

"You two are wise enough to deal with that. I'm talking about truth." I held back a moment, then said, "Thanks for the lecture on bullshit."

With the single open door and no power for air-conditioning, the airplane quickly turned into an oven. We were the last two off. I hadn't showered in Miami. Before we got to the portable stairway, I smelled like I had spent the morning rolling in the hay. Indeed.

Even with sunglasses the brightness hurt.

"A greeting committee," I said. Monty Aghajanian and Chicken Neck Liska stood behind chain-link at an employees' gate. Liska in a broad-collared shirt, bell-bottoms, white belt and white shoes. The Fear: they were here to arrest me. Billy Fernandez's slurred warnings echoed from a corner of my brain. But Liska hated what he called dirty work, and there were no uniformed officers in sight.

"What's with that guy's clothing?" said Carmen. "He left everything in storage while he did twenty years in the Navy?"

"He prides himself in being a walking museum. I know for a fact that he practices moonwalking in front of his bathroom mirror." I recalled the Key West fire chief in the 1970s who wore red polyester clothing and red leather shoes. He also wore rose-colored dark glasses, red silk socks, and a ruby pinkie ring. In any other city in America, these civil-service captains would be laughed out of their jobs. Liska's abilities might save him. The fire chief changed professions after selling drugs to a federal agent.

"Your taxicab awaits you, ambassador." In open sunlight Monty still looked crisp and neat. The FBI ought to have been laying roses at his feet. "We'll run you out to the county jail," he said. "You can help us make our pitch for Sam's innocence."

Again, the Fear: They'd drop me off and split. The joke would be on me.

Monty knew Carmen from the years he'd lived on Dredgers Lane. He introduced her to Liska. As we passed through the gate area, an instrumental version of Queen's "Fat Bottomed Girls" warbled through the music system.

Carmen held me back while the other two walked on. "He moonwalks?"

"I, too, have problems with the truth."

Their unmarked pale green Taurus occupied a "No Parking" zone. Monty unlocked the passenger-side doors. Chicken Neck went for the front seat. Monty opened the rear door for Carmen, closed it after she had gotten in, then ushered me around to the other side. "Bernier said he'd filled you in," he muttered under his breath. "Don't mention Anselmo to Liska."

The FBI trusts Monty but not his boss?

I opened my door. "Can we drop Carmen at her house?"

On South Roosevelt bike riders, Sunday strollers, and Rollerbladers cruised the County Beach strand, basked in warm breezes. To the southeast a shrimper headed into Stock Island as a yawl departed under motor power. A Bertram, its tuna tower swaying in the roll of inshore waves, overtook the sailboat. Farther down A1A, a yawning young couple climbed from the back of a station wagon, he in a slingshot bathing suit, she in sweatpants and a tie-dyed tank top. Across from the first condos a fellow slept on the sand, a newspaper tent over his head, his bicycle chained to his leg.

Even at full blast, the car's air-conditioning did not help much. Liska checked a bikini on a ten-speed. "How's your lady friend doing?"

"Perfect. She needed a vacation. She's sharing a house with a couple of gay guys, and she's got the pool to herself all day long."

"Wish you'd been here last night," said Liska. "Cootie Ortega was boozed on Spanish brandy, so we had to use that county photographer, that fruit out of Marathon. Put Lester Forsythe up against a tattooed, matty-haired, toothless street-freak dirtbag in Key West, Lester's the weirder of the two."

"Where did Mary Alice live?"

Monty half-turned around. "Three doors down from Sam at the far end of Elizabeth. Between United and South near . . . I don't know what it's called now. Used to be Lord's Motel. Did you know that she and Sam had a thing, too?"

"Nope." Small world.

"They had a fling after she divorced that guy from Bell South. He said she didn't like to go out much. Afraid of running into her ex. They wore a path between their houses. It lasted about a year."

Why hadn't Sam ever said so? Had Mary Alice Noe mentioned me to Sam?

Sam Wheeler . . . ? I wanted off this train of logic.

I suggested that we drop Carmen in front of Cobo Pharmacy. An official vehicle in Dredgers Lane might interfere with Bernier's surveillance. After a moment's thought I expressed concern for her safety.

"Somebody jumps me," she said, "I yell and my daddy blows his head off."

We kept an eye on her until she had turned up the lane. Monty eased up Fleming and turned south on Frances.

Liska tilted his head toward the south side of the island. "Stock Island will wait. We've got to run to Elizabeth Street."

Mary Alice's house? "My cameras are in my house."

"You're not on the clock today. You're donating your time to an ongoing investigation. This is civic duty."

"We had some unusual problems this morning, Alex," said Monty. "The representatives of the Monroe County Violent Crimes Task Force were a little whacked out. Naturally, we don't appreciate having county detectives screwing around with city cases in the first place. This whole Task Force deal that the state dreamed up has a crowding effect. But they showed up and Avery Hatch was walking around like a loadie on Quaaludes. 'Disoriented' would be accurate. Billy Fernandez was charged up like a drill sergeant. Showered and shaved, fresh shirt, shined shoes, trimmed mustache. A million things at once, all very proper, all very organized. Not at all like Billy."

The last time I'd seen him, late Saturday afternoon, Fernandez had looked like a wino walking on ball bearings.

Liska became adamant. "They were just plain fucked up. At seven-fifteen A.M. They looked around the murder scene for what . . . four minutes, maybe five?"

Monty nodded.

I sensed that Liska had told this before. "They went outside, had a chat, checked the address against something on a clipboard, then walked down to Wheeler's house and rang his doorbell. Woke him up. Got Sam out in the middle of the street in a pair of Levi's with no shirt, no shoes. Then they drove away. No goddamned explanation. They left Sam standing there and drove away."

Monty glanced over to prompt further details.

Liska obliged. "It was so strange that I broke down and called my ex-wife. My ex-wife who is now married to the ugly son of a bitch. She tells me he's been wacky for almost a week, stumbling around the house like a cuckoo bubba, and now she's sorry she left me. I didn't need that kind of bullshit an hour and half after sunrise, I tell you."

"An hour later," said Monty, "they arrested Sam at his dock. We sent the city attorney out to the county jail. No word yet."

"Bernier told me another tidbit," I said. "Pepper Neice was detained."

"You'll love this." Chicken Neck and Monty got on a short laughing jag and Liska continued, "He checked into a motel up in Boynton Beach. I guess he needed a piece of ass but he was too broke to buy a whore. He goes out to the pool and pulls down his pants and sticks his dick in the suction hole for the water recirculation system. Gets it stuck in there. These motel pools have high-rate pumps, to clean out all the kiddie pee. So his pork's in the suction hole, and he starts yelling for help. You got to picture this. Somebody tells the desk clerk, the desk clerk calls 911, and right away they got fifty motel guests, a crowd from the lounge next door, and two TV stations with video crews."

Liska's stopped to catch his breath. His laughing was contagious. "The next morning on the news clips they got bystanders yelling, 'Send him home to his goat!' and 'Throw a bucket of water on him!' Shit like that. Some lucky fireman had to get down there and squirt KY all over the man's unit. The anchor lady speculated on whether or not the motel would have to drain the pool to reduce the risk of AIDS. Meanwhile a city cop runs the name that Neice had registered under, and finds out it's a fake. Didn't take long to find out who he was. The poor bastard."

"Poor bastard?" I was still laughing. "Think how the pool felt."

"That's not what he meant," said Monty. "Neice didn't know his daughter was dead."

We stopped in front of a three-bay shotgun house on Elizabeth, a few doors south of United. A dour, overweight Key West police officer sat on a weathered pine porch swing in the shadows of a gumbo limbo tree. Bright yellow DO NOT CROSS tape encircled the building and yard. The broken window behind the officer had been knocked from the inside outward. Birds chittered on the utility lines.

Over on South Street, traffic, especially high-pitched mopeds and pickups with bad mufflers, raced in both directions. The world went on around us as we approached another room where time had stopped for someone else.

"Freeman, we're going in for a few minutes," Liska said to the uniformed cop. "If anyone shows up, ask 'em to wait."

"Yessir." His voice came from somewhere in his mouth, but the man did not move a single muscle, even as he spoke.

Mary Alice's living room was white wicker furniture, pastel cushions, and small throw rugs with geometric designs. A pure-white stereo system. French doors faced a small plant-filled deck at the rear of the main room. A chubby sand-colored cat with a floral collar lay on a wood-slat bench. Nothing familiar until I looked closely at the framed art on the walls. I remembered the night she had led me to her place in the Strunk Apartments. She'd owned an impressive collection of local work, much of which she'd acquired inexpensively, early in the artists' careers. She had not stopped accumulating. There must have been thirty pieces on display. The work had appreciated. The four A. D. Tinkham watercolors would pay the house rent for six months, maybe a year.

"Okay," said Monty. "Except for that window, everything's placid in here. We haven't said a thing about any of this because we want you to look and tell us your impression. The body is gone and there's dust from the lab crew all over, but everything else is untouched."

I looked at Monty, then at Liska. They both deadpanned. I was either their biggest clue or biggest suspect. For the third time I felt that my spark of fear at the airport had been right on. They wanted me to incriminate myself. A setup, out of the wild blue yonder. All too tight. My innocence gave me little comfort.

Chicken Neck opened the bedroom door. The room looked like the aftermath of a hurricane. Two broken lamps, busted glass in the frames on the wall—more photographs than art in here—drawers pulled from the bureau and turned, a large potted palm on its side with sphagnum and dirt and vermiculite spilled across a genuine-looking Oriental. Blue and beige wallpaper torn near the doorframe. The four-poster bed at an angle; one leg broken under the frame. Rope secured to each post. The loose ends cut clean by the ME squad.

"Say anything you like," said Monty. "You've photographed the Albury scene and viewed the Balbuena and Guthery scene details in Lester's photographs. By the way, Mary Alice's face was duct-taped like Ellen Albury's, and her robe lay open like Sally Ann Guthery's. She had on a short nightgown, like a teddy. Whatever they call it. Victoria's Secret type of thing."

I went into analytical overdrive. The hitches on the near side posts looked right. A bowline on the footpost. A rolling hitch high on the headpost. On the far side of the bed the knots mirrored the first two. Same height, same rub marks in the dark veneer. The son of a bitch had done it again.

I shifted my attention around the room as if framing evidence shots. The place didn't have the same feel as the others. The extreme messiness had something to do with it. I looked again at the knots. The braided rope was fresh. It could not have come from *Barracuda*. Something on the far headpost caught my eye. I walked around the bed for a closer look. The knot that I'd taken at first to be a bowline was a simple slip knot. I checked the footboard post. The hitch was more like several half hitches and a clove hitch. A sloppy knot that happened to have a multiple definition. The first knots I'd inspected were correct. The knots on both far posts were wrong.

"Shaking your head," said Monty. "Sympathy for the victim?"

"These two knots held, but they're the first ones that aren't correct." I held the clipped end of the rope. "Plus this. Brand-new. The Albury house rope was weathered sisal. In the Julia photos it was frayed polystyrene. Lester's pictures of the Guthery scene showed sisal, but I couldn't tell if it was old or new."

Monty kneaded one of the other ropes. "I hear what you're saying, but how could we have a copycat with no details on the street?"

"Where's the ex-husband?" I said.

"He was hunting in Texas with Mayor Gomez and Doc Wicker," said Liska. "They're on a plane back here right now."

"You know what else is wrong?" I pointed at a rectangle of

wallpaper on the wall opposite the west-facing windows. "That spot isn't faded. If the blank space was a photograph . . . Has anything been missing from the other scenes?"

Monty looked behind a cushioned bench that sat against the baseboard under the faded spot. "Not that we know of. Nothing's back here."

"Hold it." Liska puffed up his cheeks and let a long exhale escape through a slit between his lips. His gaze drifted toward my face, but did not meet my eyes. "I like your knot ideas, Rutledge, but don't push the detective act. Let's get the fuck out of here."

I looked around once more, looked again at the blank spot on the wall.

Bienvenidos to the Lord's Motel.

23

"One last thing on Pepper Neice." Monty Aghajanian drove the slow lane up North Roosevelt Boulevard. "This wasn't on the television. He had 'Yo Papa' tattooed four inches below his belt line, right across the top of his pubes."

Chicken Neck Liska shook his head and stared out at the strip of fast-food restaurants and car dealerships. He'd obviously heard about Ellen Albury's tattoo and Pepper Neice's history with children.

Just before the boulevard curved southward to Cow Key Bridge, the stark-white Monroe County Detention Center dominated our view to the northeast. Set back from the mangrove shallows on the shore of Stock Island, the huge jail provided a cultural and scenic landmark for vacationing families at the Comfort Inn, Econo Lodge, and Holiday Inn. The only windows on its west wall were at the forty-foot level: administrative offices. There were no windows on the lower levels or on the other external walls. I've always believed that if every inmate breathed in at once, the roof would cave in. The place is a perfect companion piece to its neighbors, the dump called Mount Trashmore, and the rust-colored stacks of the waste-processing plant.

Monty turned onto the two-lane that snaked off Junior College Road to the jail compound. Fortified transport vans waited near portals marked INMATE INTAKE and INMATE RELEASE. Dejected-looking trusties carried brooms and pole-mounted dustpans in the asphalt parking area.

Dozens of ages, colors, and shapes had crowded into the jail's triple-glazed vestibule, more a cage for the free than a waiting room. Children displayed runny noses, ill-fitting dime-store attire, and their own little mean streaks, their own lost gazes. Girlfriends and wives had nasty attitudes and unwashed hair. The few men in the room looked like uncaught accomplices, and the attorneys acted like gamblers staking an errand against the slim chance of compensation. The jailers looked bored and resentful. On our entrance fifty eyes focused on Liska's clothing and accepted Chicken Neck as one of them. The moment gave me a better understanding of the man's success as an investigator.

Liska flashed his badge and a guard slid a battered clipboard under a glass partition. Monty and I relinquished our driver's licenses and signed civilian waivers. With a loud electrical crash a door unlocked and a bright red strobe flashed above the door until we had passed through and it closed behind us. A barrel-shaped man with a crew cut, large ears, and the name ROLLE on his plastic name tag accompanied us.

"Where are we at with this, Coco Butter?" said Liska to Rolle.

"Not sure, Chicken Neck." Officer Rolle spoke in the requisite monotone, enunciated as a military subordinate might report to a commander. "The man had to jack off this morning so they could match him to an evidence sample."

I'd never seen Deputy Rolle before, but he had the thick accent of an old-time Conch. I realized I was listening to a detective named Chicken Neck talk to a jailer named Coco Butter. Only in Key West. Rolle continued, "He couldn't get it with *Playboy.* Don't know why. We had to finally send in *Letters to Penthouse.*"

"Results?" Liska's voice echoed in the hall. He managed to maintain a straight face.

"Ain't heard. They runnin' the analysis past all them murders. Looks like the perpetrator shot his load every time. All over the area of the tits."

Monty and I looked at each other, deadpan. It sounded like the forensic puzzle piece I had hoped for. I had no doubt that the guard believed "tits" to be an accepted term in law enforcement.

Liska kept his mouth shut and nodded, urging Rolle to say more.

"This don't happen that often," continued Rolle. "Man claims innocent and the personnel in this facility believe his ass. We hear that sweet tune every day. We ain't fools. This one, I don't know what's with them deputies."

I caught a glimpse of Sam Wheeler standing with two jailers at the end of the long hall. He faced into a doorway talking to someone in an office. Just as we reached speaking range he stepped into the office and the door shut behind him. Rolle steered us into a briefing room. A tall young woman I took to be Marnie Dunwoody leaned against a stained table that held two coffee urns, Styrofoam cups, sugar packets, and jars of powdered cream. She had more of a suntan than most Key West working women.

Monty introduced me, then added, "Thanks for the article on my certification screw job. Every little bit helps."

Rolle attempted to maintain command. "'Preciate you wouldn't repeat all that stuff to the reporter here, Detective. Sheriff'll talk to her hisself."

Ignoring Rolle, the reporter offered her hand and expressed concern about Annie Minnette. A lanky beauty built like a volleyball player, Marnie had straight medium-brown hair and wore an oxford-cloth blouse, wheat-colored jeans, and new-looking deck sneakers. A casual but classy approach to looking professional with minimum maintenance. She gave a curt nod to Liska.

"Always a pleasure," said Chicken Neck. It did not sound like the truth.

"How can you stand the smell in here?" said Monty. "Piss and sweat and Pine-Sol."

Marnie twisted her nose, grinned, and shrugged it off. "In spite of what the officer has told you, you are free to speak to the press anytime you choose to do so. I believe permission is included in the Constitution, a piece of paper located in a northern state. Lord knows, no one else around here has told me a thing." She turned to Rolle. "Is Tommy Tucker going to show before I turn into a pumpkin and make up my own story? I've got a press deadline in an hour and forty-five minutes."

"I'll go check, ma'am."

I turned to Rolle before he hit the door. "Can you get a message to Mr. Wheeler? Tell him Rutledge is here? See if I can help him in any way?"

"You a lawyer? Man refused to hire one."

"I can find him one fast."

"Well, he may not need one if he gets out of here today. I can't say nothin' for sure, you follow?" Rolle disappeared into the hallway.

"Miss Dunwoody, I hate to say this . . ." Chicken Neck did not appear to be apologetic. "I need to talk to Sheriff Tucker before you do. Business."

"Like what I'm here for isn't business."

Monty raised one finger: the press liaison officer mends a fence. "Maybe Tucker'll talk to us all at once."

"Oh, sure." Marnie extracted a scratch pad from her belly pack. "And Stock Island will turn into Hilton Head. Screw it. I'm out of here." She flipped some pages of notes and turned to me. "Mr. Rutledge, will you be at 298-8798 later today? That's your home number, right?"

"I'll be in and out. You might get my machine, but I'll try to call you back."

"I understand Miss Minnette is out of town."

"As far as the newspaper is concerned, Miss Minnette doesn't exist. You understand this is for her own safety."

Marnie closed the pad. "You understand it is my job to tell the truth."

Sheriff Tommy Tucker, in civilian clothes and chomping a large unlighted cigar, stuck his head into the room. "Gentlemen from the city are welcome to join me in my office. The civilians will have to stand by. Sorry, little lady."

Marnie raised one hand to eye level and extended four fingers upward. "This many questions, Sheriff. Has this man been charged? Is he the only suspect? Are there suspected accomplices? Is there a known motive?" With each question one finger folded downward. "I'm going to fill that front page with hearsay and loose fiction if you don't leave a message on my voice mail."

The cigar wiggled up and down as he said, "You bet." Either the sheriff didn't believe her or didn't care.

Monty looked exasperated. "Alex, can you sit tight awhile?"

Rolle appeared in the hallway behind Tucker. He caught my eye and said, "The man 'preciates your coming out. Says he's okay. Wants you to buy a bag of charcoal and a bunch of steaks."

Sheriff Tucker rolled his eyes.

Marnie nudged me with her elbow. "Can I give you a ride home?"

"Perfect. I've got a duffel in the city vehicle."

Monty pulled out the car keys and gestured for us to follow him. "I'll be right back," he assured Liska and Tucker.

I reclaimed my driver's license and walked into the heat of the afternoon. For all I knew the day's air was clear and clean, but I couldn't erase from my mind the smoldering stench of the dump. I imagined that I smelled it every time I hit Stock Island.

The Monroe County Health Unit's main clinic sat in the shadow of the incinerator stacks. I was surprised to see shrubs and trees still living.

Along with my travel duffel, the trunk of the Taurus held an arsenal of guns, aerosol weapons, and shields—enough to fend off an invasion force. Monty handed me the bag and slammed the lid. "Talk to you later. You call me. For sure."

Marnie Dunwoody drove a bright orange Jeep Wrangler with black foam padding on its roll cage. She started the engine as I climbed in.

"I need to go to Sam Wheeler's house on Elizabeth Street, if that's okay."

She flipped a thumbs-up and drove toward the road. I reached back to grab an angle brace in the roll bar. For the second time in a week I felt vulnerable and exposed in an open vehicle, an odd sensation for a cycle rider.

"Redneck boys in authority outfits." Marnie grimaced with disgust. "At least I don't have to work in that gymnasium stench. The government has rules for every detail of their lives. The width of the safety tread on the stairways. The thermostat setting on the central air. They have to measure out their dental floss at home."

It's always a surprise to get an inside look at any profession. This woman had built up her share of cynicism. She stopped at the light where U.S. 1 splits into North and South Roosevelt Boulevards, and slid into the left-turn lane. "One of these days, Tommy Tucker is going to get a 'little lady' lesson in black-belt karate. He's a major malfunction on two legs, and I can't put that in print." She stopped for a moment, then added in a surprisingly pleasant tone, "I may not have the greatest job, but at least I'm not on the outlaw assembly line."

It was that time in mid-afternoon when the sun reflects off rear windows of cars, the chromed bumpers of pickup trucks. Two dogs slept in shade under a bus-stop bench. In the right lane a young woman on a motor scooter waited for the light. Marnie pointed. A tiny poodle rode the scooter's floorboard.

"Known Sam long?" she said.

"Six or eight years."

She hesitated, then asked, "What's he like?"

I didn't like the question. "Is this human curiosity or fodder for a story?"

Marnie turned onto Flagler without slowing and without reacting to my tone. "Interesting guy," she said. "I met him three days ago. He came into the office with a story that's turned into a minor scandal. Suddenly he's dragged in for suspicion of murder."

"Phony charge."

"Of course it is. He was in bed with me all night. He sure as hell didn't have time to go hurt somebody. I barely let him go take a leak."

That stopped me short. She'd been hiding Sam's trump card. "To answer your question," I said, "he's intelligent and quiet and humorous. He doesn't get involved in much beyond fishing and having one girlfriend at a time. He won't let his clients keep the fish they catch. It's all 'tag-and-release' on his boat."

She slapped her forehead with the palm of her hand. "I hope that's not his policy with his women."

I understood Sam's willingness to sacrifice his virtue.

"Do me a favor?" I said. "Pull into Luani Plaza? I need a pay phone."

"I'll swing around to Winn-Dixie and pick up steaks and charcoal while you make your call." We found a coin unit on the front wall of the grocery.

Miami. Raoul Balbuena answered.

"Just checking in," I told him. "You know about the latest victim?"

"I understand a man is in custody." He sounded preoccupied.

"Let me guess. Monroe County Sheriff's Detective Billy Fernandez is standing right there, ready to collect his substantial reward."

"Let's pursue that a little farther."

I'd hit the nail on the head. "The man in custody has a rock-solid alibi of the female variety. He was too much of a gentleman to reveal her identity, but it's a fallback if he needs it. Other facts in this case and the other cases prove his innocence. I just left the Detention Center. The so-called suspect is a half hour from freedom. I will be happy to accept ten percent of the check you do not have to write to Billy Fernandez."

"I appreciate your thoughtfulness. Consider it done at this end."

"I think Fernandez tried to kill me two days ago, right after he found me scene-snooping at Bahia Honda. My death would've looked like a car accident. I still think Kemp murdered Julia. Regarding Kemp's ability to vanish, his identity, it's possible that Witness Protection is involved." I instantly sensed that I'd made a mistake in revealing that last piece of info. Too late.

"Yes. Thank you." Curt, but businesslike. The line went quiet.

Why had he said yes? Could he have already known?

On the drive to Elizabeth Street in Marnie's Jeep I found myself wondering if Annie had gone to West Palm Beach. I pictured her tooling around the landscaped suburbs in my noisy Shelby. If she had gone, I did not have to worry about the car's being exposed to weather or to theft. Her parents would want it out of sight, in the garage.

Sam Wheeler's house was surrounded by a six-foot wooden fence and a wall of tropical bushes that had been allowed to ramble. At center front, the tiny roof of a mini-gatehouse protected the mailbox and a locked doorway. Sam kept a gate key dangling from a string behind one slat in the fence. Over the years he had filled the yard with tall cacti and palmetto trees, with crotons and hibiscus along its perimeter. It was a shaded, tropical blend of freshness and decay. Even in daylight hours the fragrance of frangipani filled the air. He had strung colorful fishnet floats across the front of the house. Three sawhorses in the side yard supported the hull of a plastic-wrapped flats skiff. I went looking for a trash bag to hold the ashes from the last time Sam had used his outdoor grill. Marnie and I had not been there three minutes before a car pulled up out front.

"Yo-ho! Yo-ho!" The gate door flew open and Wheeler barged in. Ten feet behind him a pink taxi spun a wheel in the dirt as it departed. Sam carried two twelve-packs of beer under one arm. Using the open bottle in his other hand as a microphone, he struck a Presley stance and sang, "I fought the law and—hah—the law *lost!*" His hip thrust was imperfect.

This was a rare Sam Wheeler, at the loose end of his spectrum. Of all the times not to have a camera . . .

Marnie walked across the yard. She gave Sam a kiss and reached into the open box of beers.

"See?" Sam toasted me. "An alibi of last resort." He dropped the beer on a yard chair so he could hug the smiling woman. "Oh, the price I paid to cover your professional standing in this two-bit town."

She assumed an eye-fluttering coy expression. "Did you have to put your hand in your trousers?"

Sam scowled. "Talk about stretching a man's fantasy. Pulling your pud in the Detention Center."

"Oh, shit," I said. "Hair on your palms and you'll go to hell."

"Hell's never bothered me," he said. "They told me when I was five that hell was where it was hot. They talked about fires and heat and sweat. Even at that age I knew that heat and sweat are pains in the ass, but cold just plain hurts. If they'd told me that hell was cold, with frozen toes and icicles and blue skin, and

211

everyone aching and shivering, I would have lived a different life."

"Except for last night." Marnie offered a sly grin.

"Except for last night. Is that my phone? The goddamn newspapers want my life story already."

His phone was ringing.

"Tell them I'm out in my garden singing 'Born Free' a cappella. No, better yet, tell them I've sold all of my belongings and donated the proceeds to the ACLU."

I got to the phone before the answering machine clicked on. Bob Bernier, looking for me. "You know a Laura Tate?"

"She was one of the women I warned yesterday."

"Can you come over here to your place?"

I didn't want any more bad news. "Is she dead?"

"Not hardly."

24

We rode across the island in Marnie Dunwoody's Jeep. I sat in front. Sam had stationed himself next to a coolerful of iced beer in the backseat. We took back streets, dodging Sunday-evening church traffic on Truman and Simonton. Warm late-day sunlight angled through the tall trees, brilliantly illuminating houses on Grinnell and Frances, especially those trimmed in Caribbean pastels.

"Weather looks like shit," said Sam.

I looked upward. "With this warm, gentle breeze in my eyes, I'm having trouble locating those storm clouds."

"Color of the sky. The sunset'll dazzle 'em, morning'll be crap."

It struck me odd that Sam's spell in lockup could prompt manic behavior until I considered the twenty-four hours during which he'd found a new lady friend, learned that someone had murdered an ex-lover, then been accused of committing the murder. Marnie, to her credit, had given room to Sam's mood. There was always the chance that her attentiveness had more to do with a scoop and a headline, but she hadn't projected the aura of shark. I hoped her interest was genuine. Sam deserved a good woman, though he'd made little effort to join the hunt. "I find it hard to believe," he would say, "that the future Mrs. Wheeler is waiting for me on a barstool in Key West, Florida."

Often he'd add, "I don't want a red-eyed drooler with smoky-smelling hair." He would always tack on his rule of the decade: "Never love a woman with more mileage than you."

I guided Marnie to a spot in front of Carmen's cottage. We hiked to my house. Bob Bernier, Monty Aghajanian, and Laura Tate sat mute in my living room. Laura looked steamed but cute in a parrot-patterned Hawaiian luau shirt and a white miniskirt. Within a minute of our arrival we'd all noted her neon-green panties covered with yellow smiley faces. I wondered if straitlaced Bob Bernier had scoped them out.

"Laura's calmed down since she first got here," said Bernier. "What, about a half hour ago?"

Laura was not calm. She sat forward on the rocker, pouting, breathing through her nose. "Shit, I don't know, man. It feels like five hours." She turned to me. "If I didn't believe you yesterday, Alex, I sure as hell knew something was up when I come here. I mean, you sit in my house and tell me about Ray Kemp, dead women, I don't know what to think. So I come here to tell you something that pertains."

She wanted an acknowledgment. Credit for making the effort.

"Okay," I said. "I'm glad you came."

"I see your door closed, I know you aren't here. I sit on your step to write you a note. Ol' Bob here springs bad outa nowhere, you know, like those SWAT teams on the tube, tumble out a van and surround the place? So I get my own personal cop show in your crabgrass, on my tummy with my hands behind my head, my derriere sticking up like a big ol' beach ball." She paused for a swig of beer. "Shit. No wonder those 'alleged perpetrators' bitch about gettin' cuffed. Worse than twenty-five pushups in PE class with some chunky gym teacher screamin', 'Keep your butt down! Keep your butt down!' "

Bernier had learned more about the panties than I'd suspected. Marnie's mouth hung open. She'd been mesmerized by Laura Tate's monologue.

I told Laura I wanted to know what pertained.

Bernier raised his hand to stop the action. "Miss Dunwoody, it is FBI policy to not discuss cases in progress. Can this meeting remain in the background until we determine its bearing on the whole mess?"

He'd been watching too many TV shows about Washington reporters.

"Consider me off the clock." Marnie looked away from Bernier and tilted back a beer.

Bernier gestured to Laura Tate, inviting her to continue.

She sneered at him and turned back to me. "I'm at the Packet Inn for the noon shift because the boss dreamed up this stupid fucking promotion to sell tequila sunrise with breakfast. He called it the hangover-cure concept. Imagine the bluehairs slamming Cuervo to kill their headaches. Anyway"—she nodded to the others—"I got this boyfriend, Tripper Wilbanks, who had to go away but he got out early. You know, all this publicity about felons getting early released for behaving in prison. Like what else are they going to do in there? But Tripper's not dangerous, so that's okay, except he's dangerous to himself I guess." She turned back to me. "Okay, so he and his brother come in the restaurant. As it happened, they had monster hangovers. And they tell me this totally spooky story, because of what you told me yesterday.

"So, anyway, the boys are driving down I-95 Friday night on their way home from Union Correctional, which I think used to be called Raiford, right? And they stop in this restaurant near St. Augustine, somewhere up there. And Tripper recognizes some guy from the old days in Key West. He sees Ray Kemp sitting in a booth. Tripper tells me this, I'm like, 'What is this damn coincidence?' It was like you described, fat and a beard, but Tripper knew it was him. Except he plays dumb and refuses to recognize Tripper."

I said, "Did he claim to be someone else?"

"He was like, 'I don't know you boys,' and 'Quit fuckin' with me'—pardon my Portuguese. He pays his bill at the register and takes off. Tripper's like, 'Something's weird here.' He doesn't make it obvious, but he follows Ray to the lot. Ray pulls away in a pickup truck full of boxes and shit. Tripper watches him get on I-95, heading toward Jacksonville."

I felt pieces slipping into place. I didn't know how big they were. "Tripper didn't happen to get a license number, did he?"

"He said he don't know why he read that plate. It was getting dark, but he did. Except he forgot the number. I guess he was already celebrating with the beers. I bugged the piss out of him and give him about five free coffees and he says, 'Mitsubishi, Georgia plates. Jackson County, Georgia.' "

A moment of silence let everyone adjust to the news.

Bernier gestured to Money and to me. "One more little tidbit. The Bureau determined there was no coverage of the Balbuena murder outside of Florida. Even in Washington State, the *Twin Peaks* connection didn't warrant curiosity. Ray Kemp didn't read about Julia in any paper up there."

"What have we got?" I said. "A phony name on the Miami rental car, the bullshit about flying in from Washington for the funeral, the Witness Protection Program, nautical knowledge, and a pickup heading north. Add it up. If he walks like a duck . . ."

Wheeler sprang out of his beer daze. "The biggest thing is what we *don't* have. Say you're right. And the court of logic is on your side for the moment. Ray Kemp killed Ellen Albury and Julia Balbuena. Ray Kemp put the bomb in the VW convertible. I'll buy all of that. But it's a sure bet he didn't do Mary Alice Noe. He was heading north from St. Augustine at sundown. That's eight hours away."

Monty rubbed his chin. "Time of death before midnight was all they knew for sure."

"So," said Sam, "even if he turned around on I-95 and drove back to Key West, he would've been too late. Unless he chartered a plane . . ."

I said to Monty, "Where'd you leave Chicken Neck?"

"Talking to his ex-wife, Mrs. Hatch. Out at the jail he called Avery to talk about the fact that Sam had been released. Hatch had told his wife he was going somewhere to clean out a storage shed. She figured he was in a dark bar getting screwed up. She wanted to talk to Liska face-to-face. He was already hung up on the talk he'd had with her this morning, so he asked me to take a cab on the city's nickel. Then he closed himself in an office in the Detention Center. I took a cab. I presume he called her back. If I'd known five minutes earlier, I could've shared the taxi with Sam."

Bernier motioned me over to my telephone. The LED window on my answering machine showed four messages.

I punched the "play" button. The first three for Annie: Ellen Albury's mother, about the bike; Benjamin Pinder: "Please call"; Marnie with questions. The fourth for me: Raoul Balbuena. "Now that I have a moment to myself, I would like to thank you for your professionalism and your honesty. Perhaps we can meet again under happier circumstances."

Raoul sounded as if the case were settled, the killer found. Bernier raised his eyebrows and looked me in the eye. I thought back to my slip of the tongue regarding Kemp, my mention of Witness Protection. I elected not to share my transgression with Bob.

No word from Annie.

Next to the laptop computer in Bernier's briefcase was a cellular phone with a keypad as complicated as one of those scientific calculators with cosines, logarithms, and exponential keys. After typing a short memo on the computer, he pressed several buttons on the phone. Screen prompts and windows confirmed that the memo had been encrypted, compressed, autodialed, and sent by burst transmission through a secure cell network. "Next thing you know," he said, "I'll think about taking a leak, Miami will E-mail permission."

"Wait till Washington tells you you've already taken it."

Bernier cracked a reluctant smile. "I'll retire to Costa Rica."

"What are we communicating to the outside world?"

"If Laura's friend Tripper is correct . . ."

"Tripper knows his pickup trucks," said Laura.

". . . and Kemp's license tag isn't phony," continued Bernier, "we should, in a couple hours, get the name and address of every registered Mitsubishi pickup owner in Jackson County, Georgia. I'm going on the chance that Kemp built the explosive device that crunched the Volkswagen, that he transported the device from Georgia . . ."

Marnie interrupted. "That makes it a federal violation?"

Bernier leaned forward. "Enough to justify Bureau jurisdiction. Our people in Georgia will do some legwork. When we establish residence, provided we can cough up sufficient corroborating evidence at this end, we'll get a warrant and make an arrest. By Wednesday or Thursday, Kemp will be explaining himself to us in person, in detail. Which leads me to an important request. We need media quiet for a few days. This joker decides to become a fugitive, we could have more murders. As my boss says when we're forced back to square one, it's 'dog ate dog.' It's all in the past tense."

Marnie nodded. "The runway behind a jet pilot."

Bernier smiled for the second time in two minutes.

"I'm not a scoop artist," she said. "I just want an exclusive."

"Done," said Bernier.

Sam said, "Rutledge, one thing you mentioned didn't hit right. What are you talking, Witness Protection?"

I looked at Bernier. He scanned the faces in the room, then said, "Kemp got busted on a federal conspiracy fifteen years ago. Anselmo was the prosecutor. He cut Kemp a testimony deal in exchange for Witness Protection."

Marnie Dunwoody's eyes snapped wide, as if she'd been slapped.

"We don't know much else yet." said Bernier. "Files that old are still being entered into our database. For some reason, the hard-copy folder was checked out of the U.S. Attorney's library last night. It's still in their secure area, but we've got to pin it down. We should have it in the morning."

Grinning, Marnie addressed Monty. "I've spent three days scrounging on Anselmo. One funky real estate transaction. My next path was past cases."

Monty looked doubting. "I don't think prosecutors have to go public on their finances."

"Public records. He bought a house in '79 for ninety-six thousand, and sold it in '84 for three eighty-five. That's a hell of a lot of improvements for a man making forty-seven grand a year." Marnie turned to Bernier. "One other thing. I haven't heard a whisper of motivation for any of these killings. No thefts that we know of. Sam told me about the peripheral connection to Alex, but what's the motive, down deep?"

Bernier shrugged. "That's not my department. We got people in the bureau we call Agatha Christies. But you'd be surprised how seldom we peg a motive. Even serial killers—and the worst claim innocence to the end—rarely reveal, you know, the urges, whatever, that took them over the edge. They'll blame it on the full moon or make up something spectacular. Something to add to their own headlines. A lot of the media fall for that crock. No offense."

The briefcase computer issued a faint beep. Bernier shielded the keyboard to enter an access code. "Bad news," he said.

"Georgia's DMV computer is off-line for system maintenance until midnight."

A black Chevy Caprice sedan stopped in the middle of Dredgers Lane. Dark tint blacked out its windows; thick blackwall tires and plain wheelcovers gave it away. Here on the island, it stood out like a snowplow.

"You called for a ride?" I asked.

"I pressed an orange button." Bernier patted the briefcase. "Thank you for your hospitality. Thank you for your assistance."

"Yeah. Mucho gracias, sweetie." Laura Tate tipped back her beer.

Bernier started out the door. "One last thing, Rutledge." He leaned toward Monty and me. "That Walther .380? Your bookcase is a bad hiding spot. I liked the movie *Legends of the Fall.* I noticed your hardcover first edition, autographed, no less. I slid out the book, there it was. B-and-E boys, if they have time, love to riffle through book collections because people hide cash between the pages of classic novels. That gun'd be a goner. The wrong hands for sure."

As the Caprice backed out of the lane, Sam popped tops and handed out beers. I pulled my tattered road atlas from the shelf under the coffee table. Sam pointed at it. "You thinkin' tonight or tomorrow?"

"You in?"

"From here on, I don't hear a thing," said Monty. "I don't know anything."

Marnie peered over my shoulder. "What are you talking about?"

Sam put his arm around her. "An extension of a chat Alex and I had several nights ago, talking about frustration, the working out of same. Seems to me that Wednesday or Thursday is a long time from now. The man said the FBI needed 'corroborating evidence at this end'? So, nothing special. We'll go somewhere, we'll look for a pickup truck."

Monty shook his head but didn't say a word. Marnie's face showed concern and a trace of admiration.

"I'm outa here," said Laura Tate. "Nap time back at the hacienda."

25

There was no way to get short-notice seats on a Sunday flight to Miami, especially in the evening. Too many three-day tourists heading north to face the new workweek. Sam called a commercial fishing captain named Ellison who owned a Cessna 172. Captain Ellison said he'd take us, but he couldn't leave until eight. That gave us time to book two seats out of Miami, reserve a rental car in Atlanta, eat Cuban food with Marnie, Carmen, and Maria, pack our ditty bags, and drive to the airport.

Typical of pilots, Ellison had arrived early. He was doing preflight, testing his control surfaces, topping off his tanks. But he'd become grumpy and claimed to have had second thoughts about flying into Miami International after dark. There also was some question about headwinds he'd encounter on his return.

Sam pulled me aside. "Not to worry. Ellison isn't happy unless he's pissed off."

"Oh, I get it. He's an asshole. Why isn't he a light-tackle guide?"

"He's also a great pilot," said Sam.

We were in the air by 8:05. The lights of U.S. 1 pointed us to Miami. The Gulf Stream had its own traffic corridors of freighters, tramp cargo haulers, and tanker ships. In the bay-side mangrove country northwest of the highway, small boats ran the shallows in darkness, headed for port after a day on the salt. The moon lit cloud tops. Its reflection off the water raced along with us. Strobes on distant microwave towers and mainland airport beacons flashed like teasers on a giant pinball machine. To the east, heat lightning zipped cloud lines where warmed air had drifted offshore, over cooling water. None of us spoke until the pilot quietly asked us to double-check his approach frequencies and runway chart. Lights on a dozen airliners blinked around us. Ellison griped about being a mosquito in an aviary, but his final approach was a well-executed speed run with no flaps. He taxied out of the realm of the 737s and L1011s and stopped next to a private charter terminal. Wheeler handed him a short stack of fifties. We went looking for a taxi to the main terminal.

After we'd checked in and pocketed our tickets, I called West Palm. Annie's mother, evasive: "She's gone out for a while. Can I take a message?"

It would last ten minutes, nuances would be lost, details scrambled, intent edited. "I guess not," I said.

At 1:15 A.M. we arrived in Atlanta during a violent rainstorm, worse for wear. I'd grabbed an hour's sleep. I would have been better off without it. Sam woke when the airliner jerked to a halt at the gate. The courtesy van to the rental lot was on its after-midnight schedule. We waited twenty-five minutes in an empty departure lounge. Our growling stomachs echoed off floor-to-ceiling glass walls. After we'd shuffled paperwork with a graveyard-shift snarler at a rental-car counter, we hit the I-285 loop south of town. Unlike Keys rainstorms, this downpour felt like it would hang around until morning or longer.

It had been several years since Sam had rented a car. "People wonder why I never go north of Jewfish Creek," he muttered. "Pay phones, jukeboxes, Coke machines, pinball machines, drop the coin in the slot, facts of life. The pay toilet went away with dime phone calls. Pay TVs in waiting rooms. Don't

223

those people ever read a book? Now I pay for extra fucking insurance, I carry my own gas so I don't get gouged, I buy permission for you to drive if I fall asleep at the wheel. Next thing,
we'll be downtown, they'll charge us to loiter."

I patted him on the back. "Okay, Ellison."

He headed us east on U.S. 78. He drove as far as a one-story
cement-block motel near Monroe. Three A.M., we looked like
derelicts in the rain. The owner surprised us by admitting to a
vacancy. We asked for a six-thirty wake-up call. By my body
clock, the call came ten minutes later.

Sam turned into Mr. Military, ready for action, the man
with the plan. "Shower, yes, shave, no. That phone book, por
favor."

Ten minutes later we were inbound to Athens. Five minutes
after that we pulled into a Mitsubishi dealership.

"A two-pronged attack," said Sam. "I'll take the front office.
You'll describe Kemp better than I will, so go around back,
bribe a flunky. He's got to have brought it in for at least one repair. A warranty freebie or something."

"Mechanics aren't hired for their memories."

"What time of the morning does your positive attitude
kick in?"

He was right. It didn't cost me a penny to have a muffler
technician sneak into the service manager's computer. I described the truck that had hit my hunting dog and fled the
scene. I wanted to give the veterinarian's bill to the slimy bastard
that owned the truck. Ezell, the mechanic, understood the prin-
ciple behind justice for a good hunting dog. I mentioned the
salt-and-pepper beard.

Ezell snapped his tool chest shut and wiped his hands on his
coveralls. "I remember that dude. Sort of a yuppie hippie, talkin'
Yankee like you, but he push hisself around like big money.
He'd be the dog-hitting type. I think he just bought that truck
a few weeks back. Had a damned Dale Earnhardt sticker on the

224

back window. He come in here to have it checked for a long trip."

Ezell zipped through the computer, found a service memo, and scribbled an address in Albertson, Georgia. He warned me not to speed in town. "They built a Little League stadium on people doin' thirty-eight in a thirty-five." The name above the address was Delray Crane.

I returned to the car and waved Sam outside. He'd been head-to-head with an officious "customer-privacy butthead" in the front office. But he'd caused enough commotion to keep the service manager away from Ezell's charity.

"Pay dirt?" he said.

I described my ruse.

"Yep, Kemp'd be the dog-hitting type," said Sam.

Sam drove a mile or so, veered into a convenience store lot, stopped next to a bank of coin telephones. "I'm going to buy some insurance. I'll leave this name Delray Crane and the address on my answering machine. If the shit hits the fan, at least there'll be a trail."

"We could call Bernier."

"He'd order us to back off. You come this far to back off?"

We took a bypass around Athens, turned north on 441, and drove ten miles before passing the Maple Tree Palace Night Club, then the Albertson city limits sign. We were pleased to learn that the town had produced the State Champion Girls Track Team ten years earlier. As Sam slowed for the Albertson business district, a crow flew over the windshield, a garter snake hanging from its beak.

"Any ideas on who murdered Mary Alice?"

Sam flinched at the name, shook his head. "Couple of cars been parked down there the last few months. Some kind of Lexus or Infiniti—I can't tell you squat about Japanese stuff— and a late-model GM car, an Olds or a Buick. For a long time I thought she was paranoid about her ex-husband. She didn't want to go out anywhere, wouldn't go out to eat. Didn't want to go out anywhere."

We needed directions to Rural Route 3. Two old boys in the Shell station knew nothing about postal routes. The Albertson post office wouldn't be open for another twenty minutes. At town center we found a secondhand clothing store, an outboard-motor repair shop, a restaurant called the Luncheonette. Inside its twin picture windows, bathed in the off-chartreuse cast of vintage overhead lighting, sat a half dozen representatives of the hitch-up overall crowd, a couple of businessmen in short-sleeve shirts and ties, and a lady school-crossing guard wearing a clear plastic rain bonnet. An ideal spot to spend nineteen minutes. We angle-parked next to the building. We had to jog around puddles to the door.

Stares from the regulars. The booths were claimed. The place smelled of bacon grease and overcooked oatmeal. We settled for a table where someone had left a morning paper. A grandmotherly waitress peered over the top of her spectacles, her face a question, her stance an urge to hurry.

"Cream," said Sam.

"Black," I said.

Sam checked the weather map on the back page of the front section. "Like I predicted, the weather in the Keys turned to crap. I ain't missing a thing."

"Was Noe a wife beater?" I said.

"She never said. I figured out she was still in love with him, so I made some excuse about my work schedule and stopped going by. I couldn't quit thinking about her. I kept catching myself looking for her in the yard, letting myself get bothered by those cars out front. I guess she fell into that category that you described for Julia Balbuena. I always held out for the impossible reunion."

I knew words would fall flat right at the moment.

226

"On one hand," said Sam, "Bruce Noe had no reason to kill his ex-wife. I'm not positive. I don't think there was alimony going out. He was the one wanted out of the marriage."

"That leaves out jealousy, maybe. What's on the other hand?"

"He's tight with Steve Gomez and a couple of the commissioners. He hangs around with cops. He had an above-average opportunity to pick up details on the other murder scenes, if he wanted to put it to use."

"He was out of town for the weekend. If he was behind it, he had a helper."

Sam agreed. "Someone who didn't know his knots, who didn't know that he was supposed to pluck his twanger and leave a calling card."

"The detail that never leaked out."

Sam looked me in the eye. "She said she knew you."

I nodded again.

"She on the list of ex-girlfriends, Alex?"

"Technically, yes," I said, then paused to consider my phrasing. Was Sam going to become angry over an event that happened years before he even met the woman? "In a practical sense, we hardly knew each other. We took drunk a few days before her wedding. What a gentleman would call a half-night's stand. Her idea."

Now Sam was shy of words. I had told it straight. I hoped he would drop the subject. He did. "This rainy day in Georgia is lame and ugly," he said. "We should have brought walkie-talkies."

"Low-tech?"

"We get separated, one of us gets his ass in a sling, practical. Low-tech is duct-taping somebody's mouth and nose shut."

"How about weapons?" I said.

"What'd you come here to do?"

"Deliver the shitbird to justice."

"Well, yes. One must presume that he does not wish to come along."

We still had ten minutes to wait when a middle-aged man in a postal clerk's uniform walked into the luncheonette. He brushed raindrops off his shoulders and stamped his feet on a rectangle of carpet near the door. The waitress had prepared a cardboard tray. Four coffees with lids, stir sticks, a mess of sugars, several cream thimbles. Sam approached the man and asked directions.

"Y'all wouldn't believe how many questions like that I get," he said. "The government needs to change the system, get rid of rural route numbers. Go north out of town to a shut-down Gulf Oil, take a left. One mile along, go right where it says 'Karma Farm, Two Miles.' That's County Five, but it's Postal Route Three."

"Karma Farm?" said Sam.

"Longhairs," said the postal clerk, knowing that the word explained itself. It would break his heart to learn that ninety percent of the nation's longhairs are on Country Music Television. On his way out the door he turned to ask what box number we needed.

"Thirty-five," I said. "Name of Crane."

The clerk scowled. "That boy with the satellite scoop? What's he havin', a yard sale? I sent two Mexicans to that place twenty minutes ago, Puerto Ricans, they all the same. Danged wetbacks sneak into the country, drive a shiny-paint Mercedes-Benz, gold hubcaps. I gotta buy the wife a used Toyota . . ." He chewed his lips and kicked at the doorsill. He'd pronounced it "Tie-ota." The door closed behind him.

Sam said, "You look like you just crapped your pants."

"Let's save time and head back to Atlanta. If the Benz had Dade County plates, Kemp's having a soul talk right now with

Julia's brother and his father's pet thug. There won't be anything left for us to do."

Sam dropped several dollar bills on the table. "Let's go get in line. Maybe Kemp needs us to run for Band-Aids."

We hurried through the drizzle to the car. Sam pulled into an alley behind the restaurant, found a side street, then accelerated onto the main road. He crooned a soulful ". . . was a rainy night in Georgia . . ."

I suddenly figured how the Balbuenas had found Ray. "Talk about the Cuban network," I said. "What'd Bernier say last night, that the Kemp file had been checked out?"

Sam turned at the empty Gulf station, an old oil company approximation of art deco. "Miami is complicated," he said. "You need money to survive. After that, your human value is based on connections."

"It didn't work for Julia."

26

The Delray Crane address fell among a string of brick ranch-types spaced apart in hilly country not fully recovered from winter. Most properties had a mobile home or two out back. Wedged between two clumps of oaks and set twenty yards off the two-lane, the two-story frame farmhouse looked especially neglected in the rain. It needed more than just paint. The front porch was filled with dead plants and weathered furniture, and the yard had not received its first mowing of the year. The driveway's twin ruts flowed with red dirt runoff. An empty two-stall carport behind the house looked ready to collapse into the crabgrass. A row of chicken coops ran along what I guessed to be the back boundary of the property. Noticeably out of place was the Direct TV receiver dish between the house and carport. The well-maintained silos on the rise to the north probably belonged to a neighbor.

There was no sign of the Mercedes-Benz or the Mitsubishi pickup truck.

Sam eased into the driveway, then onto the grass to keep from hitting potholes under puddles. We stopped next to a broken wheelbarrow full of magnolia sprouts. The front door of the house was ajar. In spite of the dim light, there were no lights inside. Sam turned the key and stared out the windshield.

"Not a warm welcome," I said.

"Wish I'd worn a jacket," said Sam. "I also feel naked without a pistol."

"Honk the horn a bit. See if anyone comes out."

"We're not even sure this is Ray Kemp's house."

We knocked on the doorframe and yelled hellos. We peered into the gritty windows, seeing nothing in the darkness. We finally invited ourselves in. Sam went down the center hallway. I crept up a creaky stairwell and caught stale smells of mildewed vinyl upholstery and furniture stuffing. A twisted bedsheet lay on the floor outside one bedroom. Another room was full of boxes and junk: an ironing board, baseball equipment, a Seagull outboard motor on a stand. The bedroom had all the personality of the motel in Monroe, Georgia: a thrift-shop dresser with two drawers left open; magazines stacked around the bed; an old Princess-style telephone on the floor, tipped on its side, off the hook. A bright orange athletic jersey had been tossed in a corner.

Upside down in a cheap frame on top of the dresser was a photograph that looked at least twenty years old. I turned it over: an older couple in aviator-type sunglasses and Bermuda shorts standing next to a '76 Cadillac convertible.

An upside-down photo?

Sam's voice from downstairs. "Nobody here but us bulldogs."

I didn't want to leave fingerprints. I snagged a sock from the top open drawer, wiped the photo frame and hung up the Princess phone.

Sam had Ziploc baggies over his hands. He opened kitchen cupboards, one by one. "If we hadn't dropped in, the house would've burned down. That pot was boiled down to the last half-inch of water. My guess is, ol' Ray left in a hurry."

"I wonder how it feels to ride a thousand miles in the trunk of a Mercedes."

"Let's get the fuck out of here."

"Give me another minute to look around." I figured the house had to hold some kind of clue to the murders, or to Ray Kemp's motives. A copy of *Sports Illustrated* sat on the arm of a lounger. On a Formica table in the front room was a manual called "How to Write Effective Short Stories." I slid a tattered bookmark from between its pages. Dated 10 May 80, it was the boat owner's copy of the customs and immigration form that Ray had submitted on our return to Key West from Mariel on *Barracuda*. It bore his name, Julia's name, my name, and the names of the twelve strangers who had been delivered to freedom on that day. Strange that he would keep a souvenir of the Boatlift. It had not been a banner day for the captain. Any one of the refugees would have appreciated it more.

"We've got the right house," I said quietly.

Sam opened the drawers of a battered metal desk. "No utility bills or check stubs. Like he's already moved out."

"Maybe he wasn't home when they got here. Maybe Charlie Balls flipped on the stove to leave his signature on the place."

The kitchen wall phone rang. I wasn't sure what to do. After the second ring I walked the short hallway, stuck my hand in a Ziploc, and picked up the receiver. I heard a snap and then silence. I hung it up.

"Check out these old postcards," said Sam. I walked back toward the front door. Suddenly Sam's face filled with disbelief. He pointed out a front window. Two vans and six sedans sat in the front yard. I glimpsed the initials on the back of a man's nylon jacket: FBI.

A hundred ball-peen hammers slammed into my back. The explosion in the kitchen blew us both out the door and off the porch. Twirling fireworks filled my vision, and I was flat out on the wet grass with my arm twisted under my body and the taste of blood in my mouth. Two of the hammers had struck my ears directly. When I tried to sit up and move my head, splinters of glass sprinkled from my hair to my forehead.

"We alive?" Sam's voice sounded far away but I felt an elbow hit my ribs.

I leaned to one side and shook shards off my eyelids, then opened one eye to see Sam crawling away from the porch.

A voice quivering with forced calm said, "Get a move on. There could be another bomb. The whole place could go." Someone grabbed me under one arm.

My eyes were full of grit. The baggie was still on my right hand. It hurt to move my mouth. We figured later that Sam's shoulder had caught the front door framing and we'd been spun off the porch in a tangle of wicker strands and parts of a plastic clock that had hung in the hallway. Our heads had banged together—that's how I wound up with a black eye and a broken front tooth. One of my shoes had landed twenty feet away.

I remember being propped against the trunk of a dark blue Crown Victoria, watching a black-clad SWAT crew exit Ray Kemp's house. The team looked to be at parade rest; they had discovered what we knew: that the lights were out and nobody was home. My lights had been knocked halfway to Tennessee. I kept thinking how much I wanted a Dustbuster so I could clean the crap out of my hair. At one point I thought I saw Sam walking around the yard, picking up the postcards he'd wanted to show me.

"Too bad you aren't carrying a gun," said a thirtyish frat-type in a cable-knit crew-neck sweater. "We could have you on an even-dozen state and federal charges." On second glance he looked like the kind of mean-spirited pretty boy who'd beat up his Pi Phi sweetheart for shaking her fanny too much at the sock hop. "Just don't try to bullshit us," he warned. "Don't try to tell us you learned how to make bombs by copying a recipe off the Internet."

I did not want to be this boy's friend. I heard myself moan, then whisper, "I was cleaning it . . . and it went off."

I believe at that moment I faded out again.

The next thing I knew, I was being helped into our rental car. Covered with mud, holding the shredded remains of my shirt, I rolled into the front seat. Sam opened the driver's door, flopped his butt on the seat hard enough to bounce me, threw a wad of muddy postcards on the floor, and finally got the ignition key in the slot.

"Don't say a fucking word until we're out of here," he said without moving his lips. "Keep quiet. Just don't talk."

And then we were driving away from the ruined house and the squadron of federal agents. I noticed only one other thing. None of the neighbors on the rural road had come outside to investigate the explosion.

A map in the glove compartment showed the quickest route to Atlanta was up to I-85 and straight west. It hurt to move, but I slowly gathered the old postcards from the floor of the car. Lithographs from the late forties or early fifties. A collection of old linen cards, from tourist traps in the eastern part of the country. Identical to the mysterious cards that Michael Anselmo had been receiving. But why would Kemp have sent threatening notes to the man who had provided him freedom in Witness Protection?

"Why are we free to go?" I said. "That one schmuck was already reserving us rooms in the Federal Prison System." Every time I said an *s*, my broken tooth whistled.

"You owe Bernier a favor," Sam said solemnly. "Size large."

"What, to fit his hotshit ego?"

"No, to wrap around his heart. I suggest you call him from the first pay phone we see."

"I need a shirt to wear on the airplane."

Before we got onto I-85, just outside of Commerce, Georgia, Sam swung into a beer-and-candy store attached to a filling station. I got on the phone.

"Took a chance on you," Bernier said brusquely. "They were playing with the idea that you rigged your girlfriend's car with Tovex."

"How do you know it wasn't me?"

"The lab techs determined that the jury-rig couldn't have been installed at an earlier date and set to blow later. It was probably hooked up during Ellen Albury's funeral. You were stumbling around the beach at Bahia Honda about then, and your witness was a Monroe County deputy."

"So you checked me out . . ."

"You want more? The night the Guthery girl got killed, you were drunk on your ass in Louie's Back Yard. Kim, the pretty bartender lady, told me you sat at the service bar in the lobby until she closed it down. She had to call a taxi for you. You couldn't have squashed a cockroach, much less gone to Stock Island and murdered someone. Now tell me what the fuck you and Wheeler are doing in Georgia."

I explained the events of the past two hours. "Until the bomb went off, I figured Kemp had been abducted. Now I don't know what to think. Either the bomb was meant to get him, or else Kemp rigged it to get anyone who might come after him."

Bernier hummed while he thought. "Could go either way. If the Cubans grabbed him, the bomb may have been set to blow when the phone rang. That way they could rank out the evidence and confuse the issue. Or else, like you said, Kemp set it to blow as soon as anyone answered an incoming call."

I felt my brain wobble from one moment to the next. I had no confidence in my powers of reason. But one more fact lumbered into my consciousness. "Bob, there was a phone upstairs, off the hook. I hung it up two minutes before the downstairs phone rang."

"Cute. Hanging up probably triggered a phony incoming call. That's a new one, but it's simple as hell. That makes me think the bomb was meant for one of us. We're having trouble nailing down a serial criminal profile, but let's run on the idea that Kemp's still at large. Why don't you two come back and let the real cowboys do their thing?"

"Okay. We've saved the American taxpayer thousands of dollars. Now we're not qualified."

"That's not it. Your friend is out of jail on his own recognizance. He's not supposed to be outside of Monroe County. If you want to get precise, you were trespassing and interfering with an ongoing federal investigation. Truth is, the Georgia State computer is still down. I wouldn't have had that Kemp address in Albertson until five this afternoon at the earliest. Now get your ass out of there."

"How about Raoul Balbuena's home address?"

"No way."

"I wanted to send a sympathy card."

"You didn't get this from me."

I wrote as he dictated, then hung up and tried to reach Annie again.

"I'm afraid she's off to meet friends for breakfast." Her mother's officious voice especially grating when one is fighting gnats in the middle of nowhere. "May I ask her to call you when she gets back?"

"Mrs. Minnette, I'm alongside the highway in Food Court, Georgia. I'm searching for the man who blew up Annie's Volkswagen. He may be responsible for several murders. He's also threatened another of Annie's acquaintances, Mr. Michael Anselmo."

"I haven't spoken to my daughter since you last called."

"Okay, Mrs. Minnette. I'll be flying into Miami this evening. I would like Annie to meet me in North Miami, at the house where she stayed last week. If she can't be there, I'll call from Key West later tonight."

"Wasn't she about ready to trade in that old convertible?"

27

A service station with civic spirit. While Sam used the phone, I pondered the two choices on a wobbly T-shirt rack wedged between the Doritos display and a shelf full of crocheted toilet-paper covers. Extra large only, white lettering on black cotton/polyester fifty-fifty. I picked "The Big Word in Commerce is ME." The other shirts read, "I'm with Buckhead."

Sam headed us toward Atlanta. He'd connected with Marnie Dunwoody at her office. "She tried to call Anselmo to follow up on Monty's decertification. Anselmo had gone to Miami for some kind of meeting. She requested a callback and she got it."

"What did the buckhead have to say for himself?"

"She's got Caller ID at her desk." Sam paused long enough to warn me. "Anselmo dialed in from a West Palm exchange."

"Aw, Jesus." Annie must have invited him up. What had she been doing with her hands on Sunday morning, gauging the thickness of my skin?

"Anyway," said Sam, "he had no comment. Claimed he couldn't remember the case."

"Her mother said she was having breakfast with a friend."

"How much does Annie know? What's she saying to him?"

"Unless he tells her, there's no way she could know that he put Kemp into Witness Protection. She knows about the threatening postcards, she knows that Kemp is a strong possible in the murders. She can't connect them, but if she talked about both topics, and Anselmo's the bad guy, he'd know we were on to him. Depending on his level of panic, that might be dangerous to her. And Kemp could still be out there, too."

"This is getting beyond weird."

I couldn't argue. "As long as we're out in left field on this thing, where was Anselmo when Mary Alice Noe was murdered on Saturday night?"

Sam shivered with disgust. "This goddamned mess grows a brand-new dimension every twenty minutes."

"Over in right field," I said, "I've got to tell you something."

"This sounds like a confession."

"I've tried to jam this into the back of my mind, but it keeps popping out. Annie knew the names. Julia, Sally Ann, and Shelly."

"She didn't know Mary Alice?"

"Nope. No way."

Sam had to pay attention to traffic as we neared the six-lane loop around Atlanta. Citizens flipped us off because we were doing only eighty in the fast lane. South of downtown we began to see signs directing us to the airport.

We had progressed from looking like derelicts to resembling washed-out photographs of corpses. My head had begun to ache. We finally found a ticket agent who would give us two seats on a late-afternoon flight into Miami. Sam reserved a standby slot on a Key West puddle-jumper. He also bought a shirt that looked like a Jamaican party joke. We spent ten minutes in a men's room scraping dried dirt from our trousers and shoes.

My seat was seven rows behind Sam on the Miami-bound plane. A perky flight attendant informed me that he'd paid for my first four drinks. She brought the first two rum and sodas immediately and promised to deliver the second two the minute I gave her the signal. I fell in love with her, in spite of her wedding band. I spent the next hour wondering why someone just earning a paycheck could show me such consideration while my alleged lover treated me like a cold slice of week-old pizza. When I attempted to order drink number five, the young woman named Tiffany, after the retail outlet I presumed, brought coffee instead. I gave up on her and buried my face in a magazine article. The best mutual funds to hold for the next ten years. If I hit nothing but "home runs," I could quadruple my savings and ease into the Luxury Life. I should tell the magazine's editor that my future financial happiness depended entirely on my having enough to pay property taxes in Key West.

It had been a week since I'd thought about earning a living. Nothing like six ounces of rum to snap the world into focus. Our plane descended into Miami over the northern edge of the Everglades. The bleached saw grass, the few trees and fewer birds appeared to belong to sagebrush territory, to the rural West. Our final approach above the Tamiami Canal, a man-made slough, helped explain the plight of the River of Grass.

I called from the terminal and had trouble saying "Thadd" with a broken tooth. My "big black motorbike" was right where I'd left it. They'd had no word from Annie. They offered to come fetch me but I told them not to bother, I'd grab a cab. I realized my mistake when the meter clicked past thirty dollars.

The perfect host, Thadd ushered me into his home and offered a cocktail "for the ditch." Then he looked at me more closely and understood that he was too close to the truth. "Your eye looks like a hurricane map."

"I bumped into a door."

"And your tooth. You've been hanging out in the wrong kind of bar. When David comes home like that, we call it heat stroke."

David left the kitchen and returned brandishing a pair of my undershorts. "The maid found these in the bedclothes. We presumed they belonged to you and not your lady friend." The skivvies had been washed and ironed.

They were humoring me. Did I look that awful?

I asked to use their phone.

"Alex, I'm afraid she's gone out to dinner." Cleo Minnette, always afraid of something.

"Did you warn her about the dangers I described?"

"I couldn't swear to it, Alex. Things get so confused around here whenever Ann is home."

"Please ask her to call me in the morning. If she's still alive."

I presented Atlanta Braves baseball jerseys to Thadd and David to thank them for their extended hospitality. Light rain began to fall as I decamped the Enchanted Forest. My first stop was at a 7-Eleven to buy a city street map.

Raoul Balbuena lived on the edge of Coral Gables, in a modest concrete block house not five blocks from St. Joseph's Catholic Church. A four-foot stucco wall surrounded the property. Green-tinted gravel had replaced the grass. Orange lights illuminated the iron bars that covered each window and the front door. An intercom was set into a panel next to the door. When I pressed the call button, a spotlight blasted my face. I was being monitored by a closed-circuit TV camera. I pulled off my helmet and held back the temptation to dance a soft shoe for program variety. Behind me the rain came down harder.

Raoul's voice through a speaker: "Good evening, Mr. Rutledge. I'll be right there."

He appeared surprised by my rough appearance but said nothing about it. He ushered me into the house, into a large room full of heavy, dark furniture. The walls were hung with small religious icons. One small photograph showed the old cathedral in central Havana. The furniture looked worn but not trashy. Raoul appeared to be the only person in the house.

There was no offer of refreshment. "What brings you up from Key West?" he said.

"I just flew in from Atlanta. I've been touring Georgia."

I got the stutter of silence that I'd hoped for. I sat in a broad leather chair.

"Have you turned yourself into a policeman, Mr. Rutledge?"

I knocked my knuckles against the top of the helmet. "I'm the same person you met Saturday. Have you turned yourself into a criminal, Mr. Balbuena?"

He looked me in the eye. "Your check is in the mail."

"Is that like, 'Don't let the door hit me in the ass . . . ?' "

"Last Saturday we exchanged information and we asked for your help. You had a goal, but no ideas. Information can be expensive to obtain. Now you have acted on some of that information."

"And you've acted on my information, too. You need to know that I was not alone when I saw your Mercedes in Albertson."

"Thank you. Now we are back to level ground."

I wanted to push him over the edge. "One more thing. A file is missing from the criminal division of the United States Attorney's Office. If, by any chance, you have access to it, you should arrange for its immediate return."

"You're one point ahead. It's nice to sit and talk to an old friend of Julia's. Do you have anything else for us?"

"Did Julia have any other old friends that I need to know about?"

"Good guess, Mister Rutledge. Fair is fair, so you may play with this. After she left Key West, almost fifteen years ago, she met and spent almost two years sharing a condominium with Michael Anselmo. Now we're even again. Do you need any cash for your trip home?"

"No." I stood to go.

He looked me up and down. "I don't suppose the clothing stores are open this late, anyway." He showed me to the door. The lock on the iron gate buzzed as I reached to push it open.

Ray Kemp had either a rival suspect or a cohort. Billy Fernandez had tried to kill me but Michael Anselmo had been intimate with both Ellen and Julia—two murder victims—and with Annie, a near miss with the bomb. Kemp could be tracking Annie through Anselmo, or Anselmo could be setting her up for Kemp. She could be two-timing, lying her ass off, running her own agenda, and sleeping with the enemy. If she desired the man she had described to Carmen as not much of a straight shooter, the man she'd caught boffing her roommate on a kitchen floor, so be it. There is always a tragic element in physical attraction. But she didn't deserve to be harmed by a lunatic or a lunatic's accomplice.

I had two choices. I could call for the eighteenth time and try to warn her. Or I could ride to West Palm and attempt to find her. Either way I ran the danger of having her blow off my warning. With Choice Two I couldn't imagine a more perfect situation to set myself up as idiot of the year. What was I going to do, wait in the driveway for Annie and her date to pull up? Hide in the shrubs and pounce out as Annie ushered Anselmo into the house? Park down the street, out of sight, waiting for her to arrive? I didn't want to be some guy standing in the rain next to a motorcycle. The dog walkers would go haywire. Neighborhood Watch would have gendarmes on my butt in a flash. Or I could go sit with her parents, watch them mix and drink their nonstop gimlets, watch the local car crashes and gun accidents on the eleven-o'clock news, make small talk to fill the long, vicious minutes until the lovebirds waltzed in the door.

I wasn't thinking perfectly. It was the fifth day in six that I'd awakened at an uncivilized hour. I had a black eye, wet clothing, a chipped tooth, the leftovers of four rum drinks in my belly. One fact shone through the mist of indecision. Rain is always colder when you're riding northward. I stopped at a booth and dropped another quarter.

This time Annie answered. "I got your message," she said. "I called Carmen. She said that you and Sam had gone to Georgia."

"We acted quicker than the long arm of the law. But our lead fizzled out. Kemp is still on the loose. What's going on in West Palm Beach?"

"It's pretty boring. I'm sitting around the house. I've gone shopping with my mother a couple times."

Horseshit. "Well, at least you're safe."

"Safe but bored. Is Sam still in trouble?"

"No, he's not."

"Where are you? Why are you talking with a lisp?"

"Rolling down U.S. 1 on the cycle. Thadd and David say hi."

"I hope this is over soon. I need to get back down to Key West, too."

"Work piling up?"

"Always, Alex. You know that."

I wanted to ask if she missed the balalaika. Or me. My martyrdom was being trampled in the muck of ruined truth. "Look, I don't know how to tell you this. I don't own you and I don't care to boss you around."

"You've never bossed me around."

"I don't want you to think that I'm trying to interfere with your life."

"What are you trying to say?"

"There's a chance that Kemp and Anselmo are linked in this mess."

"Michael is not a killer, Alex."

"They go back fifteen years, and they may have been in

244

touch in recent months. There's another angle. Michael and Julia once lived together, after she left Ray."

She had to think about that for a moment. "Michael came here today to talk about the future. He said nothing about Ray Kemp, and he left for Key West an hour ago. I assure you I am unharmed."

"We don't know where Kemp is, however."

"Are you suggesting that I go back to Thadd and David's?"

"I think you should go somewhere. Anywhere. Until this blows over."

"Thank you for calling. Thank you for being worried about me. If I decide to go anywhere, I'll call Carmen."

I hung a chevron on my Good Intentions merit badge. The Kawasaki took me down I-95 as if it had gained a hundred horses. Typical of Florida squalls, the rainstorm blew out over the Gulf Stream. The lump on the back of my head was rubbing my helmet liner, and an exposed nerve in my tooth started to scream.

I had accumulated too much knowledge in too little time. It wasn't sorting well. My search for clues had been jumbled by my concern for preventing more attacks. A serial killer could be sitting in Albertson, Georgia, laughing about how he'd outsmarted vengeful Cubans, amateur sleuths, especially the FBI. Or he could be in the trunk of a car that would reach Miami about the time I hit Key West. Maybe my visit to Raoul had saved Kemp's life. Perhaps it was already too late. He could have been removed from the trunk after dark, pitched into a north Florida swamp or taken for a one-way boat ride out of Savannah or Jacksonville.

I was bothered more than ever by Annie's blasé attitude, her cryptic admissions, her Swiss-cheese explanations.

Below Card Sound Road I passed Barefoot Cay Marina and rode between scraggly walls of mangrove. Moonlight reflected off the flats around Mile Marker 112, where three yachts lay at anchor in the open bay to the east. Tension lifted, the spaces between cars widened. The air became warmer and thicker, and a salty film began to paint my exposed skin. It smelled more like home.

I stopped at the Holiday Inn at the Key Colony turnoff. The lounge was dead. A young female bartender was cutting fruit, prepping for the next day's business.

"What can I get ya?" she said. New York accent.

"Nothing to drink," I said. "I'm apartment hunting. My girlfriend was in for cocktail hour Tuesday. Said the bartender knew a cheap two-bedroom. I'd like to talk to whoever it was."

She shook her head. "I'm new on the job. That bartender skipped to the Yucatán on Friday. Management'd like to talk to him, too."

So much for confirming Annie's story about the night of Ellen's death.

I rolled into Key West around midnight, opened my windows to air out the house, then walked far enough down the lane to determine that Carmen had gone to bed. Wafts of frangipani drifted like clouds of intoxicating ground fog. Foliage muffled the sounds of crickets and the hum of air conditioners. A few blocks away a sports car with straight exhausts ran up through two gears and back down again. It repeated the process, stop sign to stop sign, across to the Atlantic side. The island dogs were quiet. One rooster with an off-kilter body clock crowed. A breeze rustled high in the older cabbage and coconut palms.

A hot shower in the yard darkness put warmth into my bones. I dropped into the lounge chair on the porch and drank a beer to lift the edge off my nerves while I counted muscles in my back as they went off duty. Moments like that, as much as anything, defined Luxury Life, taxes be damned. Except for basics, comfort had little to do with wealth.

246

Things could be so simple if they weren't always so complicated.

It made sense at the time. About two-thirty I woke up numb in the chair to the sound of haranguing frogs in the yard. I called Chicken Neck Liska's office, left a message on his machine, then stumbled into the bedroom.

28

Eight-twenty, a good porch morning, two sips into my first Cuban coffee, birds singing in the trees, about to sort my mail. Paul Desmond music on the CD.

The phone rang.

Chicken Neck Liska: "I had a long meeting with Aghajanian yesterday on my day off, to catch up on things. Now this message says you want to bring me up to date."

I hadn't even had a chance to bring Sam Wheeler up to date. "I'm moving slowly this morning," I mumbled, "but I got some shit on Anselmo."

"Don't even brush your teeth, bubba. I ain't gonna kiss you."

I wanted to tell him I had one less tooth to brush. I was lacing my deck shoes when the Taurus pulled up in front. He came to the porch in a disgusting lavender leisure suit and a broadcollared purple shirt, flicked his fingernail against my brass doorbell, waltzed in carrying a Dunkin' Donuts bag, cheerful as Fred Astaire tapping circles around a walking stick. His tan loafers were inset with the gauzy material used to make pot holders. When he sat his jacket fell open. His cellular phone snug in the shoulder holster.

"Tryouts for the New Village People?"

He grunted and plopped the bag on the table.

I went inside to pour him a coffee.

"This is not every day," he said. "I once figured if Dunkin' Donuts went out of business, the whole Key West City Police Department would lose a minimum of twelve hundred pounds in two months. Doctor told me to quit. My physical, a while back, I was afraid he'd take me off booze, tell me to exercise, eat yellow peppers. He said no more Dunkin' Donuts. I can live with that. For nostalgia's sake I give myself one bag of these gut bombs a month. Doctor wants to tell me I'm cutting my life short, I'll say permission to turn right on red added time to my life. One minute here and there, they add up. Until the seventies, only California allowed right turns on red. It all balances out."

He'd arranged six doughnuts on top of the flattened bag. Any one of the six would feel like a bowling ball in my stomach five minutes after eating it. Liska motioned for me to make a selection. I picked the smallest jelly doughnut, then settled into what must have been my fifteenth retelling of the facts as I knew them: Kemp's house, the Mariel receipt, the bomb, the conversations with Raoul. I mentioned that Anselmo had been with Annie in West Palm, then dropped the bomb about Julia and Anselmo sharing an apartment many years back.

"I love getting this shit on the assistant federal prosecutor," he said. "Ever since he screwed Aghajanian, I've prayed for a way to clean his clock."

"That wheel goes around," I said. "I'm not into broadcasting philosophy, but sooner or later everybody's got to pay their own tab."

"That's what keeps me from getting discouraged about my job," he said. "Year after year. A lot of people can't help themselves. A lot of other people help themselves to whatever's not attached. That old theory about the sharks and manatees? Manatees are forever endangered. I'm here to hold back sharks."

"Anselmo's in the latter category?"

"Anselmo's hogging the latter category."

The cellular phone buzzed. Liska pulled it from inside his coat, bit into a huge sugar-glazed bomber and didn't try to finish his mouthful. "Yes. Oh, shit. Oh, shit." White sugar sprayed the leisure suit. "Okay. I'll be right there." He clicked off the phone and turned to me. "I need help, bubba. You got a piece?"

"We have to shoot people?"

"Avery's locked himself in his garage. He's been a loose goose the last few days. My ex thinks he's got a shotgun in there."

I stepped inside, went for my camera bag, but thought again. This was not the occasion for news photos. I also decided to leave the Walther in the bookcase. In spite of Bob Bernier's warning, I hadn't had a chance to move it. I sure as hell didn't want to shoot a Monroe County Sheriff's Department detective.

Liska already had the car started and turned toward the top of the lane. The right-side door hung open. I fell into the passenger seat. The interior was hot as a furnace. The Taurus lurched onto Fleming.

Liska hit the siren and fumbled under the seat. He pulled out a fist-sized blue light connected to a long cord. "We haven't got time to stick this fucker on the roof. Hold it in your hand, high."

I groped for the shoulder harness, trying to shield my eyes from the blue strobe. We snaked down White Street, using both sides of the road. Twice Liska sideswiped parked cars. Near Olivia he had to slam the brakes for a bicyclist in a bathing suit whose earphones had kept him from hearing our approach. I don't know how we made it through the red light at Truman without a multiple-car pileup. The light at United was a snap. Liska raced out Washington, blew the stop sign at Tropical. He shut down the siren.

"This fucking island," he said. He turned on one of the streets before the dogleg at George, cut across Flagler, turned east on a side street, then pulled over and parked against traffic in front of a plain stucco-walled house. Two, perhaps three bed-rooms. Chain-link fencing. Real shutters on hinges. A short driveway led to a single-car garage. "It used to be mine," he said. "Smelly old carpeting. Worn-out sunporch. Now it's Avery Hatch's. The fucker dies, I get the mortgage back. Along with her."

Mrs. Hatch—the ex-Mrs. Liska—stood inside the aluminum-screen front door. Face drawn, hair askew, skin pasty, as if her blood had drained out a hole in her foot. Her hands were balled up into little white rocks. Panic sparked her pale blue eyes. "God help us, Fred . . ."

I hadn't heard Liska's real first name since a municipal court case long ago.

Liska peered over her shoulder into the house. "He's still in the garage?"

"He started the car. It's still running."

He reached inside the door, took his ex-wife by the upper arm, and tugged her outside. "Gayle, it's gonna be all right. You go by Mrs. Sweeting's and stay put. Stay inside."

Mrs. Hatch ran across the street, crossing her arms to support her ample breasts. Liska beckoned for me to follow him back to the Taurus.

"The County's Intervention Team?" I asked.

Liska flung open the driver's-side door and shook his head. "It'd destroy his career. He'd lose his job and he'd be just as dead as pulling the trigger." He reached into the glove box and snatched a remote garage-door opener. "I meant to drop this off someday." Then he pulled a pair of portable two-way radios out from under the front seat. "These cheap-ass walkie-talkies do the job when you need 'em." He flipped them on and keyed each, listening for static in the other. "They're on Channel Eight," he said. "Press this button to talk. We get interference, switch to Channel Five. But Eight ought to work okay."

I clicked the buttons to make sure I knew how to operate it.

Liska looked at his watch. "Go behind the house to the circuit-breaker box. In a couple minutes I'll say the word 'check.' You hear me, you cut the master switch. I don't want dueling door controls. I want that damned garage to stay open. Then come around front. Stay away from the door. You hear his shotgun, I'm a dead man. Get your ass out of here and call 911. Other than that, just wait."

I stood in direct sunlight next to a shaded Florida room. Dark green lizards ran the screening, looking for lunch. The central air conditioner came on with a loud electrical thud. The place was identical to all the other cement-block homes that were built north of Atlantic and west of Bertha in the late 1960s. Most had carports and basic trimmed shrubs, though a few had become overgrown. The neighborhood was one of the last strongholds for older Conch families. Security fences and "Bad Dog" signs had gone up in the 1980s.

The radio crackled. Liska's voice: "Check, check."

I snapped the master circuit breaker. The whole world went quiet as the A/C compressor spun down to a stop. I jogged to the garage side of the house, suddenly wondering if Chicken Neck wanted to calm Hatch or wished to rile him further.

Liska's voice on the radio: "I could use some help in here."

Was he injured? Would showing my face at the open garage door invite a shotgun blast? I could not hear the car running.

Liska again on the walkie-talkie, calmly: "Rutledge, come here a minute."

I wished for the Walther, stooped low, and stuck my head around the corner. They were on the far side of Hatch's Buick sedan, Liska standing, Hatch in the car. A pump-action shotgun lay on the garage floor behind the rear wheel. An access hole in the ceiling explained Liska's entry into the garage. He'd crawled into the attic through a trapdoor in another part of the house.

"Please put that in the backseat of my car." Liska pointed at the gun. His voice was mellow, his choice of words easygoing. "Then come on back because Avery needs another friend to talk to. And please bring me my telephone."

I felt supremely antisocial ambling through a quiet residential area at 10 A.M. on a Tuesday carrying a loaded shotgun. The only neighbor in view was Mrs. Sweeting. Her front door was cracked an inch, her face in the opening. I placed the weapon on the rear floor of the Taurus, took Liska's keys from the ignition, grabbed the phone, locked the car, and walked back to the garage.

Something about the Buick tweaked a vague memory. The lavender leisure-suit jacket lay on the car's roof. A pistol had replaced Liska's cellular phone in the exposed holster. I hadn't seen him make the switch.

Avery Hatch was in dress trousers, an undershirt, and bedroom slippers. His hair was disheveled. A faded anchor tattoo decorated his upper arm. Liska had wound a garden hose around him to keep his forearms down and his legs together. An impromptu straitjacket, but Hatch didn't mind. His powerful shoulders slumped in defeat. Sweat poured from him, with a foul odor to match. I had seen men like this in the Navy, men who had been running on adrenaline and whose adrenaline had run out. They'd been men who had welcomed their disorientation, their mental escape, however temporary.

"So where are we on this, Avery?" said Liska. "How do you see it?"

"Oh, man. I don't know. I told him about the Stock Island murder." Hatch's voice a monotone, depleted of emotion. His eyes darted toward me and away.

"You told him. Okay. Who is 'him'?"

"Ray Kemp. Whatever his name is now. It's all my goddamned fault."

"What do you mean, told him about it?"

"I described it, the Sally Guthery murder scene, the knots, the rope. He got all entranced by the details. I guess he copied them . . . But all he wanted with the lawyer lady was sex."

Liska patted Hatch on the knee. "You're getting ahead of me, Avery."

"He wanted to pork the girlfriend, the lawyer."

Liska looked behind himself, found two folded yard chairs, and handed them to me to open up. "Why did he want to do that, Avery?"

"Good clean fun. That's what he told me. Just to get even."

"Even for . . . ?" Chicken Neck sat down.

"For starters, the man stole his woman. Made a fool of him."

Liska looked up at me, then back to Hatch. "So his way to get even was to have sex with Miss Minnette?"

Hatch nodded.

"And he believed that Rutledge here stole away Julia Balbuena?"

Hatch looked up at me. He started to nod, but said, "No . . . No . . . Rutledge saved Kemp's life. That dickhead federal prosecutor's the one. Anselmo. He took up with Julia up in Miami after she split with Kemp. Somehow she got Anselmo to cut Ray a Witness Protection deal for a quarter million cash. A year later Ray got popped on another Fed beef, under his new name, right in Miami where he wasn't supposed to be anymore. That time Anselmo sent him to the slammer. No way out of that one. They both had to keep quiet about the other fix."

Puzzle pieces dropped into place. The Anselmo/Julia link confirmed. *Two* busts. The threatening postcards.

Liska leaned closer to me, holding a handkerchief to his forehead. "This is flying at me too fast. You saved Kemp's life?"

"Mariel." I sat in the chair next to Liska. "I saved my own life, along with some people who didn't deserve to die. Kemp just happened to be aboard at the time. The boat he bought from Avery. He didn't seem grateful at the time."

I figured out the Buick. Sam had noticed a late-model GM car parked near Mary Alice Noe's house.

"So, Avery," said Liska. "You're talking Kemp didn't kill Sally Ann."

"We know the shrimper who did her, but we ain't caught him. Previous manslaughter in Port Arthur, Texas. Asshole left prints on empty beer bottles in Sally Ann's trash."

Liska sat back in the chair. "Now I'm confused, Avery. You're saying Ray Kemp didn't kill Sally Ann Guthery, and all he wanted was sex with Annie Minnette?"

"That's it. No murders."

I caught another waft. Concentrated locker room.

"How did he know who Annie was?"

Hatch rolled his eyes and wheezed his lungs empty of air. "He had me over a barrel. He wanted to know did Anselmo have a lady friend. I went and found out he was seeing the Minnette woman. I described her. I described her car. I told him where she worked, where she lived."

"Why did you do that?"

"He threatened to blow me out of the department. Also I owed him for saving my ass. Those Colombians were going to cut me up. He pulled me out of that one, way back then. But he didn't say he'd kill her. He was just going to . . . He didn't say he'd attack the wrong woman."

Liska's voice became sympathetic. "Why were the Colombians mad at you, Avery?"

"That load I took near Cay Sal Banks? I got scared. I pushed the pot over the side."

"Was Ray Kemp on the boat with you?" Liska acted as if this kind of news came his way all the time.

"He was on the dock with Billy. They set it up. I heard the Coast Guard on the radio. I got scared, I dumped the load. It was my fault."

"Billy Fernandez?"

Hatch nodded yes. I thought: Confirmed. Billy Fernandez knew Julia.

"When was this, Avery?"

"In '79. Nineteen seventy-nine. I got scared."

"What did the Colombians want?"

Hatch weaved and fiddled with his short, fat fingers. "Half the value of the load. Kemp bought my boat so I could pay them. He saved my ass. But, damn it, I didn't know he was going to kill any girls. I just didn't know."

Liska sat back and looked at me. He tilted his head toward Hatch, offering me the chance to throw him some questions.

"Ellen Albury was killed by mistake," I said.

Hatch nodded yes.

"So Ray tried to blow up Annie Minnette's car?"

Hatch's eyes began to water. "Yeah . . . before I could tell him she was really your lady and not Anselmo's. Look, he threatened to rat me out. He's . . . Aw, shit . . ." Tears fell down his face.

I gave him a moment. "Where did Ray keep his gear from *Barracuda?*"

"Wagner's Sheds on Summerland. All this time I paid the rent. He kept everything he owned in there. The other day I went in there just to check it out for rats and leaks . . . It was cleaned out. Except for some scraps of plastic, like the stuff he wrapped around the Balbuena girl."

Was Avery blaming Kemp to cover for Billy Fernandez? Maybe Billy hadn't tried to kill me after all. "Do you know why Kemp killed Julia?" I said.

Hatch shrugged. "He didn't tell me he wanted to murder anybody. I think she had something to do with his second arrest. He went up for fifteen years. He learned a lot in jail. Now he's out, he kills people."

"How does Kemp figure into Mary Alice Noe?" I said.

Hatch winced, shook his head and shivered. "It was Billy. He couldn't take it when Mary Alice fell in love with Anselmo.

She sent Billy away. But then, you know, Anselmo found your lawyer lady, so he dropped Mary Alice. Billy heard about it, he wanted back in. I knew he'd killed her the minute we walked in that bedroom. I couldn't say shit." More tears rolled down Hatch's cheeks. "I'm in so fucking deep. I can't do anything. Fucking Ray Kemp kills Ellen Albury because he thought she was Anselmo's girlfriend. He copies the Stock Island knots and rope. I know he killed Julia. That same rope was in the shed. Then the bomb goes off before I can tell him to back off the Minnette girl. Fernandez copies the knots and rope when he goes bonkers with the Noe girl. I can't arrest either one because they both know about the pot runs. I can't do my job without losing my job. Picture me in jail. I'd last two days. I'd be queen of the cornholes. I'd have razor marks on me like a road map. I can't do nothin', I can't think straight . . ."

The late-model GM car had been Billy's Olds Cutlass. The pieces fit.

Hatch began to struggle against the garden hose. Liska gave me a wave, indicating that I should back off. He gave Hatch a moment or two to realize he couldn't get loose, then his voice returned to soothing tones. "Avery, why did you go to Rutledge's house to ask about Julia?"

"I had to find out who knew about the old days. My God, the shit was stacking up and I was sinking. I didn't know he'd kill them. I sure didn't want to take his fall. I wanted to lead people to him, so someone else could make the bust and I wouldn't take the blame for that, either. If I busted him, he'd still blow the whistle . . ."

"Did you know that Ray Kemp would hurt anybody?"

"No."

"Do you know where Billy is?"

"No."

"Do you want to die?"

Avery Hatch closed his eyes, took three deep breaths,

opened them, and looked me in the eye. He looked at Liska. He shook his head.

"When's the last time you ate a decent meal?"

"Days."

"When's the last time you had decent sleep?"

Hatch shrugged and shook his head.

"You want to know what I think?"

Hatch stared at him, a flicker of fear in his eyes.

"I think you're one of the best detectives in the state of Florida. I wish you'd stay the hell out of our city business, but out in the county you're great."

Hatch's eyes rolled up toward the ceiling.

Liska activated his cellular phone and punched in a number. "You start delivering yet?" He paused. "One-eight-zero-three Laird. H-A-T-C-H. A large pepperoni-and-green-pepper with double cheese. Two six-packs of Cokes . . . I don't give a fuck if they're Pepsis. How long?"

Liska clicked off the phone, reached for his wallet, extracted a twenty. "Here's the deal, Avery. I'll buy if you'll eat pizza until you can't eat no more. Then you go to bed until you can't sleep no more. You want this fucking rubber hose off you?"

Hatch looked at me oddly and said, "What the fuck happened to your tooth?"

I couldn't help thinking: If Avery Hatch had pointed Kemp to Ellen Albury, mistaken identity or not, he was an accessory to murder. He should have been arrested.

For the moment, I deferred to Liska's judgment.

29

We'd advised Gayle Hatch to remain with her neighbor, Mrs. Sweeting, and we'd locked Hatch's shotgun in the trunk of the Taurus. As Liska drove over the Garrison Bight Bridge, he said, "For now, that was between us and Avery. You gotta understand, when crazy shit happens, people go crazy."

"What'll we do about Billy Fernandez?" I said.

"The key word is 'we.' From here on out, everything in this case is between the city and the feds. No deputies allowed. 'Course, I ain't sure where you fit in, Mr. Freelance."

The Taurus's air-conditioning needed to be dropped off the bridge, fed to the fish. We passed Grinnell Street, the turnoff to my house.

Liska said, "Need to be home for anything?"

"Brush my teeth."

"You smell great. You smell better than my husband-in-law. Ten years of cigar residue come out his armpits. You damn sure smell good enough for the courthouse."

A social call on Anselmo? "You want me along?"

"Not who you think. He's in court anyway until eleven forty-five. I need to visit that two-shoes from the Bureau, to get more ammo so I can bring Michael Anselmo down hard, for keeps."

Traffic was slow on Eaton. Simonton's traffic had backed up

from the light at Caroline. A Conch Train full of tourists was caught between two low-rider pickups with stereos thudding Richter-scale bass tones. The train's PA system fought rap at one end, reggae at the other. Liska cut over the curbing and took a slot reserved for a federal judge.

The Federal Courthouse guard acknowledged the badge flash and waved Chicken Neck around the metal detector. One look and he pointed me through the arch. We found Bernier in a cubbyhole second-floor office filled with law books and journals. He wore a pin-striped short-sleeve shirt with dark slacks. His tie was embroidered with pink conch shells. Newspaper clips detailing arrests filled a bulletin board near the door. Bernier remarked on my appearance, then got down to business. "It's a good thing you and Sam didn't root around much more up in Georgia."

"Ka-boom?" said Liska.

Bernier nodded. "Homemade Claymores full of nuts and bolts and roofing nails. Much worse than the one you tripped. They found eight snuff movies in an ammo box. A hundred and seven thousand dollars in thermos bottles buried in the chicken coops. We still haven't found the pickup truck. We're assuming he's in it. We're also assuming he's come back to South Florida."

"No sign of the Mercedes?" I said.

"By the time we got on it, once it hit Palm Beach County, there are so many cars like that. Turns out the Witness Protection file had been checked out by mistake. Some bank-fraud investigator had it. A Cuban guy. Thirty-year man. Honest mistake."

About as honest as an Uzi at an ATM. Raoul Balbuena blackmailing thirty-year bank fraud investigators in addition to other activities.

"They also found a box of manuscripts. A friend from my early days in the Kansas City office was on the crisis team up there in Georgia. He called me about them. Short stories, by the same person on the same typewriter, with six or seven pseudonyms. They're about men who've been degraded, belittled by authority figures, who get revenge mainly through murder. Ray Kemp has quite the creative mind."

Liska exhaled a long breath and sat down in a wooden armchair. The air system in the courthouse wasn't much better than the squad car's.

Bernier checked a notepad. "One story had a kid badgered by alcoholic parents. It wasn't physical abuse, but the mental stuff was perverted, competitive, mean—you name it. His father made fun of him when he had a hard time learning to swim. His mother called him a jerk in front of his junior high playmates. Another was about a high school football player who was browbeaten by an aggressive coach. After an error in an important game, the coach berated him on the team bus in front of the team and the cheerleaders."

"The grief a million kids go through every year," I said.

Bernier nodded. "Except this part is different. Ray Kemp's parents were killed during a home robbery in 1975. Beaten up and slashed with broken beer bottles. His high school football coach in North Tonawanda, New York, was found murdered in 1976, trussed up with Ace bandages, strangled to death with a jockstrap. We've begun to track Kemp's movements over the years through the author pseudonyms. See if he's evened the score on any more family members or friends. Looks like he flew under the radar in respect to our criminal profiles."

"So Anselmo put a psychopath into Witness Protection?" I said.

Bernier nodded. "On Thursday Anselmo will visit Internal Revenue Hell. The agents claim they aren't pushing lifestyle investigations, but this case will lift the lid off anything he's been covering up. Marnie Dunwoody's digging into that old real estate transaction helped. It sure didn't correlate to his claimed income. If he was peddling Witness Protection, it'll get real obvious real fast."

"Put him into the DBA Club," said Liska.

Bernier gave him a puzzled look.

"Dis-Barred Attorneys. There are dozens in Florida—arrested, convicted, and done their time. Now they're the highest-paid paralegals in America."

I wanted to know if Hatch's story matched up. "Does the Bureau agree that Kemp couldn't have killed Mary Alice Noe?"

Bernier settled back in his chair. "I wasn't around then, but I recently heard a story." He turned to Chicken Neck. "You remember a local situation called the Jacuzzi Murders?"

Liska lit up. "City case. I worked it behind Eddie Brown. Nasty case, years ago. I'd been a detective three days when it started."

I remembered reading about it. I couldn't recall details. Something about women being found drowned in hot tubs, screwed up on bourbon and cocaine.

"You remember an Ivy League dropout confessed?" said Bernier. "Some upper-middle-class guy in his twenties from Connecticut?"

"He confessed to the first two murders," said Liska. "He stood fast on denying the third. We couldn't package the deal, so it's still open. Shit, we were lucky to catch him and solve the first two. Found the kid drunk in his car at Mallory Square."

Bernier sat back. "Larry Riley knew the young man couldn't have done the third one. Some kind of scientific mismatch."

"Right," said Chicken Neck. "The prosecutor waffled. We couldn't close the case."

"Riley also had a suspect. But Riley was new on the job, like you."

Liska flinched. "Did he suspect a cop? Is that where this is going?"

"What made you think that?"

Liska considered his answer. "Local gossip."

"Concerning a law-enforcement officer?" said Bernier.

Now I knew why Riley had played his cards close to his chest. He didn't trust anyone in Key West except the feds.

Liska rubbed his cheeks as if checking his morning shave. "I am told by unimpeachable sources in the housewives' telegraph that Mary Alice Noe once had a relationship with Billy Fernandez. At the Noe crime scene, Billy was not his usual lazy-slob self. He was inspection-perfect at the crack of dawn on a Sunday. He ran around like he'd already had fifteen cafés cubanos. He showed no emotion. He never mentioned an affair."

Bernier stood and leaned against his desk. "I gotta say, you folks live in an offbeat little city."

"I think Billy got himself in a little jam on Sunday," I said.

Both men looked as if they might not tolerate a know-nothing civilian.

"Right after Sam was arrested for the Noe murder," I said, "Billy tried to screw Raoul Balbuena out of a five-thousand-dollar reward. Raoul offered it to both of us on Saturday in exchange for information. I told him I didn't want his money, but I called yesterday to tell him that Wheeler's arrest was bogus. I got the impression that Fernandez was there with him. 'Course, if Billy's innocent I may have to pay for that one down the road."

We spent a minute or so studying the inlaid marble flooring. Offices down the hall provided background music. Two or three metal file cabinet drawers slammed shut, a beeping telephone went unanswered, a dot matrix printer scratched and growled, someone coughed loudly.

"Speaking for the American taxpayer," said Bernier, "I hope that Billy Fernandez and Ray Kemp are enjoying the tender, loving care of the Balbuenas. Cut our expenses on prison and courtroom time. Speaking as an enforcement professional, we should assume that Ray Kemp is loose and has more nastiness on his agenda. Finding him is the toughie. Fernandez'll be easy. He probably still thinks he's got us all fooled."

"And I get to take the heat." Liska stood to leave. "It won't go down as popular, me going out to the county and dragging in a sheriff's detective for questioning."

"We'll look into nailing him on a civil-rights complaint," said Bernier.

I thought of one more thing. "Bob, did you check the phone company records on that call into Kemp's house?"

Bernier frowned. "Pay phone in Athens."

Had Kemp laid the trap for Carlos and Emilio, or was it the other way around?

Liska and I walked to the courthouse parking lot. A tearful young woman sat on the Simonton Street curb nursing a skinned knee. A blue moped lay in the gutter, its handlebars cocked at a sharp angle. Liska turned away when he saw a police car approach.

"Liska!"

Bernier stood on the courthouse steps, a white-shirt beacon in the sunlight, ignoring the police activity around the injured woman at the curb. He waved us into the shade of the portico.

"Problem?" said Chicken Neck.

"That five-thousand-dollar reward? Fernandez collected." Bernier's voice dropped a level. "You know how certain faiths of Caribbean persuasion believe that animal sacrifices invoke the gods of judicial leniency? The carcass-retrieval team found Billy's body two hours ago in Miami. Dumped on a loading platform behind the Federal Court House. Tossed in there with the dead black chickens and slaughtered goats."

Liska winced. "Jesus Christ."

Bernier continued, "His heart had been removed. The operation was clean, like a surgeon did the job. They stuffed five grand in twenty-dollar bills into the cavity."

Fernandez had warned me about "Ogunito." I described Billy's rundown of bad-boy Carlos and Emilio, worshiper of sharp edges. "Are we the first people on the island to hear this?" I added.

Bernier looked offended. "I was the first. You two are the second."

Liska dropped me off on Fleming at the head of the lane. I found six wilted doughnuts, two unfinished coffees, and eight messages. I wanted a shower but things were happening quickly. I needed to reach Annie or Carmen. I found a legal pad, a felt-tip pen, and pulled up a chair.

The first two calls were for Annie. Mrs. Embry, still looking for that bike, and a client looking for some paperwork. Sears wanted to sell me top-of-the-line aluminum siding. Duffy Lee Hall had an OM-2 and two lenses for sale. Laura Tate said to come by the Packet Inn for a drink later in the week. The police needed photographs of vandalism at their K-9 Training Center. Another business message for Annie. The final one was from Marnie. I called her back.

"Bernier gave me the green light on some of the stuff we talked about the other night," she said. "So I rang that state representative who tried to buy me away from bothering Anselmo."

"You lay out the skinny on the payoffs?"

"Laid the skinny on thick, if you can do that. About his granting Witness Protection to a noninformant, the possible payoffs, his meddling in Florida Department of Law Enforcement board activities. Plus, Sam told me about Anselmo's trip to West Palm. That means the taxpayer paid for his clandestine rendezvous with a lady friend. 'Course, it's your lady friend."

"Her status is under review."

"Good. Anyway, this political toe dancer backpedaled ninety miles an hour. Changed his tune big-time, and said he'd personally look into the Aghajanian decertification case. He would also petition the governor to reconvene the Board of Training and Professional Standards to initiate reinstatement proceedings. He said he'd report back to me on a daily basis until the entire matter was cleared up to the satisfaction of the voting and taxpaying public."

"Sounds like a load of shit."

"Loads of shit are what these people deal in. I've been rolling in it, secondhand, for years. This is a good sign, believe me. You got lunch plans?"

"I've got a date with a bar of Pure and Natural. After that I'm a free man."

"Monty says he's buying. An early celebration of getting his badge back. No matter what he says, Sam and I are picking up the tab. But I don't know where we're going. We'll come by and get you."

"Call Bob Bernier first. Billy Fernandez was found dead this morning. Off the record, there's a chance he killed Mary Alice Noe."

"Oh, God. What is happening in this little town of ours?"

"His body was found in Miami. My guess is the Balbuenas."

"We're selling so many newspapers, we had to delay printing three of the contract weeklies. People are scared to leave their homes. Even the grocery stores are losing business. Now this."

"Maybe this will be the end of the storm."

"I hope so. Take your time in the shower. It may take a while for me to file this story. After that we'll all take the rest of the afternoon off. I promise."

30

Shower time. Bernier's people had not fixed my hot-water heater. Lucky to be in Key West. The cold spigot was warm enough to make a production of it. A moral dilution obvious: I suspected that an FBI agent had swiped my shampoo.

Someone once wrote a tongue-in-cheek song about playing the field in the singles scene: waking in sundry apartments, not looking for the ideal mate, but in search of the perfect shampoo. The world turned on surplus and scarcity. Some people had buckets of shampoo and no mangoes. I was out of shampoo in a yard with a tree. Some people have too many lovers. I had been accused. I kept thinking about Chicken Neck and Avery Hatch fighting over their wife. I tried not to think about Michael Anselmo, the four-for-four, wide-swath cocksman.

I had fashioned a drainage system from PVC pipe that funneled runoff to the bougainvillea and fruit tree. I'd hung a spring-hinged door and lined the stall with teakwood hooks for loofah sponges and shelves and soap caddies, plus a fancy mirror. There was room for two, standing up or sitting on the slat bench. For a while, stereo speakers had hung under the eaves. But there was no way to change tapes during a shower if the music failed to match or improve my mood. The speaker cones had rotted in the island humidity and I'd tossed them. I could sing in the shower if I needed music, my own bluesy opera under the open sky.

I bobbed around in my redwood cubicle as a breeze rattled surrounding treetops. I tested pattern and angle of spray, did the conditioner, lathered the body scrub as sunlight stabbed through high fronds and the mango tree's lower limbs, watched fuzzy shadows dance the rear wall of the house, dared invisible mosquitoes to dive-bomb exposed skin. A long rinse. Birds flew overhead. A line of slender cumulus clouds to the north, a twin-prop plane on eastbound final to the airport. When I got a chance I wanted to sit and think about the strange and sudden tragedies of this town, to ponder reasons for all of its lunacy. To answer nagging questions about logic and timing and motives.

If Avery's convoluted tale was accurate, for instance, and if Ray Kemp had structured his revenge scenarios to match affronts, as his pseudonymous short stories suggested, why had Kemp killed Julia in the style of *Twin Peaks*? For that matter, why had he killed her at all? Why hadn't he killed Michael Anselmo, strangled him with a bra, or beaten him to death with a forty-pound law book?

Why hadn't Anselmo done anything to protect himself after he'd received the cryptic postcards? I had warned Annie about Kemp, so Anselmo must have learned through Annie the source of those threats.

Why had Billy Fernandez, a former smuggler who'd covered his tracks with a law-enforcement career, a man with a kid in the Little League, arranged to have me crushed by a dump truck on U.S. 1? All he stood to do was beat me out of five thousand dollars. With his knowledge of Palguta and Carlos, their violent ways, why would he try to scam Raoul for a measly five grand? Why would he go for small potatoes? Why would he dare scam Raoul at all? Or did he have some other knowledge that might be worth bigger money?

Why, for another half-assed instance, was Avery Hatch not

around when Sam Wheeler was being detained in the Monroe County jail? Why, suddenly, did he have to check out that storage shed? Unless he wanted to make sure that all that gear in the shed was finally gone. Unless he just wanted to get away from the action back at the jail.

Why had it taken me three years to realize that Annie's refreshing beacon of honesty came equipped with a dimmer switch?

One thing about a cold shower, the water doesn't get any colder. A bird I couldn't identify warbled in one of the taller trees. A cloud floated under the sun. On a cool draft under the cloud I caught a whiff of something sweet, nonfloral, like one of Liska's vintage discotheque colognes. I've never been able to identify scents, but a name drifted in with this odor. Why did the men who used Brut always wear too much?

Like a bad tune on the stereo speakers, the heavy smell yanked me out of my mood.

I turned off the shower, toweled my hair, and wrapped the towel around my waist. The shower had delivered its therapeutic relief. I checked the faucets to make sure they didn't drip, stuck my toes into the rubber sandals and pushed open the shower-stall door. Carlos Balbuena was sitting in the yard pointing a gun at my chest.

I was about to die in my flip-flops.

Balbuena's neck remained nonexistent. His dark face was relaxed but his eyes were focused, sharp as ice picks, ready to witness my death. He'd started a beard. A small gold ring hung from each earlobe. A Polo logo on his shirt.

"I don't get it," I said.

He didn't care. "Get it, worm. You the smart one, we the dumb ones." With each sentence he lifted his head, poked out his chin. The universal badass.

"I did your father two favors last night."

"You so dumb to think Raoul might eat that bullshit about

some other man there in Georgia to see me and Emilio. But that man got no name. You say that shit to protect your ass. We hear that ten million times."

The neighbor's spaniel whimpered through the fence. Something—a lizard or a palmetto bug—crawled across my right foot. I didn't dare look down, away from Balbuena's icy hard gaze. Keeping Carlos locked eye-to-eye prolonged his bragging session, prolonged my life.

"I've had twenty-four hours to tell a lot of people about it."

"Right. That's how a story work. But not how it work in trial and with the testimonies. You not there in that court, bubba, they got no evidence. Zip shit. No witness, no conviction. Right? Who's smart, bubba? Who's dumb now?"

He was right. Brains don't mean shit without evidence. I had no leverage. My mind shot off on eddy currents, thinking how Annie might not grieve, how no one would understand the value of my Shelby. Sam had found a good woman. Monty would get his job with the FBI. Laura Tate was a missed opportunity. I'll take a rain check in heaven. If I thought about those nipples I'd lose my focus on talking Carlos out of this.

"We know you hungry for the five K that other boy tried to fuck us on."

"He got it straight through the heart."

"Ahh. That's another case, bubba. No proof, with you gone away."

The mango tree hovered over us. In periphery I saw everything in the yard. Under the expensive new tarp, my toys, the Kawasaki and the Cannondale. Long spears of midday sunlight painted the patchy grass. My own world, a long way from facing down a Kalashnikov and wrestling a Gulf of Mexico nor'wester. I couldn't vouch for fun in either episode. The Mariel Boatlift was forty percent of my life ago. Nothing was different. I would leave thousands of slides with no copyright stamps. My legacy would become public domain. Fat ladies sang of a shampoo shortage in the mango opera.

I groped for a way to reach him. I heard my phone ring. "Your sister knew I was a friend."

He lifted the gun a fraction of an inch. "All this Key West bullshit kill that pretty little girl. You just as bad as that cuckoo man with the phony name that twisted her neck . . ."

"So it was Kemp who killed her?"

"That coward cry because we show him what happen to worms."

"You punched his ticket?" The phone rang again.

Carlos grinned as if recalling a dirty joke. "Fuckhead having trouble walking. I'm hungry for my fuckin' lunch. I gotta go." His eyes had not lost their evil glint. Carlos leveled the gun, pointing it at my nose. The tendons in his forearm bulged, his fingers moved, clenched the pistol grip, settling their alignment for the squeeze. Any emotion he might have possessed fled his expression. He had expelled me from humanity, turned me into a cardboard target. I waited for my life to flash before me, waited for my lights to go out. All I got was an intense view of the backyard. Time slowed. A third ring from the phone. The machine would get it next time. The sun glistened on individual leaves behind the man. Wind in one shrub, then another. Why wouldn't the dog bark, just once? Why was I lost for anything to say, anything to prolong the talking, to add an extra minute to my life, an extra thirty seconds? Suddenly I got a brainstorm about the identity of the murderer. No use now. The fourth ring cut short by the machine.

The gun went off.

The whole right side of his head went away. Charlie Balls Balbuena tipped sideways, looking puzzled by where his life had gone. He rolled into the sandy grass, shaking the gun as if it were stuck to his hand, hot as the blazing sun. A small hole next to his left ear dribbled blood. I felt cold, out of breath.

Monty Aghajanian crouched in the shadows alongside the screened porch, the satin black Walther firm in his hand. He slumped forward and squeezed his forehead with his other hand, then jumped up and ran toward Carlos with the weapon extended. He kicked the pistol out of the man's lifeless grip and leaned down to confirm that he was dead.

"Thanks for leaving this in your bookcase." Monty laid the Walther on a plastic table.

"Did you have to make it so dramatic?"

"I barely had time to plant my feet."

Someone would have been listening to my voice on the answering tape the instant I died.

31

My life had not flashed before my eyes. No reruns, no grim reminders, no highlights of yesteryear. I sat on a cobwebbed redwood chair under the mango tree with the towel around me, wondering about the parameters of luck. In the past three days I had dodged a bomb and a bullet. I wasn't given much time to be introspective. City police swarmed into my yard. Two accusatory officers I didn't recognize started to order me around. Monty backed them off with some departmental mumbo-jumbo. I went inside to get dressed.

Marnie was on the phone to her office. "Look," I heard her say, "if you won't bump down the dogcatcher story for this, Russell, I'll file my piece with the fucking *Miami Herald*. Don't think I won't, you kiss-ass dipshit."

Sam sat in the front room, pensive and distant, an arm's length from the window fan though sweat drenched his denim shirt. He nibbled hangnails and stared at a magazine. The police had blocked Dredgers Lane to traffic. Bright yellow crime-scene ribbon snapped in the wind like party decorations. The flat-toned speakers of two-way radios broadcast constant chatter. All the activity prompted indignant barking from the neighbor's dog.

Cootie Ortega arrived and unpacked a bag of dirty cameras. I offered a packet of lens-cleaning paper and let him do his thing. Larry Riley's team from the Monroe County ME's office arrived in two white Cherokees and a van. An EMS vehicle bore a bumper sticker: HAVE YOU FLOGGED YOUR CREW TODAY?

Marnie went out to get statements from Riley and the neighbors. Hector Ayusa ambled across the lane to make sure everything was okay. He lifted his guayabera shirt to show us the pistol stuck in his belt, to assure us that he could handle any aftershocks. Sam hurried Hector back over to his house.

"Weird," said Monty. "All this revenge and no arrests."

"Only paybacks," I said. "How'd you know Carlos was about to send me to Happy Hour?"

"I had to drop some papers at Nathan Eden's office, so we came up Eaton instead of Fleming. When Marnie turned onto Grinnell, Sam noticed Dade plates and gold hubcaps on a green Mercedes parked by the Paradise Cafe. A man was in the car. Sam guessed the other guy was headed for your house. Marnie made the light at Fleming and turned left, out of sight of the Benz. I sprinted up Fleming and Sam ran back to the pay phone in front of Cobo's."

The ringing telephone.

"How'd you find us in the yard?" I said.

"I sneaked onto the porch and heard his voice out back. I almost couldn't remember the name of that book that Bernier said was in front of the gun."

"Legends of the Fall."

"I remembered."

"Did Emilio get away?"

Sam opened the porch door and cracked a grin. "Marnie made the ultimate sacrifice. I was on the phone at Cobo's when I heard the gunshot. The boy in the Mercedes heard it too. He cranked up his car and floored it up Grinnell, ran the light and hooked a left onto Fleming. Marnie timed it perfectly. She whipped her Jeep away from the curb and crashed the Benz on the left front wheel and the driver's door. She played it like she didn't know who he was. She got out and acted hurt and stumbled around. I'm running up from Cobo's, the bad guy scoots out the passenger side of the Mercedes with a big nasty gun in his hand. She's leaning over, whimpering, holding her ankle. Next thing you know, she karate-kicks his Adam's apple. Out went his lights, just like that. Whammo."

"I believe you've got a keeper, Sam," I said.

"Superwoman. I'm in love."

"Where's Emilio now?" said Monty.

Sam laughed. "We grabbed his keys and stuffed him in his trunk. It smelled like puke and piss in there. Kemp must've had a nasty ride. I looked down the lane a minute ago. Emilio's in the backseat of a cruiser, bunch of kids standing around sticking their tongues out at him."

Monty asked to borrow my micro-cassette recorder. His civilian permit to carry a weapon would get him off the legal hook on the shooting, but the department would require a statement. Why spend an hour, he said, pounding the computer? Or two hours writing a police "white paper" in longhand? He walked into the bedroom and closed the door.

Sam went back to his chair by the fan.

As I put away the clean dishes that Bernier's team had left in the sink rack, I watched the yard through the kitchen window. Every uniformed city cop wore a mustache. Someone had appropriated the tarp from my Kawasaki to cover Balbuena's body. As if the city couldn't afford their own body blankets. To hell with it, I thought. A small price for being alive. It wasn't as if I couldn't hose off the stains. I'd have all day tomorrow to put my world back into kilter. All week next week. All year long. I could buy a replacement tarp. Carlos couldn't.

I felt no desire to call West Palm Beach to tell Annie what had happened. Judging by Carlos Balbuena's comment about having taught Kemp a lesson, I figured Annie was out of danger from that direction. If we could believe Avery, Anselmo

275

never had been a threat. She could read about it in the newspaper, or watch TV. Still, in all the confusion, something didn't ring right. I felt convinced that Kemp had killed Ellen and Julia, and had planted the bomb in Annie's VW. That much was clear. But I couldn't shake the feeling that a piece was missing from the puzzle. I tried to recall what had occurred to me just as Carlos was pulling his trigger. I didn't know what it was or where it went.

Carmen stuck her head in the front door, her face a funereal grimace. "My mother called me at work. That Cuban boy tried to kill you?"

"He was deep in the process of killing me."

Carmen gave me a hug. It lasted long enough to let me know that I needed it. "Monty had to shoot him?" she said.

"Monty found out this morning that he's probably going to get his badge back," I said. "I don't think he wanted to celebrate like this."

"This is probably old news," said Carmen in a quieter tone. "And I'm sorry I waited to tell you, but I talked to Larry Riley the other day like you asked me to. He said, quote, 'Your friend's on the right track.'"

The place was turning into Grand Central Station. Bob Bernier barged in with his all-purpose black FBI briefcase. "We found Kemp in Marathon," he said, out of breath. "Fishermen's Hospital, intensive care. A beachcomber found him at the south end of the Bahia Honda Bridge, right where they found Julia's body. He was wrapped in plastic. They castrated him. He almost bled to death."

"Good God," said Marnie.

"Good," said Carmen.

Emilio's scalpels had gone to war.

Monty came out of the bedroom. "Paybacks."

"I hope he makes it," said Sam. "Anglo castrati get all kinds of preferential treatment in prison."

"They think he'll pull through," said Bernier.

"Good," said Carmen.

"By the way," I said to Bob Bernier, "Carlos bragged on two things while he was waiting to pull the trigger. He implicated Palguta in Billy's death, and he knew for certain that Kemp had killed Julia. I don't know how he knew it . . ."

"Maybe Ray admitted it after they cut off the first nut," said Sam.

I needed to make a call. I ducked into the bedroom. As I closed the door, I caught an inquisitive look from Monty. I looked up the number and hoped that Anselmo was back in his office. Bad luck. It rang four times and a voice-mail tape grabbed the call. Shit. Leave a message or not? As the beep sounded, I heard someone pick up the receiver.

"Anselmo here."

He did not sound surprised when I identified myself.

"What can I do for you, Alex?" The perfectly modulated voice of the legal professional. As if nothing out of the ordinary had been happening for the past thirty days.

"A favor," I said. "I got dragged into the periphery of the Mary Alice Noe murder case. I don't mean to pry into your personal life, but I understand you once dated the woman."

This time he hesitated. "Okay, let's say I did."

"She ever discuss her previous gentlemen friends?"

"No. I didn't appreciate that topic of conversation. My job, every minute, every day, I deal with near-term history. I prefer to deal with the future in my friendships."

"Did you tell her that, Mr. Anselmo?"

This time a long wait. I looked out the window to the side yard. All of the uniforms were gone. Liska and Riley were talking. Chicken Neck still wore the bad-lavender trousers and purple shirt. He also wore a grim expression.

Anselmo cleared his throat. "I don't recall exactly what I told her."

"How about pictures in her house? Any where she'd been photographed with male friends?"

"Yes, one. I found it upsetting, and she discarded the damned thing."

I made a sniffing noise, then remained silent. He knew the next question without my asking. The name he gave surprised me at first, but I realized that it confirmed a deep, almost subliminal suspicion. I thanked him and hung up. Have fun with the IRS, pal. And all your future friends.

I slid open the window. "Detective Liska, you got a minute?"

I met him at the porch door and ushered him toward the bedroom. Sam, Marnie, and Carmen were out in the yard. Monty sat in the chair near the fan, staring at the Pearlcorder. I was glad that he'd saved my life. I also was glad it wasn't me who'd had to kill a man.

"What's up?" said Liska.

"I need you to call Sheriff Tucker. He won't give me straight answers."

"What am I supposed to say?"

"Ask him what time he heard about Fernandez being found dead. Ask him what time he told Avery about it."

Chicken Neck looked puzzled, then suddenly deflated. He sat on the bed and nodded, slowly recovering his swagger, as if things were adding up for him, too. "I was just talking to Riley. I brought up the Jacuzzi Murders. That boy's got some heavy secrets locked in his head."

Liska dialed a number I did not recognize. After he'd spoken with Tucker he looked worse. "Why am I a goddamned detective?" he said. "I accept Avery's shit about Mary Alice Noe. I check out the Guthery suspect. That shrimper'd lived with the woman for months. Naturally his fingerprints were all over the place. But he also had a previous manslaughter charge. I figure that part of Avery's story was legit. His Ray Kemp details made sense, too. I never would've bought the pizza . . ." He shook his head. "My ex-wife is gonna be pissed."

"You go with your gut . . ." I said. "Avery knew Billy was toast. We didn't."

"I could tell before he said good-bye, Tucker knew how big a shitstorm would hit his department. He'll blame the messenger." Liska paused, then said, "He can't fire me. I don't work for him. What made you think . . . ?"

"When Sam got picked up on Sunday, was Avery the arresting officer?"

"Yeah."

"I figured so, since Billy was in Miami trying to hustle Raoul Balbuena for five grand. So I wondered why Billy was worried more about reward money than covering his tracks for a murder. Then I wondered why Avery would arrest Sam on a total long shot, especially if he secretly knew that Billy was the killer. The detail that never locked tight was the GM sedan that Sam used to see parked by the Noe house. Billy's Oldsmobile, Avery's Buick . . . There was one too many GM sedans. Sam can't tell one GM sedan from another, but Avery didn't know that."

Liska shook his head. "He knew the charge against Wheeler wouldn't hold, but he needed him cooped up and shut up . . ."

". . . until the Noe rap had come down solidly on the late Billy Fernandez."

Liska bit his lip and punched the mattress. "A nervous breakdown. He tells the wife to call me instead of 911. He confesses to crimes too old to prosecute, tells the truth about Kemp's crazy spree, then passes off the Noe murder on his dead partner. What do you think, he went over for a piece of ass?"

I shrugged.

Liska rolled with the thought: "I'll bet he raped her to get his nut, then killed her to protect his career. My old lady is gonna be pissed."

"Avery's going to miss his cigars."

279

"Gonna miss his wife, too. We better go wake his ass up. You want to bring your cameras?"

"If you say so. Who killed Sally Ann Guthery?"

"One thing at a time," said Liska. "What the fuck happened to your face?"

32

The arrest did not turn out to be a dignified, Monday-afternoon, "Let's go now, Avery," *Murder, She Wrote* affair. It didn't come close.

Before we left my cottage, Chicken Neck phoned the duty-desk sergeant to request that two black-and-whites and an unmarked unit meet us at Flagler and White. He specifically demanded that no one use the police radio to discuss the rendezvous. Then he asked Monty Aghajanian to use his personal car, a red Geo two-door, to scope Hatch's house on Laird and meet us at Flagler and White. Bob Bernier opted not to join us, claiming lack of jurisdiction. After garnering for *The Citizen* a promise of exclusivity and first choice of any photos I might get, Marnie Dunwoody agreed to wait with Sam Wheeler two blocks from Hatch's house. She'd get a call from Liska's cellular the minute something happened.

Liska drove the Taurus down White, the same route as the lightning-bolt trip I'd survived that morning. This time the pace promised fewer dents on parked cars.

Only the two black-and-white prowl cars were waiting at Flagler.

"Shit," said Liska. He turned right and parked it. "I need a car at each end of the street and one with me. We don't fucking need to be waiting around." He got out of the Taurus, so I did, too. "Very Key West," he said, leaning his rear on the front fender. "We got too few; they'll send three more, we'll have too many."

"Like mangoes and shampoo," I said.

"What the fuck is that?" snapped Liska.

"Why am I here, anyway?"

"You had a rough day. You don't want to be here, walk back home. Take you twelve minutes."

"That answers my question?" I said.

Liska gazed down White Street, the direction from which we'd come. His profile was that of a man freshly reacquainted with good posture, and with a chip on his shoulder. The afternoon sun had begun to work on Chicken Neck's polyester. Sweat beads covered his upper lip, the furrows in his forehead. "I only had one wife in my life, Rutledge. You're the one with all the dead girlfriends."

Hardball, zipper-high. "You missed my drift."

Liska laughed and shook his head, but was not humored. "No, I didn't. You helped out, you want praise. It ain't over yet, and go back six notches, Rutledge. Contrary to common gossip, Avery Hatch didn't steal my wife. I let her slip away. You might even say I pushed her away, but she happened to slip in his direction. We never had no kids . . . no family, I don't know if I was ever in love with the woman. 'Course, I didn't foresee the outcome—that she'd wind up with a douchebag like Hatch. You think I resent it, you bet your ass I resent it. So, say I've got a personal stake in this . . ."

"Getting back to my . . ."

He turned to face me. "You got a dork ten streets away who killed a friend of yours. Then he tried to hang the beef on your buddy Sam. You want revenge? You fucking can't have it. You're in line behind me, and we can't have revenge because he's a murderer and we aren't. The best we get, which is better than most people get, is we get to push his face up next to the fan when the shit starts to fly. Mick fuckin' Jagger can't get no satisfaction. We get ours, even if it ain't of the first order. You follow?"

"Okay."

"And . . . I'll fucking say it," Liska added, "I couldn't have gotten this far without you. It'll be my bust on your sweat. Wheeler's, too, I guess."

I slapped my knee and grinned. "That's what I wanted to hear."

He gave me a disgusted look. "You bastard. You get off on this?"

I didn't, and I didn't want to carry it any farther. I dropped the smile. "I'm a photographer, also with a personal stake. You really want pictures?"

"No. I want that buddy-buddy shit that worked this morning."

The unmarked car drove up from the direction of the Casa Marina. A black-and-white behind it.

"My prediction." Liska, disgusted.

Monty cruised down Flagler and stopped his red Geo coupe. "Hatch's Buick is in the garage," he said. "The door is open, the car is pointing outward. The whole neighborhood smells like gasoline."

"Shit," said Liska. "Plan A and Plan B down the toilet."

I spoke up: "Does it cross your mind, he killed Mary Alice Noe, he might harm his wife?"

Liska nodded and looked away. "Also, if he bullshitted me about Fernandez killing Mary Alice, he might have bullshitted me about wanting to live. He could be in a mood to take himself out, and other people along with him."

"You figure your ex-wife's in the house with Hatch?" said Monty.

"Call Mrs. Sweeting on your walk-around phone," I said.

Liska closed his eyes, pissed that I'd thought of it first. He dialed information, then Mrs. Sweeting. The uniformed officers gathered around Monty's car.

Liska clicked off. "Half hour after we left, Avery came across the street, all showered and shaved, in go-to-work civvies, carrying a cold pizza. He talked her back into the house. Then he backed out and drove away, but returned fifteen minutes later and backed it in. As of right now the Buick's still facing the street. No sign of movement."

"In fifteen minutes he went where?" I said. "Six minutes each direction, max, three minutes to do what he went to do. What did he need that he didn't have?"

"Gasoline," said Liska. "Or the bank for cash."

"Either way, something's happening. He's not taking a long nap."

"We're playing 'Beat the Clock' with a cuckoo bubba," said Monty.

Liska made one more phone call—to Marnie—then huddled the uniforms and laid down Plan C procedures. Fewer than fifteen minutes passed before Liska and I walked from Marnie's Jeep to Hatch's front door. An officer in a tree behind a house on Rose Street had a clear rifle shot at the door. Cruisers blocked the intersections on George Street at Johnson and Rose, and at Venetia and Bertha. An EMT van and a pumper truck had been alerted to stand ready behind the Conch Train Storage Depot over on Flagler. Two officers hid behind the wooden fence that ran the rear property line. Most of the neighbors had been shuttled out of their homes to safer turf.

Marnie sat bravely in the driver's seat of her vehicle, a Kevlar vest under her T-shirt. I, too, wore a borrowed vest; Liska's service .38 was tucked into my belt. Both were covered by a Gators sweatshirt we'd found in the Jeep. One of my cameras hung from a strap around my neck.

"Don't press the doorbell," Liska said firmly. "We don't know what's been rigged." A digital radio in his shirt pocket was open-keyed on a noncop freak: the pseudo-SWAT team listened in. "Lemme knock, Rutledge. You stand back, over here. Jesus, the stench. If the asshole torches the place, don't let me be a hero." He rapped his knuckles against the doorframe. "Avery, Candygram!"

No sound inside. Liska rapped again and tried the screen door. Unlocked. "Hey, yo, Detective Hatch," he shouted. He held the door open. "It's me, Liska. Wake up for the media, hotshot. Ten minutes of fame out here."

No response.

Softly into the mike Liska said, "Weimer, that Buick starts to roll, take out the radiator first, then a front tire."

Liska rattled the handle. "Avery, you okay in there?" Locked. "You all right, Avery?" Liska pulled a key ring and tried one. The big door swung. Gas fumes poured out of the house.

Marnie shouted, "Fire in the garage!"

Liska pulled it shut. Into the mike, fast: "Flames in the garage. Hit the back and get her out. Take him down if you have to." He motioned me to the side of the house away from the garage. "Don't break a window unless you see her."

I slipped as I rounded the corner, landed flat on my belly, the wind knocked out of me. The camera had bounced against my chipped tooth. I stayed low and scrambled. A metal-framed window, open miniblinds, flowery curtains, dark in the room. I pulled the pistol and fitted my forefinger to the trigger. I felt wholly out of my league. Half-crouched, I pressed against the wall. Above me, a loud whoosh and a roar.

Hell, an F-18 inbound to Boca Chica. Not part of this war.

The window toward the rear clattered. The lower half jittered upward. Her head poked, then Mrs. Hatch's whole body came out. I scootched and pulled her sideways as a uniform somersaulted. His feet brought the whole upper window casing with him. Broken glass flying, he didn't give a shit. Had her like a rag doll, over the fence, out of sight in a heartbeat. Fumes out the window. Sirens from all directions. No idea where Hatch or Liska might be.

Over my shoulder, Marnie no longer in her Jeep. Behind me, a young cop in a KWPD nylon jacket, gut crawling, gesturing toward the open window. "I don't know who you work for, man, but I hope you're writing this circus report."

Splashing. I looked behind me. A rainbow: the fire truck arcing spray. Is that how to fight a gasoline fire? Water dripped from a sabal palm next to the fence.

Liska's voice inside, distant, getting louder: "Avery, you don't want that."

Mumbling, probably Hatch. A shout more like a bark. Breaking glass, more like dinner plates than another window.

Louder still: "Look at it, Avery. It's not what you need right now."

Sounds of scuffling. Quiet outdoors. The fire truck shut down. Inside, a door slammed. A loud whoosh. The curtains blew inward, then back out. Along with the curtains came Avery. The KWPD guy jumped and cuffed him. Out came Liska, facing upward, his arms full of garden hose, the ass of his pants on fire. He rolled across the lawn and sat in a puddle under the palm. I knew he was hurt. I managed not to laugh at the steam rising from the purple trousers.

Liska looked at Hatch and shook his head. "The asshole shot his own Buick with a fucking flare gun. What the fuck did that prove?"

"He's going to miss his cigars," I said.

The pumper truck revved again. Marnie and a female EMT ran to Liska. I wanted to get away from Avery Hatch. I barely had the strength to stand.

I wished I'd eaten one of Chicken Neck's doughnuts at eight-thirty that morning. On the way back to my house we stopped so Wheeler could make a munchies run into the Sunbeam. Two remote broadcasting trucks from Miami TV stations had set up on Fleming. At the house a city investigator named Strauglin took my statement and the tape that Monty had recorded earlier. We consumed beer and junk food in lieu of lunch. Carmen went to meet Maria's school bus so the little girl wouldn't be hassled by onlookers.

Later in the afternoon Bob Bernier called and asked for Monty. Two things: Word had been passed up the ranks regarding Monty's heroics earlier in the afternoon. And the FBI in Miami had arrested Raoul Balbuena for complicity in the murder of Billy Fernandez. Monty called to let his wife know that his future with the Bureau looked promising. A while later he went on home. Sam and Marnie went out and rented a movie. A current-day spy-versus-spy epic with submarines and computers.

I have no idea what time I fell asleep or how I got into my bed.

33

At first light I heard a car door slam. A foreign reverberation. It was not a car from Dredgers Lane.

Or else it was in front of my house. Something alerted my sleeping mind. I no longer had protection; the police had taken Sam's Walther. I didn't need any more surprises. I heard a car pull out of the lane and roar up Fleming. The clock said six-forty. My head ached.

I checked the front window. When I walked outside to inspect my Shelby, I apologized to the car for not recognizing the solid thunk of its door. As much as I could see in the half-light of dawn, everything was intact. Annie had stuck her handwritten note under the driver's-side windshield wiper. I carried it inside to read by the kitchen light.

Dear Alex,

I didn't want to wake you early. I've got mucho many errands in addition to packing stuff and driving back to Florida this P.M. Start new job—Pompano Beach—on Monday. Benjy Pinder batshit over my departure. The new firm wants me in office tomorrow to start health-insurance papers, Sonitrol, etc., and I need to find apartment. Don't worry that Michael is helping me today. It is you in my heart, dear soul, but you have been through so much this

past week . . . I will come back between 11 and 12. Hope
you are home then. Yes, the balalaika belongs in Key West.
     Love and a tushy swat, A.

This breakup reminded me of her old morning routine. She
was not getting out of bed, showering, slipping into her clothes,
leaving for work. But she had talked herself into the past
tense, covered herself in memo form, with no eye contact, no
touching.

The phone rang. Carmen said, "I saw your light on. I know
you're supposed to go fishing, but I'm in a jam."

"Fishing?"

"Last thing I heard, Sam was taking Monty to the Marquesas to make up for the trip they missed last week. You and
Marnie were going along."

"News to me. What's the jam?"

"I'm already late for work. And I can't miss another day.
Maria's got a sore throat, and today is my mother's day to vol-
unteer at the MARC home. Can you baby-sit? I'll say it just
once. Please."

"This ought to be good for a toss in the hot tub."

"In chain mail, you bastard. But I will take that answer as a
yes, and we can negotiate later on terms of the deal. There's
Cuban coffee here."

"Okay, go to work. Tell Maria I'll be there in five minutes."

"Thank you, Alex. I still can't believe they cut his balls off."

"Have a good day at the post office."

I came off the front porch carrying a box of cereal. Marnie's
Jeep rolled up. The three of them, dressed out for a day on the
flats. Long sleeves, sunscreen, long-billed ball caps.

Sam laughed. "You going to chum with Raisin Squares?"

I admitted my failure to recall the morning's plans, and explained my agreement to watch Maria. The anglers promised to
return with food for the table.

I read old newspapers while Maria slept until after ten. She didn't look sick when she bounded out of bed. I wondered if the previous day's events hadn't piqued her curiosity and inspired a marginal illness.

Our first get-well project was to read a new book she'd received from her Uncle Cruz Ayusa. *A Prayer for the Opening of the Little League Season* by Willie Morris. One page prevailed upon the Almighty to stand by the umpires, the poor guys who have to make the calls and enforce the rules. In that short passage I saw room for people like Liska and Monty and Bernier as well. They had to do a job that most people would shun, to do it alongside poisonous elements like Hatch and Fernandez. They needed our patience, our encouragement to keep clear of the poison.

I had a strange craving for seafood that I couldn't lose. Either the lunch I had missed yesterday or the promise of fresh fish from Sam's boat had me going. I also did not want to encounter Annie when she came to pick up her "stuff" during the noon hour. I suggested to Maria that she might feel better if she helped me stow the Shelby in the garage behind her house, then rode her bike with me to the Half Shell for lunch.

It wasn't a tough sales job.

It took less than ten minutes to move the Shelby and pull its car cover into position. I padlocked the garage and walked as Maria pedaled across the lane. She reached my porch, then shouted indignantly: "Alex, your phone is ringing."

I knew who it was. The answering machine could earn its keep. "I'm too hungry to talk business, Maria," I called out. "I'll get a message later." I entered the yard. "Soon as I unlock my bike we're out of here."

A child's mind questions the injustice of grown-up logic. "But you're right here. You can answer it."

I'd left the volume turned up. My recorded voice barked through the screening, "Alex Rutledge. Please leave a message."

I walked quickly past the porch. I did not want to be tempted by Annie's voice.

From the machine: "Alex, Bob Bernier, ten minutes before noon. Look, I've put together some information that should interest you. Our friends in Georgia checked a stack of phone records . . .

I snatched the receiver. The machine cut off. "Alex here."

"Rutledge . . . Did you catch what I said? We found records of a call from Albertson, Georgia, to Hatch's home three weeks ago. You want more?"

"I've always said, you can't tell the players without a score-card."

"Well, we wouldn't be this far along without you. I wanted to fill you in."

"I'm not sure it'll change much in my mind," I said. "Maybe it'll answer some questions down the line."

"You tell me when you want me to stop, okay? Ray Kemp is still under sedation, in the hospital up in Marathon. Raoul, Palguta, and Hatch all retained lawyers. We've started to interrogate them and they're spewing details like crazy, trying to shift blame. Maybe they're looking for reductions. Ultimately, they're incriminating themselves. Anyway, we've pieced together a sequence of events starting when Ray Kemp came to the Keys two days after that call, which would be eleven days before Ellen Albury was murdered. Kemp revealed to Avery a plan to 'even some old scores,' as Hatch described it, and leave clues on purpose, to link the crimes to his boat, *Barracuda,* and his legal problems that led to prison time. Kemp intended to kill Michael Anselmo, Anselmo's girlfriend, and Julia Balbuena."

"That fits those short stories that you found." It also meant that Kemp had not intended to even a score with me.

"Right. And Avery felt powerless to stop him because of a blackmail threat regarding an old smuggling exploit . . ."

". . . the story that he gave to Liska and me."

"Okay. Anyway, once Hatch had been told how Kemp would carry out these crimes, he apparently decided to settle some grudges himself. Sally Ann Guthery had rejected him after a brief affair, so it's our guess that he raped and killed her in the manner that Kemp had planned for his attacks."

"The *Barracuda* clues . . ."

"Right. And the investigating officers—Hatch and his partner—elected not to reveal crime-scene details to the press. Kemp had no way to know that by using knotted rope, duct tape, semen stains, whatever, in his attacks, he'd be setting himself up for complicity in the Guthery and Mary Alice Noe cases."

"You think Hatch killed them both?"

"No doubt in my mind."

"How about the bomb in Annie's convertible?" I said.

"Kemp. When the story of Ellen Albury's murder hit the newspaper, he knew that he'd killed the wrong woman. The bomb was a hurried attempt to make up for his mistake. Fragments in the VW matched the homemade bombs our team found at his place in Georgia."

"What about Billy Fernandez?" I said.

"Palguta said that Fernandez pieced together clues from the Guthery and Albury murders, caught on to Avery's act, and assumed Hatch'd killed Julia, too. Fernandez went to Miami to deliver Avery's ass to the Balbuenas. Meanwhile, Avery was arresting Sam and you were telling Raoul what he already knew, that Julia's killer was Ray Kemp. Raoul also was aware that Fernandez knew Julia from the old days, but Billy denied ever knowing her. Fernandez thought he was gouging dumb rich people for a reward. He wanted a whole lot more than five grand. Naturally, Palguta claims that it was Carlos who carved up Billy."

"I still don't understand why Kemp killed Julia."

"Palguta says she handed Kemp to the DEA on the second bust. It was a currency rap. After she and Anselmo had rigged the Witness Protection deal for Kemp's first bust, Julia found out her little brother had been dragged into one of Ray's operations. Ray had bought him a car and a condo, and made him a runner. The deal went south. They found the poor kid in a drumful of used cooking oil behind a Burger King. Not long later, Julia discovered that Kemp was heading for St. Barth's with a new identity and seven hundred thousand dollars. So she turned him in."

"You have any idea how Anselmo escaped being attacked?"

"Dumb luck and timing. Last Thursday night he started drinking at one of the hotels, despondent, he said, over his love life. He drove over to your house to confront Annie, looked through your porch and saw her cooking dinner for you. He resigned himself to the situation, went back to the hotel bar, got drunker, couldn't drive home, so he rented a room for the night. Next morning, closer to noon, he straggled home and found a scribbled note that read, 'Don't make yourself so scarce.' The handwriting matched threatening notes he'd been getting in the mail."

"Are Sam and I clear regarding Georgia?"

"It never happened. But yesterday afternoon, a place called Sinclair Lake near Milledgeville, south of Albertson, bunch of boxes and bags start popping to the surface. Kemp's stuff. Divers found his pickup in twenty feet of water. We figure Kemp thought he was cute, going to the funeral as part of his revenge. But you blew his deal by recognizing him. He raced back to Albertson and began to pack everything he owned. He almost made it. Palguta and Carlos snagged him before he could split. They rigged the place to blow up, sank the truck, and took Kemp south. Palguta operated, again claiming it was Carlos."

"Thanks for the call, Bob."

"One last thing. The Bureau's not going to wait for the state of Florida to reinstate Monty's badge. He's already got a tentative date to report for training at Quantico."

Sometimes people who get the wienie get reprieves.

I hung up, locked the door behind me, and went to get my bike. I hadn't heard the car drive up, the new-looking Honda four-door. Annie Minnette was hunkered down in the side yard, chatting with Maria.

I gave Maria the key and sent her into the backyard to fetch my bicycle.

"So, you've got things sorted out in your mind?" I said.

Annie shielded her eyes from the sun, but didn't focus on anything in particular, least of all my face. "It's not you, Alex. It's this damned town."

"What you're saying, then, is you didn't get tired of me, you got tired of Key West."

"Yes, that's exactly it. All the craziness . . . People either not giving a shit, or screwing each other royally."

"Well, I just wondered," I said. "Because you didn't go to bed with another city. You went and slept with another man."

She almost caved in. I hadn't meant to be so strong.

She turned and looked me in the eye. "I guess I had trouble defining my desperation. Michael helped me understand that I needed a change of scenery more than I needed a new lover."

"He's going to have some changes himself."

"I think he realizes that. He said he's been waiting for the doorbell to ring for a long time."

A change of scenery. It occurred to me that Annie had been too focused on her own ennui to chip in assistance tracking down her roommate's murderer.

"Whose car?" I said.

She looked at the Honda. "Benjy Pinder's. I rented a truck. Michael's going to help me drive it up tonight."

"Middle of the week. Ought to be a snap." I couldn't believe I was talking about traffic conditions. I felt something nudge the back of my leg. Maria, with the Cannondale, my key in her open hand.

Annie slipped her arm around my waist and kissed my cheek up next to my ear. "It's been a great three years," she said softly. "You changed my life for the good. There's a chance that the next three years won't compare . . ."

"There's a lot in those three years I wouldn't have accomplished without you," I said. It was the truth. We'd been a good team. I kissed her forehead. "Drive carefully."

"Okay." She smiled. "I'll leave your house key in the kitchen after I load up my stuff." Her arm slipped away. She watched Maria and me ride away.

I laughed to myself. Whether he realized it or not, Michael Anselmo would get talked into driving the rental truck all the way to Pompano Beach.

Then I realized that I would miss her tremendously.

At the Half Shell, Peggy Sue Peligrosa steered us to two barstools next to hers. It was her day off. "Yes, ma'am, buddy. This is a happy camper," she said to Maria, as if two big girls were about to share confidential information. "I went shopping this morning for a Wonderbra, and the saleslady told me I plain didn't need one. I am one happy camper."

Maria giggled at that one.

"Now," said Peggy Sue, "I happen to know that you're in Mrs. Fox's third-grade class with my little girl Holly."

"No. I'm in Miss Gualtieri's fourth-grade class with Buddy."

"Okay, I knew it was one of them. So I need to know why you're playing hooky. This island may be a vacation paradise for some folks, honey, but for us normal people it's real life."

I ordered two grouper sandwiches with slaw. A Coke for my recuperating friend and tea for me. I reminded myself to buy shampoo. The ice in the tea froze a nerve in my broken tooth. I shuddered and wondered if Annie had remembered to return Ellen Albury's bike to Mrs. Embry.